SECRET OF THE
DRAGON CROWN

DEDICATED TO

Shannan Haas, Civi, and Michelle,
for all your support.

Shadow Dragon Saga

Curse of the Dragon Shadow

Legend of the Dragon Soul

Rise of the Dragon Sworn

Blood of the Dragon Throne

Reign of the Dragon Born

Secret of the Dragon Crown

First Edition
Published by Fairies and Fantasy Pty Ltd 2024

ISBN: 978-1-922390-93-6 (paperback)

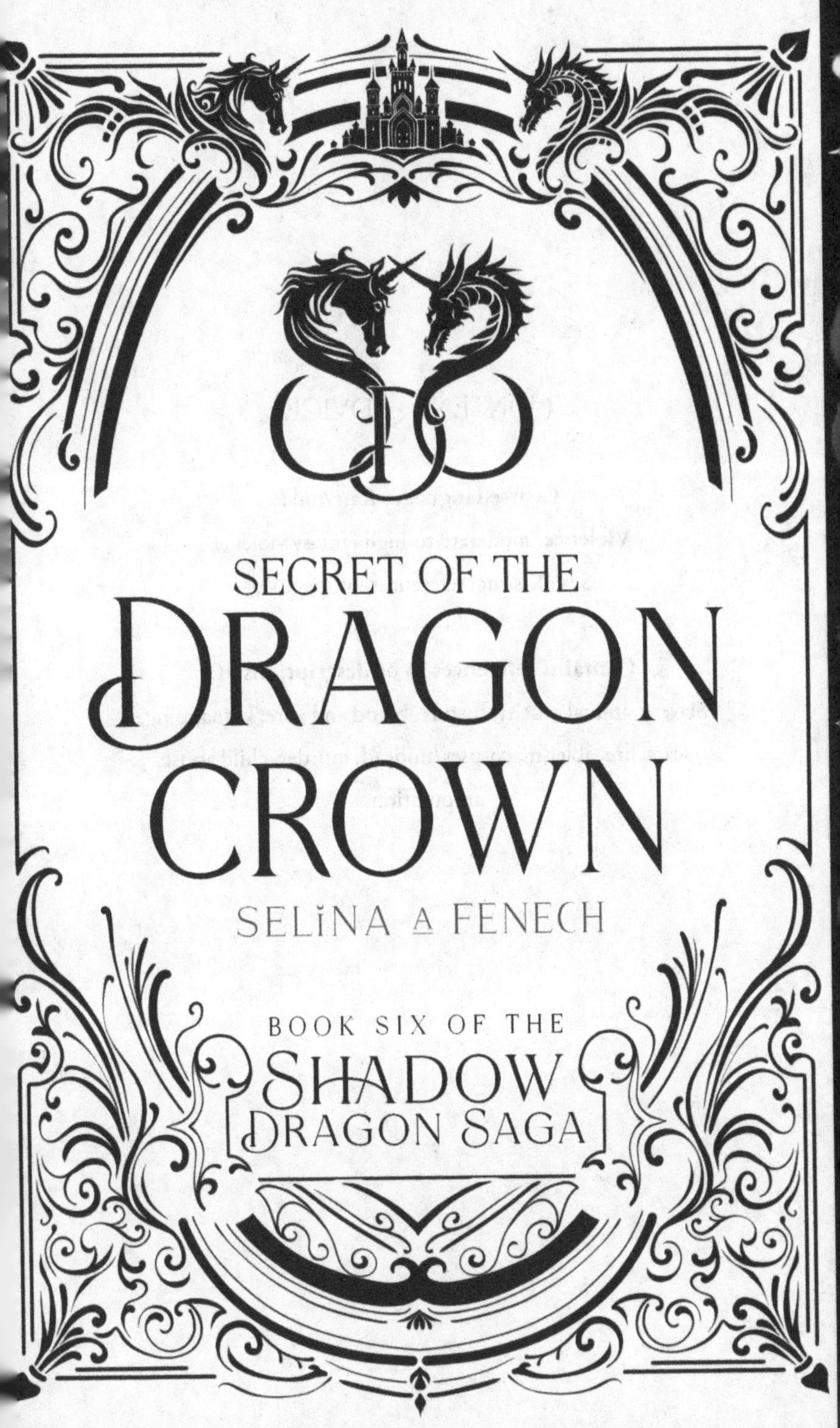

SECRET OF THE
DRAGON
CROWN
SELINA A FENECH
BOOK SIX OF THE
SHADOW
DRAGON SAGA

CONTENT ADVICE

Coarse language: Rare/mild

Violence: moderate-to-high fantasy violence

Sex: Kissing, references, off-page sex

Contains references to or descriptions of:
Slavery, animal cruelty, torture, blood and gore, kidnapping, scars, fire, ableism, corpses/undead, murder, child abuse, amputation.

CONTENTS

Dragon Keeps

1. Braigwenkeep (Trade Hub)
2. Nevrynkeep (Mining)
3. Ardahnkeep (Trade Harbor, Old Rolanian Capital)
4. Tjollaskeep (Mining)
5. Salixkeep (Fishing)
6. Ulfrenkeep (Mining)
7. Ylvakeep (Farming)
8. Leskakeep (Farming)
9. Pryshakeep (Farming)
10. Dastmyrkeep (Glass)
11. Tarrickeep (Mining)
12. Gerichkeep (Lumber)
13. Skaellakeep (Farming)
14. Idrakeep (Penal)
15. Hjelzahnkeep (Training)
16. Eslindekeep (Incomplete)

NORTHERN ALDERKIN DEPTHS
(Nerrun Deemfret)
Gris Hofen
(15)
(8)
Lorg Sesstra
Nord Myrr
(9)
EYLE NORDCREST
(14)
Seasong Shores
Lorg Eldstrom
Lorg Draeka
Sunborn Range
Draeskull Crags
Serpents Run
Mestra's Horn
EASTERN ALDERKIN DEPTHS
(Ilst Deemfret)
Stonewing Crest
(4)
Starris River
(7)
DRAEKHAN'S REST
CENTRAL ALDERKIN DEPTHS
(Luis Deemfret)
Eishowl Peaks
(6)
Etherflame Plains
Bovin Steppes
Graud Hofen
DRAEKHANHELM
Unicorn Tears River
(13)
SKYBREAK SEA
(5)
Erst Hofen
The Red Cliffs
SOUTHERN ALDERKIN DEPTHS
(Sous Deemfret)
Talon Bluffs

ALDERKIN
DEPTHS
UPSLOPE
Relic
Lower
Wet
Descent
Whisperwind
Passage
DragonMaw
Descent
Stores
1.
Upper
Flats
The Curtain
2.
Relic
Upper
12.
The
Grand
Arch
9.
3.
11.
Flowstone
Steps
Delver's
Circuit
Crystalline
Reservoir
STONESHIELD
GATE
Livestock
Root
Farm

THE UNDERCITY
Mushroom Farms
CURSED DEPTHS
DOWNSLOPE
Orphans' Den
UNICORN GATE
FIRSTMAN'S PASS
5.
7.
10.
4.
8.
6.
1. Temple Tower
2. Grand Column
3. Frostwork Column
4. Dragonwing Tower
5. Satinstraw Tower
6. Slowflow Flats
7. Rimstone Flats
8. Shimmervein Tower
9. Grand Arch Markets
10. Downslope Markets
11. Curtain Markets
12. Sinking Stream Lake

ONE

The Dragon King's fingers squeezed around Lyrrin's jaw, digging into her soft flesh. She tried to pull away, but he held firm in a way that could crack bone.

Still shivering from the cold flight there, she held his gaze and it made her shudder harder. There was something wrong about his stare, with those bottomless black irises and silver-bright pupils. It curdled her stomach and brought the sting of tears.

"Don't think you are so special that I will tolerate your disobedience, child." The tips of his fingers clenched. His voice rattled her insides and thundered around the walls of the empty throne room.

Lyrrin could feel her skin bruising.

Beside her, Yensen kept his eyes forward, as though

nothing was happening at all. Over near the throne, the queen cast furtive looks their way and remained so still she didn't even seem to be breathing.

No one is going to help me. Lyrrin wanted to keep defying the man but was already regretting her words that had made him angry. She had to be smarter.

Tilting her chin up so high it stretched her throat, the king asked, "Are you going to cooperate or should I have this grayglim dispose of you here and now?"

Through gritted teeth, Lyrrin mumbled, "I can't tell you what I know if you break my jaw."

He didn't let go. "Of course you can. What I break can be fixed. As many times as we have to until you learn your place. But there'll be no need for that, because you're going to cooperate, aren't you?"

A sharp zing of terror cut through Lyrrin's stomach. Teary and tired, she nodded once. It was barely a movement at all, locked in the king's grasp, but he would have felt it.

He released her, and she gasped in relief. Her head flopped forward and a tear splashed free.

Stalking back to the throne, Yeonard Draekhan flicked a hand toward his wife. "Leave us."

The queen bobbed a curtsy once, then strode briskly to the door without questioning the order. The tight angle of her shoulders looked like fear to Lyrrin.

The king leaned back in the throne, as though resting after a leisurely stroll. He addressed Yensen. "Tell me how

the hybrid creature was made."

The grayglim cleared his throat and went over everything, the entire story of how Riony had healed the broken dragon egg with the vial of silvernix Lyrrin had decorated.

The king kept Lyrrin locked in his terrible gaze. "What runes did you carve on the glass?"

"I don't remember." Her voice came out small and breathy, scared she'd be seen as not cooperating again.

But it was only the truth. All she remembered was that she'd just learned about the magical runes in the undercity and was so enchanted with them that she wanted to draw her own ones on the silvernix vial to make it pretty and protected and magical too.

But whatever I did, Riony wouldn't have known what it was, how to activate it, or even known there was something to activate.

The king didn't look happy with her answer.

She shot a pleading look toward Yensen, but his only response was a slight narrowing of his eyes.

She rambled. "The markings I carved probably didn't do anything anyway. It was years ago when I did them and I didn't even know how to use any runes back then. And my sister didn't activate the rune when she used the silvernix."

Lyrrin's thoughts raced, going over the details. Riony may not have activated it when she used it, but had Lyrrin, when she'd carved the runes?

Could it have affected the silvernix then?

"So the carvings may have had nothing to do with the process." Lyrrin's grandfather looked at her as though she were a disappointing plate placed in front of him at lunch.

Stay useful. Stay cooperative. Don't give him too much. Don't let him work out how to get more unidragons.

Lyrrin's head hurt. Maybe the carvings did have nothing to do with it. They were on glass, not crystal, and how could it have had any magical charge for it to work?

Maybe it was something else entirely, to do with Dracuni's parents or that specific batch of silvernix?

Lyrrin chewed her lips and settled her thoughts. It didn't matter that she didn't know how to make more unidragons. All she had to do was keep the king thinking she did and keep him busy trying ways that weren't going to work until she could escape.

"The carvings must have done something," Lyrrin said confidently. "Because we tried making another hybrid with just an egg and silvernix and it didn't work."

Elumon. I hope he's okay.

Lyrrin's chest ached with a strange hollowness at being away from the hatchling.

The king didn't reply, only pierced her with an assessing gaze.

Overwrought, Lyrrin turned to Yensen. "Tell him. Tell him we did."

Her voice strained up into a high-pitched whine as the

grayglim didn't even look at her. He opened his mouth but the king spoke first.

"Stop looking to him for assistance, child." Yeonard reclined further into his throne. "He is not your friend or ally or anything other than my loyal hand, as every grayglim is."

Lyrrin's lips pulled in and she kept her eyes on Yensen.

He had betrayed Eslinde for the king, but Lyrrin also knew not every grayglim was totally loyal. Brishan had abandoned his duties to be with Niskina's mother.

And there was also Lady Hjelzahn. She'd become the wife of a Hjelzahn heir, although she had remained a grayglim afterward too, so it was unclear where her loyalties lay, even before she became possessed and killed him and two of her children. Maybe she wasn't a good example.

Still, Lyrrin was only asking Yensen to confirm what was true, not commit treason. "Yensen, please tell him how we couldn't make another unidragon."

Yensen's jaw tightened. "It is true, my king. The dragonling created in the test did not have silvernix blood."

"Grayglim," Yeonard Draekhan scratched the side of his hooked nose. "Take one of your knives and pierce the palm of your hand with it. All the way through."

"Yes, my king."

Lyrrin's jaw dropped. "What? No!"

Yensen moved fast. His right hand swished across his belt and he plucked a slim dagger from a sheath.

The blade flashed in the flickering blue light as he raised it, then brought it down into the palm of his other hand. There was a sickening tearing sound as the blade went through right to the hilt.

"Why? Why did you do that?" Lyrrin shrieked, both at Yensen and the man smirking down from his throne.

The Dragon King rose and strolled casually toward them. "Because the grayglim knows whom he serves, the only person he serves. Because he understands unfailing loyalty. And because you, my granddaughter, need to know that I have *hundreds* of grayglims just as loyal, all willing to do anything for me."

Yensen's jaw tensed and a sheen of sweat spread over his forehead, but he made no other movement. Lyrrin couldn't take her eyes off his hand, the blade going through it, the trembling twitch of his fingers, and the blood dripping onto the floor.

The king had ordered it, and he had done it, without hesitation ... I have no friends here.

All of the shuddering cold and curdling fear and stinging nausea within Lyrrin met and merged in a rush of sickness in her throat.

She knew she could swallow it away. She could ...

But maybe she didn't want to.

Heaving forward, Lyrrin emptied the contents of her stomach onto the Dragon King's boots. The splatter of her vomit echoed in the stark throne room.

The king inhaled sharply through his nose and glared at her in horror.

He raised a hand. His fingers, each ringed in ornate gold rings studded with multiple glassy gems, clenched into a fist, then opened flat again.

Lyrrin wiped her mouth and put on her smallest, most childlike voice. "I'm sorry. Blood makes me sick. I think I might ..."

She made a convulsing motion with her chest and the king stepped back.

"Get her out of here. Now!"

Lyrrin did her best not to smile. It had been only a small act of rebellion, maybe, but one she was getting away with.

"My king?" Yensen asked, as though unsure the order was for him, despite him being the only other person in the room.

"I want you watching her. She's your responsibility."

Yensen nodded once, then pulled the dagger from his hand as quickly as he'd put it there. His face was pale. "Where do you wish her kept?"

Lyrrin made a gagging sound and puffed her cheeks.

Stepping back again, the king's face twisted. "I don't care, just take her away. Tomorrow we'll begin trials for creating more hybrids. I'll need to get more silvernix. We'll need more than we have on hand here, so deal with getting her cleaned up before then."

Yensen bowed, then grasped Lyrrin by the back of

the neck with his uninjured hand and steered her briskly to the exit.

They pushed out through the doors, with Lyrrin trotting to keep up with Yensen's long strides. Two more grayglims flanked the doorway, and Yensen gestured to one who fell in beside him. They whispered together for a moment, then the other grayglim split off again, hurrying down another hallway.

Yeonard Draekhan's booming voice, yelling for servants, echoed all the way to Lyrrin as Yensen pushed her around another corner and they began climbing steps.

She sighed in relief to be away from that awful man, whom she never wanted to consider her grandfather. Now she just had to get herself all the way free.

"Where are you taking me?" Lyrrin asked.

"Eslinde's chambers. They are secure." Yensen removed his hand from her neck.

Despite being released, there wasn't anywhere for Lyrrin to go other than up or down, and she doubted she'd have much luck simply running for it. Her legs felt weak and wobbly.

The thought that they were going to her mother's room also drew curiosity from Lyrrin. She wanted to see that space, find something of her mother's to hold on to. So she kept going up the stairs.

Yensen drew a black strip of fabric from a pouch and bandaged his hand.

"Does it hurt?" Lyrrin asked.

Yensen gave her a flat stare and returned to his work.

"Sorry. Of course it does." Lyrrin grunted in disgust. "I can't believe he made you do that! I can't believe you did that!"

Yensen tied off the fabric, pulling it taut with his teeth. "I'm grateful to my king that he spared me after my failure."

"Don't be grateful to him! That was cruel. Him choosing awful pain instead of instant execution isn't something to be grateful for."

They reached the top of the stairs, and Lyrrin groaned to see another long hallway lined with arched niches ahead of them and more stairs beyond. The palace was huge. Who needed this much space?

"He is my king, and yours." Yensen nudged her shoulder to keep her moving. "We are both lucky to be alive, and you haven't been harmed. As long as you behave, it will be fine."

Lyrrin snorted. "I am *not* going to behave. And you shouldn't either for someone who makes you stab yourself. Did Eslinde ever make you stab yourself? I doubt it."

Yensen didn't reply. His expression was as stony as ever, but his silky black hair hung messily and there was tension around his eyes, giving him a pained, haunted look.

Is he thinking about her? Did he ever really care for Eslinde?

They continued on in silence. The passage was lined with statues of angry-looking people posing with weapons,

looming out of each arched alcove. Lyrrin sneered at them and the harsh, cold stone all around. There was no warmth there. No plants or animals, no pets or personal touches of a home lived in and loved. The whole place felt lifeless.

A pang of sadness hit Lyrrin as she remembered the small two-room dwelling she and Riony had shared in the undercity, with its soft blankets and broken door and often some critter or another Lyrrin had tempted in with food.

Is Riony still in the undercity now? Did she and the others manage to help? Are they okay? Do they know what happened to me yet?

Lyrrin wished she still had her heart stone, to feel her sister's heartbeat again.

At the top of the next flight of stairs, Yensen pushed a door open, and then pushed Lyrrin inside. He reached to a strange toggle on the wall, and with a click the room illuminated.

"Servants with food and clean clothing are on their way. Don't do anything stupid. *Behave,*" he said.

Lyrrin stuck her tongue out at him.

He closed the door, locking it between them.

Lyrrin stared at the solid doorway as she took a few deep breaths and then turned around.

Eslinde's room ... No, Eslinde's *chambers*. Lyrrin hadn't expected how big they would be, how many rooms were involved. There were four doorways splitting off from the vast central living area she'd stepped into, a space draped in

books along every wall, like a waterfall of tomes all around, spilling out from the shelves in piles on the ground.

Only a few other pieces of furniture occupied the space. A small table with two chairs beside a large window at one end, and a lounge and armchairs—Lyrrin hadn't seen those before but knew about them—around another low table, covered in books. A patch on the floor near there had a dark stain marring the polished tiles.

Lyrrin scurried over to the lounge and pulled a blanket from it. She draped it over her chilled shoulders and brought it up to her face. It smelled like her mother.

Pulling it tight around her, she quickly checked the other rooms, looking for weapons or exits. The first she tried was too dark to see into.

Lyrrin noticed another one of the toggle switches near the door. She tentatively flicked it, and light crackled from the lamp fittings in the same eerie blue of the rest of the palace. It was cooler than the cyan glow of the Alderkin light stones.

Inside was a bathroom. So different to those in the undercity, with hot spring water running perpetually into stone baths, filling the air with steam. This one was cold, with a shining steel tub and metal pipes and taps.

But it contained no windows or exits, so Lyrrin moved on. Behind the second door was a storage closet. The third was a room even more filled with books than the living area, creating a maze across the floor. Lyrrin flicked the

toggle, but the lights in there didn't work.

A large window on the other side brightened the room with the last dull purple light of day. Lyrrin made her way there, growing eager as she saw the balcony beyond the glass. The massive window had a door built in, and Lyrrin grinned when she pushed and it swung open easily.

Her smile faded, though, as she stepped out onto the balcony, so, so far above the ground below with nothing on the slick marble walls to climb down. Someone would have to be desperate to try to get down from there.

Against the dusk-bruised sky, something massive moved, flying off to the northeast. A dragon, bigger than she'd ever seen. Its wings seemed to stretch from one side of the city to the other, four times as big as any dragon Lyrrin had known. Bigger than the shadow dragon itself.

A dragon that big could swallow someone whole.

Cold wind gusted against Lyrrin's face. She pulled the blanket closer again and went back inside. The fourth and final room was the bedroom. Her mother's bedroom. Lyrrin traced around the walls, hoping for some secret doorway to reveal itself, as she avoided the desire to crawl into the massive bed in the center of the space and curl up and cry.

She followed the boundary all the way around and back out of the room and to the front door again, dragging her fingertips along the wall as she went. Nothing but slick, streaky marble all the way, with no seams or buttons revealing a concealed escape route.

The texture only changed when she reached the front door, where ornate carvings surrounded the threshold. And as her fingers passed over a section of them, she felt the stone there sing.

Lyrrin stopped, blinked, and backtracked. She ran her fingers and eyes over the area, heart pounding. Within the swirling lines and intricate patterns a different sort of design became clear.

Alderkin runes.

She touched the symbol hesitantly, feeling how it sung to her, a reverberation deep in her chest.

Alderkin runes on ... crystal? It had to be charged crystal for it to hum like that, but it looked just like the surrounding stone. Lyrrin leaned closer and saw the careful layer of paint and the edges of the carved section.

Prying her sharp fingers into the gap, Lyrrin grasped the crystal and pulled.

The long, thin shaft slid from the wall. Beyond the painted cap, the transparent quartz glowed softly. A cavity in the middle held a small vial of silvernix.

"Sparks, yes!" Lyrrin whispered breathily.

There was a crystal she might be able to work with and silvernix to keep her safe. They felt like a gift from her mother, waiting there for her, to give her hope, to give her a chance to get free.

She examined the rune. She'd never seen one like it before, so she wasn't sure what she could do with it.

I'll work it out soon enough.

But what she wasn't sure of was how the crystal was still charged. They were a long, long way from any shrines there.

Lyrrin remembered Shael's words when they had been talking about the standing stones and how they charge the crystals.

There's only one way that works without—

Her mother knows already. Alleem worked it out for her, to keep her safe.

Lyrrin dropped down to the floor, cradling the crystal on her lap. She turned it in her hands, and along the bottom was a line of swirling shapes. Alderkin writing. Lyrrin wished she knew what it meant.

Did my father make this? For Eslinde?

All her plans to carve that length of crystal into pieces and test out rune combinations shattered as surely as if she'd pelted the stone onto the floor. She couldn't do it. She couldn't destroy what might be the last thing in the world her father had left behind.

She had so little of anything left of those she loved. Riony and Eslinde and Dracuni and Aishena and Benjin and Elumon and Niskina and everyone who had become her friends and family felt a world away from her and suddenly all she wanted was to be squeezing her doll she'd left in the undercity tight in her arms as Riony squeezed tight around her.

I'm going to see her again. I'm going to get out of here.

But even the voice in her head sounded weak and scared and all the pain and fear of the day hit her like the smack of a dragon wing.

Because how could she stay strong in this awful, lifeless place, all alone? How could she stay safe around a man who would make even those loyal to him stab themselves through their hand?

How could she survive against that sort of cruelty and power?

TWO

The silken plates of Dracuni's scales jolted against Riony's back.

Teetering on the edge of sleep, Riony woke with a start, her heart cracking into a sprint as she was hit by Dracuni's fear and her own all at once. She grasped around nearby until her fingers closed on the hilt of her crystal sword, heavy and uncharged.

She scrambled blindly to her feet. "What is it? What's wrong?"

Riony scrubbed the palm of her free hand into her bleary eyes, trying to clear them. The unfamiliar room was lit by a single glow stone, left activated because Dracuni didn't like the complete darkness the caves otherwise provided. Lyrrin never used to like it either.

Elumon slept on a blanket on the other side of the tiled floor, undisturbed. Cool air from the open vent nearby blew the frayed edges of Myrwa's shawl that was draped over Riony's shoulders, tickling her bare arms. Nothing else moved.

The unidragon's flanks heaved with gasping, sobbing breaths. ***Nightmare. I'm sorry.***

The tension in Riony's sword hand eased, but her heart hadn't gotten the all clear message yet, still rattling hard. "Same as usual? Flying?"

Yes. Flying. Falling ... The fear rushing into her from Dracuni changed to a deep aching shame and sadness. ***Losing little sister.***

Riony turned around and leaned into Dracuni's neck, holding her and stroking a hand over her pale rainbow scales.

"It's not your fault. It's okay."

A truth and a lie. Riony didn't blame Dracuni at all. But it wasn't okay.

Lyrrin was gone.

It had been over a week since they'd sealed themselves into the Alderkin depths with an army of dragonriders outside. Over a week since Lyrrin had been taken away.

Over a week since Riony or Dracuni had managed any semblance of proper sleep, until Niskina and Aishena had ordered them home at midday to take a nap before they passed out on their feet.

Riony wasn't sure what time it was, but the low murmur of the sounds of the undercity rumbling through the stone walls suggested everyone else was still awake.

Dracuni's lilac eyes glimmered with the reflected cyan glow, her eyelids drooping heavily.

Ruffling the tuft of hair above her horn, Riony sighed. "Come on. Back to sleep. You need it."

Riony expected resistance, but Dracuni's head lowered down to the ground and her eyes squeezed closed, pressing loose a tear. It didn't take long for the exhausted unidragon to fall asleep again with Riony stroking her eye ridges and whispering calming words.

But Riony's own hopes of sleep had once again been lost.

She left her sword beside Dracuni and tiptoed out of the room. Now that the panic of startling awake was gone, Riony knew they were safe in there. Only approved people could get in. The chambers she'd been given were deep within the Delver's Circuit.

These huge razing chambers.

Riony had originally wanted to go home to her tiny apartment at the top of Dragonwing Tower, but Dracuni wouldn't fit in there. So she'd gotten what she'd wanted for so long. The spacious, rich home of a delver. Fully furnished, the chambers even had proper beds, a large dining table, and lounges. Riony hadn't even seen a lounge since leaving Heithorn estate.

Every inch was beautifully decorated, the doors and walls carved with flowing organic patterns. Everything from the plumbing to the ventilation, hot and cold, all worked. No sticky door mechanisms there.

She was neighbors to the Hjelzahns, with enough room for Dracuni and Elumon and Sir Butterfur and all the pets Lyrrin could want, and it all felt cold and empty because Lyrrin wasn't there with her.

Out in the large living area, the air was muggy, steamed by the hot spring bath at one end of the room. Riony rolled her braies up to the knees and stepped into the scalding water, then sat down on the edge.

"I don't have any treats," she said, as Butterfur sluiced through the pool toward her, sniffing around her thin undershirt.

The cave otter looked up at her, then looked over her shoulder on one side, then the other, as he often did. Searching for someone who wasn't there.

Butterfur twitched his snout accusingly, then swam off, disappearing into a pipe that a creature his size had no right fitting through.

Riony scooped a handful of water and splashed her face, then swiped through her hair. Or what was left of it. It had grown long in their time aboveground, the deep red picking up gold highlights from being under the sun. But one too-close puff of dragonfire burned away half of it.

Riony had raggedly cropped the rest herself.

Zeina promised her she was still hot, but even that praise hadn't stirred anything in Riony.

Her toes tingled in the steaming water as she pulled the heart stone from where it hung beneath her shirt, now missing its other half.

She sat there staring at it, willing it to miraculously burst to life again and show her that Lyrrin's heart still beat. In a haze of exhaustion, she thought she might have done it when there was a low thump and a dull grinding sound.

But it was the entrance door rolling open behind her.

She half turned, squinting at the strange silhouette quietly stalking in, backlit by the corridor's lighting.

"Sparks," Riony growled low under her breath.

The last person she wanted to see or be alone with.

Ever since coming back to the undercity, since the fight against the riders … since the whipping post … Riony found she couldn't look at Kess. Holding her gaze on the wolf girl was like staring at the sun. A strange, dizzying, deeply scarring sensation.

She simply couldn't do it. Every time Kess was around or within view, a churning pressure seemed to fill Riony like a pot boiling over, if the pot also lost all emotional coherence and ability to think straight. Which would make sense because it was a pot. But Riony found the experience overwhelming.

So she'd been making sure she saw Kess as little as possible.

The way Kess also eschewed eye contact made Riony think she'd noticed the avoidance.

Kess cleared her throat. "Sorry. I thought you were sleeping. I was just going to drop these off and go."

Riony lifted her gaze from the ground to see Griskin, Kess's legs, and an overflowing woven basket balanced on those legs. She lowered her eyes quickly again.

"Drop what off?"

"Your belongings."

"I don't have …"

The clink of glass and rustle of blankets from within the basket cut off Riony's words. Griskin sniffed and whined as he brought Kess closer.

"Someone else had moved into your old place. But one of your neighbors kept these for you, in case you came back." Kess lowered the basket down in front of her.

Riony's shoulders slumped as she saw the familiar woven blanket, carefully folded on top, spotted with burn holes. Her nose wrinkled as she moved it aside to find neatly stacked glass jars filled with dried herbs, crystals with experimental runes carved on them, and an old straw doll with an age-dulled red ribbon.

With the threat of the siege, not enough food to feed the dragons they and the defeated riders had brought underground, the Alderkin vanishing, and Eslinde locking herself away, utterly heartbroken, Riony had been too busy to check what had become of her old home.

Or too scared to go back there without Lyrrin. To hold these remnants of their old lives when Riony was so far away from holding Lyrrin herself ... It hurt like a knife in the heart.

"Thanks," she choked out, staring at Griskin's feet.

The wolf snuffled and pawed at his nose.

"It's nothing." Kess and Griskin turned away.

Riony reached into the basket, grasping a cold glass jar in her hand. Her head spun as the smell of wild animal and honeyed wilderness that Riony had come to associate with Kess drifted across to her. Kess and the wolf were almost at the door again when a sound that was barely a word stuttered desperately from Riony's mouth.

"Wait," she managed to say more clearly. "I ... can put something together for the pup. To help him with the fungus allergy."

They padded back silently to her side. "Do you have what you need?"

"Yeah, I should. Tried to always have the supplies around for if Lyrrin had a flare-up." Riony's throat closed over her sister's name.

She lifted her legs from the water and turned around to face the basket completely, leaning over and digging through, bringing the jars out and lining them up beside her. She only needed two herbs for the mix, three for best results.

She found the genjermint quickly, but the blue pine

was being more elusive. Her search revealed a half-filled jar of hennan and her thoughts shuddered to a stop as she remembered applying the muddy paste made from it to Lyrrin's hair to darken away the bright-blue tone.

If only I could have disguised all of us, somehow. Kept Dracuni hidden from everyone. I've made so many mistakes.

She closed her eyes to force away the tears. In her moment of hesitation, Kess moved closer and slid down from Griskin to sit on the ground beside the basket.

Riony took a shaky breath, found the herbs she needed, then turned around again so she wasn't facing Kess. With her back to the pool, she worked on pulling corks from the jars and sniffing them to make sure they were still potent enough.

Kess murmured, "I have ..."

A quick glance to the side showed Kess holding one hand in front of her, clasped closed around something small. She was way too close and Riony's body felt hot and disjointed the way it had when she'd poisoned herself with corpsefoot.

She grimaced and almost dropped a jar.

Kess withdrew her hand and Riony heard a belt pouch clasp open and closed. "I should go. You need to sleep."

No kidding. But it wasn't going to happen. Riony hadn't told anyone, but she'd been having nightmares too.

Every time she closed her eyes, she saw the faces of the people she'd killed, the burning enclaves, the destroyed keep, the whipping post. Only keeping busy had kept those visions away, but she was being betrayed by her body's physical desperation for rest.

Her hands had stilled on the jars and her eyes were unfocused.

Kess spoke softly. "I'll go. I'll come back later when it's ready, or you could give it to someone else to pass on to me."

Kess shifted, and Riony dared to look at her back as she moved to remount Griskin. She swallowed hard.

"Are you ... okay?" Riony felt awful that whatever was going on inside her meant she hadn't checked on Kess after what she went through.

Kess stopped and turned back. "Me?"

Riony flicked her eyes to look at the ground again. She busied her hands with mixing the three herbs she needed into the emptiest jar.

"After ... what Kife did. After almost drowning."

"I'm fine. You used silvernix on me. I'm completely healed."

"But are you *okay*?"

Silence stretched out between them. Riony couldn't be sure, because she refused to look, but it felt as though Kess moved closer.

Kess asked, "What would you give for what is most important to you?"

"Don't answer my question with another question. I'm too tired for mind games."

"No. I really want to know."

Rolling her eyes, Riony begrudgingly thought about it. Then she decided not to think and just let her mouth take over and trust its truth.

"My life. If I knew that giving my life would change this world in a way that mattered, I wouldn't hesitate." Riony's eyes filled with tears that didn't fall as she suddenly felt as though her small life was so insignificant in the face of all she wanted, all she hoped to save, the scale of what she faced.

Her head dropped forward, shaking. "I want Lyrrin back more than anything, but there is so much more to consider now, so many more lives at risk that I feel like I could save if I just push a little harder."

"Push any harder and you'll destroy yourself."

"We all destroy ourselves for something. All that matters is that we choose a worthy cause to destroy ourselves for."

The only sound in the room was Kess's trembling breath, then she whispered, "That's how I feel too. Whatever I suffer, whatever I've been through, it's worth it."

Riony flinched as a hand came near her face, brushing along the flame-cropped hair. She snatched the wrist from the air, tight in her own, and instinctively turned as though toward danger and came face-to-face with Kess.

Kess froze, eyes round like prey, but not without defiance. Mouth parted, nostrils flared, cheeks red.

"I'm sorry."

Her hand tugged, trying to move away again, but Riony didn't let go.

Their gazes met and Riony's world swirled down to nothing but those icy-blue eyes staring back into hers.

The overwhelming sensation flooded her. The tingling pressure squeezed her heart and rushed up her spine and spread across her scalp and blurred her vision with the heat of emotion.

Riony's breath stuttered, and her fingers flexed, opening and closing around Kess's wrist as though trying to let go but held in place by an unseen force. Once, twice, three times she tried to release, then her grasp locked tight and pulled, bringing Kess into her.

Their lips crushed together.

Riony pressed her mouth against Kess with an all-consuming need, and for a heartbeat, Kess was frozen, motionless under her touch. Then the kiss was returned with a frantic yearning that sent Riony mindless.

Releasing Kess's wrist, she tangled both hands into Kess's stormy hair and drove her whole body into the kiss. The smaller body beneath her crumpled, falling back under her assault and together they thumped onto the floor, lips still joined.

Riony felt the sharp inhale of air into Kess's mouth and she chased that breath.

When Riony opened Kess's mouth with hers, pressing deeper, Kess arched up against Riony's chest. Riony slid her hands under the small of Kess's back and pulled her in tight with all her strength, needing her closeness as though any distance between their bodies wounded her very soul.

Kess released a gasping, songlike whimper that made Riony's heart beat so hard she felt ready to pass out. She pressed her mouth over the cry with a low moan.

Hot air gusted over the back of Riony's neck, followed by a vicious, rumbling growl.

Riony froze. The only movement she made was the shaking from her frantic breath and rampant pulse. She slowly lifted her hands and lips away from Kess in surrender as bared teeth pressed against her skin.

Kess stared up wild-eyed at Riony and the wolf at her neck.

"Gris! It's okay. She's ... she's not hurting me."

The wolf growled again but backed away enough for Riony to move without fear that she was about to be decapitated by wolf bite. She sat up, kneeling straddled across Kess's thighs, breathing like she'd been fighting for her life.

Sparks. What did I just do?

"I didn't?" Riony's mouth went dry. "I didn't hurt you, did I?"

"No, not at all." Despite the words, Kess looked utterly devastated.

Eyes glistening, lips and cheeks flushed.

Riony had rarely seen her like that, her emotions so

clear and vulnerable on her face.

What did I just do? And why did Kess let me?

Riony felt horrified that Kess's pledge somehow extended to *this*. Allowing Riony to do that to her, even if she didn't want to.

I pledge my life to you and your cause. For whatever good it can provide you.

Where was the boundary? Riony was a world away from knowing what she wanted right now but she didn't want *that*.

"Sorry. I'm sorry. That wasn't right. I shouldn't have." Riony shifted onto her haunches and reached to help Kess up.

Griskin growled again. He shoved into the space in front of Riony, pushing her back onto her rump as he nudged Kess to sit up, licking her face.

Is she okay? What did I just do?

The boiling-over sensation still ran rampant throughout Riony. The way Kess had kissed her back ... She had, hadn't she? She hadn't just imagined it?

What sort of love had Kess meant back when she'd said, "That's the Riony I love?"

And was that also what this overwhelming feeling was?

What did I just do? And why do I so badly want to do it again?

Kess, red-faced and chest heaving and eyes averted, climbed onto the still growling wolf's back. "I should go."

Riony nodded drunkenly from her seat on the floor. She spotted the jar of mixed herbs beside her, knocked on its side but unspilled. She recorked it and thrust it up toward Kess.

"Here."

Kess reached for it. Their fingers touched and it felt like a bolt of lightning. Riony bit her tongue to keep quiet as every part of her wanted to tell Kess to stay. Even if it meant being mauled by a wolf.

Confused and ashamed and drowning in a kind of wanting she'd never experienced before, Riony watched Kess leave.

When the door closed, she flopped backward onto the ground. Her head fell over the lip of the pool, lolling into the warm water, and she swore loudly. For an aching hazy-sweet moment, all she could think about was the kiss.

That kiss. With Kessara Razing Heithorn. *That kiss.*

And then all her other worries returned in the crush of a landslide.

THREE

Ambushed. Again.

Kess and Griskin stepped out of Riony's room to find Niskina waiting for her in the hallway. The curvy woman leaned against the wall and swung her poleaxe lazily like a pendulum in front of her.

"If you're here to warn me away from Riony again, then ..."

Then Kess didn't know what.

A few moments ago, she would have said it didn't matter because Riony was already avoiding her like she'd avoid a plague-ridden pile of manure.

Until she *wasn't*.

Until she was doing something entirely different than avoiding.

Kess's hands shook with the thud of her fired-up pulse and her cheeks felt hot as her mind relived the kiss in a loop. She let it. She never wanted to forget how every touch felt, every press of skin to skin, the curve of Riony's mouth under hers.

Kess's lips had become a reliquary, haunted by the sensation of Riony's kiss.

Brushing back her tumbling hair, Niskina narrowed her eyes on Kess. "Are you okay? You look sick."

"I'm fine," Kess snapped.

Hiding the heat in her face behind her hair, she pushed Griskin onward down the passageway. "I'm late getting to scouting for the day."

"I'll walk with you, then." Niskina fell in beside her.

Griskin growled, and Kess shushed him, rubbing his ears.

Niskina widened the gap. "What's got him all riled up?"

Hands in my hair, around my waist, falling back under Riony's weight.

Kess swallowed. "Nothing. Did you want something?"

"I've been wanting to talk to you. Alone. But haven't found the chance."

They'd all been busy since the siege began, working to make sure the undercity was safe.

The Alderkin had done some magic to block the main entryways to the depths before they disappeared, but there were other barricades and defenses that had to

be built in case the army of dragons outside managed to dig their way in.

Kess's main job had been regular trips out through the hidden mountain exit to spy down on those keeping them imprisoned, then reporting her findings to the others.

Which Kess had made sure was the only time she spent around Niskina and the guilt her presence evoked in her.

She sighed. "Here we are, alone. Get to the threats already."

They moved through the quiet hallways of Delver's Circuit, the private tunnels carved between the exclusive homes there, but would soon be out onto the busy streets of Upslope. Kess hoped Niskina wouldn't try to murder her before then.

Niskina frowned slightly, and her full lips popped open. "No threats. I just wanted to say ... ugh. Look. What you did for Riony, taking that whipping instead of her ... I've seen her scars. She has so many scars. And I know Ri is the type who would have taken more, but it means the world that she didn't have to."

Kess nodded, muted by the depths of her agreement.

Niskina snorted and shook her head. "And I still can't believe it was *you* who saved her from that!"

"I live to defy people's expectations, I guess."

Niskina grew solemn and her words rambled. "Aish has been telling me things. And after what you did to Kife too, well, I know he deserved it in every way, but he was your brother. And still you didn't hesitate to do what had to be done."

Kess pressed her eyes closed for a moment, rocking gently in the darkness as Griskin kept them moving forward.

Kife. Her brother. The last of her family, gone. For the better, and even the wolf she rode on was more family than any of them had ever been, but that didn't reduce the pain that rebounded within her chest as though she were hollow inside.

Kife's body had been recovered the day of his death by a competent swimmer, to make sure the water reservoirs weren't tainted. He was burned without ceremony.

Kess opened her eyes. "And I'd do it again. I meant my pledge."

Niskina reached out, grasping Kess around the arm and bringing her and Griskin to a stop. "I know. I can see it now. You really have changed. I'm sorry I didn't believe you before."

Niskina's touch was gentle and warm. The touch of a friend. A touch Kess had so rarely felt.

She blinked rapidly to clear the wash of salt water on her eyes. "I'm sorry too. I'm sorry that I didn't change sooner. I'm sorry you lost your father because of me."

Niskina's nose flushed pink, and she fluttered her eyelids too. "We don't know what would have happened, even if you were on our side. We don't know ... I decided to redirect my ire toward Lady Hjelzahn for now, although apparently she's possessed or something?"

"You could blame the shadow dragon, then," Kess offered.

Niskina half smiled and held out a hand.

Kess reached back, shaking it, offering a nervous, thin-lipped smile. Silently, they both turned and continued on together.

Leaving the guarded exit of Delver's Circuit, the bustling hum of the undercity loudened, and Griskin sniffled.

Kess looked numbly at the jar clutched in her hand, trying to focus on the *here and now* and not the *there and Riony's kiss*. She dug around her pockets for a handkerchief.

Niskina cleared her throat, but her voice still came out low with concern. "So, how was she? How's Riony feeling?"

Feeling our bodies pressed together, feeling the warmth of Riony's skin through her thin shirt.

The glass jar slipped in Kess's fingers. She fumbled, catching it at the last moment.

"She's upset ... tired. I think she's too tired to be thinking straight."

That had to be it. Why what happened, happened. Riony was just exhausted and overwhelmed and seeking comfort from the closest body.

Kess was sure Riony didn't like her, in *any* particular way. Riony only allowed her to be around, only done what she'd done to help her because she would have done that for almost anyone. It was just who she was.

That moment together ... Kess couldn't assume it meant anything.

No matter how real it felt. *How it felt ...*

Niskina hummed agreement. "I know losing Lyrrin is hitting Riony hard, but she's not going to be able to do anything if she doesn't take a break and look after herself. Do you know how hard I had to bully her to even take a few hours to go and catch up on some sleep?"

Sleep she wasn't getting, even before my visit.

"We all destroy ourselves for something," Kess whispered.

"Huh?"

Kess shook her head. "Riony would do anything, give everything for others. That's why she needs us. She can save the world, but we're here to save her."

Niskina hummed again in thoughtful agreement.

Kess uncorked the jar and a bright, cool fragrance emerged.

She shook some of the herbal mix into the handkerchief on her lap and recorked the rest for later. Knotting the corners into a neat bundle with a piece of string, she then leaned forward and tied it to the front harness of Griskin's saddle.

The scent wafted around them.

Passersby gave her and her wolf space, stepping away

as they saw them and Niskina coming through. Niskina received respectful nods and even a salute or two, with wary glances reserved for Kess.

When Kess and Griskin had explored the undercity the first time, the richer areas of Upslope had been quiet and sparsely populated. Exclusively for delvers—which Kess had recently learned about—and others with the money or means to separate themselves from the masses packed in Downslope.

Not anymore. Upslope was as densely filled as the rest of the undercity. The town square area beside the long curtain of stone that ran across the cavern had become a training ground, where Aishena, Zeina, Benjin, and some delvers were teaching melee combat to anyone willing.

Overhead in the gaps between the towering stalagmite apartments and the dripping stalactites far above, dragons flew. All the smaller treedarts that remained after the invading riders were defeated had been gathered up, and the even more daring undercity volunteers were receiving training from Vance, Dashiel, and Jaym on how to fly.

And the dragons too big to fly easily in that space, Viska, Gleem, Hux, and Ambri, were attracting even more people in to where they were being housed on the Upper Flats, just to see them.

Kess and Niskina reached the top of the flowstone steps, and an arm raised above the crowd nearby, waving them down. The people parted, revealing Jaym, grinning a dazzling, crooked smile. His pocket-hawk, Teeka, perched on his shoulder, preening the man's golden blond curls.

Cute little thing. But also another thing that I will protect Riony from. Even Riony's name in her thoughts made Kess feel ready to combust like dragonfire again.

Niskina stilled, waiting for the Rebel Rider to reach them.

But she kept her eyes on Kess and narrowed them suspiciously. "Riony didn't say anything to you, did she? Do anything odd?"

Kess choked. "What do you mean?"

"I'm just worried she's secretly plotting a one-woman rescue mission again, like when she went off after you."

Kess frowned. Would Riony do that? She'd gone after Kess; of course she'd go after Lyrrin. Although Riony only had to get through Kife to reach Kess, for all she knew when setting out. Rescuing a captive of the Dragon King was something else entirely.

"If she is, why would she tell me about it?" Kess asked.

"I think she opens up to you more than the rest of us sometimes."

"She probably cares less what I think about her."

"Maybe." Niskina didn't sound convinced. "You better not be in on letting her endanger herself. You've been acting weird ever since you came out of her room and—"

"Look at these two majestic heroines!" Jaym reached them, arms wide in greeting.

Kess exhaled her relief as her heart continued to race and her mind kept reliving every touch shared between her and Riony. Acting weird was the least of her concerns. She felt lucky she hadn't keeled over on the spot from the intensity of her feelings.

Niskina scoffed at the Rebel Rider. "You're such a flatterer. But you know it doesn't work if you do it to everyone."

"Oh, I think it still works." He winked at her and then turned and gave Kess another, even more conspiratorial wink.

Niskina rolled her eyes, but a grin grew across her lips.

Jaym leaned in and looped a finger around one of the steel rings on Niskina's leather harness vest. "You and I have that meeting to get to, the one before the other meeting with everyone else later."

"So many meetings." Niskina sighed dramatically, still grinning. "If I must."

A rough voice barked from nearby, "If it's such a struggle for you, let someone who's capable take charge!"

The neatly coifed man stood flanked by two others, looking more like bodyguards than companions. His silver tunic was spotless and lay under a glow stone that had been fitted into a decadent gold necklace.

It wasn't the first time Niskina and the others had been challenged for the work they were doing in the undercity. Generally by people who all looked much like this man.

They were few and far between, but tensions were rising with the dragon army outside and risk that they might get *inside*. But people were coming together too, helping each other, learning how to defend each other.

Dracuni had also decided she wanted to help. She'd seen people suffering and argued with Riony for days before Riony agreed to bottle her blood.

And so the ill and injured were offered access to the silvernix supplies 'belonging to the benevolent princess' who had come to the undercity. Kess thought it was a good idea. They needed as many healthy bodies as possible for what might come next. And Dracuni's blood helped so many.

But still, some people weren't happy.

Niskina raised her eyebrows at the man. "I'm not in charge, for starters. I'm doing the work I can to be of service. And I'm sure I remember you were happy with the services I offered the undercity when I was able to get crystals recharged."

The glowing crystal pendant swung as the man huffed. "That was before you brought in all the riffraff, letting them into Upslope."

"There was space there, and people need a place to live." Niskina shrugged.

The man stepped closer, his brown skin deepening red. "And now people are saying you're going to start rationing food?"

A crowd was building, watching the exchange. Rowdy voices muttered their agreement as the man yelled into Niskina's face.

Kess slipped a dagger from where it was sheathed on her bracer and turned Griskin around for a better angle, preparing to take on the mob that was forming.

Niskina huffed, hands on her hips. "We're *under siege*, if you haven't noticed. The undercity is fairly self-sufficient, but there are so many more people here now."

The crowd surged, grumbling and arguing. Kess tensed, prepared to fight.

Jaym raised his voice, calling like a town crier over the crowd. "People who were saved from the terrible massacre of Midwinter's Eve by this very brave young woman right here! That night ... you wouldn't believe the horrors we were witness too."

A hush fell over the surrounding people and their eyes turned to him.

Jaym lowered his voice, melodious and solemn. "Some of you know. Oh yes. Some of you were there. You, maybe? Or you?"

He pointed vaguely into the crowd, not at anyone particular. A few people still grumbled but were hissed into silence by those around them.

Kess's fingers loosened around the bone knife. Jaym had the crowd transfixed.

Hopping up onto a step, the Rebel Rider's voice carried

over the audience. "Some of you weren't there, but you've heard the tales from those who survived. And how did they survive? Only through the actions of the heroic beauties here before you."

Kess's eyes widened at being included. But the glances her way weren't the kind she was used to. They were curious and awed. Some of them were openly reverential. The man leading the assault sputtered as the crowd jostled him and his cronies away.

Niskina sidled over beside where Kess watched Jaym spin his tale about the night the enclaves were attacked, with all his embellishments, especially about Niskina's role in the heroics. He made it sound like a grand legend of old, a far cry from the tragic, messy atrocity that it was.

Smirking, Niskina whispered, "Yep, he's as good orally as he is in print."

The man's words worked like magic, soothing the crowd and clearly raising both Niskina and Kess in their estimations.

But Kess's own estimations of herself had dropped. When presented with a problem, she had as ever been ready for violence, but Jaym had found another solution.

Jaym finished his story and the crowd dispersed, a new energy humming through them. A positive energy.

Niskina folded her arms and lifted her chin at the man. "Does this mean you're going to write me into one of your stories?"

His grin in return was broad and hungry. "Maybe, but we'll need some more to write about first. Now ... that meeting?"

Niskina nodded a farewell to Kess and followed Jaym away down the street.

Kess watched for a moment, taking in all the faces around her.

Would she have taken lives if things had turned nasty? Added more marks to all the others tallied in her brutal past? She was a killer.

She'd even killed her own brother.

Sighing, Kess slid her bone dagger away and urged Griskin on again, heading to the passageway up into the mountains.

The scent of the herbal parcel thickened again as they moved, and Kess's heart felt heavy. The intoxication of the kiss had worn off, and only questions that felt as though they were traps designed to maim her remained.

Did the kiss mean anything? Of course not.

Could it happen again? Of course not.

Did Riony actually care for her?

How could someone like her ever love a killer like me?

Back at Eslindekeep, Lyrrin had talked about how they don't attack, they protect. Kess had liked that. The kid was smart. Hopefully smart enough to survive the Dragon King's captivity.

In her time surviving aboveground, Kess had done

anything she had to do to protect herself. She'd done it for so long that she'd gotten too used to it. She'd become hard and vicious and deadly in defending herself and only herself.

She had more to protect now, could be someone who protected instead of attacked. She had been that for Riony, and she would continue to be. No matter what.

Griskin moved through the cave and reached the iced-over waterfall. Kess used the cutting athame Riony had given her to clear the hole that had closed over since her last trip out.

She'd volunteered them for the task of scouting since she knew the mountain range well from her time stalking the mother dragon. She knew where she could go to get a good view down over the entrances of the depths, and she doubted anyone without their own wolf to ride would be able to make their way to that peak.

Stepping out into the blistering winter winds, a strange sensation washed over Kess. She squinted at the smoky skies that rained ash onto the snow and made the alpine landscape muddy and gray.

She'd had that feeling every time she'd come out of the depths. A strange mix of longing and anger and shame which felt basically the way Kess usually felt, but still somehow unfamiliar.

Nothing moved in the sky, so Kess pulled a pale blanket from a saddlebag and threw it over her back.

Griskin crunched upward through the snow.

The leather delver armor that she'd been given was warm and chosen because it didn't glint in the sun the way the golden scale mail from Eslindekeep did.

But Kess still preferred to cover herself entirely, lest even the small metal rings on the harness catch the eye of one of the riders below.

It was a hard climb to the highest peak. Rocks skidded beneath Griskin's paws as he leaped them from narrow ledge to narrow ledge.

They settled on a rocky outcrop, backs to a cliff, and looked down. Kess squinted through the seeing stone Riony had loaned her.

Just doing the same as they've been doing every day.

The majority of the dragon army were camped on the slopes below, tents and dragons alternating in a pattern around the entrances. A few flew patrols, far closer to the ground than even Kess's perch.

There was always a team of five or six dragons at the Alderkin depth gates, trying to force their way inside. They burned and clawed and dug, but so far the stone of the gates, and whatever the Alderkin had done to it, held strong.

The strange sensation tugged on Kess's senses again. Closer.

"I know you're there!" Kess yelled into the wind. "Show yourself!"

A trickle of ice and pebbles cascaded down the rock face.

Above Kess, a large shape moved, casting a shadow over her. Claws appeared, clutching the top of the cliff, and a dusky purple head snaked down. Griskin whined, his back foot slipping from the narrow ledge before he caught himself.

Kess rubbed a hand on his neck to reassure him. "If Lyomir wanted to roast us, he would have done it by now. He's had plenty of opportunities, following us around up here. Haven't you?"

The dragon huffed. *Maybe ... I wanted ... to get closer first.*

The words came through slow and disjointed, as though the dragon were still finding his voice after so long without one. But those words, slicing into Kess's mind so clearly, made her gasp.

"You're close enough now," Kess challenged.

The etherdart's eyes narrowed as he moved even nearer, taking in Kess and her wolf with an eager curiosity that washed from him to her. He didn't speak again. Or burn them alive.

"Why did you follow us here?"

From the very first day they had rushed to the undercity to defend it against Kife, Lyomir had followed them. At a great distance and out of sight, but Kess had sensed his presence. As she had every time she'd come out scouting.

You ... interest me. Compel me. Lyomir closed his hazy green eyes in a slow blink as though he didn't like that fact one bit. ***You make me hear ... song.***

The echoing, gravelly voice in Kess's head hummed four notes.

Kess cringed, suddenly embarrassed. "I sang to you. After you were born. Before you were tamed. *Close your eyes, and dream so deep, while dragons sleep, while dragons sleep.*"

A Rolanian lullaby. The only one Kess had known at the time, learned from Riony. Kess's parents had never sung to her.

Lyomir sighed deeply and the hot air warmed Kess's face. ***My memories, thoughts ... all chaos.***

"I'm sorry." Kess had no idea what it would feel like, living through being tamed, then waking up again after so long.

Lyomir's head shook in a shiver and his teeth bared. Kess braced herself. Then his eyes met hers.

But I see you in the chaos. Singing. Freeing me. Joining me in the air.

"I see it too," Kess whispered desperately.

Since Kess had first flown on Lyomir in her attempt to stop him attacking their tamed dragons, she had longed to fly with him again, dreamed of sharing the sky with him.

She'd felt a connection between them, but it was one so raw and delicate that she feared even examining it would make it vanish.

But as they spoke, his words inside her felt like strands of thread weaving into her soul, tying them together. She could feel his every shift in emotion and how they were reacting to hers. The sensation dizzied her as it all accumulated into a single resounding thought.

We're bonded.

A deep thrumming sound reverberated in Lyomir's throat. Kess's fingers trembled, and she reached up. Lyomir balked, pulling away.

Kess exhaled roughly, a wry smile on her face. Bonded maybe, but the purple etherdart radiated only the barest tolerance for her.

I'll take it.

Kess lowered her hand, and Lyomir moved closer again. He sniffed at her, then Griskin, making the wolf growl softly.

"Now that we're on speaking terms at least, is there anything you need? Are you safe out here, from all the dragons down the hill? I can't get you into the caverns below through the tunnel I came out. It's too small. But I'll be out here often."

Lyomir's head tilted side to side. *I ... owe ... to you.*

"You don't owe me a thing."

You freed me.

It was the Taenish way, to owe and repay debts. How Kess had been raised. And then there was Riony, willing to give anything for those she cared about and everyone else,

never asking anything for it. Something Kess was getting used to. Something she preferred.

"I only returned to you what was taken from you unjustly. I only made things right."

Lyomir watched her steadily with his huge eyes, her own image reflected within them, so small.

Kess straightened up as she stared back.

Small, but mighty. More than anyone had ever expected her to be.

With the kiss from Riony still burning on her lips and the voice of a dragon in her mind, Kess felt capable of anything. And she knew if she didn't want Riony sneaking off to go and save Lyrrin on her own, something had to be done about it.

"You owe me nothing." Kess squared her shoulders and stared up at Lyomir. "But ... There's something important I need to do. Somewhere I have to go. Not as payment or as a master's command. It is for you to choose."

My choice? Hmph. Lyomir's eyes narrowed, looking out at the gray skies around them, then back to Kess.

From her heart, she asked, *Will you fly with me again?*

FOUR

The heavy stone rolled toward Riony, pressing her between it and the doorframe.

She grunted and matched its pressure, pushing back the other way. All the muscles in her back and arms coiled and strained.

"I know you're—mmph—in there!"

Putting her shoulder against the stone, she forced the gap wide enough for her to stumble through into the dismal room beyond. Only a small, single glow stone lit the space, half lost within a mess of blankets, clothing, and dishes of old food scattering the floor. The smell wasn't great.

"Go away," a feeble voice called from somewhere buried beneath it all.

Catching her breath, Riony grumbled, "You can't hide

in here forever."

"I can, if you simply leave me be."

"Yeah, I'm not going to do that."

Riony stomped across the space, clattering the ceramic plates in her wake. She grabbed a handful of woven wool and pulled it up to reveal Eslinde curled up beneath.

The princess's hair was tangled, a cloudy haze of silver around old, loosened braids, and her eyes were puffy and bruised as though she'd cried and not slept in equal amounts. She tried to grab the blanket back, but Riony wrenched it off her and tossed it clear.

Eslinde made a pitiful sound and turned her face away.

Exhaling deeply, Riony lowered herself down to sit next to her, pushing aside a barely touched bowl of mushroom stew. She wondered who had been delivering the princess food. Probably Vance.

"Listen, I'm sorry, really. I wish I could leave you be. I wish I could let you get through this however you need to get through this. Stars, I wish I could be in here wallowing with you. But there is so much to do, and we are drowning out there. We need you."

Eslinde looked honestly shocked. "Why? I am a curse. I can be of no help to anyone."

"Because, as you dared to point out to me once, we are just children. And we've got a whole lot of people looking to us for solutions to a whole depths-damned siege that's happening right now, and we could really use the advice of someone who might know a little bit more about politics and warfare and all of this sort of thing. Someone maybe like a princess."

Eslinde groaned and rolled over the other way.

Riony put a hand on her shoulder. The woman was small, thin-boned much like Lyrrin, but she'd lost more weight recently.

"I know how you feel. Believe me. I want Lyrrin back as much as you."

A sob racked through her small body. "Then I have hurt you as well. I brought a traitor in and lost my daughter. Again. All those around me are destined to suffer or betray me. I can trust nobody."

Riony made a rude noise. "You can trust me. You can trust Kess. And Vance and Dashiel. And Aishena and Benjin. And Niskina."

Eslinde made a similarly rude noise, sandwiched between silent sobs.

"*And* most of all, you can trust Lyrrin. You know how clever she is, how brave she is. She's probably running circles around her captors, giving them more trouble than they bargained for. You can trust her ability to survive."

The soundless tears ceased, and Eslinde looked up at Riony from the side of her eye. "Do you really think so?"

The words had originally been meant only as a comfort to Eslinde, but as Riony challenged their meaning within her, she found she had no hesitation. "Yeah, I do."

Lyrrin would survive. She'd fought and outwitted slavers and dragonriders and undead. Riony just wished she knew how long her sister would have to survive without her, before they could rescue her, somehow.

She had been trying to work out a way that she could go, but none of her plans came close to being even as good as the worst ideas she'd ever had.

Riony squeezed Eslinde's shoulder. "But I don't know if *I'm* going to survive the complexities of organizing a community of refugees into a defensive force while keeping the peace during a siege. This isn't what I'm built for. I'm only built to hit things with a sword and look hot."

Eslinde slowly rolled into a sitting position, then looked up and held Riony's gaze. "I think you are capable of far more than you think."

A sudden soft, warm feeling in Riony's chest surprised her. It was so close to how she'd felt when her amma would praise her for being able to identify herbs correctly during their studies together that it left her flooded with complex emotions.

She shrugged bashfully. "We'd still really appreciate your input, though. There's a meeting in ten minutes in my room. It's right around the corner. Will you be there?"

Eslinde's eyes shimmered, red-rimmed, and her lips pulled into a tight line. Then she nodded once.

"Do you ... need any help cleaning up?" Riony offered awkwardly.

Eslinde's back straightened and there was a spark in her eye. "Who is the child here?"

Riony rubbed her chin, thinking about it. "Does that mean you're taking over and I can lock myself in a room for a week? Because I'm down for that swap."

Eslinde scoffed. "You wouldn't even if you could."

Riony wasn't sure whether Eslinde would actually show, but she was the first one there.

Her face had been washed, her hair pulled back into a neat bun, and the dress which she had seemed to have worn since they arrived at the undercity had been changed out for a neat and simple military uniform brought from Eslindekeep.

She gave Riony a grateful but still sad smile and took a seat at the long dining table that ran down along one side of the living area. The Alderkin-made chairs were high-backed, inlaid with agate and crystal with finely woven cushions.

Eslinde was dwarfed by them, and despite the richness of the room being beyond anything Riony had ever known, she felt as though they were all children playing tea parties rather than people who could manage the scale of issues they faced.

How are we going to get through this?

Eslinde was quickly joined by Aishena, Benjin, and Niskina. And then Dashiel, Vance, Jaym, and Zeina arrived. They were all surprised to see the princess there and greeted her happily.

"Where's Kess?" Eslinde asked, edged with concern.

Riony was wondering the same thing. She hadn't seen Kess since the day before, and her nerves had been strung tight at the thought of seeing her again after that. Maybe Kess was now avoiding her.

Ouch. That thought hurt.

As though meeting a challenge, her mind offered up other ideas for why Kess wasn't there that hurt even more.

What if something happened to her? What if she's hurt? What if she's never coming back?

Riony dropped into her seat, suddenly lightheaded.

Aishena seemed less worried. "She's late. We should start without her. We have a lot to go over."

Riony glanced to the front door once more, willing it to open, before turning to the others. Dracuni and Elumon were curled up across the room on the other side of the softly steaming pool. Pangs of hunger came from Dracuni, and Lyrrin's hatchling had become lethargic without a regular stream of food.

Vance, Dashiel, and Jaym began their report on how the rider training was going, and a twinge of embarrassment joined the other emotions Riony was sharing with Dracuni.

Dashiel had taken her to practice flying that morning, but Dracuni returned early, sullen and silent.

Riony directed her attention to the unidragon, extending her thoughts.

Did you get to do some flying?

The space is too small. With sharp rocks everywhere. Her thoughts were laced heavily with shame and fear.

She'd only flown that one other time. The time she still had nightmares about.

I'm sorry I was busy this morning. What if next time I go with you?

Fly together?

Yeah. What do you think?

Riony's shoulders dropped as the unidragon's overwhelming emotions calmed.

I'd like that.

Dashiel's voice pulled Riony back to the meeting. "It won't matter if we have everyone flying like masters if the dragons are all too weak from hunger to do anything."

"So I might have thought of a way to deal with the food issue," Riony said. She lifted both hands in front of her, framing her words. "Cave spiders."

"*Cave spiders?*" Zeina cringed back in her chair. "Stars, I hate it down here."

Dashiel had gone an off-green color. "Wait. Is that a type of food down here? I thought the street vendor was teasing me. What did I razing eat?"

Aishena shook her head. "It's one thing catching the occasional spider for a snack—"

Dashiel turned sideways to bend over and put their head between their knees. "I'm going to be sick."

"—but it would take the delvers weeks of chasing around, picking the creatures off to get enough to feed the dragons." Aishena patted Dashiel on the back in a *there-there* motion.

"Except I know where to find a whole heap of spiders all in one place. Remember where I got my sword?" Riony had shared the tale of her and Kess's adventures through the depths with her friends before, but it was clear they thought she was grossly exaggerating.

Aishena frowned thoughtfully. "How many are we talking about?"

"Enough for all the dragons to have a solid feed." Riony leaned back, folding her arms. "Not an easy mission, though. We'd have to get past the revenant conglomerate. But I can lead the way. I know what it's like down there."

"I want to see the rev king!" Benjin said, far too eagerly.

Eslinde watched the entire exchange, aghast. "You're going to try catching enough *cave spiders* to feed the dragons, after fighting a ... a *rev king*? This is your plan?"

Riony walked her fingers in the air. "I'm kind of hoping we can just sneak past it. I don't want to see that mountain of bones again."

Eslinde rubbed her forehead. "Blessed sun, maybe it

is good I'm here."

Vance chuckled wryly.

"If it's as bad as you said down there," Aishena sounded skeptical, "you'll need a bunch of good fighters with you. Some of the ones we're training are ready."

"Ready?" Zeina barked a laugh. "Ready to sometimes land a decent blow on an unmoving training pole. If the things I've seen the vendors selling are spider legs—and I will be thanking my ancestors tonight that I haven't eaten any—"

Dashiel made a gagging sound.

"Then those blighted things are *big*."

Niskina rolled her eyes. "They aren't even venomous."

The sound of the door rolling open shot Riony up in her seat. Her heartbeat became frantic with a mix of relief and embarrassment and something else even stronger as Kess rode in on Griskin.

"You're late," Aishena snapped. "And why are you *wet*?"

Kess ignored her, riding right up beside Riony. Her dark hair was flattened to her scalp and sopping wet, and all her clothing glistened with water. Griskin remained dry, except for where Kess dripped on him. She carried something long and thin on her lap.

Kess laid the item reverentially onto the table in front of Riony. It took a long moment before Riony could tear her gaze away from Kess to see her dragonguard sword lying before her.

Riony gaped at it. She touched her fingers lightly to the cold, slick steel, to be sure it was really there. Around the table the others whispered in confusion between themselves. They didn't know what that sword was. What that sword *meant.*

How for all their talk of perilous missions and rev king's and cave spiders, that small, incredible, wolf-riding girl had just faced them all alone and returned with something Riony had thought was gone forever.

And Riony found she didn't care one bit about that piece of metal that used to mean so much to her. She cared far more that Kess had risked her life for it.

I could have lost her.

"What were you thinking? Going down there alone?" Riony surged up to her feet. "Why would you do that?"

Kess didn't flinch. She raised her chin and said firmly, "I went to recover your sword because I wanted to prove that I can retrieve things that are important, no matter how impossible it may seem."

Riony wanted to yell at her, to scream that she didn't need to keep proving herself, didn't need to continue her pledge or put her life second to it. Riony didn't want any of that. She just wanted Kess.

She wanted Kess.

Unsteady on her feet, Kess's next words knocked Riony right back into her chair.

"Because I'm going to go and get Lyrrin back for you."

Riony could only gape at her.

Eslinde's head shook, and her voice trembled. "How?"

Riony's ears felt clogged and eyes blurred as Kess explained her plan. How the purple dragon had followed them, was outside the siege and willing to fly Kess to the capital. How Kess knew some of the layout of the palace, enough to find her way around. How Griskin would help sniff Lyrrin out.

How she was prepared to leave immediately.

Kess no longer looked at Riony, pitching her scheme to the rest of the table. "It makes sense that it's me who goes. Alone."

Riony felt as though she could choke on her heartbeat. "What? No! You're not going alone. And if anyone is going to get Lyrrin back, it should be me. I should go too."

Niskina sucked in a breath through her teeth. "It does sort of make sense for Kess to go. She sounds like our best chance to save Lyrrin. And we need you here."

Riony slapped her hands on the table. "You just want her gone because you don't like her."

Niskina glared back. "It's not like that. Just think for a moment. It's a good plan."

Aishena gave Riony a pitying look. "She's right. It is a good plan. Kess should do this."

"Aish," Riony pleaded.

The stern young woman locked Riony with a stare that seemed to look right into her soul, understanding every part of her.

She nodded gently. "But I don't think she should go alone. Chances of success will be higher if Benjin and I go with her."

Benjin silently pumped a fist.

Dashiel, who had recovered from their nausea, cleared their throat. "If you're taking more volunteers, I'd like to go too. I know the city inside out and much of the palace too. I can help."

"If you're going, I'm going," Vance said.

"Not this time, brother. You and Jaym need to stay and keep up the training without me."

"You just want to get away from the cave spiders," Aishena said.

"Stop," Dashiel replied, swallowing hard.

Kess shook her head. "It's too dangerous. I'm going alone, and I'm going now."

Aishena gestured to Benjin and they both rose from their chairs. "It is dangerous, which is why we're coming. We'll go and prepare now."

The two of them were out of the room before Kess could argue again, with Dashiel following quickly after.

Eslinde looked around the table. "I should go too. I want to go. I know the palace better than anyone."

Kess, already looking put out, shook her head fiercely.

"I'm sorry, princess, but you don't have the skill set for this mission. The Hjelzahns and Dash will, I suppose,

be helpful."

"Then let me go too," Riony grumbled again through gritted teeth.

Niskina leaned forward across the table and pulled Riony's hands into hers. "I know you're desperate to get Lyrrin back, but we need you to lead the mission to feed the dragons. And Dracuni needs you here. You can't leave her alone, not with an army outside trying to reach her."

Riony felt torn into three pieces as she looked between Dracuni and Kess and into her heart where she held Lyrrin. She was desperate to get her sister back, but she could also see clearly now how desperate she was to keep Kess by her side.

A great, dreadful clarity about just how she felt for Kess hit her like the beat of a dragon wing.

All her attention turned to Kess and the bright daring of her eyes and the scatter of spots across her cheek and the soft pink of her lips.

In a husky, low tone, Kess said, "Trust this to me. Let me do this for you."

Riony reached for the hilt of the sword lying on the table before her. She clutched the dragonscale patterned metal tight, feeling the familiar shape of it in her palm.

"I can't talk you out of this, can I?" Riony murmured back.

Kess searched her face. "Why would you want to?"

The whole table fell silent, awaiting the answer.

Heat flushed up Riony's neck and all her words failed her.

Jaym clapped his hands together, breaking the spell.

He spoke joyfully. "We have successfully planned two missions today! Two! Better progress than most of our meetings, I have to admit. I'm feeling good about this."

He slid his seat back, signaling the end of the meeting. Vance hurried away, and Niskina gave Kess a long look and single nod before Jaym slung an arm over her shoulders and they left together with Zeina, arguing about the quality of undercity food.

Eslinde spoke softly with Kess for a long moment while Riony remained trapped in place, caught within the gravity of her feelings.

She didn't want Kess to go. Kessara Heithorn. The wretched gremlin. The person Riony would have once put high on her list of most deserving a painful and humiliating death. She wanted Kess there, with her, right beside her and even closer.

Riony wasn't sure what Eslinde saw in her face as she approached their conversation, but the first heir stepped away, leaving Riony and Kess alone.

Face-to-face again, Riony still couldn't find her words. What could she say? Would Kess stay if she begged her to? And what would that mean for Lyrrin?

Stomach churning, Riony lifted one hand up between them. Kess tilted her head as she looked at it, then grasped it with her own. There was a soft tremor there, and she tensed as Riony stepped closer. Her legs pressed up against Griskin's flank. With their hands gripped tight between their chests, Riony pressed her forehead to Kess's.

The uneven panting of Kess's breath merged with Riony's.

"Come back to me, okay?" Riony whispered.

"I will. I'll bring Lyrrin back for you."

Riony shook her head, forehead wobbling against Kess's. Riony turned her head to the side and their cheeks touched.

"You too. I need you to come back to me too. Do you understand?"

Kess pulled away, the corner of her lips brushing Riony's as she did. Mouth parted, she frowned at Riony as though she didn't understand at all but nodded anyway.

With her free hand, Riony grasped one of her string necklaces and pulled it off over her head. The acorn pendant dangled as she reached over Kess and placed it around her neck.

Kess's eyes widened into bright pools.

"We're ready." Aishena's voice cut through from the doorway. "The sooner we leave, the better."

She, Benjin, and Dashiel were armored and carrying packs.

Eslinde pushed back in and wrapped Kess in an embrace, and Riony farewelled the others.

Then everyone was gone, leaving Riony alone with Dracuni and Lyrrin's hatchling. On wobbly legs she went and flopped onto the ground between them.

She patted Elumon down the back of his maned neck, so much liked Dracuni's. "Lyrrin will be back with you soon. I hope."

He blinked at her and made a sad croaking noise.

Riony leaned back into Dracuni, seeking the warmth and comfort of her silky scales. It all felt like too much, understanding how she felt about Kess only to have to say goodbye. She wanted to chase after her, do the reckless thing that old Riony wouldn't have hesitated to do.

But she understood more now, about the world, and responsibility. She knew protecting Dracuni, keeping Dracuni fed and alive, was more important than anything else, even her own heart.

Dracuni turned her neck around and laid her head on Riony's lap with a soft sigh.

"You've been quiet. Are you happy Kess is going too?"

No. She is a friend now. I've just been thinking.

"What about?"

The depths. The spiders. The bone monster. Other things.

Riony could feel her worrying about it all like a weight in her stomach.

"It was pretty scary for you last time we were down there, wasn't it? We'll be more prepared this time. I'll be

fine."

Dracuni snorted. *Actually, I had an idea. Something to help with the meat problem.*

"Yeah?"

Yeah. But you're not going to like it.

FIVE

Yensen held Lyrrin in place with a firm hand on her shoulder, right in front of the maw of a dragon with teeth as long as Lyrrin stood tall.

She fought her fear. The dragon was tamed, it shouldn't—*wouldn't*—act without orders.

But what if it does get orders?

She knew as soon as they walked onto the flight deck that the immense silver and gold dragon could only belong to the Dragon King. That it was the same one she'd seen flying through the darkening sky on her first night in the palace.

And if she displeased the man, she could be dragon food within seconds.

Yensen had already given her his daily warning, about

how their king was good and kind and just and would remain that way as long as Lyrrin behaved for him. Lyrrin held serious doubts. Good, kind, and just people didn't become cruel when someone misbehaved.

For now, though, the king was occupied with other matters.

A stream of servants loaded metal crates and fabric-wrapped furniture onto the back of the dragon, overseen by the queen.

The dragon—an etherflame probably, but Lyrrin was still getting used to identifying dragon types—had its head and body lowered, and staircases on wheels were rolled up beside it. It didn't have the normal cap of a taming spike in the center of its head, but instead, a polished length of wood emerged from just above one eye.

The end of a spear. It was the first tamed dragon. No wonder it was so big. It was over eighty years old.

Eighty years enslaved to that man. Poor thing.

One servant climbing the stairs fumbled the crate she carried, and it slipped, clattering in her hands as she caught it again before it crashed to the ground.

The queen howled, "If you drop that, I will have you flayed strip by strip and your ribbons hung out for the birds!"

The king only kept half an eye on the loading work. Before him, a man in a very simple but tidy gray tunic delivered a report in a long monotonous string. They both stood beside a small table that seemed to be a temporary office desk, strewn with papers, quills, and a small chest.

Whether Yensen had brought her in too early or the messenger's delivery had taken too long, nobody paid any attention to her as their continued their work.

Lyrrin strained to listen to the report but found the queen's business far more interesting than glassworks production numbers (lower than expected) and defenses at the king's external factories (weakened, with so many dragons away under other orders).

There was so much furniture, ghostly and bumpy in its protective shrouds, getting stacked and roped onto the back of the dragon, but the palace itself hadn't seemed any barer for the lack of it. How did they have so much? And where were they taking it?

The Dragon King had a whole additional private palace along with his one here in the capital. Eslinde had shown it to Lyrrin on a map once. It lay on the coast to the northeast.

Maybe they were moving things there. But Lyrrin also remembered Niskina's reports of dragonlords packing all their precious belongings and fleeing Elundrae entirely.

The messenger's tone changed to one more somber, drawing Lyrrin back.

"Dastmyr, Salix, and Skaellakeep have been breached."

"All three?" Yeonard Draekhan sounded more skeptical than concerned. "Small breaches, perhaps."

The messenger seemed to shrink, and his voice wavered. "Overrun, my king. There weren't enough riders left to defend them, and the numbers of undead have risen dramatically."

"My heirs?"

With a bowed head, the messenger delivered his news as though his head was on the executioner's block, and they were his final words. "Unknown. Presumed dead."

"Hmm," the king grumbled without any emotion.

That was all? Lyrrin studied the man with ferocious eyes. Three of his children could be dead, and all it got from him was a polite grunt?

The king turned back to the messenger, and Lyrrin expected him to say something about his heirs, about all the people lost in those keeps along with them, about any plans to do something about it.

He said, "Any updates from the undercity siege?"

Lyrrin held her breath. Not what she was expecting, but news from the undercity was something she desperately wanted too. She leaned in closer.

The messenger seemed equally confused about the change of subject.

He stuttered, "The rider army you've sent are trying all they can, but the entrances haven't yet been penetrated."

Yes! Lyrrin smiled grimly. She didn't know for sure whether Riony and her friends were still okay, but she assumed they must be within the undercity, with Dracuni, if the Dragon King was trying so hard to get in. And failing.

Yeonard Draekhan's awful eyes turned on Lyrrin then, and she hid her smile a second too slow. He dismissed the messenger, and the man bowed stiffly and skittered away in obvious relief.

All the pressure of the Dragon King's attention fell on Lyrrin, and goosebumps prickled over her with the fear of what that attention would bring.

Because it was clear he wasn't happy.

The queen came to her husband's side and seemed to notice Lyrrin's presence for the first time as well.

She looked her up and down, mouth twisted. "Well. Our little grandchild cleaned up well. It almost looks sweet. If I didn't know what it really was."

Lyrrin offered her most saccharine smile in return, fluttering her lashes over her startling blue eyes—the one thing that the flurry of servants who had cleaned and dressed her couldn't change.

They had forced her into a chair and covered her scalp with a horrible stinking gunk, so different to the earthy paste Riony used to dye her hair.

Lyrrin didn't want her hair changed. She'd become proud of the shimmering blue color that was growing in, that it was *her* hair, her family's hair, undisguised, for once in her life. Now it was a harsh black. She hated it.

She also hated the horrible, dull gray dress they wrestled her into. It was too tight around her chest and draped too long over her feet, tripping her up.

The servants had looked at her pointed nails and planned to try to trim them, but Yensen explained she needed them for the work she was to do for the king.

Instead, they found new gloves for her, fancy silk ones. The tips of Lyrrin's nails already pierced through the fragile seams.

But she passed as fully human.

Strange that was how she had to appear when the qualities the king wanted from her were from her Alderkin side.

"She appears well, and yet she continues to defy me," Yeonard Draekhan said in his booming tone.

"I'm not—"

"All ten of the first batch of trials failed. Ten vials of silvernix wasted. Ten hatchlings wasted."

Lyrrin turned cold from scalp to toes. The hatchlings ... he didn't ...

"I tried—"

"Did you?"

The disappointment in his tone actually hurt.

"I told you I don't know how I did it before. I tried all the runes I know, and some combinations. That was trying. What else could I do?"

"Do it the way you did before. Stop stalling, stop trying to trick me. I need you to make this work. The land needs you to make this work. How many people must die because we don't have the resources to tame enough dragons to defend against the shadow dragon's blight?"

The queen hovered nearby, her forehead wrinkled ever so slightly as she listened, but she didn't question anything.

Lyrrin did, though. The fire of defiance burned through her at the king's words. How dare he blame any of that on her? The keeps were falling because they weren't defended, because the Dragon King had moved all the riders he could find to the undercity.

"You know the shadow dragon's curse will only get worse if you keep taming more dragons," Lyrrin challenged back. "You know all those people could be saved and the curse ended, if you just stop fighting against those of us who are trying to do exactly that!"

"You have too much of your mother in you," Yeonard said. "With the same ridiculous dreams. Elundrae as we know it cannot exist without tamed dragons."

He turned away to the portable desk and picked up the small chest there. "And we must have the means to continue making more."

He pushed the chest into Lyrrin's hands.

She already knew what was inside. The first ten vials had been delivered and returned in that same jeweled box. But she opened the lid anyway to see the line of glittering bottles laid out on velvet within.

"I expect this next round of trials to succeed, or there will be consequences."

Lyrrin's mouth puckered. He could expect all he wanted. It wasn't going to work.

But he hadn't punished her for failing the first time. He still believed she could do it. He still thought she was valuable to him.

Running her fingers over the vials, Lyrrin decided she was feeling bold enough to test just how valuable he considered her.

She stroked the gloved tips of her fingers over the teardrop-sized glass, holding the precious silvernix. She'd hoped she could use some to do her own tests when they had been delivered to Eslinde's rooms the first time, but she had been watched the whole time she had them, the vials counted in and out.

"I can do my best, that's all I can promise," Lyrrin said, and then she let the chest tumble from her fingers.

She feigned an attempt to catch it, juggling it in the air and flinging the vials out all around. Yensen, the king, and queen, all started forward in their own attempts to save the precious contents. But the rain of glass already clinked and cracked onto the ground.

Lyrrin gasped dramatically. "I'm so sorry! These gloves, they make me so clumsy."

She stepped around in a circle, acting flustered and bending to collect the now empty chest. The last couple of intact vials crunched beneath her shoes and she spread a trail of shimmering unicorn blood across the floor in her wake, making it unclear which spots were broken vials, and which were her footprints.

As she stood back up, the king stood over her, his arm mid swing.

"You stupid creature!"

The back of his knuckles cracked against her cheek, filling her head with ringing pain. She shrieked in outrage, her temper flying free of the bonds of her good sense, and she swung her clawed hand back in response.

Her nails, poking through the tips of her gloves, scratched across the king's upper arm. They cut through the weave of his tunic, into his skin. Blood stained through the frayed fabric.

Lyrrin froze, staring at what she'd done. Her cheek ached and ears rung with her pounding heartbeat and a triumphant voice crowed within her at the knowledge the king's blood brought.

He's just a man. And he can bleed.

But she'd also just attacked the king, and he looked ready to murder her.

His fist was raised, but before he could strike, hands grabbed Lyrrin from behind and dragged her out of reach.

Yensen held her tight, restraining her arms and panting out his words. "My king, forgive me that I didn't protect you from this creature sooner."

The king glared from Lyrrin to the silvernix spoiling on the floor. The bright shimmer was fading as it lay on the streaked, glossy marble.

Taking a slow, threatening breath, he lowered his fist. Moving his thumb within his fingers, he crushed something then wiped the palm of his hand directly over the bloodied area on his arm.

And then he glowed. Lyrrin had seen her sister glow like that more times than she'd have liked. She knew what it meant.

Scowling at the wound, as though the torn and stained clothing were a bigger issue than the injury Lyrrin had given him, he wiped his hand clean on a handkerchief his wife hastily passed him. As he worked it around the rings on all his fingers, Lyrrin's eyes widened.

Was every one of the silvery gems on those rings a dose of silvernix?

The Dragon King could bleed, but not for long.

"Take it back to its rooms," he muttered to Yensen. "I'll send more silvernix soon. And maybe I'll send something else too. Something to encourage the wild beast to behave. My late son Hjelzahn had a man in his employ who is very skilled at getting results out of people who are being defiant. A man very good with his tools."

Lyrrin kept her mouth squeezed shut. She didn't trust herself to say anything else that wouldn't get her into more trouble, and luckily Yensen kept her hands pinned behind her as well.

Both she and the grayglim sighed in relief when the

king turned away and left.

As the fury that had fired up Lyrrin cooled, the throbbing in her cheek grew stronger, and she licked her lips, finding them split and bloody. But as she rubbed the fabric of her glove around her fingers, feeling the small bumps inside, she knew it was worth it.

The queen seemed locked in place, her chest rising and falling in short breaths. Yensen bowed to her and tugged on Lyrrin to move her away.

"How dare you?" The queen gasped her words, scandalized to breathlessness. "How dare you strike the king?"

Lyrrin pulled out of Yensen's grasp. "He hit me first."

The queen's cheeks darkened as though they were as bruised as Lyrrin's. "But you never *strike back*!"

Yensen grew very still at Lyrrin's side, but Lyrrin was twitchy with fury.

"He should never have hit me to start with!" She had expected consequences, possibly even worse ones, for destroying the silvernix. Even if it was seen as an 'accident.'

But she was still angry that it had happened. It was still wrong.

She shook her head in confusion at the woman. "How could you marry someone like that? Someone who hits children?"

Queen Vellira's back straightened and her streaked black-and-white hair swished behind her. "Of course I had to—wanted to marry him. He's *the king.*"

Lyrrin stared at her grandmother. It felt absurd to call her that. She barely looked older than Eslinde. How young had she been when she married the king? When he halted her aging with silvernix as he had halted his own?

Servants still moved around behind them, casting surreptitious glances at the royal quarrel.

The queen stepped closer to Lyrrin, her voice a threatening hiss. "He is our king, and if you keep defying him, he *will* bring his torturer in, whether you're a child or not."

Torturer? Is that what he meant by the man with the tools?

Lyrrin tried to keep her voice strong, but it broke over her words. "I didn't think you cared."

"I don't." Vellira dropped the words like a blow, then turned her back on Lyrrin. "It's only that your failure is Eslinde's failure which in turn is my failure, and failure isn't tolerated. The king will only accept disappointment so many times before there are consequences, no matter how important you think you are to him."

She placed both hands on her stomach as though she might throw up.

Lyrrin looked at the side of the woman's face, the blotchy pink and pale skin. Was she sick? Surely if the king was spending so much silvernix on trying to make more unidragons, he'd have enough for his wife.

"I'm sorry I broke the silvernix," Lyrrin said gently,

carefully. "It was a terrible accident. I know how rare and precious it is. There mustn't be much left."

"The king still has plenty."

Lyrrin smirked at how easily the queen offered the information.

She pushed a little further. "Are you sure? Have you seen it yourself?"

Yensen grasped her arm, squeezing a warning.

The queen shrugged a shoulder. "Only the king has access to the main supply."

"But you must have seen somethi—"

Yensen tugged Lyrrin backward sharply. "Your Majesty, I will remove this creature from your presence now."

Vellira half turned but didn't look at them. "Please do."

With a shove in the center of her back, Yensen moved Lyrrin at a fast pace across the flight deck.

She craned her neck back, staring at her grandmother, the massive, mindless dragon, and the stacked-up furniture, and a frown wrinkled her face.

"You're pushing your luck," Yensen hissed to her once they were in the corridor outside.

A hysterical chuckle escape Lyrrin's bleeding lips. "Am I? What have I done wrong? I'm trying my best, doing what the king wants. You know that I don't know how to do it, so what do you expect to happen?"

Yensen scoffed and gave her another nudge. "You can fool the others, but I know that wasn't an accident."

Lyrrin pulled her gloved hand closed in panic, and her footsteps stumbled and caught on the hem of her dress. Yensen caught her by the back to keep her upright.

He kept her in that grip and bent to whisper in her ear as some servants passed by. "You're foolish to be prying into things you shouldn't. Getting rid of all that silvernix just to get information on the king's supply was a transparent ploy."

The tightness in Lyrrin's chest eased. She was happy for Yensen to think that was all she was doing.

"I'm the foolish one?" she asked. "You're the one pledging your loyalty to a man who hits children. Who threatened me with his torturer."

Yensen's face grew stony, and he looked straight ahead up the stairs.

Lyrrin wasn't going to let him ignore her. "And it's not just me, either. How many children died in the attacks on the enclaves? How many people are dying in the keeps that are unprotected because all *your king* cares about is getting Dracuni?"

"He's doing what is most important in the long-term. He needs Dracuni to repair this world. I trust his plan."

Lyrrin made a rude noise. "I trust he's a cruel old man who has no value for life other than his own anymore."

They reached the entrance to Eslinde's chambers, and Yensen opened the door and tried to push Lyrrin in.

She turned on him, pleading with her eyes.

"Eslinde trusted you. She believed in you, cared for you. You could still be out there right now, helping them, making a real difference in the world. If you'd just help me ..."

He pushed her again, sending her stumbling back, and slammed the door between them.

"Fine. *Fine,*" Lyrrin seethed under her breath. "I don't need you anyway."

Muttering curses under her breath, she hurried to the room with the large balcony window and floor filled with books. Even though she knew Yensen couldn't see her, even if he was peering through the keyhole, she still ducked down behind a large stack of tomes as she carefully peeled her silk glove off.

The soft tinkle of glass sounded as three tiny vials landed in the palm of her other hand.

That was all she'd dared take, pushing them up into the holes at the ends of her gloves before dropping the others. That was all she'd dared allow missing as she obscured how many other vials were smashed on the floor.

Three vials. That was plenty to do some tests of her own. Three vials of silvernix ... but no crystals.

She hadn't worked out yet how she was going to get her hands on crystal. The only one she had was the locking rune, but she didn't want to ruin it with her experiments. Being able to lock her prison from within could also come in useful.

The runed crystal had been made by her pabba for Eslinde. She couldn't bring herself to carve it up, even for her escape.

Besides, she had another idea she wanted to test.

She crouched down beside the towering window and picked one of the diamond-shaped panes close to the floor. The hazy orange light of a smoky midday streamed into the otherwise unlit room. With her bare fingers, she began carving a line around the edge of the glass.

It had to work ... Lyrrin didn't know what she'd carved on the glass holding the silvernix that created Dracuni, but she knew now that runes on glass worked as well as on crystal.

The king's first trials had also been Lyrrin's first trials. She had carved every rune she knew and carefully activated them. The one with the light symbol lit up like a tiny glowfly. The burn rune vial warmed.

There wasn't enough surface area for them to do much, like the tiny shard crystals she'd cut from larger stones when she was low on resources. But it worked.

"And now I'll see if it works on something bigger."

The pane popped free. It was a decent size, larger than her splayed hand. She cut a second, as the chilled winter wind from outside whistled in, making her shiver from the cold and anticipation.

Once she had two panes laid out on the tiled floor, she considered her options and decided to play it safe.

She carved a light symbol onto one. The glass made soft, screeching sounds under her nails, and she kept checking over her shoulder as she worked, but nobody burst in to see what she was doing.

Just to be sure, Lyrrin wailed some fake sobs to cover the noise.

The next step she wasn't so sure about. She tried resting one of the vials on the glass the way the vial on the locking rune crystal sat on it.

She traced the rune to activate it.

Nothing.

She tried setting all three vials on the glass. Nothing She sat and waited a few minutes in case it needed time to charge. Still nothing.

Maybe it needs direct contact when it's glass instead of crystal?

She knew silvernix spoiled quickly when it wasn't encased in dragonglass. But just how encased did it have to be? She carefully pulled the stopper from one vial and released the shimmering drop onto the middle of the unmarked glass, then as quickly as she could, she sandwiched the runed pane over the top.

The opalescent fluid squeezed and spread between them, creating a mirror. It didn't reach to the edges and spill. It remained sparkling and moonlit.

Holding her breath, Lyrrin traced her fingers over the rune.

And the dim room lit up bright with a soft cyan glow.

Biting back a yelp of delight, Lyrrin bounced in place where she sat. She held the diamond of sandwiched glass over her head in triumph.

It worked. It worked, it worked, it worked!

Lyrrin's mind whirled with the possibilities. She had magic again. She had power again. She could make her escape. She sat there for a few long moments, enjoying the familiar cool glow.

As she brought her finger back to the rune to deactivate it, she frowned.

Was it dimmer than before?

"Already?" she whispered.

She hastily traced the rune again and the light went out. Holding the glass in front of the window, she angled it back and forth in the light. The silvernix still glittered, but it had dulled noticeably.

It wasn't fully enclosed. The gaps all around the edge seemed to be allowing the silvernix to spoil. Not immediately, but far too fast.

Without access to larger bottles or a way to seal the edges with glass, Lyrrin wasn't sure what to do. She hadn't been allowed any glass drinkware, not allowed anything sharp, as though she were a dangerous criminal.

The flat panes were all she had.

She activated the light rune again, and the air rushed out of her at how much dimmer it was already.

She doubted it would last another few minutes.

She had magic again, but it didn't last long.

And she only had two more vials of silvernix available to make her escape.

SIX

The red glow of fire brightened the ground far below. Sunset had passed recently, and smoke filled the dusky sky, sharp in Kess's lungs.

"What's down there? Can you take us lower to see?" Kess called to Lyomir.

He didn't reply. He had kept a sullen silence ever since finding out he wasn't flying only Kess and Griskin, but also Aishena, Benjin, and Dashiel as well. He had allowed it, but he clearly wasn't happy about having other humans riding him.

He stretched his wings out to glide down slowly.

"That's Tjollaskeep," Aishena said from further along the purple dragon's spine.

Lyomir hadn't allowed any saddles, so each of them

had roped themselves in between the double row of spikes down his back. Griskin was carefully tied between Kess and Aishena, with Benjin and Dashiel at the back. Except for the wolf, they were all kitted out in dark leather delver armor and flight goggles.

Although the scale armor they had from Eslindekeep would have offered more protection, wearing shimmering rider armor in Eslinde's colors didn't seem the most covert option.

As they grew closer, the walled city spread beneath them. A couple of buildings burned, the last embers smoldering like red eyes in the dark. But mostly the keep was simply empty. Unlit. Lifeless.

"Maybe they evacuated?" Dashiel said.

Kess shivered. Dragonkeeps were meant to be impenetrable. A safe haven from the undead blight. Protected by their massive walls and dragonfire. But Kess had seen Gerichkeep fall to the revenant army. She'd prayed that it was an anomaly, that something had gone wrong there that could never go wrong again.

Seeing another dragonkeep broken and abandoned shook Kess to her core.

All the people flying with her were also once dragonlords too, raised to believe in the strength of their defenses against the undead. The tense silence suggested they all felt the same way about what they saw.

They flew on to the east, and the full moon rose red

above them, ringed in a ghostly glow from the ever-present haze.

"Look," Dashiel said, voice cut short with emotion.

Under the bloody moonlight, the ground churned with motion. The revenant army, marching onward. Uncountable in its multitudes.

"Ardahnkeep is just ahead," Aishena said. "They're heading right for it."

"It'll be protected, though, won't it?" Dashiel asked. "I mean, it's *Ardahnkeep*."

The shape of the city appeared, silhouetted on the horizon like a jagged tooth. The firstborn heir's dragonkeep, formed around the old Rolanian capital, and second biggest city in Elundrae.

Although Ardahn himself had died long ago, his descendants kept the dragonkeep in high regard as equally populous and flourishing as the capital.

"I don't know," Aishena replied. "From the numbers of dragons besieging the undercity, Eslinde thinks the king has drawn riders from every keep to be there. Maybe not all of them, but Ardahnkeep isn't going to have much more protection than their walls."

"Which doesn't help much when some of those revs down there are flying." Kess urged Lyomir onward with her thoughts, eager to be away from the ocean of undead below.

They flew high, where the air was chilled and thin,

and between them and the ground there were large shapes hovering over the rev army, worn wings beating unevenly.

"Can we help them? The people in Ardahnkeep?" Benjin asked.

Aishena's voice replied, hushed, "I don't think us and one dragon are going to turn the tides for them in any meaningful way."

Kess frowned. She'd also come to this painful conclusion.

They needed to push on. They needed to fulfill their mission and get back safe with Lyrrin, and then they could work to do more toward breaking the curse.

They couldn't let the Dragon King hold access to someone with so much knowledge of Alderkin magic and Dracuni. If he found a way to use Lyrrin's knowledge to tame more dragons, things would only get worse.

But most of all, Kess needed to bring Lyrrin back for Riony.

Kess lifted a hand to touch the lump beneath her leather armor where the acorn hung.

I need you to come back to me too. Do you understand?

The way Riony had pulled her close, forehead pressed against hers ... It was just the same as how she farewelled Aishena and the rest of her friends and family.

It warmed Kess beyond measure to think that maybe she had raised herself in Riony's esteem to that same level. But still her greedy heart wanted more. It yearned for how that kiss had made her feel.

Not just tolerated, not just friend, or even family, but *wanted*. Wanted in the kind of crushing, all-consuming, too-much way that Kess had always wanted things, a way that she sometimes thought only she knew.

The way she felt about Riony in return.

Benjin cleared his throat as they passed over Ardahnkeep and continued onward.

"Do you think Hjelzahnkeep is okay?" His voice had grown deeper recently, but now it rose high, breaking over the words.

"I'm sure it is. It hasn't been in this army's path," Aishena replied in a tone far gentler than she usually used.

They all grew silent again.

Kess directed Lyomir, skirting out over the water, along the shoreline of Grand Hofen. When she'd asked this favor from him, she'd explained all about where they needed to go and what they needed to do. He'd somewhat uncomfortably told her he didn't know the land, didn't know where anything was. He had no real memories of the places he'd been while tamed.

All recollections of his life existed as though through a grease-smeared lens, dulled and gray, lacking clarity or emotion or anything other than the ability to follow orders.

So he allowed Kess to guide him with her thoughts and gentle touches of her hands to his neck. It mirrored how she rode Griskin, how she would give him direction, but he would choose whether he would follow it, and how.

It wasn't long before Draekhanhelm loomed before them.

Lyomir swooped in low then, coming in over the soft waves of the harbor. Ocean spray fell across Kess's face, salty on her lips. The dragon's wings remained still and silent as they glided up over the keep's walls and between the tallest of the buildings.

Kess was on alert for dragonriders on guard spotting them, no matter how elegantly stealthy the purple etherdart moved through the dusk. But no dragons appeared.

They flew over unguarded streets that were mostly quiet, but some were lit by torchlight and pounded with the angry chants of crowds.

Not even any city guards on treedarts emerged to deal with the unrest.

"Well, that was easy," Benjin said. "I thought we were going to have to fight our way into the keep."

"Don't jinx us," Kess hissed back.

"He's right though." Dashiel's expression was drawn tight, scanning the air around them. "There should have been at least a couple of riders with eyes on any unscheduled arrivals. But this place is entirely unguarded."

Benjin pulled his crystal-studded staff and looked through a clear section at the end. "The Dragon King wouldn't have sent all his riders away, surely. He wouldn't leave all these people defenseless."

"The rev army isn't quite on their doorstep yet. Maybe the riders that are still here are taking a night off," Dashiel offered.

"Let's hope so." Kess guided Lyomir up a little higher, out of the cover of the buildings. "The palace is just up ahead. Be ready."

The dark stone blocks and spires of the palace rose skyward in their path. The last time Kess had flown in, she'd been too panicked to really take in the scale of the structure.

The bulk of the palace formed a half-circle shape, like archways tipped flat and stacked unevenly upon each other, creating deep gaps where courtyards lay. Along the curved top, towers jutted upward. The whole thing was reminiscent of the Dragon King's crown.

Lyomir moved in silently, and Kess looked for somewhere he could drop them off. They didn't want to risk landing in a flight deck.

Then swift, dark wings cut through the sky. A black-and-white dragon rose in front of them.

Kess swore, and Lyomir's surprise and anger also slammed into her.

Silent, brainless thing!

She could feel his strong urge to continue forward, to clash with that dragon and pull its taming stake free.

Kess pushed back with her own thoughts and feelings. *Turn, turn away!*

They hovered there, dragon facing dragon, as Lyomir growled.

Metal glinted on the back of the black-and-white dragon as the rider brought something to their mouth. A piercing whistle blew. Within seconds, two more smaller dragons emerged from a flight deck on the upper levels of the palace.

"It looks like not all of the city was left unguarded," Benjin said almost matter-of-factly.

"I told you not to jinx us!" Kess replied.

Lyomir turned then, looping sharply to the side and downward. Kess's stomach lurched, and Griskin whined behind her.

Three more pips from the whistle blew, then the king's rider was after them.

Lyomir's wing membrane rippled and fluttered as they skimmed one high wall of the palace, then they were shooting along a wide street, low to the cobblestones.

Kess angled around to keep an eye on their pursuer. The black-and-white dragon was close behind them, close enough to hit them with their breath. But nothing came.

Black and white ... what breed is that?

Seasongs had black scales. Snowshimmers were regularly white, but never black. Dracuni's seasong mother had been silver and black, but this dragon was too small to be purely seasong.

"Is that a seashimmer?" she yelled back to Dashiel.

"Yeah, weird choice for a rider."

Kess hadn't seen that hybrid breed before. They were generally only used in ice production.

"They must have scraped the bottom of the barrel to be riding that thing," Aishena said. "Its cold breath is useless against revs."

"It is fast, though." Kess tugged the end of a throwing knife, then pushed it back into the sheath.

The rider was within range, but she didn't have to take their life. She just had to get away from them. Narrowing her eyes, she scanned their path ahead. The seashimmer may be fast, but all of its reactions relied on signals from its human rider.

Kess leaned forward, both hands flat against Lyomir's scales. She cleared her mind of everything except their connection, the feeling of oneness it brought.

Okay, we're going to lose these clowns. You know what to do. I'll spot for you.

Lyomir lifted straight up, wings gusting out and bringing them to a sudden stop. Benjin cried out as he slipped sideways, dangling from his rope. Dashiel caught him and hauled him back up.

The black-and-white dragon shot past them, then far down the wide street and corrected to come after them again.

Kess spotted a dark gap between buildings ahead, and without more thought than that, Lyomir turned that way. With wings tucked close, he dove down the narrow alley, beneath covered walkways that cut from building to building above them.

Kess leaned right, and he whipped the same way, pumping his wings hard as he broke across a wide square, then behind a building lined with columns.

Two more sharp turns within the city streets, and Kess could no longer hear their pursuer. She brought Lyomir to a stop under the cover of a large arched gateway. The two smaller dragons from the palace circled high above, but none were coming directly for them.

"Nice flying." Dashiel looked flushed and worked to tighten the ropes holding them in place.

Kess patted the purple scales. "It was all Lyomir. I knew he was an incredible dragon from the moment he was born."

The dragon's sides were heaving with deep breaths, and there was a slight thrum of pride washing through from him to Kess. He snorted grumpily.

"We're not going to be able to get into the palace by air, it seems," Aishena said. "We're going to have to work out another way in. On foot."

Kess wrinkled her nose. She'd hoped it would have been faster and easier than that, hoped she would be back by Riony's side again soon. But nothing was ever that easy.

She reached back to Griskin, ruffling the fur around his neck. He tail thumped happily, as it always did the moment they were no longer in the air anymore.

Aishena watched the surrounding streets with narrowed eyes. "We need somewhere to hide out. We need to let those guards give up their search before we attempt to breach the palace."

Dashiel winced. "I know a place. Zarram dragonhold is just around the corner from here. I don't know what state it will be in, whether anyone will be there ..."

"It's worth checking out." Kess undid the ropes tying her in place, then turned around to work on Griskin's. "Lyomir, will you be able to fly out of here without trouble from those other riders?"

The purple dragon huffed as though even the question was an insult. Kess could have sworn he rolled his green eyes.

She half smiled and climbed onto Griskin, then all of them got down from the dragon's back and onto the street.

Lyomir peered out from under the gate's archway, stretching his wings.

I'll stay close. Call when you need me.

He didn't wait for any kind of reply. Air gusted around Kess and ruffled Griskin's fur as the purple dragon took off and disappeared into the night sky, with the king's riders chasing after him.

Stay safe. Kess sent her thought to Lyomir like a wish, already missing him.

Even though she knew that with a dragon no longer

on their team, it was her own chances of getting in to save Lyrrin and out again safely that had dropped dramatically.

SEVEN

The mountain of conglomerated revenants rumbled up the slope, bones clattering on the stone in a horrific percussion. Glowflies filled the air, fleeing in a hum of shooting light.

Riony ran ahead, leading it after her.

She huffed deep breaths between bellowing over her shoulder, "Come on, you mess of tangled tailbones. You remember this dance. Come and get me!"

A chorus of roars replied.

"Now!" She reached the summit and dropped, skidding between Dracuni's legs.

And the unidragon breathed.

It was so much larger than last time.

A storm cloud of silver flame burst through the cavern

and across the charging monster.

But it had the same effect.

The rev king's advance faltered, slowed, then came to a juddering stop as the bright shimmer of fire spread across it and through all the gaps between its bony mass.

A wet, crackling sound filled the air as the revenants' roars became screams. Human and animal and cries that sounded like neither echoed through the cavern.

Over the glowing bones, organs and flesh reformed, bodies long dead surged with life as they were healed with the power of Dracuni's magic.

Riony squeezed her eyes closed and turned away as all those creatures, those poor animals who had once died and were brought back undead, had their bodies returned only to remain dead.

Dracuni had been right. She didn't like it at all.

But it was a good idea. It would create meat for the dragons and get rid of all those revs in one blow.

Behind the unidragon, Vance swore in a rough, awed voice. "It's working. It's actually working!"

"Greaaaat," Riony mumbled, trying to hold back the rise of sickness that heated through her chest as she got to her feet.

Amma. She could still feel the bony claws of her dead mother's hands ripping into her skin, still see her mother's soft face reforming, piece by piece under Dracuni's fire, only to fall still again. It hurt less now. But 'less' was still enough to make Riony want to curl into a ball.

Niskina squeezed between the tunnel wall and Dracuni in order to reach Riony. Her lips turned down, and she wrapped Riony in a hug. Riony leaned into her. She wanted Lyrrin or Aishena or Kess—*sparks, I want Kess?*—to seek that comfort from, but they were all gone. Niskina also knew, though, what this meant to Riony. She squeezed her hard.

Farther back in the tunnel, Jaym eyed the entangled mass of skeletons and corpses spilling across the cavern in front of them under Dracuni's continuing flame. "That is quite the magic trick. But I don't think we're going to get as much meat out of this as we'd hoped."

Riony half turned in Niskina's arms, glancing for a moment but unable to keep her eyes on the scene for long.

Jaym was right. The revs that were less degraded, that had even a little skin clinging to their skeletons, regrew more flesh, but those that had been picked clean by the spiders twitched and moaned, then fell still without healing.

Riony moved out of the embrace and patted Dracuni's neck. "That's enough."

The stream of fire slowed, then sputtered out. The unidragon made a wheezing sound, and her head slumped. "You okay?"

Yeah. Just ... tired. Really tired.

Her legs shuddered and folded beneath her, and her flanks heaved with labored breaths.

"Whoa, easy." Riony helped support Dracuni's bobbing head.

I'm okay. Just feeling weak. Need to rest.

"Some food will help her recover quicker if she's anything like a snowflame," Vance said softly. "Which she seems to be, with how much flaming affects her. The flame's fuel must be being drawn directly from her bloodstream."

Riony gestured to the renewed corpses. "Given its effect, I'd say that's a good bet."

Vance moved closer, examining Dracuni's eyes and snout. "You said her mother was a seasong, though? She couldn't be all seasong, or she wouldn't flame at all. I would have said she had a snowflame father, but considering they're a human raised and tamed breed, I don't know how that could have happened."

Dracuni's worry leached into Riony's senses. *Don't snowflames have shorter lives if they breathe too much?*

"You're okay. I'm sure that just hit you hard because you were already hungry. And we're not going to need you to use your flame again anytime soon." Riony patted her mane, then clarified to Vance, "She's worried about how long snowflames live."

Vance bent over to look Dracuni in the eye. "One big burn can use up a snowflame entirely if pushed too far. Next time, keep to smaller, controlled puffs when possible so that you're keeping a gauge on how you feel in between."

Dracuni's nerves settled, and she gave a small nod.

"Watch yourself!" Niskina barked.

Riony spun around to find the skeleton of a bear dragging itself weakly across the ground toward her. Its back half had reformed with the dead weight of skin and organs, but the regenerating magic hadn't worked on its front half. The rev slowly clawed her way.

Given a few more minutes, it could have taken a chunk out of her leg if she'd kept her back to it. Now, Riony was ready to put it out of its misery.

She drew her dragonguard sword in one hand. Her crystal sword was with her as always, sheathed on her back. But as it was out of charge, she figured she'd change things up. Her old sword felt so familiar in her grip, but also so strange in how lightweight and flexible it was compared to the weapon she'd become used to.

She brought it cracking down through the back of the bear's spine bones, close to the skull, and the bones fell apart, lifeless on the floor.

Niskina pushed past her and hammered her poleaxe down on another still twitching rev.

"Here you go." Riony grabbed the meaty back leg of the bear and dragged it close to Dracuni. "Eat up, I guess?"

The unidragon sniffed the meat with equal amounts of distrust and starved appetite. The flesh was new and fresh and smelled fine, and after a tentative bite, Dracuni flushed with happy feelings as she joyfully devoured the rest.

Riony turned away. Meat was meat, but this whole

situation still felt kind of icky.

In the spill of entangled skeletons and reformed corpses, a few revs still clung to the last vestiges of animation, and Riony, Niskina, and Vance moved through and made sure they were all put to rest.

Riony paused beside one, waiting to watch whether it burst back to life again as the revs aboveground now regularly did, but it stayed dead. Maybe they were too far away from the shadow dragon's call down there to have been made stronger in that way.

"Looks like we'll have enough to give all the dragons one decent meal from this." Vance poked at the pile with his boot as though checking for any more signs of life.

"And if we need more, we now have a clear path through to the nightmare of spiders beyond," Riony added joyfully.

Niskina poked Jaym playfully as he cringed at the mention of spiders.

She looked over Riony, still with a flicker of sympathy in her expression. "We can finish up down here. Now that Dracuni has done her thing, we can bring others in to finish the work. You don't need to be around all this."

Riony squeezed Niskina on the shoulder in thanks. The whole experience down there left her feeling as though a snake was coiling around in her stomach. She was also eager to hear if there was any news yet from the rescue team.

It's only been a day. Stop freaking out.

Dracuni finished her food and was standing again on

shaky legs. Her stomach rumbled.

Riony raised her eyebrows. "All good?"

I feel even hungrier than I did before.

"Come on. The others will bring you some more meat soon, but you've got to go and rest now."

The two of them made the slow journey back through the tunnels to the collapsed section, where delvers had set up ropes and pulleys and a platform big enough for Dracuni to ride on. Riony pulled one of the ropes, ringing a bell far above, and before long they were slowly edging their way up the deep hole.

At the top, Riony passed on the message that it was clear for more helpers to go down and help with the meat collection. She had no way to explain to the delvers and volunteers working with the dragons exactly how all those fresh carcasses appeared down there.

It was the best they could do to make sure no one saw Dracuni use her flame and keep the source of the meat between a small group of more trusted workers.

The corridor leading back to the main cavern held an odd, nostalgic feeling. The swirling, floral engravings that decorated the neatly carved limestone and the temperate air, suffused with cyan light and just a hint of fungal scent, all felt like home.

Riony had ventured out through this same tunnel the day she found the dragon nest and had run through it blindly on the day she and Kess had been washed away into the depths. She had snuck in through it on the day they'd defeated Kife, and she'd come back there to be alone and cry after finding out Lyrrin had been taken.

Today, she and Dracuni walked in tired silence, and as they came to the end of the tunnel, Eslinde stood waiting for them, flanked by two tall, robed figures.

Riony knew who they were, and it made her itchy with anger.

"Oh, *now* you decide to finally pop up again?"

Priyune and Yrik had the grace to bow their heads lower.

Eslinde returned a fire-bright glare. "Riony, listen. They have returned with something to share."

"Maybe they could have shared a bit more earlier on? Like before Lyrrin got taken? Maybe that would have helped?"

Dracuni bumped her shoulder. **Be nice. She was their family too.**

Not like she was ours. Riony knew she was being unreasonable. She was also hurting.

"We are sorry for our absence." Priyune stepped forward and drew a symbol in the air with her long fingers. "But we were working. We had much to do with only four hands, and we don't yet know whether it has worked."

"Please let us show you." Yrik gestured for her to follow.

Riony remained where she was. "Dracuni needs to rest."

Eslinde moved close and looped her arm around

Riony's. "Dracuni needs to be there for this too. Come. You'll like it."

Riony snorted air through her nose but sighed her agreement. She expected to continue out of Whisperwind Passage, but the Alderkin led them all back in and around a couple of short turns into a circular chamber.

"Oh ..." Riony mumbled as the large geode slice sitting in the center of the space came into view.

Niskina had moved the gateway up from the depths, but since it was out of charge, nobody had really bothered checking on it since then.

"*Oh*," she said again, taking in the ring of massive standing stones around the edge of the room, apparently freshly carved from crystal-streaked limestone. "Is that ... are they going to work?"

Yrik bowed apologetically. "We don't know. We had no access to core crystals of the size that would have been used for shrines in the past. But we hope there is enough crystal within these stones to work."

Priyune tilted her head to Dracuni, who hovered at the entrance, one front paw lifted in hesitation. "We will know shortly."

"Go on, go in," Eslinde encouraged.

Dracuni stepped into the circle. There was no immediate feedback, no visual sign or sound that indicated anything was working the way shrines normally did.

But when Riony followed Dracuni into the ring formed

by the stones, a zing of energy tickled up the back of her neck.

"Try the gateway," Riony said in a hushed breath.

Yrik bowed low before the oval crystal, bending to place his forehead against the base before tracing the rune. A small, wavering glow built within the symbols around the edge of the gateway. Yrik selected one, and the gateway shimmered to life.

Dracuni trilled with excitement. Eslinde let out a yelp of celebration, and the Alderkin both raised their hands and drew a wide, swirling shape with them.

Riony grasped the sides of her head in her hands and let out a long breath.

This is huge. They had a working gateway again. They could get people out of the siege.

But where could they send them that was safe?

"Dracuni, can you fit through?" Riony eyeballed the size of the unidragon compared to the gateway.

The last time she'd fit through was the night of the enclaves attacks, and it was a tight squeeze then. As she moved up to the crystal now, she couldn't even wriggle her front shoulders through.

She backed out again, looking bashful.

"This is still good, though. This means a lot. If people want to leave the siege, they can. And ..." Riony's eyes popped wide.

She wrestled her crystal sword free from its sheath on

her back and held it in front of her. Quickly skimming her finger over the rune, the blade glowed purple and the weight floated away.

"Yes, yes, yes!" She kissed the glowing crystal. "Oh, I've missed you!"

And not just her sword. All of the used-up crystals throughout the undercity could be brought in and recharged. There would be enough light and warmth and weapons for everyone.

Riony walked over to Yrik and Priyune. She wasn't sure of Alderkin etiquette and hoped she wasn't overstepping as she pulled them both into an embrace with an arm each.

"Thank you. This is going to change everything."

She was startled when they held her back just as tight.

"You were right. We should have shared more, sooner. And if we had done so, we might have saved my granddaughter, your sister." Yrik's gravelly voice rumbled near her ear.

He pulled back and looked at her with eyes so similar to Lyrrin's. "After suffering that loss, after seeing how far into death our land has fallen, we have made our decision. We will share everything now. Any of our magic that can assist, we will give it, in order to keep what we can of the world alive, human and otherwise."

Riony offered them a sad smile. Fishing for the string around her neck, her heart clenched, thinking of the other string, now gone along with Kess.

I hope she's okay, that she hasn't needed the silvernix in that acorn.

At the end of the remaining string, the flat slice of crystal hung. The remaining unpaired heart stone.

"Here. You should have this back."

Priyune lifted both hands together to receive it and then clasped it close to her chest. "I'll return it to the warrior's tomb."

"Yeah ... just maybe wait until we clear out the spiders down there first."

Riony looked at the gateway again. A few more of the shrine symbols around the outside had gone dark since the last time she'd seen a working gateway.

"The shrine just down the hill is still active. We could send scouts out that way to check on the situation outside. I don't like not knowing what's happening out there," Riony said.

Without Kess and Griskin, they hadn't had anyone game enough to climb the frozen mountain peak to bring back a report.

"You may not need to travel so far," Yrik replied. "We used to have a way to oversee our exits without needing to go outside."

Eslinde's eyes remained on the shimmering gateway, a slight crease between her pale eyebrows. "That sounds useful indeed."

Yrik deactivated the rune at the base of the oval crystal.

"It will take time to recreate, though. It's a complicated array of runes. The previous setup was destroyed when the battle for this deemfret was lost."

As though snapped out of a spell, Eslinde turned to them, blinking rapidly. "If only we could have done this at Eslindekeep …"

Priyune and Yrik shared a long look between themselves and whispered tersely in their own language.

Then Yrik bowed. "We didn't have the resources then, even if we had the will. But there was a way we could have kept the gateway there active, and we will live with the guilt for what could have been if we'd shared that knowledge earlier."

Priyune placed both hands palm outward in front of her face. "There is a way to keep crystals charged without shrines. Aleem discovered it in his work for the unicorn slayer."

Holding her strange stance, as though hiding behind her own hands, she explained how bottled unicorn blood kept close to crystals could keep them charged.

"Stars." Riony shook her head and moved closer to Dracuni. "I can understand why you didn't want anyone to know that bit of information."

More reasons people will want my blood. Wonderful.

The unidragon's head was lowered, exhaustion drooping her eyelids.

"We did not want to use Dracuni that way," Priyune said it like an apology and lifted her hands higher. "It would have taken more than a few drops to keep a crystal that size charged."

Eslinde watched as Riony rested a hand on the unidragon's neck. "Even if the gateway had still been working then ... Yensen was clever. He had me so thoroughly tricked. I'm sure he would have just found some other way to get what he wanted."

"He had us all tricked." Riony circled around the nearest standing stone, brushing her hand over the sharply carved limestone.

Lightning-bright zigzags of clear calcite shot through the milky stone.

She noticed how the rough surface formed into a repeating pattern, scratched with fine lines she'd never noticed on the time-worn crystals surrounding shrines aboveground.

Every part of the massive stones was covered in hair-fine runes, barely visible in the low light. It must have taken the two Alderkin every waking moment since they got there to create them.

And they had achieved their goal. They had a working gateway again.

Riony's breathing grew ragged with the rampant energy that filled her.

I could go after Lyrrin, catch up to the others.

She moved toward the gate as though she could leave right away and then stopped. Perhaps in the past, she would have.

Now, all the working pieces of what lay before them turned more clearly in her mind.

She had no way of contacting the rescue party to meet up with them again.

She didn't have Griskin with her this time to help her get into the capital dragonkeep, to help sniff her way to her goal.

There were more revs than ever.

It was impossible, and as much as she didn't want to care, as much as she wanted to be the Riony again who threw herself mindlessly at impossible things, she knew there was something greater she had to put her strength behind now.

Dracuni.

She had to be protected, for all she could provide the world.

This humming circle of magic they stood in was proof of that. It was going to mean so much to the undercity community.

Riony couldn't run into a trap and leave Dracuni behind. Not even to save Lyrrin.

She was going to have to trust Kess's promise that she would bring her sister home. That they would both come home.

I do. I trust her. Came the thought Riony never would have thought she would think.

Riony turned back to face the gateway, narrowing her eyes.

No, she couldn't travel through it to chase after Lyrrin. But it could be used for other things.

EIGHT

Kess hugged the shadows with Griskin, avoiding streetlights as they moved through the quiet nighttime of the city.

She wasn't sure how recognizable she'd be to anyone who may peer out a window, seeing as she was riding on her wolf, but she was sure there would be those in the capital who still believed she was the heir slayer.

"This way." Dashiel adjusted their backpack and took the lead, hurrying down the quiet stone street.

Around another corner, the streets became familiar to Kess. The last time she'd seen them they had been filled with floodwater and rioters. Soon they reached the front entrance to Zarram dragonhold and found it scorched and barricaded closed.

Aishena thumbed one of the athames at her belt. "I don't think we're getting through that."

"But on the good side, it doesn't look like anyone else has been getting through there either." Dashiel almost sounded cheerful, but their eyes were sad. "Let's see if we can get in through the back."

They hurried up the street. Only moonlight and the occasional streetlamp lit their way. The clatter of metal startled them all. A couple of cats that could fit in the palm of a hand circled an old milk can.

The gate to the stockyard came within view. It was bent and broken but chained closed in an upright position. Dashiel reached it first and gave it a shove. It rattled but didn't open.

Aishena pulled her athame and it lit up yellow as she traced the rune. She sliced through the links, and they pushed the whining metal open just far enough to squeeze through.

No bovin brayed and no stream washed down the pathway as they made their way down to the building this time, but still ...

"This all feels too familiar," Kess said. "What are the chances someone has fixed that drop gate of yours?"

"I don't think it's going to be a problem." Dashiel pointed.

The external gate was still down off its hinges where Riony had left it, and the heavy metal internal gate had

been propped up on a pile of splintered furniture. There was enough room beneath to crawl under.

They went one after another into the darkness beyond, keeping a wary eye on the heavy gate above. Once they were inside and away from any prying eyes, Aishena activated a glow stone at her belt.

Griskin sniffed at footprints in the dirt there and growled softly.

"I'm less sure now that this place is unoccupied," Kess said.

"It doesn't exactly look like somebody else has moved in. This is a mess." Dashiel's expression darkened, and Aishena moved closer beside them.

Inside, scorch marks marred the walls and litter was strewn along the corridor. Kess pushed the nearest doorway open, checking inside.

"Is that room secure?" Aishena asked.

Kess couldn't see everything in the dark chamber, but Griskin wasn't bristling, so she nodded.

Aishena touched fingertips to Dashiel's arm. "Stay here. Benj and I will do a sweep to make sure we're alone. Kess, look after Dash."

"What makes you think I'm the one who needs looking after?" Dashiel called toward Aishena as she walked away.

She threw back, "Because you don't have a wolf."

Dashiel shrugged. "I suppose that's a fair point."

Kess opened her own mouth to argue. She and Griskin

could have the building cleared far faster than the other two. But Aishena rounded the corner up ahead, the paired blades she always carried strapped to her pack but never used glinting before she and Benjin disappeared.

Kess activated her own glow stone and turned to Dashiel to suggest they do their own scouting, when she noticed how pale their face had become.

They had moved into the room, kicking dully at the papers strewn across the ground, blackened and crisp. Cabinets along the walls had been wrenched open, doors hanging askew and anything of value cleared out. A couple of low cots were piled near the entrance, out of place in what seemed to be a storeroom.

Dashiel dropped down to sit on one of them and soot puffed out.

"I'm sorry," Kess said. "It must be hard, being here."

"I think the hardest part is that I never thought I'd come back here. That I'd never have to see it like this." Dashiel half smiled at her. "And that it doesn't hurt nearly as much as I feel it should. Does that make me a terrible person?"

Kess brought Griskin closer, and the wolf settled down on his stomach so that Kess was closer to Dashiel's level. "Coming from someone who watched their own home burn to the ground as well, I actually understand exactly what you mean."

Dashiel nodded eagerly. "It's just a place, and one with

so many conflicting memories. Home came with me when I left. Home was Vance and Shiff, Eslinde and Viska."

That Kess didn't understand. She'd been flung from her home with nothing.

Dashiel watched Kess's faltering expression with a frown. "And you. You're family now, too."

A rush of warmth filled Kess, watching Dashiel's kind, eager eyes. She remembered the first time they'd met after the taming ceremony, how easily Dashiel had accepted her, befriended her, taken her flying, and held her when she broke down crying afterward.

Before then, nobody but Riony had ever treated Kess with that care. Dashiel had shown her what friendship could be, outside of the complications Kess and Riony's relationship held.

"You are too good for this world," Kess said through a fierce grin. "Now stop it. I'm meant to be cheering you up, not the other way around. Although it may be a mission I'm woefully inadequate for."

Dashiel glanced toward the door. "Listen, I don't mind a little overprotective energy. But I don't need looking after. Wolf or no wolf. Now, let's work on our plan so we can show Aishena that we're half as good at this stuff as she is."

Kess snorted, reminding herself instantly of Lyomir, then dug around in her saddlebags for the map of the palace Eslinde had given them.

The princess had drawn it up in a hurry herself and

chased after them to hand it over before they'd left.

It was rough but had notes on potential entrances, guardrooms and grayglim lodgings, and places prisoners may be kept. Kess held the parchment flat between her and Dashiel.

"Our first problem with moving around on foot is that we're all kind of recognizable," Dashiel said. "Me, the rare Rolanian dragonlord, you and your wolf. And the Hjelzahn children half the kingdom and one possessed grayglim have been hunting for."

Kess didn't know what Lady Hjelzahn was doing now. She just hoped she was doing it far, far away.

"So we'll need disguises. We can fit in as commoners or beggars around the city while we work out how to get into the palace. After that, we're going to need something more."

"I'm not sure Aishena and Benjin are going to pass as commoners or beggars at the moment."

"Maybe we should have gotten them to dye their hair before we left. It's gotten very pale." Kess cursed her hurry to leave so fast and that she'd brought the others with her.

The Hjelzahn siblings' hair was its natural silver tone again, a clear mark of their royal lineage.

Kess's own hair, streaked through with long strands of white from all the silvernix her parents had spent on her in her youth also stood out, but still had enough black that the telltale brightness could be hidden more easily.

Dashiel smiled softly, some color returning to their cheeks.

"I do like Aishena with her silver hair though."

Kess closed the map in her hands. "Oh, really?"

"Okay, I like her either way." Dashiel's tone was dreamy. "Have you seen how good she is at … pretty much everything?"

"Well, yes," Kess admitted sourly. "Does this mean you're no longer competing for Riony's affections?"

Dashiel rasped a laugh. "I think that competition is over."

Kess's heart kicked up its pace as though she were staring down a sword point. Over? Was Riony with Zeina? Someone else? What had Kess missed?

"What do you mean?"

Dashiel leaned in close and gestured at her with both hands.

Kess shook her head, frowning.

This made Dashiel laugh harder. "Stars, Kess. Have you not seen the way she was looking at you after she pulled you from that lake, and honestly every moment since?"

Kess had only noticed how Riony had been trying hard *not* to look at Kess since pulling her from the lake. She'd noticed the avoidance, the sharp tension in Riony's shoulders and lips whenever Kess came too close.

"What way? Is she angry at me?"

Dashiel broke into laughter so hard tears squeezed

from the corners of their eyes.

Kess wanted to reach out and shake them. "What do you mean, Dash?"

"I feel improper even being in the same room as that look. If that look could be bottled, it'd be worth more than silvernix. That look, Kessara."

Heat flushed through Kess. "*What look?*"

She had no more time to force an answer because Griskin rumbled a warning growl and surged up to his feet.

"What is it?" Dashiel drew their sword and dagger.

Footsteps approached, more than two sets. The door swung open and Aishena stepped in, dragging a tied-up line of three prisoners behind her. Benjin followed at the back, staff glowing red and held high.

Aishena gave the thin silk rope a tug. "We found this lot camping out in the living chambers upstairs. Otherwise, the place is empty. What should we do with them?"

The bound people cowered from the heat of Benjin's staff and the wolf in front of them. There was a brown-skinned teenager close to Benjin's age who hadn't yet lost the soft cheeks of childhood, a bronze and freckled woman, and an older man with a stooped back and bushy hair who stood protectively in front of them.

"Azri, is that you?" Dashiel lowered their weapons.

The man squinted over the wolf's back. "Dashiel? I thought you were dead!"

"I've just been gone for a while." Dashiel stepped

around Griskin and clasped the man's hands. "It's okay. Let them go. I know them."

Aishena maintained her hold on the end of the rope. "They've *seen us*."

"Azri and his family worked here, for my family. We can trust them. They're good people."

Aishena's nose twitched, but she brought the end of the rope in and worked on the knots binding each of her captive's wrists together.

With his hands free again, Azri bowed to Dashiel. "I'm sorry we've been living here without permission, my lord. Nobody else would hire us after everything."

Dashiel grasped his shoulders, urging him back up. "I'm sorry, and don't worry. You can stay here. We're just ... visiting."

The woman and teen were freed, and the teen's eyes remained wide and locked on Griskin. The mother equally seemed frozen in fear by the wolf.

They must know the city well. They could help us get disguises too. A couple of growls from Griskin and they'd give us the clothing off their own backs.

Kess sighed inwardly. That was how she used to work, when faced with smugglers and slavers. She hated that it was still her first instinct.

She brushed her hands over Griskin's ears to settle him. He lowered down again onto his belly and panted happily.

"He's not going to hurt you."

"*Is he a wolf?*" the teen whispered dramatically.

Kess smiled in what she hoped was a friendly way. "He's a good boy. You're safe."

Kess pulled a loaf of the brown root-flour bread from the undercity out of her bag and broke it, handing half toward the three newcomers. Dashiel, Aishena, and Benjin followed her lead, sharing supplies they had brought.

Azri bowed. "Thank you."

Kess shrugged. "That's okay. You'll all need your strength for when the rev army reaches the capital."

"The what?" the woman balked, choking on her first mouthful.

Kess frowned. "The revenant army? That's marching this direction?"

Blank looks were returned.

Aishena added, "The one that has destroyed more than a couple of dragonkeeps in its path already?"

The family looked at them like they were crazy.

"You haven't heard anything about it?" Dashiel asked gently. "Nobody has said anything?"

Azri shook his head. "A friend who works for another dragonlord had some crazy gossip about why their lord was leaving for Elgartha, but nobody believes it. There's been no news in the daily sheets."

Kess and Dashiel shared a look. They didn't know. The whole general population didn't know what was coming for them. It was being kept quiet.

Dashiel ran through everything that had been happening, the size of the revenant horde, and the destruction left in its wake.

Azri scoffed. "The Dragon King will protect us if there are any revenants around. Keeps cannot fall."

His wife shoved him in the shoulder. "It's been weeks since I've received a letter from my sister at Gerichkeep. What if they're right?"

"We're right. We've seen it with our own eyes," Dashiel said.

Azri's mouth turned down. "All the riders are away at the moment. The skies have been so empty. What can we do? What do we do if the revenants get in?"

Kess remembered the inferno that had become of Gerichkeep when those remaining there had tried to fight back. "Hide. You should hide. Don't try to fight back or burn them. They don't burn anymore."

"*They don't burn?*" the teen whispered, aghast.

Kess continued. "When the revenants reach the city, get somewhere secure that you can barricade yourselves into."

"The flamesong stalls here would work well," Dashiel added.

Kess nodded. "Stock up with as many supplies as you can to last as long as you can before having to come out. Start now."

Azri shifted side to side on his feet, glancing at the door. "Yes, *now* now," Kess confirmed.

Azri bowed once more to Dashiel, eyes wide, and then herded his family to the door.

"And spread the word. Tell everyone you can to do the same," Kess called after them.

Benjin thumped the end of his staff on the ground and deactivated the burn rune. "We're just going to let them go? They were my first prisoners."

Aishena patted him on the top of the head.

Dashiel's mouth was pulled thin. "Do you think it's going to make any difference? If the revs get into the capital?"

Kess pictured the swarming masses of undead they'd seen heading this way. And if Ardahnkeep fell first, the army could be twice as big again when it got there.

There was no point telling people like Azri and his family to fight back. Not when the revs wouldn't burn, wouldn't stay dead. There was nowhere else for them to run.

Hiding made the most sense. But Kess wasn't sure it would help at all while the rest of the city was defenseless.

NINE

The pocket-hawk keened, the shrill whistle cutting through the low hum of industrial clatter and braying of bovin. Riony flinched as the bird appeared in a flutter before her.

"Relax." Niskina reached her arm out horizontally, creating a perch for Teeka to land.

Riony cringed at the beady-eyed creature. "I wish Jaym hadn't brought that thing along. It's a bad omen."

"Only to you with your weird bird issues. I think she's cute, and she's also part of our plan." Niskina pulled a small scrap of blue fabric from the bird's beak. "The others are ready."

Riony adjusted her crouched position on the ground behind the scrubby bushes, eying the high-walled factory ahead. Her hands were sweaty with anticipation. She dusted them in the ashy dirt and tried to focus on what they were about to do.

It had been over a week since the Alderkin had gotten the gateway in the depths active, and since Kess and the others had left to find Lyrrin.

Stars, what is taking them so long? I should have gone with them.

More than a couple of times, Riony almost charged off through the gateway to go after them. But the people of the undercity needed her. The hungry dragons needed her. Dracuni needed her.

The last big meals of revs and spiders didn't last long, especially for the younger, still growing dragons. And what Dracuni got back barely covered the energy she'd expended in flaming the rev king.

So Riony came up with a plan to get more meat.

She glanced behind her. Her heart panged at not seeing Kess there at her shoulder, or any more familiar faces.

Instead, she addressed a team of strangers—delvers and new recruits from the undercity. "Remember to leave the dragonrider guards to us. Stick to those on the ground."

They nodded as one, watching Riony intensely. A crystal slab provided by the Alderkin hung on each of their torsos like badly made chest armor. Their gazes settled heavily on Riony, filled with expectation and awe.

Sparks. What tamebrain put me in charge? Riony still

wasn't used to being looked at as the leader, even if it was just for this mission. She hoped she'd prepared everyone well enough.

Niskina scratched the palm-sized raptor around the neck, then gave her a piece of red fabric. Teeka took it in her beak and launched back into the sky. "Not long now."

Jaym, Zeina, and Vance led the second team, coming in from the back of the large compound.

There was no gate or ground level entrance into the glass factory ahead, since all transit in and out was done by dragons. There were only walls that jutted two stories high all around the interior buildings and smokestacks that belched smoke in long columns.

The whole place was as large as Heithorn estate, with dormitories, living areas, and its own stockyard of bovin to feed the working dragons within. After Riony had the idea to raid factories' food supplies to feed their own dragons, Eslinde helped with a list of options for factories still running outside of keeps. And there were plenty to choose from.

Niskina leaned closer to Riony and whispered, "How are you going to celebrate when we get home after our heroic mission? Do you and Zeina have plans?"

Riony's palms felt slick again. "Um ... we're not ..."

"What? You have a Rebel Rider, right there, who seems perfectly willing. Isn't that the dream? Why aren't you on that?" Niskina assessed Riony's wincing expression.

"Stars, girl. Jaym and I have been going at it since day one of him getting to the undercity!"

Riony blinked a couple of times. "Wait, is that what all the *meetings* have been?"

Niskina smirked and bumped her shoulder against Riony's. "I love you, but you can be slow to catch on sometimes. Is that the issue with Zeina? Are you not getting her cues? 'Cause I'll do you a favor and tell you right now that she wants you bad."

Riony pressed her hands into the ground, staring at the dry dirt. "No, it's more that maybe I'm not as into her as I thought I'd be. That maybe ... maybe I'm into someone else."

"Aishena? I thought you'd learned your lesson with her already. When she's not interested, she's not interested."

Riony swallowed hard. "Someone *else* else."

Niskina's eyes remained locked on Riony for a long, silent moment.

Then Niskina shrugged lightly. "Kess ... isn't that bad."

Riony huffed a relieved breath. "Wow. That's high praise from you."

"I mean, you could do better."

Despite Niskina's playful smirk, a defensive anger flared inside Riony. "I'm not so sure I could. Kess is ..."

Riony's mouth went dry under the weight of all that Kess was to her, all she'd become. All the qualities and strengths held within that one body that she could now

see so clearly since the bitter veil of hatred had been pulled away.

All they had survived together, because of each other. All Riony would be willing to suffer just to continue having Kess at her side. All the dragonflame-bright emotions within her that burned at being apart and at imagining being together again.

"She is the star my heart reaches for." Riony exhaled the words roughly.

Niskina's eyebrows crept upward, a soft smile forming on her lips.

Riony coughed. "Also, she's hot ... and stuff."

"Then I hope you and your star are reunited soon. Now, let's get to work." Niskina pointed upward.

Jaym's pocket-hawk circled above in the clear winter's day sky. It was time to move. Niskina gave the signal to the ten others waiting behind them.

A moment later, Riony had her glowing sword in her hand, rushing forward on light feet, leading her team toward their target ahead.

A purple glow shone from each of their crystals, and as the stone fortifications rose up in front of them, they jumped.

As a group they soared high over the scorched ground surrounding the factory, arcing toward the top of the wall.

Riony's feet planted onto the stone walkway first. She turned back, making room for those following her.

Niskina landed, wide-eyed and gasping. "Sparks, these float runes are fun."

The team landed lightly all around. One middle-aged man with a rust-toned beard flew high, his trajectory taking him up over the other's heads instead of onto the wall. Riony thrust out a hand, catching him around the ankle. With a quick tug, she had him down on the wall with the rest of them.

"You good?" she asked.

He brushed himself off and stood tall. "I swear this is shorter than what we'd practiced."

Riony chuckled quietly. "Love your enthusiasm."

Across the other side of the facility, the soft glow of purple shimmered through the midday air. Less obvious than if they'd come at night, but they were still plenty visible to the guards standing watch at the ends of the fortification walkway.

Riony directed three of her team that direction as the guards reached for the alarm bell. The metal clanged as Riony, Niskina, and the rest of the team dropped down the other side of the wall into the factory yard.

Riony had scouted the area three times that week in preparation for the raid. She knew there would be guards on the walls. She knew they would sound the alarm.

She'd counted out the eight guards and twenty slaves, the one overseer, and two dragonriders. Without a ground entrance and with all their own dragons stuck in the undercity, they were never going to get in less detected than they just had. So they just brought double the numbers.

Riony's team swarmed down through the stockyard, running between the pawing bovin, upset at the intrusion into their pen. As guards came into view, running out of the buildings at the sound of the bell, her team split into groups of two and three to set upon them.

Vance and the Rebel Riders' team would be doing the same, coming in from the other side.

Riony kept on straight ahead, rushing the central tower in long strides, ignoring the guards and smaller scuffles around her. Her targets were larger.

The first of the dragons appeared from an open archway at the top of the tower. A yellow etherflame. Its rider yelled something lost under the growing clatter of battle.

Riony sheathed her sword, still lit, onto her back, and pounced like a cat onto the side of the tower. She grasped a protruding waterspout and swung around it, throwing herself higher. Her fingers latched on to a window ledge, and she kicked up again, her float rune carrying her.

Her hand slipped on the next hold and her chest hammered. But she had to reach the dragonriders before they roasted the teams below.

Go, go, go.

She dug her toes and fingers into the vertical stone and scrambled skyward as the yellow dragon emerged and spread its wings. As it dropped from its perch to glide over the grounds below, Riony pushed off the tower with both feet, sending herself flying for its rider.

The woman wasn't nearly as surprised by Riony's airborne attack as she deserved to be. She pulled a short sword in time to smack it weakly across the blue and gold scale armor Riony wore. Dodging to avoid a better aimed second blow, Riony skidded down the dragon's back, between its beating wings.

Steadying her feet against the beast's spine, she drew her sword. A shadow fell over her, and she only had a split second to drop out of the way of the second dragon's snapping maw. The smaller bronze etherdart shot over them, circling around to come up behind Riony again.

The goggled rider smiled viciously as their dragon bore closer.

Riony braced, turning to face the approaching beast with her sword drawn. "Easy to feel superior while you're hiding behind all those scales and teeth. Come down here and fight me one-on-one!"

The dragon's mouth opened, aimed right for her.

A dart of red-brown feathers shot in from the side, colliding with the rider's head. Riony ducked under a bronze wingtip as the dragon swerved away.

The pocket-hawk screeched as she clawed into the rider's face, her wings out, fluttering as the man tried to swat her away. Blinded by the bird, his dragon slammed into a chimney, wings tangling as it and its rider tumbled to the ground.

Okay, maybe I don't hate the bird entirely.

The diminutive hawk circled again, her head angling around and beady eyes on Riony.

She still creeps me out, though.

Riony shook off the near-dragon-bite adrenaline and turned back to the rider she shared a dragon with. The woman's attention was off Riony now, bringing the yellow etherflame down over the stockyard below where Riony's team fought the guards. The dragon's chest swelled.

"You'd burn all of them, friend and foe, wouldn't you?" Riony barked.

The woman spun around, reaching for her sword again. But Riony already had her fist colliding with the woman's temple. Her flight goggles flew off as her head snapped away from the blow.

She slumped in her saddle.

And now here I am, up in the air with a whole dragon to manage.

The yellow dragon was still following through on its signal to burn. Riony stepped over the unconscious rider and slapped her hands over the dragon's neck, poking and prodding until the dragon lifted its head away from the people below, releasing a jet of flame into the air in front of them. The heat blew back over Riony as the dragon continued to glide onward, out over the facility walls and away from the others.

Riony had sat in on a couple of lessons that Vance and Zeina gave to the new undercity riders. She hoped it would be enough to get the dragon under control and back where she needed to be. She shifted her position, pressing more purposefully against the dragon's scales.

Riony let out a whoop as the dragon circled, turning toward the factory again. Soon they were approaching the walls where Zeina stood, waving up at her.

"A little help?" Riony yelled down as she passed over.

With a running jump, the Rebel Rider came flying her way. Riony caught her with an outstretched hand.

"Need me to get you back on the ground?" Zeina grinned.

The rider who was slumped between them groaned, and Riony pulled a rope to quickly lash her hands before she regained her senses.

"Me, not so much. The dragon, yes." Riony shuffled around, letting Zeina in front.

"Happy to handle it for you." Zeina's eyes glittered.

Riony patted Zeina on the shoulder, grasped her sword tight, and jumped down to the nearest roof. Her eyes darted around, taking in their progress.

The two dragons were dealt with. The second team had met up with the first, working on bringing together and binding up all eight guards. Jaym and Vance were dragging the overseer kicking and cussing out of a building to the side. Slaves watched in small huddles around the yard and

through doorways, whispering excitedly together. One spotted Riony, pointing to her as though he knew her.

From her perch on the roof, Riony could see the stores at the back, mountains of white sand and other minerals in heaps mined from the neighboring quarry. Down through the high windows of the long building in the center of the grounds, a dozen juvenile etherflames were chained into small cages beside glowing red furnaces.

The bovin in the stockyard, disturbed by the clashing humans, cowered in one corner, braying, despite being twice as tall as any of the creatures that had scared them.

Riony jumped down beside Niskina, who was bent over the man with the rusty beard.

"We all good? All clear?"

"Sure are. And just one injury." As Niskina straightened up, the man glowed.

He sputtered as the silvernix did its work, hands clutched over red wetness at his side. "Sorry, got a bit too carried away. Again."

"Lucky the princess has been so giving with the silvernix she brought from the capital," Niskina said, eyes on Riony.

"Yeah, lucky."

It wasn't clear whether anyone was believing their lie about where the influx of silvernix had been coming from recently.

Dracuni had been offering more and more of her blood to others, healing those in the undercity who needed it, making sure there was a supply for those going on risky missions.

Without the food she needed to replenish, it had been weakening her a lot.

"I'm sure the *princess* will be really grateful in return for the food we bring back," Riony said.

Vance already had the team moving. A slave showed them to a building on the side where carcasses of freshly slaughtered bovin hung. They loaded as much as they could into a cargo crate for Zeina to take to the nearby gateway with the yellow dragon.

Coming to join Riony and Niskina, Vance said, "The people here want to come and join us in the undercity. Jaym has gone to see if the bronze dragon is still good to fly as well, then we'll get all the people and meat out of here and call it a good day."

Riony bent over to help up the healed man. "Our fresh recruits did really well. They're going to be off running raids without us in no time."

The man turned red around his beard. "We couldn't have done this without you. You took down those dragonriders! You ..."

Overcome, the man made a series of swishing, exploding noises, his hands gesturing wildly.

Riony shrugged and patted her sword. "I've just had more practice with this. You'll be taking down dragons yourself soon."

"This was also all your plan," Niskina told Riony. "Don't sell yourself short. You'll be giving Aishena competition for strategy if you keep this up."

"I'm not sure my plan was that well thought out. I'm not sure what we're supposed to do now with all of this lot." Riony gestured to the tied-up guards and remaining bovin.

Niskina and Vance discussed the logistics of getting the rest of the bovin out, whether they could get them through the gateway to the undercity alive for future use. The guards they'd leave behind. Someone would fly in to check on the factory and find them at some point.

Riony turned to face the building holding the working dragons inside, her mind chewing over a thought that had been with her since she first started planning the raid.

She—and Jaym's bird—had taken down two more riders and their tamed dragons that day. After the dragons were used to help carry out what they needed, those dragons would be freed. They had a couple more doses of silvernix with them for that purpose.

The riding dragons were one thing, but there were another dozen tamed dragons inside, locked in cages.

All of which could be untamed, far more easily than taking down those with riders one at a time. When Eslinde had helped her find a target for this raid, she'd shown her locations of factories all over Elundrae.

If they could gain control of each the way they had this facility, they could free dozens and dozens of dragons at a time. They could work toward the numbers of untamed dragons needed that might make an impact on the shadow dragon's curse.

Riony's chest felt heavy, and she shivered as her sweat chilled on her skin.

They could do it. They might finally be able to make a difference. But every untamed dragon required more of Dracuni's blood.

Ten

Lyrrin pushed the carefully stacked pile of books over in an avalanche, frantically kicking the last few out of the way.

The section of wall hidden behind them had deep score marks in the stone from her nails, marking out a rough circle just large enough for Lyrrin to squeeze out of.

Or she hoped it would be, once it broke through to the other side. Which had to happen now.

The torturer was on the way.

She gave the stone a push, but it was still firmly attached, despite the hours and hours of work she'd put into carving the escape route. She needed something more to get through to the other side.

The handle of the entrance door turned and rattled.

"It's locked!" a deep, unfamiliar voice yelled from the other side.

It sure is.

Lyrrin had made sure of it the moment she'd overheard that the torturer had arrived. The rune lock her father made for Eslinde worked well, sealing up every entrance to the chambers.

Lyrrin ran for the nearby window and popped out two panes she had cut free and set back into place earlier. She carved her rune into one and placed a drop of silvernix sandwiched between the glass.

Back at the carved wall, she traced the rune again and it lit up yellow. She'd have to work fast before the charge ran out. She only had one vial of silvernix left after that.

Pushing the point of the diamond panes toward where she'd already carved, the cutting rune magic pressed into the stone like toes into sand. She pushed until there was no more resistance, breaking through the other side, and then ran it around the whole circle.

The front door shuddered loudly as something large smashed against it.

"Open this door immediately!" the deep voice yelled.

"How has she locked it?" another grumbled.

"I'll keep trying to get through. You go and get help."

Neither was Yensen. Her ever-present warden was only rarely off duty for short breaks.

Would he let he torturer take me, if he was here?

No matter how the guards hammered on the door or jammed things into the keyhole, the magical lock held. Lyrrin focused on her cutting. The golden glow faded with just a hair's breadth of stone left uncut.

She grunted shrilly and tossed the used-up glass aside. It shattered where it landed.

"What's going on in there?" The door shook again.

Lyrrin leaned back on her elbows. She hitched up her gray dress and kicked at the cut section with both feet. The shock of hitting the stone jarred up through her bones. She struck out again.

Crack. The cut section shifted. Leaning forward, Lyrrin pushed the polished marble with her hands and wriggled it through and out the other side. She tentatively put her head through the hole.

She didn't know exactly what she'd find there, only that from her observations of the palace layout, there was something through that wall other than a long drop down.

A chilled, narrow hallway lay beyond, illuminated by torches that sputtered from the winter wind howling through open slit windows in the walls.

Some kind of secret passage? Or was this where the servants appeared and disappeared from? Lyrrin rarely saw them moving around the main corridors. Whatever it was, it continued in both directions, turning a corner and dropping down stairs to the left. Hopefully to a way out.

Lyrrin squeezed the rest of her body through the hole,

cursing at her gown as it caught beneath her. Once on the other side, she checked on the final vial of silvernix and two pieces of blank glass she had wrapped in a scarf in her pocket, and then ran. The thumping at Eslinde's chamber door chased after her.

Down on the next level, doorways began appearing along the passage. Lyrrin tried one, cracking it open carefully. The clang of pots, crackle and spit of cooking, and hum of working voices came from beyond. She shut the door quickly and ran on.

She'd seen so little of the palace, and the place was huge. These tunnels felt like a maze within a maze.

Where do I go?

A doorway up ahead caught her eye. Made of a heavier metal, with the dark stain of damp footprints marking the ground around it.

Lyrrin gave it a hesitant push and found the dull purple of evening light and sappy scent of freshly pruned hedges beyond. A courtyard, wide and geometrically trimmed, and empty.

The garden was walled in on all sides, but it still felt like *outside*. That gave Lyrrin hope.

She tried to sneak through the shadows beside hedges and keep out of sight, but the polished pebbles there made a terrible crunching sound, so she moved back to the middle of the stone path and tried to walk casually as though she were meant to be there.

Two stories of windows looked down onto the courtyard, cold blue lighting shining from within, and a bell tower stood at one end, shooting up into the star-spotted evening sky.

An old memory surfaced, of the much smaller bell tower in the village she and Riony had grown up in, the sound of the bell marking time throughout the day, or used to warn of any signs of a revenant attack. Lyrrin hadn't heard any bells ring since she came to the palace.

From the window right at the top, a dark silhouette peered down at her.

Lyrrin gasped and ran again.

Arched entrances stood on three of the four walls of the courtyard, and Lyrrin had picked one at random. She reached it and peered inside. Two palace guards marched in time up the hallway within, their neat, quilted armor rustling with each step. Jolting back, Lyrrin ran for the entrance on the other side of the garden, her heart pounding.

She startled again when faced with more figures, but these didn't move. They were the statues she had seen before lining corridors in the castle. She recognized the one holding a long spear overhead from when she'd been taken to Eslinde's chambers.

If that way leads to where I was, maybe the other way might get me out of here.

Running on soft feet, she paused again at the next intersection, checking to see if it was clear. She sighed as the hallway lay empty beyond, leading to another stairway down. A spark of hope warmed her, and she stepped forward again.

A hand landed on her shoulder.

"What is this? An heir, wandering all alone?"

The voice chilled Lyrrin right through. She spun around, staring up into the merciless, dark eyes of Lady Hjelzahn.

Lyrrin backed away from Aishena and Benjin's creepy mother and hit the wall behind her. She reached for her pocket where the glass and silvernix were held.

In a flash of steel, the tip of a blade pressed against Lyrrin's hand until she stilled again and raised those bare hands in front of her.

Lyrrin stared up the length of the sword to the statuesque woman beyond. "Are you going to kill me?"

She only questioned it because Lady Hjelzahn didn't immediately strike her down, as Lyrrin thought she might. Instead, her dark eyes flickered and eyebrows knit.

"Who are you?" she asked.

"I'm Lyrrin Eyfarr," she said, without hesitation.

"Eyfarr?" Lady Hjelzahn lifted her blade, making Lyrrin tilt her face up to avoid it.

The woman wore full grayglim armor, the shadowy scales muted in the cool light. With her dark skin and sweeping eyes, she looked so much like her daughter, except for her black hair pulled back into one single long braid

and the inhuman coldness her presence exuded.

She inspected Lyrrin with a scrutinizing glare. "I saw you, in the caves with my children. But now you're here? How? Why?"

What had been a calculating, murderous look in Lady Hjelzahn's expression now showed hesitation, confusion.

Lyrrin pushed her lower lip out, letting it tremble, hoping to leverage that confusion, if not draw out some sympathy. "I don't want to be here. I'm being kept prisoner by the king. I'm trying to get away."

The grayglim's eyes seemed to look right through her. "You're born from the blood of the king. You're one of them."

"I'm not like them," Lyrrin grumbled.

"You are an heir. I can *feel* it. I can feel how you have to die. But you are also ... something else." The tip of the blade dropped a fraction.

"You can feel it?" Lyrrin lowered her hands, and the woman didn't react.

Her eyes became glassy. "It's all I feel. All I can think about, all I care about. I wait and watch for any opportunity to kill those who enslaved the dragons, as though if I kill all of you I could ... I could stop feeling so sad."

She shook her head and brought the sword tip up against Lyrrin's sternum.

Lyrrin ran her words fast. "No! I don't have to die. You don't have to kill me. Please listen. You're possessed by the spirit of the shadow dragon. That's why you're being driven to kill heirs. It's not who you really are. You could fight it."

The corner of the grayglim's mouth twitched.

"Every one of you must die." Lady Hjelzahn breathed the words like a prayer and plunged the sword into Lyrrin's middle.

Lyrrin's eyes popped wide. A sickening, flame-laced agony exploded through her.

"No!" The voice that screamed wasn't her own.

Lady Hjelzahn hissed and extracted her blade from Lyrrin's flesh in a swish of movement that hurt as greatly again in reverse. The world turned blotchy and dim.

Pounding footsteps grew louder. Lady Hjelzahn ran the other way, vanishing into the shadows. Lyrrin panted pained breaths, and her legs gave way beneath her.

Scale armor rattled as an arm caught her. Yensen swore under his breath as he inspected her wound. His dark hair hung loose around his face.

Other figures, blurred in Lyrrin's vision, moved around him.

He barked, "You two, continue pursuit."

More movement and thundering steps. Lyrrin's mouth remained open, locked in a silent scream.

A grayglim Lyrrin didn't know bent over them, looking more irritated than concerned. "How did she get out? She was locked in her chambers. That's why we came for you."

"Go quick. Inform the king. We need silvernix. I'll take

her there directly." Yensen rose up to his feet in a smooth motion, but even that made Lyrrin whimper, feeling cut in two.

Silvernix. I have silvernix! Lyrrin opened her mouth to tell Yensen where it was. She couldn't even feel her own hands to find it herself. She just wanted this hurting to stop. From her stomach to her ribs, everything felt seared and slippery and wrong.

Then she clamped her mouth shut again. *It's my last vial. My last chance.*

Yensen said he was taking her to silvernix. She could wait. She could make it.

Would she make it? It was hard to think.

Then they were moving, and the jostling of Yensen's swift steps blinded Lyrrin with pain.

"You're going to be okay." Yensen held her cradled tight to his chest. His voice was low and surprisingly gentle. "Our king will have silvernix for you."

Fear chilled Lyrrin. What if he didn't? He'd been using so much on the trials and often said he had to collect more.

Her words gurgled, "Will ... he ...?"

"The palace always has a supply. The king never lets it run low."

Light and dark flashed in Lyrrin's hazy vision and fire and ice warred within her, making her shiver and sweat. She coughed and tasted blood.

Yensen cursed again. "How is that blighted woman

still here? I told the king Kverra Hjelzahn was the Heir Killer in my missives, but nothing seems to have been done about it. Idra the First was found dead last week during her visit, and the king is still allowing Prysha the First to stay at the palace, for her supposed *safety*."

He was rambling like Lyrrin had never heard before. Even through her agony, Lyrrin heard the change in Yensen's tone. How *my* king had become *the* king.

"But I never thought she would go after you. I never thought you'd be out of your chambers alone." His voice cracked with worry.

For her? Or because he would be the first person punished if the king's precious half-Alderkin was lost. Lyrrin struggled to grasp the last thin strands of her consciousness as those thoughts whirled within her.

They turned a sharp corner and galloped down a flight of stairs in a way that made Lyrrin wish she'd given up her own vial of silvernix to have avoided the pain.

"Let us through!!" Yensen snapped.

They came up against a barred gate. The metal was formed into twining thorned vines that crawled and grew in Lyrrin's wavering vision. It blocked the width of the corridor. Two guards stood at ease within, in front of another solid metal door.

"Only approved persons can enter the royal silvernix chamber."

Yensen grunted. "The king will approve this. He will

want this girl to live."

"If it is our king's wish, we can escort the silvernix with you to be used in his presence."

Lyrrin stopped shivering. She didn't feel the pain so much now. Her eyelids just felt heavy. She felt much better. She was okay ... she just wanted to sleep.

"We don't have that much time. Let us through!"

The guards remained still. Not even a bleeding child in Yensen's arms moved them to break their orders.

Then with a sliding kick of their feet, they drew to attention.

"Let me see her." The king's face appeared in front of Lyrrin, and he grasped her chin, looking down with incandescent eyes.

Lyrrin wanted to swat him away so she could sleep, but her hands weren't responding. None of her body seemed to be there anymore. Everything was hazed and dim. At least three more grayglims surrounded the king, then six, then three, swimming in her vision.

Yeonard Draekhan snapped, "Open it."

There was a rustle of movement and a clang as the gate swung before them. Lyrrin bumped in Yensen's arms as they stepped through, waiting again as the two guards each moved to a slot in the wall on either side of the solid door in front of them.

"Hurry," Yensen whispered, too low for anyone but Lyrrin to hear.

Mechanisms turned and there was the grinding of metal, and they were moving again. Into darkness at first, and then with a click the room illuminated.

Or perhaps Lyrrin had died and fallen into a haunted land of death.

Skeletons surrounded her. She let out a weak wail. Arms squeezed around her a little tighter. Yensen still carried her, hurrying her toward shelves carved of the same dark, streaked stone that most of the palace was made from.

"Do it," commanded the king.

Lyrrin's eyes fluttered as something cool and wet touched her cheek.

A harsh white glare filled the space, cutting across the strange shapes all around her. The light came from her, rushing out from every part of her bare skin, streaming from her hands, mouth, eyes, blinding her. Her hearing filled with the hum of a thousand glowflies.

It hurts. Stars, it hurts! Riony had never told her that being healed with silvernix was an agony as great as the original wound.

Lyrrin screamed. Her body twisted and twitched from the pain of closing the hole through her middle. She felt every reconnection of flesh, from her navel through all the intricate parts of her insides and along the line of her back.

Her body surged as all the blood she'd washed Yensen and the floors of the palace with was renewed within her.

The light faded. She was left gasping and lightheaded,

as she stared with clear eyes at her scarlet sodden dress and the long rip in its middle.

Her hearing cleared as well, to voices speaking over her head.

"It was Lady Hjelzahn, my king. She continues to be a danger to you and your heirs. If you'd let me—"

"You'll leave her be." The king turned away, running a finger along the stone shelf in front of him.

It was tall as the king and as narrow as a hand's breadth, carved with intricate designs up the sides. A second shelf stood close by like its twin in the center of the domed room. Each held a single vial on each tier, except for where one was now missing. Less than a dozen in total.

A small supply kept on hand, brought in from wherever else the king kept the rest.

Yensen asked, "Kverra Hjelzahn ... You want nothing done?"

"Yes. Apart from this little inconvenience, she has proven useful."

Inconvenience? Lyrrin scowled.

Yensen hadn't yet attempted to put her on her feet, despite how she wriggled in his arms, fully revived. This space horrified her, made her want to run.

She hadn't been dreaming when she saw skeletons before.

The walls of the chamber were lined with skulls and bones, stacked and laid out into a hypnotic pattern.

Of all the skeletons Lyrrin had seen raised and walking, she'd never seen these. The white bones held a faint opalescent shimmer. The long skulls had a spiraling golden horn in the center of the forehead.

Unicorns. Dozens and dozens of unicorns.

There were some different skulls too, set alone on plinths that looked like broken standing stones from shrines. The skulls seemed human, but sharper.

Lyrrin brought her fingers to her own chin and cheekbones, wondering if her skull was like that too.

The room was filled with terrible trophies, from the remains of those the king had defeated to the broken standing stones, to the slice of geode gateway, broken in half, arching across the two shelves.

Lyrrin shivered, then glared at the monster that was her grandfather. "Lady Hjelzahn told me she wants you and all your heirs dead. How is that useful?"

The king didn't look at her. He locked eyes with Yensen instead. "They've all been plotting against me, you know. All of the Firsts. Ulfren and his razed cult of sun-mad worshippers was the worst. Do you know how much work it has been managing that mess? Far easier dispersing them now that he's gone."

Yensen's arms around Lyrrin stiffened but he made no other reaction.

"The First heirs were *your children*," Lyrrin said.

"One can always have more children. Sometimes it's

good to start again fresh." Yeonard Draekhan turned to Lyrrin then, looking over her as though she were nothing. An inconvenience. "Now leave. This isn't a place for you."

Yensen moved without hesitation, carrying Lyrrin from the silvernix chamber. She lifted her head to look over his shoulder, staring at the king. He watched her in return as he closed the heavy steel door between them.

His group of grayglims waited for him outside. Yensen spoke with one of them in a brief whisper. What Lyrrin could hear sounded more like a string of code words than anything she could understand.

He kept his tight grip on her as he left them and marched swiftly down the long hall.

"I can walk now," she said.

"I'm sure what you really want to do is *run*." The grayglim made no effort to put her back on her feet.

Lyrrin folded her arms over her sticky dress and pouted. "Wouldn't you if you were in my place? The king is going to use his torturer on me, and I just got *stabbed*!"

"It wouldn't be like this if you cooperated. If you gave the king what he wants."

"A unidragon?"

Yensen shushed her with a hiss, despite them being the only people in the corridor.

"And what do you think the king will do once he has one?"

Yensen's expression shifted from anger to something

more fervent. "He will repair our land! He will have enough silvernix to heal everyone, make all the dragonkeeps safe again. It will be humanity's fresh start."

Lyrrin scoffed. "I don't think that's what he meant when he said that. This is a man who doesn't even care about his own family. What makes you think he isn't going to keep all a unidragon gives him for himself?"

Yensen took Lyrrin up a flight of stairs, not half as gently as he'd carried her down them. "You kept Dracuni to yourselves."

"For her safety," Lyrrin snapped back. "Was there ever a time when someone needed healing and it didn't happen? Was there ever a time any of us could have helped people and didn't?"

Yensen's lips grew thin. He turned down a wider hallway that Lyrrin didn't recognize, lined with thin, pointed windows.

He seemed so close to cracking, so Lyrrin kept pushing. "The queen said the king still has plenty of silvernix hidden away somewhere. If the king was going to save our land, to do all these things you hope from him, why hasn't he started already?"

Yensen's mouth twitched.

"He talks of having more children as though they're just a resource to be made and spent. The way he treats me as well. Do you honestly think he's going to care more about the rest of the world?"

"He is our king," Yensen parroted as he often did, and his expression closed off.

He approached a wall and pressed something there, making a section of it swing away. He took her into a darker, rougher tunnel.

A dank smell made Lyrrin's nose wrinkle. "This isn't the way back to Eslinde's rooms."

Yensen huffed. "Rooms you've clearly discovered a way out of. I'd be a fool to take you back there."

A small chamber opened ahead, and Yensen finally put Lyrrin down to stand beside him. He kept one hand ringed like a shackle around her wrist as he struck a flint beside a torch, lighting it ablaze. A small dungeon lay ahead of them, gated with a grid of iron, with a short corridor of cells beyond. One side was a mess of warped metal and cracked stone, as though an explosion of some kind had ripped it to pieces. But a solid door with small, barred window on the other side of the passage remained whole.

Yensen dragged Lyrrin to it. "This kept your Alderkin family secure for decades. It should keep you out of trouble until you've done what is needed."

"And then?" Lyrrin challenged him, standing straight with the full length of her blood-sodden dress on display.

"Then ..." Yensen's mouth twitched. "I'm sure the king will still find you useful."

He closed and locked the door, plunging Lyrrin into darkness.

Only a small flicker of flame reached through the barred window, and Lyrrin's eyes worked hard to adjust. The ground was uneven and crunchy under her soft shoes and the drying blood all over her left her feeling itchy and cold.

All the warmth of hope her earlier escape attempt had filled her with was long gone, replaced now with a deep, sinking sadness.

This is how my father and the other Alderkin lived for so long?

The space was small, claustrophobic. There was no daylight. No glass.

She reached into her pocket and unwrapped the scarf. She sighed when she found the two pieces of glass and vial of silvernix still whole.

But the walls and door were far too thick to cut through with her final dose of silvernix. She'd have to think of something else.

There was a shuffle of movement outside.

"That was quick," Yensen said.

A gruff, haughty tone answered. "Our king wants you relieved. We'll be guarding the cell as our friend here does his work."

What work? Lyrrin frowned fand pushed closer to the door to listen.

A tense silence followed.

"Those are the king's orders?" Yensen's voice was clipped.

"He wants results, and he doesn't trust you anymore to get them."

Silence again, only broken by Lyrrin's heavy breaths as her stomach churned and fingers trembled.

My late son Hjelzahn had a man in his employ who is very skilled at getting results out of people who are being defiant. A man very good with his tools.

"Yensen?" Lyrrin whispered into the door, pleading, hoping.

A single set of footsteps marched away.

The door opened. Lyrrin stumbled back away from it, heart thumping like a trapped rabbit.

A very average man with neat black hair and tidy gray tunic stood at the cell's threshold, rimmed in the orange glow of the torchlight. He had soft cheeks and square chin and wore glasses that reminded Lyrrin of Yoskar.

A leather bag hung heavy in one of his hands, jangling as he shifted it.

He looked Lyrrin up and down, eyes moving over her clawed hands, her bright eyes, the blood soaking her dress. And he smiled widely, showing all his teeth.

ELEVEN

Griskin's ears twitched, flicking forward, alert. Kess felt every movement and tension in the wolf's neck, translating it like a second language.

Someone was coming their way.

"Shh. Hide!" she rasped to the others.

Aishena tried a door to her side, but it was locked. Dashiel frowned back the way they'd come. They couldn't go that way. They barely slipped past three guards who marched into that courtyard after them. Benjin slipped closer behind his sister.

The cold stone floor of the palace seemed to absorb every sound, but the silence felt more oppressive than comforting. The corridor stretched long and empty ahead, lamps flickering with a bluish light that cast the guard's shadow on the wall as she rounded the corner toward them.

"Behind the statues." Kess barely breathed the words, gesturing with her hands to get the message across.

Aishena, Dashiel, and Benjin ducked into an alcove each. The sculptures of golden warriors barely concealed their forms as they huddled behind them, trying to become invisible. Only Aishena managed it seamlessly.

Kess urged Griskin into their own alcove. He bumped the gilt figure as he wedged in behind it. Kess held her breath as it teetered and rocked, then stabilized. The large wolf was too big for the space, unable to hide behind the statue like the others.

It got them out of direct view down the hallway, but they'd be obvious to anyone walking past.

The guard's footsteps grew louder, reverberating off the stone walls.

Turn around, go a different way, Kess wished silently.

As the guard drew closer, Kess radiated with tension, her hand hovering over her throwing knives. The guard's shadow loomed down the hall. Kess pulled a bone blade free. The guard was only a few steps away.

Peeking from behind the golden biceps of the ancient Taen warrior, Kess prepared her shot. Blue light flickered off the guard's bare face and neat braids.

She's barely older than me. Kess's stomach churned.

But if the guard saw them hiding there, she could raise the alarm, and it would all be over.

Kess had to act. But maybe, maybe she didn't have to kill anyone today.

Hand whipping out like a striking snake, Kess threw her blade. It went wide, behind the young woman, and cracked into the glass bulb covering a lamp. Broken shards hailed to the floor and the guard yelped.

Halted mid-step, the guard turned toward the mess. The bone blade lay farther down the hallway, and Kess eyed it, hoping the guard wouldn't see it too. Hoping she wouldn't have to kill the girl after all.

The guard leaned over and kicked at the fallen debris. "Ugh, I hate these dragonflame lights! Someone has to clean this razing mess up."

With a huff, she returned back the way she came.

Once she was out of earshot, Kess and the others emerged from their hiding places.

"That was too close," Aishena said. "This is foolish, trying to sneak around a palace with a huge wolf. Maybe we should go on alone."

The three others wore padded silver and black guard gambesons but unless castle guards had started riding wolves, there wasn't much point in Kess wearing the uniform. She remained in delver armor.

"As though your disguises are going to work for anyone who sees you up close. Any one of us is going to set off alarms if we're spotted."

Kess gestured to Aishena's row of crystal athames

along her belt and twin grayglim blades strapped to her back, then Benjin, carrying his crystal-studded staff and looking barely into puberty, and then Dashiel, with clearly Rolanian features.

"*And* you two are the ones with bounties still on you. You could easily be recognized." Kess continued down the hallway, checking the intersection up ahead to make sure the guard was gone.

It had taken too many days to find a way into the palace. Aishena had done the majority of the reconnaissance trips alone, timing the guards' shifts, and stealing uniforms. But despite Aishena's solo journeys into the palace, she hadn't been able to find Lyrrin. That was when they decided to all go together.

"We just need to keep our faces hidden." Aishena hurried to catch up. "How are you going to keep Griskin hidden?"

"I can't exactly leave him behind," Kess said flatly. "Besides, he's the one who's going to find Lyrrin for us."

Griskin grumbled softly and sniffed at the polished floor.

Kess smirked. "And I think he's got her scent."

Aishena's mouth was a hard line, but she nodded and let Kess take the lead. They rushed along the cold hallways, letting Griskin follow his nose. Kess held him back at each intersection, letting Aishena clear it first.

It was such a different experience, gliding down those

long passages on Griskin's swift feet, compared to the hard and squeaking wheeled chair Kess had last traveled those spaces on before.

At the next corner, Aishena paused, ducking down and running her fingers over the floor. She held them up, marked red.

"Blood?" Dashiel asked.

Griskin sniffed at it, whining.

Benjin looked from the wolf to the red stains dripping all the way up the hall. "Is it Lyrrin's?"

Kess didn't want to answer. Her heart pounded with the fear that they were too late. That she had failed Riony.

"The blood's still wet," Aishena said. "We should move fast."

They took off at a run, Griskin chasing along the trail of blood. They no longer checked corners before they rounded them. Every second counted.

Two guards fell into their path, freezing as they were met with their strange group. Griskin pounced upon one, knocking him to the floor. Aishena vaulted over the other, landing behind her and cracking an elbow into the back of her neck, making her drop, boneless.

Dashiel and Benjin dragged the two woozy guards into a shadowed corner, and Griskin sniffed ahead. The messy trail of blood went one way, but Griskin seemed torn between that and a second direction.

Kess took the chance to get her bearings. She didn't

know what was down the corridor where the blood trail went, but she had been the other way before.

"This way," she hissed, and they set off at a run again.

Every moment of the night when Eslinde had led Kess down into the hidden dungeon to meet the Alderkin was clear in Kess's memory. It wasn't a time she'd easily forget.

When they reached the room with the secret door, Aishena said, "I've already checked, she's not down there."

It was one of the first places Kess had instructed Aishena to look.

"She might not have been down there before, but I think she is now." Kess pointed to a smear of blood on the stone that opened the passage.

Griskin also still had Lyrrin's scent, eager to rush down the dark tunnel.

Voices and the orange flicker of torchlight came from ahead. Kess and her team slowed their pace, drawing weapons. The dungeons were at a dead end. They were going to have to fight through the guards down there.

In the dimly lit chamber outside the cells, three guards clad in heavy armor stood scattered around the room, chatting in low voices. The air hung thick with the scent of damp stone and faint whimpers echoed from beyond.

Griskin growled low in his throat.

Lyrrin.

Kess signaled with a sharp nod, and her team moved as one. Aishena was the first to strike, slipping into the

shadows with the grace of a seasoned predator. She crept behind the nearest guard, clamped a hand over the man's mouth, then shoved his head against the nearby stone wall. The guard went limp, sliding to the floor.

The second two guards drew alert, scrambling for their weapons.

Before he could draw his sword, Benjin had the next man stumbling backward at the end of his burning hot staff. The red glow trailed through the dim air, reflecting in the man's terrified eyes as he tried to dodge away from the unfamiliar magic.

As he cowered back, Benjin raised the staff and cracked it down. The guard sprawled beneath the blow.

Kess and Griskin took on the third guard. As Dashiel rushed in on one side, the wolf swerved around behind the man and snapped at his ankles, pulling his feet out from under him.

Dashiel crouched over the squirming guard and knocked him on the temple with the pommel of their push dagger.

Kess scanned the room to ensure no one else was left standing.

A man called from one of the cells beyond. "What's going on out there?"

The voice caused a shiver of familiarity through Kess.

Benjin was first to where the sound had come from, the only closed cell. "The door's locked."

Aishena and Dashiel began searching the downed guards.

An anxious shiver had built within Kess. She couldn't wait for the keys. She needed to get that door open now.

Pulling the cutting athame Riony had given her, she activated it and attacked the heavy door, trying to cut through. The enchanted crystal carved and sliced, but the cell door was solid.

"Got the key!" Dashiel ran in beside her, ducking beneath Griskin to turn the lock.

The moment he was out of the way, Kess hissed, "Griskin, go!"

Understanding, the wolf reared back and pushed the door in with his front paws. It swung hard, clattering against the stone wall. Inside, a single torch lit the space.

The man in the middle of the cell, looking very neat and clean-faced, turned to the intrusion. He held a long, barbed blade in one hand.

A curious smile widened his lips. "Kessara Heithorn?"

Kess reeled back in her saddle. She almost turned and fled, faced with this man, this monster, who haunted her nightmares. Who had once taken joy in carving her open time and time again. A bag of familiar tools sat open at the man's feet.

Kess's throat jammed closed as fear overtook her every nerve.

Then she saw Lyrrin in the back corner of the cell,

shivering and drenched in blood, and her fear burned away.

A child. She's just a child!

Fury tore through Kess, heating her eyes and snorting out in sharp breaths. The torturer must have noticed her murderous change of expression. He raised the barbed blade, brandishing the wicked point toward Griskin.

Kess growled more ferociously than the wolf. Her fingers tightened around the weapon already in her hand. Her arm and eyes and fingers worked in concert, fluid and instinctual. She knew her target, she threw the blade, she didn't hesitate.

This was one life she wouldn't question taking.

Golden light shot like a falling star across the room.

As the monster of a man stood there gulping, with no blade jutting from his chest, Kess thought she'd somehow missed. The athame clattered to the stone floor.

With a bewildered expression, the man raised his hands over where his heart should have been, and they came away bloody from a hole that went right through.

He fell to his knees, then awkwardly backward onto the filthy floor, and didn't move again.

Kess tried to breathe, to still the shake in her hands, as Aishena and Dashiel came up behind her.

"Sparks. What is *he* doing here?" Aishena's voice held an edge of terror the young woman usually never showed.

"He's never going to do any of his evil work again, that's what," Kess said.

"You ... how do you know about him?" Aishena frowned, locking eyes with her. "Oh, Kess ..."

Kess blinked away the threat of tears and turned back to Lyrrin. She reached for the acorn at her neck. "Are you okay? Did he touch you?"

Lyrrin stared at them all, mouth dropped wide. "No. No. He only just got here."

"You're covered in blood!" Benjin took off his guard jacket and handed it to her.

Lyrrin put it on, the oversized fabric puffy around her.

She craned her neck to look behind where they all stood in the doorway. "It's from something else. I'm fine. Where's—?"

"Riony had to stay with Dracuni. She sent us, and we're going to get you back to her," Kess said.

Lyrrin frowned but nodded.

From far overhead, a clanging bell rang.

Dashiel picked up Kess's cutting athame and handed it back to her. "And we really need to be getting out of here, right now."

Kess offered for Lyrrin to ride on Griskin with her, but Lyrrin insisted she was fine. Far shorter than the rest of them, she still managed to keep up as they ran.

Back in the main hallways of the palace, the sounds of marching boots echoed from every direction. Kess led the way, hurrying them back along the route they'd come in. They were almost back at the courtyard that led through

to their exit when three grayglims appeared as though from thin air, blocking their path.

"The other way, go!" Aishena hissed.

They sprinted together down the corridor and a flight of stairs, the grayglims close behind. Another area Kess wasn't familiar with.

They passed a huge floor-to-ceiling window which looked out over the city and skidded to a stop when faced with another group of two grayglims and half a dozen castle guards, led by Yensen.

Kess's lip curled as her head swiveled back and forth. They were penned in.

Twelve

Kess reached for the knives in her bracers, calculating how many grayglims she might manage to drop before they were overwhelmed.

Lyrrin stepped in front of her, waving directions. "Back to the window!"

Kess pounced Griskin toward the glass, pressing close to peer out. The drop was sheer, running down the full height of the palace walls.

"You think we should jump?"

Lyrrin's face screwed up. "What? No! Do you have a death wish? You and Riony ... I swear."

"You can't get out that way." Yensen stepped to the front of the circling guards and grayglims. "Return Lyrrin to us, and we will make your deaths swift."

"Don't you mean *or* we will make your deaths swift?" Dashiel laughed nervously.

"No," Yensen said.

Kess pulled a throwing knife for each hand, and Aishena, Benjin, and Dashiel all drew their weapons too.

Lyrrin had one of her hands in her pocket but took a small step away from the window toward Yensen. "You don't have to do this. You know you're not on the right side. I know you know it!"

The grayglim sneered in response.

"Don't bother with him," Kess said. "He's made his loyalties clear."

"No." Lyrrin stamped a step closer to the grayglim. "People can change. People can be forgiven. You of all people should believe that too, Kess."

Kess's heart panged sharply, and her expression softened before she shook it off.

"No. Not everyone deserves that. Not the kind of person who would leave a child alone with that monster and his tools," Kess growled the words, directing them at the grayglim she had once trusted, once fought beside. "Do you have any idea what the Hjelzahn's torturer would have done to her?"

Yensen held Kess's stare for a long, silent moment. His chest lifted and fell in a visible breath, and he drew two swords. "Take them."

The grayglims at his side burst into motion. Kess

tensed, pushing Griskin in front of Lyrrin and bringing her hands up to throw her blades.

Then a tearing sound cut the air and the charging grayglim fell face-first to the floor in a clatter of smoke-toned scale armor.

Kess blinked, unsure what had happened. Neither she, Aishena, Benjin, or Dashiel had moved from their holding positions.

But then she saw the source of the attack. Yensen held one sword lunged forward, reddened with his companion's blood. In the moment of confusion, as cries went up from the other grayglims and guards, he struck out with his second sword, toppling a guard to his left.

Chaos erupted. The remaining four grayglims and five guards broke into action, swinging to down Yensen and the palace invaders. With one grayglim down and Yensen, possibly, on their side, they were in a better position than before.

But four was still far more grayglims than Kess felt comfortable facing, and as the clash of combat grew louder, she knew more would be on the way.

Aishena and Benjin pushed through the chaos with their glowing Alderkin weapons. An athame went skidding across the floor, leaving a burning trail as a grayglim disarmed Aishena of it.

She should be using her long blades! She's at a disadvantage with the daggers. Why doesn't she use her swords?

Kess had to dodge her own attackers, ducking under swinging blades as Griskin pounced between guards and grayglims.

Dashiel had Lyrrin behind them, backing up against the window. One of the grayglim approached, catlike, batting almost playfully at them with the tip of their sword.

Kess looked for an opening to reach them. Dashiel was a fine fighter, but not at take-on-a-grayglim-solo level. She threw her knives, teeth clenched as she felled two guards.

Yensen and Aishena had dropped a couple of guards as well, but now that the element of surprise was gone, the grayglims weren't so easy to defeat.

Behind Dashiel, Lyrrin had turned to the window, running her sharp nails over it.

Maybe she's decided jumping is preferable after all.

The sharp scrape of her claws on the glass rang through the air and Griskin whined, pulling his ears back. As he cringed from the sound, he missed a step, and the length of a grayglim's blade sank deep into his neck.

Kess wailed in horror as the wolf dropped beneath her. "No. *No!*"

More knives found their way into her hands, and she flung them—one, two, three, four, five—into the chest and face of the grayglim above her. He froze, mid-swing, wavering on the spot.

Rough, gurgling sounds came from Griskin's throat. He lay on his side, pinning one of Kess's legs beneath him.

The final castle guard stepped in beside the still wavering grayglim and swung his sword down at Kess in a swishing blow.

"Kess!" Aishena moved in, knocking the stumbling pin-cushioned grayglim the rest of the way down with a bash from her shoulder.

The other guard turned the swing of his sword away from Kess to meet Aishena instead, and they clashed blow for blow above Kess and Griskin, yellow and red light streaking from Aishena's athames.

Kess turned away, ignoring the fight. She reached an arm around Griskin's neck, feeling for the wound. "Come on, boy, you're okay. You're going to be okay."

Air wheezed from his throat and the hot metallic tang of blood filled the air. Kess knew he wasn't going to be okay, not on his own. But she could save him.

She tore the acorn pendant off and pulled it open. She knew Riony had given it to her in case she needed it to save Lyrrin, Aishena, Benjin, Dashiel, or maybe, *maybe* even herself. But there was no way she wasn't going to use it to save Griskin.

Kess pushed Griskin's fur apart and applied the precious drop of fluid to his skin.

"Get down!" Lyrrin's voice cut through the fighting.

The girl dropped to her belly on the ground, and everyone who knew what she was capable of followed her orders in an instant.

Aishena, Benjin, Dashiel, and even Yensen all hit the floor.

Kess couldn't pull her leg free from Griskin as light glimmered from beneath his thick fur and he twitched and howled. So she simply threw herself over his back as best she could to protect him from whatever Lyrrin had set off.

The grayglims and remaining guard were unable to understand that when this small girl gave you an order, you followed it. They stood, unsure, confused at their opponents' strange behavior.

Behind where Lyrrin lay, a swirl of Alderkin runes had been etched in the glass, covered in a film of shining liquid. The whole window glowed and rattled. Cracks cut across the surface like lightning.

In an explosion of tinkling sound, the glass burst outward. Shards flew across the corridor, skewering the standing grayglims and guard. Kess gasped as sharp points jabbed through her leather armor, sinking into her back. She kept her arms around Griskin, covering him as the healing light faded.

As the last clinking of falling glass faded, bodies dropped.

"Is that all of them?" Lyrrin's voice sounded small, a little ill but determined.

"How did you *do that*?" Benjin was first on his feet, staring between Lyrrin and the field of broken glass all around with his mouth wide open.

Dashiel helped Lyrrin to her feet, and Yensen stood beside them. Lyrrin offered the grayglim a tentative smile.

"You two okay over there?" Aishena called over to Kess from where she'd sheltered in a doorway.

Griskin yawned with a soft yelping sound and rolled off his side, bringing Kess up with him as he stood. The warmth of blood trickled down her back from sharp points of pain.

But all she cared about right now was that Griskin was okay.

She rubbed his ears. "Yeah, we're good."

Aishena sheathed her athames. "Then we need to—

Watch out!"

There was movement beside Lyrrin. Yensen's arms shot out, grabbing her and pulling her in.

"What are you—?"

"Stop him!"

Everyone yelled at once. Kess brought Griskin across the space in one huge leap, ready to put the traitorous grayglim down for good.

There was a tearing squelch as a blade sank into skin, and Yensen fell.

Kess blinked at the scene before her, trying to work out who had gotten to him first.

Then she saw another grayglim, punctured with glass shards but still breathing, up on his knees, his sword thrust into Yensen's chest. Right where Lyrrin had been standing

a second before. The blade slid deep into Yensen's side, between the scales of his armor.

"No!" Lyrrin cried out, trying to support Yensen as he staggered, crumpling over her.

Dashiel and Benjin grasped him from either side, adding their strength to halt his fall.

The other grayglim pulled his arm back to strike again. His eyes glowed white from within a face painted red from a hundred cuts. Then Griskin was on him, teeth around the back of his neck.

Crunch. The wolf tossed the man's limp body from his mouth.

"Do we have any more silvernix?" Lyrrin kneeled at Yensen's side. Her cheeks were slick with tears as she leaned over, pressing her hands to the gaping wound on the man's chest. "I only had one left, which I used on the window."

Aishena, Dashiel, and Benjin shook their heads.

"I don't have any more. I'm sorry." Kess brushed a hand over the sticky blood in Griskin's fur, her nose wrinkled. The wolf tensed, ears pricking up.

"We have to go," Kess said, straining to hear what Griskin had already noticed. Footsteps, pounding their way.

"Leave me. Go while you can," Yensen groaned.

"We're not leaving you!" Lyrrin shook her head, then looked around at the rest of them. "We can't leave him. He helped us. He saved me. I know where they have silvernix. We can go there."

"No!" Yensen snapped. "They will trap you in there if you try."

Kess swore as the footsteps grew louder. "Get him up onto Griskin with me. Quick! We need to get out of the palace."

Aishena and Dashiel got their arms under the grayglim, and he cried out roughly as they lifted him. Kess shifted backward in her saddle so there was room for him in front of her, wincing as pain lanced through the wounds in her own back.

Is there glass still in me? It feels like it.

Every lift of Yensen's limbs and body as the others positioned him onto the wolf left him gasping between stubborn refusals.

"You shouldn't ... just leave me ..."

"Go, go!" Kess ordered as the shadows of approaching figures filled the other end of the hall.

Yensen slumped over Griskin's neck, and Kess helped keep him from falling off as they raced through the palace, the others running at their side.

Yensen's breaths labored and sputtered, and when Kess put a hand to his neck to steady him, his skin felt cold.

Kess's lips curled as her heart raged between disgust and sympathy. She wanted to hate him for how he'd betrayed them. She did hate him, as much as she hated who she once was.

Softly, she said, "Just hold in there, okay? We'll get you

fixed up as soon as we're out of here."

Yensen's head shook, either in denial or because he didn't have the strength to steady it as Griskin ran. "You … would help me? After what I've done?"

"I know what it is to have made mistakes. Terrible mistakes that should never have been forgiven." Kess furrowed her brows as blood spurted from Yensen's side. "You're not a bad person, Yensen. You were loyal, above all. You were just loyal to the wrong cause."

Yensen bowed over farther, resting entirely over Griskin's neck. "If you … if you had more silvernix … you would have, wouldn't you? You would have used …"

Kess still held the empty acorn pendant clasped in one fist. She could never regret saving Griskin. She just wished Riony had given her enough to do more.

It had stunned her that Riony had given her any at all. They had always been so against bleeding Dracuni into bottles. Now that Dracuni allowed it, how did they stop from asking for too much? How did they say no to taking her blood when it could have meant saving more lives?

Kess tried to swallow all the aching questions away as she also swallowed away the pain in her back. "We're almost out. Come on, I know you're tough. You can make it."

Yensen didn't reply.

Griskin pounced out into the dark courtyard, and the grayglim slipped in the saddle, falling sideways.

"Whoa, whoa!" Kess grasped at his armor, trying to

catch him.

Aishena moved in quick, getting under the man and propping him back up. She held him for a moment, looking into his face, then turned to Kess.

Her lips pulled thin, and she shook her head.

"What is it?" Lyrrin skidded to a stop on the gravel up ahead.

"We tried. I'm sorry," Kess said.

She and Aishena worked together to move the lifeless body off Griskin's saddle. Lyrrin remained in place, her clawed hands flexing and eyes glistening.

Again, in a softer voice, Kess said to Yensen, "We tried. I'm sorry."

The grayglim's blank eyes stared back up at her.

"Someone's up there!" Benjin called from across the courtyard, pointing to the tall tower that rose high above them. "They're watching us."

"We really, really, really need to go now," Lyrrin said.

Kess turned, her head heavy with sorrow and dulled by her own pain. "Now you're in a hurry? Why? They're all the way up there."

"Because if that's who I think it is, it's Kverra Hjelzahn," Lyrrin replied.

Aishena grew very still. "How do you know?"

Lyrrin gestured to all the blood on her gown. "We ran into each other earlier tonight. I think that's where she's been hiding out, keeping watch for her victims."

"Then move, move!" Kess urged Griskin into a run again. They were across the courtyard when she realized Aishena wasn't following.

Her cropped silver hair swung around her chin as she stared up at the tower and the silhouette within.

"I'm not coming." Aishena's dark eyes glimmered in the low light. "I need to go and see my mother."

Thirteen

The blood on Lyrrin's dress had dried like a crackly leather. Facing the woman who spilled that blood again wasn't high on the list of things she wanted to do.

"The rest of you go, get Lyrrin out safely." Aishena checked over her weapons and stretched her shoulders. "I'll catch up when I can."

Benjin thumped the end of his staff on the ground. "No way. If you're going after Mami, I'm coming too."

"Wait, wait, wait. You can't be serious." Dashiel looked between Aishena and the exit from the courtyard that would get them out of the palace. "I feel as though we should be avoiding the near-immortal grayglim who wants the majority of people here dead."

Aishena gave her head a swift shake. "A near-immortal

grayglim who has been stalking the king and heirs for years all across Elundrae? If our goal is to also remove the Dragon King, she could be useful. Think about what she might know."

Lyrrin squinted back up at the tower. The silhouetted shape in the window had vanished. Hidden again in the shadows, always lurking, always watching.

Just what has she seen?

"Do you think you can capture her?" she asked Aishena. "Alive?"

Aishena went still, her head slightly bowed. "Either I do, or I put her down for good."

"Can you do it alone?"

"Maybe." She seemed pained to admit her doubt.

"With us helping?"

Aishena looked around the group. "A much better chance."

"Then I'm going too," Lyrrin said and joined Aishena and Benjin.

Dashiel sighed and jogged back to them as well. "As long as we can be fast about it. Just a reminder that we have a palace worth of guards chasing after us."

Aishena offered them a thin smile.

"Kess, are you in?" Lyrrin called out.

Over on the wolf, Kess blinked woozily. She winced as she straightened up in her saddle and nodded. "Griskin can help us find her."

The rumble of footsteps in the distance pulled Lyrrin's attention. "Let's move."

The wolf dashed ahead first, and Kess checked the exit out of the courtyard that led to the tower. The leather armor on her back glistened wetly in the low light and was torn in a few places. But Lyrrin had seen the glow of silvernix come from Kess during the fight, hadn't she? It had all been a blur in the corner of her eye as she'd worked on her runes, then sheltered from the explosion they brought.

"This way." Kess and Griskin led them at a run along the corridor.

Aishena ran shoulder to shoulder with Benjin, muttering quickly to him. They reached a locked doorway and Aishena sliced their way through with her cutting athame.

Inside, the small base of the tower was dusty and disused. A few old chairs sat stacked and neglected by one wall beside a coiled rope and some gardening tools. A narrow staircase traced the outside edge of the square tower, with stone balustrades edging the gap all the way up the center.

Aishena wiped the dust over the first step with her fingers. "No footprints."

"She's up there," Kess replied as Griskin sniffed the air.

That was when Lyrrin noticed how much of a trail they were leaving. Drops of blood and tacky red footprints had followed them into the tower. Benjin closed the door, then took one of the chairs and propped it behind the handle, but anyone on their trail would still know exactly where they went.

Aishena and Benjin took the lead, taking the stairs two at a time, with Dashiel close behind.

Kess put an arm out, holding Lyrrin back. "Stick close to me. I need to get you safely back to Riony."

Lyrrin's face scrunched up at her sister's name. An awful anger and sadness burbled inside her that Riony wasn't there.

She came to save Kess. Why not me?

Kess watched her with furrowed brows. "She wanted to come for you. She *really* wanted to. In her just-about-to-go-and-do-something-stupid way. That's why we came to get you for her. So she could stay and look after Dracuni. So they could stay safe."

They moved together up the stairs, following the others at a jog—fast for Lyrrin, slow for Griskin.

Lyrrin remembered when the wolf had stalked brazenly into their campsite one night. They had all drawn weapons, expecting an attack from the evil girl they thought had stabbed Riony in the back and left her for dead.

All of them except for Riony.

When it was clear the wolf was alone, that he was trying to get Riony to go with him, the argument about what to do had lasted for days. Nobody else thought it was a good idea to follow Griskin. Nobody else thought it was worth

finding out what happened to Kess, worth helping her if she was still alive.

Only Riony.

She doesn't care for Kess more than me. She had to go after Kess because she was the only one who would.

And there was Lyrrin, with four friends who had come to save her, and save her sister and Dracuni from danger at the same time.

Lyrrin pushed her anger away. "Thank you for coming to help me. And for protecting Riony, in all the ways you do."

Kess kept her eyes on the stairs in front of them. "It's what she deserves."

As they ascended the staircase, the air grew cooler, the stone walls narrowing around them. The sound of the wind became more pronounced, slipping through small openings in the tower.

Lyrrin huffed, winded from the run. "Well, you deserve more too. I hope Riony is finally being a bit nicer to you now."

Kess went pale, yet her cheeks were splotchy red.

"Are you okay?"

The clash of weapons echoed through the tower. Lyrrin and Griskin broke into a faster run.

"She's here!" Aishena yelled from a flight up.

Ahead, the stairs led to a small landing where a wooden door stood flung open. Lyrrin rushed through into a

cobweb-strewn belfry. The room was stark, with high, narrow windows that allowed shafts of moonlight to pierce through the gloom.

Benjin grabbed for Lyrrin as she stepped in, pulling her to cover behind a solid beam.

Aishena and her mother battled across the room, weaving between bells and ropes that lay discarded across the floor. Lady Hjelzahn's gaze was cold and unyielding. Her twin blades gleamed in the dim light as they flitted through the air in swirling attacks.

The woman's older swords, taken from her in their earlier battle, remained strapped on Aishena's back, untouched, as she fought back with her glowing athames.

Lyrrin searched the space with her eyes for a weapon. She patted down her clothing. She had nothing left to use. Dashiel skirted around the edges of the square room, sword and dagger drawn. Griskin stepped forward, growling.

"Don't engage!" Aishena ordered.

They held positions, eyes on the battle.

The clash of crystal against steel rang out as Aishena met her mother's strikes with her own, each blow fierce and desperate to keep her at bay.

"You never beat me before, and you won't now," Lady Hjelzahn drawled, as though the assault took no effort at all to ward off.

Lyrrin could see the strain on Aishena's face, focused in total concentration. Her athames flashed, red and yellow,

barely able to keep her mother's longer twin swords held back.

Kverra's blade caught Aishena's shoulder, slicing through her guard uniform and drawing a line of crimson across her skin. Aishena hissed but didn't falter. She hit back lightning fast, slicing through the tip of one of Kverra's blades with a swift strike of her cutting athame.

The metal clattered to the ground, leaving Lady Hjelzahn with half the reach on that side. But with a sharp twist of her wrist, she disarmed Aishena of the yellow crystal, sending it skittering across the floor.

Beside Lyrrin, Benjin rolled his shoulders, then turned away from the duel to face her. He thrust the crystal-studded staff out toward Lyrrin.

"Here. Take this."

"What? Why?" Lyrrin's fingers closed around the wood she had carved.

In the center of the space, Aishena dropped into a crouch. "Now!"

Benjin took a deep breath and rushed into the fray. With a fluid motion, he vaulted over his sister, drawing the swords from her back in the same movement and launching himself at Kverra. The clash of the two sets of twin blades sent sparks flying, then the tear of armor and flesh came as Benjin landed his first strike.

Kverra stumbled backward as his assault was joined by Aishena's. Her mask of indifference slipped into wide-eyed shock and then teeth-bared anger as the red athame sizzled across her cheek.

With a feral snarl, she kicked Benjin in the chest, sending him rolling back, but that only gave an opening for a white bone knife to fly in from Kess's hand, puncturing into the woman's neck. It didn't slow her down at all.

"This isn't working!" Lyrrin shouted, frustration lacing her voice.

No matter how they wounded the woman, she just kept moving.

Aishena's eyes flashed with determination. "It is. Trust me! Do as I say, when I say it! Lyrrin, you're up. Push her back. We need fire!"

Heart pounding, Lyrrin nodded. The weight of Benjin's staff in her hands grounded her, and she spun it in her fingers to bring the crystal with the burn rune toward her. Scratching over it quickly, she added in a float symbol and activated them both.

The crystal sung under her fingers, feeling like the home she'd been missing.

Pink flames bloomed around the stone, bursting outward. Lyrrin charged forward, staff held out. Aishena and Benjin cleared a path for her, and she pushed through between them, thrusting the magical flames at the possessed woman's chest.

Kverra dodged backward across the cluttered space toward the entrance.

The fire roared, crackling over the gray armor and Kverra's neck and face. The room filled with the smell of burned hair. Then the staff was struck by the pommel of two swords, knocking it away in a move that jarred Lyrrin's arms. The end of the staff smacked against a nearby bell, clanging loudly.

"Dash! Get Lyrrin!" Aishena commanded.

An arm wrapped Lyrrin from behind, pulling her backward as two blades flashed down toward her face. Dashiel's broadsword blocked the blow, and everyone around Kverra scattered back.

With bare hands, Lady Hjelzahn patted away the flames smoldering across her chest and neck. Her armor hung crookedly, some of the straps burned loose, but there were no injuries showing beneath.

Lyrrin watched in disbelief. "It didn't do anything, she's—"

"Kess, hip joints, now!" Aishena yelled.

From the shadowed corner of the room, two blades flew out, one after the other. They each struck deep into Lady Hjelzahn's hips. She snarled, trying to take a step forward, but her legs moved awkwardly.

Aishena moved in front of her, pressing her back with lashing arcs of her red athame. In faltering steps, Lady Hjelzahn wobbled in retreat, warding off every blow with her swords, but unable to dodge and maneuver. She backed up against the wooden door and it creaked on its hinges.

"Benj, swords!" Aishena cried.

Without hesitation, he threw them to her. She dropped her athame and snatched the weapons from the air. With a roar, Aishena drove both swords into Lady Hjelzahn's shoulders and out the other side, pinning her to the wooden doorway. No blood poured from the wounds.

The woman twitched and bucked against the steel blades, shrieking as she found herself caught tight.

Lyrrin's chest heaved as she stared at the grayglim, pinned in place like a butterfly, defiance burning in her eyes despite the blades through her flesh. "Is that it? Is she trapped?"

"I will kill you. I will kill all of you! You all have to die." Lady Hjelzahn brought her swords up, able to move from the elbows down only.

Aishena kicked the weapons from her hands. Panting hard, she watched her mother with dark, intense eyes.

Kess, looking paler and more drawn than before, rode up beside her. "That's one way to stop her."

"A little trick I learned from you," Aishena replied.

Kverra's voice went cold and low. "Conniving and unfair numbers? This isn't how I trained you, Aishena. A grayglim would face me one-on-one with honor. Free me, and we will finish this duel properly."

Aishena's angular shoulders raised up around her neck and she winced.

Her mother's inhuman voice rose louder. "I am your

mestra! You are the hand and must do as I command."

With a heavy sigh, Aishena's expression steadied, and she locked eyes with her mother. "I'm not going to fight you again. The blow will come hard enough when you understand all you have done."

Kverra snarled. She twisted her torso, pressing left and right as though she could cut right through her own shoulders to get free.

Aishena pulled a parcel from her belt pouch. "I brought this along, in case we needed it. Hopefully whatever is possessing you isn't immune to morass mercy."

Kess flinched away as Aishena pushed the fabric parcel up to her mother's face. She writhed and struggled, cursing through the wad of cloth and herbs. But after a torturously long moment, Lady Hjelzahn, Heir Killer, fell still.

Lyrrin released a long sigh of relief. "You did it!"

"We did it." Aishena put the parcel away, brushing her hands off. She watched the woman for a long moment, then her shoulders dropped heavily. "Come on, let's get her tied up, then get us all out of here."

Benjin turned away quickly, keeping his eyes averted from where his mother's body hung from the door. He gathered up his sister's athames and brought them back to her, and Dashiel brought some rope over. Once Kverra was thoroughly bound, they worked together to pry the swords free.

Aishena's hands shook around the hilts of the extracted

weapons, and she quickly passed them on to Benjin.

Lyrrin waited beside Kess, who was slumped over Griskin's neck.

"It's nice to work as a team, isn't it?"

Kess smiled back weakly. "Yeah. It is."

Lyrrin's own smile faltered as she took in Kess's unfocused eyes and blue lips. "Are you sure you're okay?"

"I'll be fine as long as ..." Kess stilled.

Griskin growled, his ears flattening back. A moment later, Lyrrin heard it too. Footsteps, many of them, thundering up the stairwell below.

Dashiel ducked out the doorway, then back in again, pushing the door closed behind them. "Safe to say, we've been found."

"How many?" Benjin swung the twin blades in his hands.

Dashiel's expression was one of utter desolation. "All of them?"

Lyrrin's fingers tightened around the staff she still held. Her gaze ran over it, cataloging the crystals she had available, what options she had. She could still fight, but Kess looked on the edge of passing out, and Aishena and Benjin were sheened in sweat and still catching their breath from their recent efforts.

The drop from the narrow windows was steep and far. There were no other exits from the disused bell tower.

No way out. They were trapped.

FOURTEEN

Kess closed her eyes and took a deep breath, willing her consciousness not to topple off the precipice into darkness. Pain radiated in throbbing waves from multiple points on her back.

She felt worried, deeply worried, in a way she didn't usually feel. She had been so close to getting Lyrrin out, getting her back to Riony. She didn't want to fail.

When she opened her eyes again, the others were all working to block the belfry door. Aishena and Dashiel had their shoulders up against a bell larger than them. It scraped disharmoniously across the floor as they pushed it toward the door.

Lyrrin and Benjin dragged some of the larger coils of rope across, dropped them into a heavy pile around the bell, then ran back to get more.

As they loaded a couple more smaller bells, crates, and ropes onto the barricade, the door rattled violently. Aishena and Dashiel leaped forward to add their weight to the blockade.

Loud thumping and shouting reverberated through to them and the wood of the door strained.

"Even if this holds, we can't stay in here forever," Dashiel groaned, back pressed against the door.

Lyrrin held up the crystal staff and pointed it toward one of the windows. "I have a float rune on here now, but it's only small. It might only get a safe landing for one or two of us if we have to jump."

Kess pulled her cutting athame and ran the yellow crystal around one of the upright wooden beams.

She called to the two kids, "Come and catch this. Dash, they might need your help."

Once the top was cut through, she indicated for Griskin to lower himself down, then bent over to cut through the bottom. Curving her back that way forced out a whimper, and starbursts of pain obscured her vision. The wounds from the glass shards were worse than she'd originally thought, or at least had become worse since, with every movement she'd made.

The athame cut through, and the three beside her caught it, taking it over to wedge against the door.

As Kess winced through the agony of straightening

back up again, more waves of worry reached her.

They were different than usual. They weren't her worries.

Lyomir?

No reply came, but she could feel his presence, distantly. He said he would stay close. He must be around the keep somewhere. Could he feel her too?

"There's one way out of here," Kess said. "By dragon."

"Do you think you can get Lyomir to come for us? Here?" Dashiel shuffled the beam, getting it positioned at a forty-five-degree angle against the door.

"I'm not sure. But I don't know what else we're going to do." Kess wiped cold sweat off her forehead.

"Try to call him." With the beam in place, Aishena warily moved away from holding the door as well.

The barricade held, and the rattling and thumping from the other side quieted down.

Lyrrin angled her ear toward the door. "What are they doing? Do you think they've given up?"

A booming crack made her jump away. A thin split ran up the middle of the door. A few seconds later, the echoing thud hit again. The top hinge popped from the wall.

Dashiel sighed. "Sounds like somebody found a battering ram."

"Keep loading the barricade," Aishena ordered, working to cut a second beam down. "And Kess, get Lyomir here, now!"

"I'll try." Kess reached out with her senses and thoughts calling toward her bonded dragon.

Lyomir? Can you hear me? Can you find me?

She pictured the tower they were in, how it had looked from outside. To reach them, Lyomir would have to fly right over the palace and into the couple of remaining dragonriders still on guard.

No words came back to Kess, only a strong surge of annoyance, like a growling *harrumph* in her head.

Kess found herself shivering. What if he didn't come for them? What if he decided they weren't worth fighting his way in for?

The crack of splintering wood cut the air. One of the planks of the door snapped and a thick column of metal, shaped like a fist at the end, pushed through. One more strike, and the vertical plank broke free, slivers of sharp wood hanging around the edges.

A guard moved into the hole, pushing an arm and shoulder through. Aishena struck out with a swift sequence of blows, forcing the man to retreat again. The battering ram slammed into the door again.

Kess moved to the window, glaring at the long drop down. If Lyomir didn't come, they might have to jump. As injured as Kess already felt, she wasn't sure she'd survive that fall. It was getting harder and harder for her to even keep her eyes open.

Lyomir, we need you. I need you.

A deeper, angrier growl filled her head. The strength of the emotion made Kess gasp. He was close.

A burst of flame lit the night sky outside. A human scream merged with the shriek of a dragon, and a massive shape walloped against the tower, shaking the walls, then crashed to the ground below.

Dark wings flashed through the air.

Puny tamed beast.

"It's him, he's here!" Kess called to the others.

They rushed to join her at the window. Lyomir circled above, and another dragon lay smoldering in the courtyard below.

"We need to get out there so he can reach us. We've got to get up onto the roof." Aishena stepped onto the sill of the narrow window, angling out over the drop and looking up. "We're going to have to climb."

Benjin thumb-pointed to his unconscious mother. "What are we going to do with her?"

Aishena frowned. "Can Griskin carry her?"

Kess nodded with a matching frown. He could but getting out through the narrow window and up onto the roof with them both would be a feat Kess wasn't confident of.

Aishena jumped back in and waved Dashiel to her side. Together they lifted Lady Hjelzahn and draped her face down over Griskin, behind Kess. Aishena pulled some thin cave-silk rope from her belt and lashed the woman in place.

Benjin and Lyrrin were already halfway out the window. A purple glow came from one of the crystals on Lyrrin's staff, which stuck out over her shoulder. The length was wedged down the back of her gown.

"The ledge is really narrow. Watch your step." Aishena stepped out beside them.

She clung to the side of the window as she helped boost the children up out of sight. One of Lyrrin's feet slipped and dangled down over the top of the window. Aishena climbed up behind her and the sounds of them scrambling onto the roof echoed down.

Dashiel waved a hand questioningly toward Kess.

"You go first," she replied, punctuated by the crack of another plank on the door splitting through.

Dashiel stepped out confidently, as though striding along the back of a trusted dragon. Aishena's hand appeared, reaching down from above. Dashiel grabbed it and was hoisted up.

"Come on, Gris," Kess moved them to the window again and pushed him forward.

He stepped up with both front paws, pushing his head through the narrow space. Kess tried to push him farther, and he whined softly. The door tore open again like rippling thunder.

Wincing, Kess climbed up his neck, pushing away his thick fur so she could see around him. The ledge on the other side was barely a palm's-width across. Enough for a

human to stand on with just their toes. A wolf of Griskin's size would have far more difficulty.

"You can do it. Just keep your claws dug in." Kess urged him forward again.

He stepped over the sill, straddling it with his stomach. His front paws skidded and scraped against the exterior wall, unable to find purchase against the narrow ledge.

"Raze it!" Kess pulled back, bringing him off the window and back into the belfry.

"Kess?" Dashiel called from above.

She turned Griskin so she could lean sideways out the window. Dashiel's face watched down from over the roof's edge.

"Get Aishena to throw down more rope. I'll tie Kverra on. You're going to have to pull her up."

"What about you?"

"I'm not leaving Griskin." Kess groaned as she pulled herself back inside and reached for the knots holding the possessed grayglim onto the wolf's back.

With the cacophonous clatter of broken wood and tumbling bells, the remains of the door burst apart. Kess's hands reached instead for her knives as grayglims and guards flooded into the room. They spread out into the space, gauging the situation, taking in the one girl on her wolf confronting them.

At least this will be one epic way to go out. Kess gave Griskin's ears a rub for good luck and felt satisfied that

she'd succeeded in one last thing for Riony.

Lyrrin was out. Lyrrin was saved. She had done that.

She only wished she could also see Riony again.

Roaring worry filled her, but she steadied herself through her pain and sent her first two knives flying.

Only one hit its mark, sending the grayglim tripping sideways as he grasped his bleeding neck. He collapsed on the ground and the whole tower shuddered as though he had weighed as much as a giant.

"What—?"

An avalanche of slate tiles and stone crushed down over the approaching guards. Griskin dodged back, and Kess flung an arm up in front of her face as shattered chunks hailed around her.

I won't let you die, small fool.

A purple claw thrust down through the collapsing roof, tearing the hole in it wider. Dust filled the air and Kess choked on it, but it wasn't the dust that made her eyes sting with tears.

Lyomir's teeth came within view, mouth open and roaring into the hole he'd torn through the tower roof. To reach Kess.

Griskin bounded forward over the shifting debris and struggling bodies of the guards beneath it. The roof had fallen at an angle, and the wolf ran up it to the dragon waiting above.

Aishena, Dashiel, and the kids were already on the

dragon's back, tying themselves in place. Griskin looped around behind the dragon, using his spine as a ramp to climb up and join the others.

They were met with a multitude of arms, catching Kess as she slumped sideways from her saddle, getting Griskin secured, moving Kverra off the wolf and into a better position.

Kess gasped and panted, pain and adrenaline warring over every short breath as Lyomir's wings *whumped*, lifting them into the sky. He moved with such swift power that it took Kess's breath away all over again.

"There's another rider behind us," Aishena warned.

Lyomir snorted.

They sped across the spires and roofs of the city like a fleeting shadow. The palace dragonrider followed, falling farther and farther behind.

Kess folded forward where she sat, pressing trembling hands against the purple scales beneath her.

Thank you.

A growl thrummed through Lyomir's neck. **Maybe try not getting into so much trouble in the first place.**

Kess huffed a laugh, then whimpered as something sharp cut deeper into her skin.

You're hurt.

You're not. Griskin's not. Lyrrin's not. I'm calling that a good day.

They sailed over the high dragonkeep walls and out

over the surrounding scorched grasslands. Lyrrin watched the trailing dot behind them through the clear crystal on her staff, then gave a whoop so loud it made everyone else on the dragon jump.

"They've turned around! We did it! We got away!" She flung herself in a hug around Aishena, who tolerated it with a grimace and awkward pat on the head. "I can't wait to see Riony and Dracuni and Elumon and everyone again!"

Kess's chest tightened at Riony's name with a longing pull, as though her heart had been bound in rope and was being pulled away.

Riony. I hope she's safe. I hope she ... I hope she wants to see me again.

"Thank you!" Without warning, Lyrrin wrapped her arms around Kess next.

"Ah!" Kess grunted as pain lanced through her.

Lyrrin pulled back quickly, turning her palms upward to reveal them red where she'd touched Kess's back. "Is this your blood?"

Aishena and Dashiel's heads both swung her way.

Kess winced apologetically. "I think I have a bit of glass in me."

Lyrrin gasped and covered her mouth. "Oh no! I'm sorry!"

"It's not your fault. Your magic saved us."

"*A bit of glass?*" Narrowing her eyes, Aishena switched places with Lyrrin, shuffling down between the spines of

the dragon. "Let me see."

Kess shook her head. There wasn't much they could do up there on the dragon's back.

She opened her mouth to say as much when Dashiel snapped, "Don't make us hold you down."

"She's as bad as Riony." Aishena tutted and pushed against Kess's shoulder.

Sighing, Kess leaned forward and submitted her back for inspection.

A bright cyan glow lit up and Aishena's fingers prodded none too gently around the tears in the leather. She hissed under her breath and tentatively tugged at one of the shards. Kess bit off a yelp. Griskin pressed his snout against her face and licked her cheek.

"That one's deep," Aishena murmured. "It'll be better to leave them in for now or you're only going to bleed more. Stay still, I'll bandage around them."

Kess remained in place. She wasn't sure she could move again if she wanted to. Every breath brought a thousand daggers of agony. Aishena pulled a long strip of bandage out and got to work.

Benjin stayed farther down the dragon's back, close to Kverra. He watched his mother warily, but there was also a sad softness to his expression. Her old twin blades he had wielded lay across his lap. Lyrrin moved down in slow shuffles to his side.

She presented the crystal staff to him. "Thanks for

letting me use it."

Benjin didn't reach out to take it back. "You know, I think you should keep it."

Lyrrin's lips turned down. "What? Why?"

"I know you made it for me, and that means a lot. But the crystals, the staff ... it was always more Yoskar's thing."

Aishena reached under Kess's stomach, passing the bandage through and bringing it around and around her middle, pulling it tight in a way that left Kess drenched in the fevered sweat of pain.

"And I always wanted to be like Yoskar, for such a long time," Benjin continued, eyes on his sister. "But not so much anymore."

Smiling, he turned back to Lyrrin. "Besides, you can do way cooler things with those crystals than I can."

Lyrrin half smiled and pulled the staff in to hug it against her chest.

Aishena tied off the bandage. "Just hold on. Lyomir is fast. It won't be long until we're back in the undercity."

Back where there was silvernix. Back with Riony.

Kess's eyes drooped closed.

When she opened them again, there was light. A shell-pink stretch of sky lay above her, tainted with blotches of gray clouds.

She felt cold to her core, and her tongue felt thick and dry. "How ... long?"

A hand was wrapped around hers, hot to touch against

her icy fingers.

Dashiel said, "Shh, rest. We're almost there."

Kess tried to sit up to see where they were. No part of her body wanted to move right.

Dashiel held her down with a hand on her shoulder. "*Rest*. I don't want to face Riony if you don't make it."

Lyomir rumbled beneath them, the leathery flutter of his wings the only other sound as they beat hard. The heave of his chest had all his passengers rising and lowering with him. The worry Kess had felt before continued to fill her head.

Don't overdo it. You've been flying all night.

Don't tell me what to do, little fool.

"There's something happening up ahead!" Lyrrin yelled from nearby.

Kess turned her head to see her sitting up in front, using the seeing stone on the staff to look down over snowy mountains below. She handed the staff to Aishena, who immediately bristled.

"What is it?" Kess asked.

"A battle. The siege dragons, they're all over the place, fighting."

"Fighting who?" Kess pushed Dashiel's hand away and sat up with a wailing groan.

Her whole body had seized up during the night and she felt weak and shivery.

"It's hard to see what's going on. It's chaos." Aishena

handed the staff back to Lyrrin.

Kess shook her head, and her heart pounded. "A battle at the undercity entrance can only mean one thing. The siege has broken. Either they've gotten in, or Riony and the undercity riders have come out. We have to go and help."

Lyomir veered away. **We should go around this mess. I'm taking you back to the other entrance.**

Taking me back to the other entrance won't help me at all if Dracuni has been caught. We're going to help them.

Aishena gave Kess a long, assessing look, then glanced around at Dashiel, Lyrrin, and Benjin. "None of us are in any condition to join the fight."

But Kess heard the uncertainty hidden in her tone. She straightened up further. "And what happens if we don't?"

"We have to help," Lyrrin said.

Aishena squinted back toward the battle. "Fine. We can at least go a bit closer to see what's happening."

Kess gave her a grateful nod. *Lyomir?*

The purple etherdart snorted loudly. But he turned back toward the battle.

Lyrrin squinted through the seeing stone as they drew closer. "I can't see anyone familiar. It's just a bunch of dragonriders fighting a bunch of dragonriders. I can't see Riony or Dracuni or any of our friends."

"Are you sure? Absolutely sure? They aren't already downed?" Kess asked.

"I'm sure," Lyrrin replied.

As close as they were now, Kess could see most of the dragons were larger breeds, none of the smaller treedarts the new undercity riders would be flying, none flying with the fluid motions of the untamed Viska, Gleem, or Hux. The battle had slowed, with a number of dragons flying away in every direction, fleeing the conflict, and others returning to the ground.

"What are they doing?" Benjin leaned around from near the back.

Aishena said, "I don't know. But if they don't have our friends, we need to get out of here before they see us."

Too late. Lyomir put on a burst of speed, taking them diving.

Behind them, four matching red etherflames swooped after them, having come in from behind while they were distracted.

The sudden drop wrenched Kess against the rope she was tied to the dragon with, and she screamed as she dropped again onto his scaled back, pushing one of the shards in her skin deeper.

Lyomir loosed a rough, frustrated growl, slowing his retreat.

I'm okay. Just get us out of here. Kess could barely think the words clearly through the fiery sting. Could he feel her pain along with her thoughts and emotions, the way she felt his?

But even through his worry for her, Kess could sense

how exhausted he was too. He'd been flying his fastest all night, for her.

The red dragons caught up fast, coming up around them on every side. Their riders didn't direct their dragons to claw or bite or flame, but they harried Lyomir from the sides, the back, and above, forcing him down, down, down.

The side of the mountain came up toward them, bright with snow and dotted in dark rocks. Lyomir landed hard, skidding across the icy surface, sending a spray of cold powder over them all.

Lyrrin, Dashiel, Aishena, and Benjin had their weapons in their hands already and cut through the ropes holding them in place on the purple dragon's back.

Kess reached for her throwing knives, but her vision swam, and her fingers felt frozen and numb. She blinked, trying to clear her sight.

Around them, the four red dragons landed lightly. Lyomir growled turning on the spot, penned in. And on each dragon sat a rider wearing Yeonard Draekhan's colors.

FIFTEEN

Dracuni swerved right, wings pulled in after a rushing burst of speed. Riony pressed close to the unidragon's neck and the opalescent hair of Dracuni's mane tickled her face as she kept her eyes on upcoming challenges.

"To the right again, between those stalactites."

It's too narrow.

"It's fine. You can do it. Just like the last one."

If I miss and knock you off …

"You'll catch me." Riony smirked. "Go on, it'll be good practice. The flying through that gap part, I mean, not the knocking me off part."

Dracuni sighed but aimed the direction Riony suggested. Riony felt the thrill in Dracuni's emotions as they zipped between the narrow rock formations, a hair's breadth away from scraping the stone.

Riony let out a whoop. "That was amazing! You're getting so much better."

Dracuni didn't answer, but a ripple of pride transferred through her senses.

Riony let her own pride rush back in return. They'd practiced relentlessly in those tight quarters, and it was paying off.

Still, the lure of open skies teased at the back of her mind—a stretch of endless blue where Dracuni could truly soar, without the looming rock and constant need to pivot at the last moment. Without being hunted for what she was.

Would she ever have that freedom?

For now, the undercity training was invaluable. They were learning to adapt, to maneuver through confined spaces—skills that might mean the difference between life and death in battle.

They wove through the forest of long, jagged limestone draping from the undercity's cavern ceiling. The air was cool and still up there, and Dracuni's scales were warm beneath Riony, riding without a saddle. The unidragon's wings beat steadily, the ripple of air over the diaphanous membrane an inspiring sound.

Riony patted Dracuni's neck. "I still can't believe how big you've gotten. I remember when you fit in my backpack, so tiny and cute."

I just remember being hungry and Butterfur

stepping on me.

"Listen, some mistakes were made, but we survived." Riony huffed a laugh. "Sparks, that little furry sausage has grown so big now too."

Do you think little sister will be bigger when we see her again?

Riony's smile faded. "She's only been gone a week or so."

It feels like longer.

"I know." Riony missed her sister keenly, like a gaping wound in her chest that only bled more for also missing Kess and everyone else she cared for. "We'll have her back soon. I'm sure we will."

They better all be back soon. They better all be safe.

They banked left around a particularly sharp turn, heading down over the Grand Arch markets, and passing another rider out training on one of the tamed treedarts. The markets hummed below, and faces turned up to watch them.

But more were focused on a commotion on the main street that people were rushing toward. A whistle sounded—the signal to call in defenses. Riony's pulse quickened.

"Down there, quick. We need to see what's going on."

Dracuni angled her wings, gliding downward. Riony strained her eyes to pick out details. Niskina was there, taking charge of the situation.

Something was definitely wrong.

Dracuni landed on a low rooftop beside the market, and Riony jumped down between a couple of stallholder's carts. She pushed through the crowd, wishing she had a weapon with her.

Niskina's voice carried to her as she went. "The mountain entrance has been revealed to the enemy. Get up there now and get it sealed! It has runes prepped for closure. You know what to do."

A small squad of delvers moved off at a jog, passing Riony as she reached Niskina.

"Sorry about that, but it was important that I got in as fast as I could. For a few reasons," a boyish voice said.

"What's happened? How—?" Riony's voice cut off the moment she saw Benjin.

The young boy's shorn silver hair sparkled in the cyan light. He wore an armored uniform that was too large for him and was crusted with dried blood.

Tracking where her gaze fell, he said, "It's not my blood. Also, don't freak out when you see Lyrrin. I mean, it was her blood, but she's okay."

"What? Lyrrin? You got her? Where is she?" Riony turned a full circle, her heart thumping its way up into her throat as she scanned her surroundings.

Beside them, Niskina sent more delvers running in all directions with orders.

Once she faced Benjin again, he shook his head, brows

furrowed. "They're outside the Shield Gate entrance. We got caught on our way back. The riders who captured us sent me in to let you know. They want to talk."

Riony's skin chilled. "Captured? Is everyone okay?"

Benjin winced slightly. "So far. Kess is injured."

The air huffed out of Riony like she'd been struck in the chest.

Niskina gestured to them both to follow her, leading them away from the crowd of onlookers. "They want to talk? About what? They just want to lure us out so they can finally take Dracuni."

"I'm not so sure," Benjin said. "Things were crazy out there. The riders were all fighting each other! Like an insurrection or something. Except I'm not sure which side won or what they were fighting about."

They moved around a corner to a quieter street. Dracuni perched on the rooftop above, watching down with concern.

"It doesn't matter." Riony was jangly and tense all over, her fingers twitching and back strained.

Lyrrin was there, just outside. And Aishena, Dashiel, and Kess ... Kess was injured.

Riony closed her hands into fists. "It doesn't matter what they were fighting about or if it's a trap. I'm going out there and getting our family back."

"They've returned? Where's Lyrrin?" From one end of the street, Eslinde rushed toward them, guided by a delver.

She carried her gown scooped up in front of her as she ran.

From the other end, the Alderkin approached, cloaked and hooded and with their own delver escort.

Benjin caught them up in a flurry of words. He finished with, "Whatever we do, we really have to hurry. We ... also brought someone else home with us too."

Riony raised her eyebrows at that.

Niskina said, "I want everyone back safe too, but we can't risk the safety of the entire undercity for it."

Eslinde's face was set in flat lines of determination. "I'm getting my daughter back, one way or another."

"We'll use the gateway," Riony said, her mind racing the way her feet longed to. "Travel to the nearest shrine downhill and go up to meet with the riders that way."

Benjin shook his head. "That's half a day's hike. I'm not sure we have that much time."

Riony's mouth felt gummed up and her heart rioted.

It was Niskina who asked gently, "How injured is Kess?"

Benjin paled and shook his head.

"Then we're going out, through Shield Gate." Riony turned to Yrik and Priyune. "Can you clear the way, get it open quickly?"

Yrik bowed his head. "We can. But we may have another option. We have been working on the runic arrangement needed to view outside our gates. It will allow you meet with those outside without risking yourself."

"I'm not worried about myself right now!" Riony

snapped.

Niskina put a calming hand on Riony's shoulder. "Then worry about Dracuni. If we open the gate and they force their way in, it will be war in here, with Dracuni the prize."

Riony turned her face up, and Dracuni looked back down at her, a heartsick pain shared between them.

She let a long breath out through her nose and addressed Yrik. "Okay, if you say we can meet with them with your magic, then let's do that. But I also want one of you getting the gate cleared and ready to open so we can bring the others in as soon as possible."

Yrik traced his finger through the air. "I'll get it done. I will make this mountain sing to bring Lyrrin home."

"Dracuni, go with him. I want you at the gate, ready." Riony didn't want to say what she needed to be ready for. She still hated asking for Dracuni's blood.

But Dracuni simply nodded once and took to the air again.

They split up, with Yrik leaving toward Shield Gate with a handful of delvers, and Riony, Eslinde, Niskina, and Benjin following Priyune.

The Alderkin woman's shoulders hunched and her long fingers were dusty and seemed worn from use. The Alderkin had followed through with their promise, working tirelessly in any way the people of the undercity needed.

Broken services were repaired, new crystals were carved.

They had provided all the float runes requested for the raid on the glass factory and other upcoming missions. If anything, Riony was worried they were working too hard.

Maybe they all were. But when the alternative was admitting defeat and the collapse of all good in their world, how could they stop?

Priyune led them through to an empty chamber close to where the gateway crystal and new shrine was housed.

Within it, the central space had been cleared, and five long, thin crystals stood around the edge, like spears jutting from the ground.

"Wait beyond the circle," Priyune directed, moving to the nearest crystal. She started at the bottom, tracing a long and complicated sequence of runes up the shaft. "Once the view of outside appears, you can step in."

"What will it do? Is this like a gateway?" Eslinde asked.

Priyune moved along to the next crystal. "Not quite. You will see the second location as though through a gateway, and you will step into it as though through a gateway, but it will only project your image there. You will physically remain within this room."

Riony twitched, bouncing on the balls of her feet, her whole body still wanting to run. "As long as it gets us out there so we can talk those depths-damned riders into giving our people back, I don't care how it works."

Niskina side-eyed her. "Pity the fool who stands between you and your star."

Priyune moved around, activating each crystal rod in turn. As she traced over the final runes of the fifth, the air between them shivered and shifted, forming a vision of a rocky plateau. Three riders in the king's colors paced there, ghostlike and hazy around the edges. They argued with no sound.

Behind them, close to the farthest boundary of the crystal arrangement, sat a huddle of bodies. Two lay prone and lifeless.

Heart jolting, Riony took a hurried step forward.

Priyune blocked her path. "Once you are within the array, they will see you and hear you, and you will hear them. Don't move too far once you are in, or you will step out again. You are not really there. Don't try to touch anything."

Riony nodded, although the words had floated through her head without finding purchase. She could only focus on the people lying on the rocky ground.

The features of all the figures were too fuzzy to identify. But there was nobody in that group she wanted to lose.

"I'm ready," Eslinde said, stepping beside Riony.

The princess clasped Riony's hand, and her fingers trembled. They stepped together into the vision, with Niskina and Benjin at their back.

"Razed skies!" A female rider whose limbs seemed carved from tree trunks startled at the sight of them. She cast her gaze over Riony's shoulder and back again a couple

of times. "How did you ... did the gate open?"

Riony glanced around. Behind her, the cavern chamber had vanished, replaced instead with the exterior of Shield Gate.

And in front of her, the land and sky extended out to the horizon. Figures became whole and details cleared.

Kess's purple dragon lay at the edge of the plateau, snout bound in rope and seething, and Griskin lay at his feet, bound so thoroughly he lay motionless on his side.

The three king's riders gawked at Riony's sudden appearance.

Aishena and Dashiel also watched, wide-eyed. They knelt with their hands bound in front of them. Lyrrin wasn't one of the bodies on the ground. She stood beside the others, her face and dress darkened with the rust of old blood, but she bounced and beamed brightly when she saw Riony.

It was Kess who lay face down, lifeless. So limp, the captors hadn't even bothered tying her up.

"What did they do to her?" Riony growled.

Benjin gripped her arm from behind as though to keep her in place. "It wasn't them."

Every nerve in Riony twinged with the desire to run to Kess. To feel for her pulse, her breath, to scoop her up and make sure she was okay. But she couldn't do any of those things. Not yet.

It took Eslinde hissing "Is that *Kverra Hjelzahn*?" for

Riony to turn her attention away from Kess to the second body lying motionless.

Benjin replied, "Mami? Yeah."

Riony's eyes popped wide. "Okay, that's a surprise you could have mentioned."

Benjin shrugged. "Well, everyone's going to get a surprise if the morass mercy we used on her wears out before we get her somewhere secure."

Eyebrows creeping even farther up her forehead, Riony nodded. "Right. Yes."

With clenched teeth, she turned her attention back to the riders who had formed up in a line before them. They all still wore bewildered expressions but weren't making any aggressive actions.

Gesturing to the gate behind her, Riony said, "We have more ways to get in and out than you know."

"So it seems. All the more reason this siege has been a farce from the beginning." The bulky woman scowled, but the ire was directed to the sky behind her, not at Riony and her companions.

"Call me Lerris." She stepped forward, one hand out as though expecting Riony to shake it.

Riony remained still. "Are we friends? Because friends don't hold their friends' loved ones hostage."

Lerris continued scowling, but Riony suspected it may just be how she looked. "No, not friends. Although I hope we can become allies."

She made an expansive gesture to the downward slope of the mountain and land beyond. Where tents and dragons had once filled the space, the remnants of a battle now marred the landscape. Fires spotted the ground and more than one downed dragon lay in the rocky snow around the entrance.

In the far distance, dragon silhouettes as small as birds were fleeing, and while there were still far more dragons and their riders sitting in wait for orders around them than Riony enjoyed seeing, it was half the numbers there had once been.

"What happened out here?" Eslinde asked.

Lerris inclined her head. "The right decision was made. One it seems you came to some time ago, your highness."

"Can we skip the formalities and get to the point?" Riony's eyes were back on Kess, willing her to move, to show any sign of life across the distance.

Lerris's eyebrows drew in. "The point is that dragonkeeps are falling. Entire dragonkeeps! All those here who fought today on our side have lost homes that we weren't there to protect because we were *here*. Here chasing some flippant desire of the man we once called our king, while the people suffer!"

Eslinde's hand in Riony's tightened.

Her voice was breathy. "How many keeps?"

Lerris shook her head, and her mouth opened but no sound emerged. She took a moment and cleared her throat.

"Too many. But we refuse to lose any more. No matter the orders. No matter old loyalties. The revenant army marches upon the capital, left defenseless. Those who refused to join our side have been chased back there, but from all reports I've heard, that won't be enough. We need more. We need every dragon we can get."

Riony took a step forward, challenging the woman's personal space. "Great. So go, then! Go and leave us and our friends who look like they are bleeding out in the dirt!"

Lerris glanced back at Kess as well. "Her injuries aren't our doing. And you can have her back, you can have them all back, if you agree to join us in the battle against the revenant army when the time comes."

Riony's eyes narrowed to slits. "Holding my injured family hostage isn't a good start along our road toward working together."

The rider folded her barrel-sized arms across her chest. "How else could we have brought you out to speak with us? We found a way and we used it. You have power in your ranks that we need."

Eslinde asked, "What do you need us for?"

"We know there are dragons in there, a lot of them. The ones the king sent with that upstart Heithorn jerk who suddenly gained his favor."

"One upstart jerk who is no longer with us," Riony said.

Lerris's lips curled up into what might count as a smile. "We've also heard stories that you're allied with the Rebel

Riders. And we know you have Dashiel on your side, and Vance Zarram, two of the best riders I've ever trained, and whom I'm glad to see survived the destruction of their hold."

Dashiel straightened up proudly. "Lerris was my mestra as I trained to be a rider. She's a good person, and what she's saying is true. We saw the army. We saw how little the capital is prepared."

"Dash. She's tied you up," Riony said.

Dashiel shrugged. "Well, yes. But what she's saying still deserves consideration."

Riony chewed her lip. Every instinct in her told her not to trust dragonriders. This had to be some kind of trap, and she hated how reasonable the woman sounded.

Eslinde gave her hand another squeeze. "I know of Mestra Lerris too. She is honorable. And we will, someday soon, have to face my father and the curse that plagues our land. One way or another. Better we do it with all these people by our side as well."

Lerris remained front and center, with two younger men by her side. Riony tried to gauge their expressions, looking for any indication of malice.

If anything, they just seemed exhausted and as worried and wary as Riony.

Riony lifted her chin at the riders. "So if we agree to help you, then what?"

"Then we will leave you and your friends alone until

the time comes and we call for you. And we will trust that you will come to our aid. I've heard tales of your honor as well."

Behind the riders, Lyrrin gave a small, hopeful nod, and Kess remained still. The people Riony loved were all there in front of her and yet felt a million worlds away. And all it took to get to them was forging an alliance with their enemy.

She looked to Eslinde, who returned a steely expression and nodded.

"Yes." Riony rattled all over with desperation. "Yes, we will help when the time comes."

With a grand flourish of her arm, Lerris signaled the riders waiting below. In an instant, they began taking to the air, one after another.

Riony watched in disbelief. They were really leaving.

"Go, go quick and get the gate open," Eslinde whispered back to Niskina and Benjin.

The three riders before them were turned away, making further signals to some closer riders. The next time Riony glanced behind her, Niskina and Benjin were gone, vanished from sight.

Eslinde spoke in a regal tone, "So, we agree to work together to face our true enemy, the shadow dragon's curse and the revenants it raises. And you will not try to encroach upon the undercity in any way before the time comes for us to fight side by side?"

Lerris snorted. "There's nothing in that dank cave we want. Whatever the king was so keen to capture, he can go get it himself. We're done with his orders."

One of the men at her side pulled a blade and marched back toward the prisoners. Riony bit her tongue bloody with worry, but the man simply cut through the bindings holding each of them.

As he turned his knife toward Kverra Hjelzahn's ropes, Aishena snapped, "If you want to live, don't touch those."

Lerris watched as they were all freed, including wolf and dragon, both growling and grumbling, then turned back to Riony. "They're all yours."

Lyrrin was first to move. She ran for Riony, arms out.

Riony balked, taking a step back and shaking her head vehemently. Lyrrin frowned but stilled before she attempted to wrap herself around Riony and go right through, revealing their illusion.

Riony wanted to hold her sister so badly, and as much as the Alderkin's spell had facilitated the negotiations, it wasn't facilitating getting Riony and her loved ones reunited in the way Riony longed for.

Aishena and Dashiel moved together to lift Kess gently onto Griskin's back.

"Is she ...?" Riony called over, keeping her feet planted.

Dashiel shook their head. "She needed urgent treatment hours ago, but she's holding on."

That's my girl. Hold on.

"See to your companions. I do hope they will all be well, and I apologize for delaying them." Lerris approached a red dragon seated at the edge of the plateau and hauled herself up onto its back. Her scowl shifting into something sadder. "You will hear from us again … I fear far too soon."

The moment Lerris and her two companions were in the air, Riony called out to the others, "The gate will be opening in a moment. We have to go, but we'll meet you inside!"

"What? Why?" Lyrrin reached for Riony, and her hand passed right through.

"That's why."

Lyrrin's bright-blue eyes sparkled as she waved her hand through Riony's middle in awe.

Riony swatted her uselessly back. "Stop that. It's weird."

Eslinde brushed a ghostly hand across Lyrrin's cheek. "We won't be long."

Aishena shouted from where she stood over Kverra Hjelzahn's body. "You better not be. Because I lost my morass mercy in our escape, and I think my mother is waking up."

SIXTEEN

The race from the illusion crystals to Shield Gate was a blur of frantic, pounding feet, interspersed with apologizing to those Riony collided with in her haste. By the time she reached the undercity exit, her pulse pounded like crashing waves in her ears, and she'd left Eslinde far behind in the streets of the undercity.

Yrik stood before the looming double doors of stone, hands pressed deep into a hole cut into the shield shaped relief. A glow of magic shone around his wrists as he worked on the enchanted mechanisms within the gate.

"He's opening it now." Benjin hovered on tiptoes near the Alderkin's shoulder, watching him work and breathing hard from his own run there.

Niskina acknowledged Riony, then joined the delvers

waiting there. With a few quiet orders, they left.

Riony knew why. They didn't need any more witnesses to Dracuni's power.

The unidragon sat to the side, tail flicking and eyes worried.

Lyomir is being very loud about Kess.

Riony nodded. Her heart was also.

The stone doorways groaned and scraped, bringing the yellow of early morning light in to merge with the cyan glow of the undercity. Griskin was first through, bolting straight to Riony, whom he had gone to for aid once before and turned to again now as Kess lay limply over his neck.

He whined as Riony moved to his side. She ran her hands over the stupid gremlin's clammy, far too cold skin, the tacky blood, the sharp points of glass poking out of her back below padding and bandages.

"Sparks, Kess. What did you do to yourself?" Riony breathed the words and thought after them, *for Lyrrin. For me.*

Riony had a vial of silvernix on her that Dracuni demanded she always carry now, but before she could reach it, the unidragon moved in beside her. She scratched the tip of her snout, then pressed it to Kess's cheek.

Kess jerked upright as starlight exploded from her. Riony caught her as she screamed and gasped through the pain of being healed. Her torso twitched and arched, and an awful squelching sound came from her back.

Long shards of glass twisted and cut through her skin as the magic tried to expel them but the bandages held them in.

Riony grasped for the gauze, wrenching it between her fisted hands and tearing it off. Five long daggers of glass slithered their way out of Kess's back, then fell and shattered on the cavern floor. With a high, gasping cry, Kess slumped forward again, and Riony was there to catch her. Kess's face rested against Riony's neck as she gasped deeply.

"It's okay. You're going to be okay." She cradled the back of Kess's head in one hand and whispered into her hair as the light faded and their breathing steadied together. A deep ache filled Riony's chest and arms, an all-consuming desire to hold Kess like that forever.

Kess shifted in her embrace. "Ri—"

"Ow!" Riony yelped.

She backed away from Kess, who was sitting up on her own now, blinking at Riony as though woken from a dream.

"You're here this time!" Lyrrin stood at Riony's side, poking her with a sharp finger. "And you cut your hair!"

Lyrrin, safe and happy and with her again. Riony bent over the small girl, then straightened back up with her trapped in a tight embrace, lifting her off her feet.

"Little moon. I'm so glad you're back. I'm sorry I didn't come to get you myself."

"It's okay. I understand." Lyrrin nuzzled into Riony

and then pushed away. "Gross. You're so sweaty!"

Riony put her sister back on her feet. "And you're covered in smelly blood. Are you going to tell me about that?"

"Are you going to tell me how you were a ghost a minute ago?"

"Ask your grandfather."

Aishena hollered over them, "Reunions later! We need to deal with this, now!"

She and Dashiel charged in, carrying Kverra Hjelzahn between them. The woman was bound around her hands and feet, but her eyes were open, and she was wrestling against her bonds.

Lyomir followed after, huge eyes locked on Kess. Kess gave him a small smile, and the dragon huffed grumpily and turned back around.

"Deal with what?" Breathing hard, Eslinde jogged up the tunnel, having finally caught up. Her eyes landed on Lady Hjelzahn. "Oh, blessed sun."

Vance followed at the princess's side and continued running straight to Dashiel, catching their sibling in a clapping embrace.

"Amma!" Lyrrin squealed.

Eslinde met the charging child on her knees and was toppled onto her back by her momentum.

"And I get a poke in the ribs. But fine, I guess," Riony muttered.

Tsking, Aishena shouted, "I said reunions later! I can't hold her on my own!"

Kverra snarled, "You won't be able to hold me for long at all."

A chill ran down Riony's back at the woman's voice, so hollow and cold.

Riony hurried to join Aishena in keeping the grayglim woman pinned. The ropes around the woman's ankles had loosened with her writhing and Riony held her feet down onto the tunnel floor.

"Weird you're complaining about reunions when you're the one who brought your murderous possessed mother home." Riony hissed as the woman bucked harder, giving no sign of easing up. "Also, it's so good to see you again."

"I have a plan." Aishena pressed all her weight down on the woman's shoulders, having to dodge as she angled her head around, trying to bite her. "And it's good to see you too."

Niskina stood as still as a statue at their side, glaring down at the woman who had killed her father. "And what exactly is your plan? Because I hope you've brought her in for justice."

"I've lost as much and more to this woman's hands as you. And if by justice you mean revenge, then yes, if my plan doesn't work, we will have no option but to end this mockery of life she's living." Aishena's silver hair swung around her chin as she bowed her head. "But first ... first

I want to try to heal her."

"Heal her ... how?" Riony asked.

With an unspoken apology softening her eyes, Aishena said, "When your mother was healed ... it seemed to me that whatever compulsion the shadow dragon had over her was severed."

"Whatever happened to my amma then, she didn't survive it."

"Because she was long dead already. I don't think my mother ever fully died, that the curse somehow made its way inside her when she was knocked down. She is still Kverra Hjelzahn *and* something more, something controlling her. And if we heal her, maybe we can break that connection."

Crouching by his sister's side, Benjin's eyes widened hopefully. "Do you really think it will work?"

Aishena's face crumpled in a display of emotion she so rarely let slip. Her mouth moved but made no sound and she shrugged.

"It's worth a try." Riony looked questioningly to Dracuni.

The unidragon was already moving closer. ***It's okay. Now that I'm bigger, it's only a little cut.***

You'll let me know if it's ever too much, if we're ever asking too much from you.

Dracuni brought her claw up to her nose again, her opalescent moonlight scales glimmering in the cyan light. Each cut she made on herself for others healed quickly, but recently there had been so many that faint scars were showing around the softer scales and skin on her snout and forearms.

She touched her silvernix blood to Lady Hjelzahn. The woman lit up bright but didn't writhe or scream as the healing worked through her body, the way Riony knew could hurt so keenly.

As the magic worked through Lady Hjelzahn, Riony's gaze drifted upward, away from her and to the beautiful young woman on the wolf, keeping to the shadows away from everyone else. She had a bone knife in each hand, in a way that once would have had Riony running. But Kess kept sharp, wary eyes on the grayglim woman.

The light faded.

"Did it work?" Benjin asked.

Kverra lay still beneath them, midnight-dark eyes darting from person to person around her.

Riony and Aishena released their hold on her, backing away.

With a smooth, easy motion, Lady Hjelzahn bent at the waist and sat up, her wrists and ankles still tied. "I feel ... better. I feel clearer, healed as though from some long illness."

Benjin beamed, but Aishena blocked him from moving any closer. She squatted down in front of her mother and grasped the long, whiplike braid of black hair at the nape of her neck.

Turning the woman's face side to side, Aishena peered into her eyes. "It didn't work. She's still possessed."

"Are you sure?" Eslinde asked.

"I know my mother. This is something else." With a slow sigh, Aishena activated her cutting athame. "Niskina will get her wish after all."

Niskina had both hands over her mouth. "Oh, Aish … I didn't want this."

Riony wanted to argue, to give her friend hope, but she could see it too. That same, inhuman emptiness she felt when she looked into the woman's dark eyes. It hadn't left. She hadn't changed.

"I am your mother and your mestra! Stop being foolish and untie me."

Aishena only shook her head as though it weighed as much as the world.

Lady Hjelzahn growled at them and wrenched at her bonds again.

Staring at the lethal weapon glowing in her hands, Aishena spoke flatly, "I assume beheading would have to put her down once and for all?"

"I'll take the children away," Eslinde said hurriedly.

"No!" Benjin snapped. "I'm staying. No matter what."

"I'm sorry. I really thought it would work," Aishena whispered and lifted her blade.

Riony's chest squeezed around her heart. It wasn't fair for them to lose their parents again and again. For Aishena

and Benjin to have had lost their father and siblings, then had to flee from their own mother who wasn't their mother anymore. Only to lose her again now, like this.

It wasn't fair that Riony had to watch her own mother die, clawed apart in the hands of the curse's creatures, only to have her come back and die again. Riony's fists clenched, nails digging into her palms at the memory.

It wasn't …

Riony's eyes widened, and she lurched forward, grabbing Aishena by the shoulder and pulling her back. "It was different! With my amma. It was different. It wasn't just silvernix, it was Dracuni's flame."

Aishena's flat look of determination faltered, and her knuckles were white around the hilt of her crystal blade. "Do you think it will make a difference?"

Riony helped Aishena back to her feet, and they moved away. "We should try, just in case."

Riony thought to Dracuni, *Will you do this for us?*

Of course. But I am feeling hungry again.

I'll get you more to eat really soon. Just a short burst, the way Vance said.

Dracuni moved in front of Lady Hjelzahn, who stared the dragon down fearlessly, although she backed up in small wriggles until she hit the wall.

"You're going to burn me? Fine, burn me, take my head. You cannot stop me, and you cannot stop what is coming for all of you. I will—"

Dracuni flamed. A short puff that started and stopped so quickly that the silvery fire came out like a bursting cloud.

It surrounded Kverra, blocking her from view as the flickering flame and bright light glared. Gasping breaths grew louder and faster, culminating in a single, heart-piercing shriek.

Then the healing flame and light were gone.

Kverra leaned with her back pressed hard into the wall behind her, her eyes open so wide that all the whites around her dark irises were visible. She stared from Aishena to Benjin, back and forth in a flutter, then her face scrunched in on itself and she fell sideways.

Her mouth opened in a silent scream, and her body curled up, shaking with heavy sobs.

"Is this a good sign or a bad sign?" Riony asked.

Aishena stepped over the shuddering woman, who made no further attempt to pull free of her bonds or attack her daughter.

Through Kverra's racking cries, the soft rhythm of hushed words escaped. Over and over. "What have I ... what have I done? What have I... What have ... What have I done?"

"I never in my life saw my mother cry." There was no emotion in Aishena's voice, only something deeply tired and final. "But that is her."

SEVENTEEN

Riony didn't particularly enjoy hearing the story of where all the blood on Lyrrin came from, how Yensen died, or how the Dragon King, Lyrrin's own grandfather, had called a torturer to use on her.

Eslinde was white-faced and drawn at the stories as well. She spoke more to herself than the others. "Oh, Yensen ... What a waste my father makes of good people."

Riony shook her head, awed. "Stars, I'm so sorry I couldn't be there for you. But I'm so proud of how you kept yourself alive."

"I learned from the best," Lyrrin said from above where she rode on Riony's shoulders.

She had only been gone for less than two weeks, but she still seemed somehow heavier. Older.

Riony squeezed her legs. "Let's not make this a 'who can survive near-death most often' competition, though, okay?"

Tell her I'm proud too! Tell her I'm sorry too, that I couldn't save her. From where she followed behind, the jittery waves of the unidragon's guilt and shame washed over Riony with almost overpowering strength.

Reaching their new front door in Delver's Circuit, Riony bent over and put her sister down.

"Dracuni has nothing to be sorry for and is proud of you too." She pushed the square stone button, and the stone door rolled open.

"Elumon!" Lyrrin cried as the doorway cleared.

The little hatchling danced there, hopping back and forth on anxious claws, expecting Lyrrin's arrival. He had gotten larger in the time Lyrrin had been away, growing fast the way Dracuni did in her early days.

Lyrrin giggled as the dragonling licked her face with a long split tongue. "I know!"

She held his head cupped in her hands and nodded along to a long and silent conversation between them. "I missed you too."

"He's not the only one," Riony said with a flick of her chin.

Lyrrin's gasp could have used up all the air in the room as there was a splash from the pool and slap of wet running footsteps.

"Butterfur! You're so big!"

The cave otter, balancing on back legs and tail, was taller than Lyrrin now. He nuzzled his whiskered snout all over Lyrrin's face as she squealed.

He dropped to all fours again and circled around Lyrrin twice, sniffing anything that might have been a pocket. With a huffing bark, Sir Butterfur Spelunkychunks slithered on his belly back to the pool again.

"Oh no. I should have brought some treats home for him." Lyrrin looked devastated.

Riony chuckled. "Don't worry, he gets plenty of food. Come on, go inside."

"Is this our new place? It has a pool! And furniture!" Lyrrin beamed up at her. Her hair had been darkened to a glossy black, and it made her bright-blue eyes stand out against her pale skin.

Only Eslinde followed in behind Riony, Lyrrin, and Dracuni.

With it being decided that Lady Hjelzahn was no longer a threat, she was left with her children. Aishena and Benjin half carried the broken woman away to deal with the fallout of her curse as a family.

After a few more brief reunions, everyone else split off as well. Vance and Dashiel, arms over each other's shoulders, went one way, and Niskina, wet-faced yet calm, left on her own. Yrik gave Lyrrin a number of long, very human hugs before letting her go, remaining behind to seal the gateway again, just in case.

Riony didn't notice when Kess left. She only noticed her absence like a spike through her heart when she found her gone. There was so much more she wanted to say to her ...

She hadn't even had time to thank her for bringing Lyrrin home safe.

And now Riony was waylaid under a ceaseless barrage of a moment-by-moment rundown of Lyrrin's adventures. And she savored every bit of it because her sister was home with her again.

"And I think she's pregnant," Lyrrin said with the sort of wired, buzzing enthusiasm only a child who'd had a night filled with far too much excitement and zero sleep possessed.

She zigzagged around the room like a ricocheting ball, looking at each chair and lounge and carving on the wall and dipping her hands into the pool, then patting Elumon again, then playing with the doorways to the adjoining rooms.

"Who?" Riony asked.

"The queen, of course! Some of the things she and the king were saying made me think it. Like they didn't care at all if the other heirs were all getting killed one way or another, how they were going to have more."

Eslinde tutted. "Who else was killed, did they say?"

Lyrrin gaped, but her mouth continued at full speed. "I'm sorry, they're your brothers and sisters, aren't they?

I kind of keep forgetting that you're part of that family because you're not like them at all. I really didn't like the king, but it was still kind of interesting there. They said a lot of interesting things. Things that gave me ideas."

"I've had some ideas while you were gone too. We've got a lot to talk about." Riony pulled Lyrrin to a stop with another hug. "And I'd love to hear all your ideas, but for now, how about getting cleaned up and resting? Benjin said you were flying all night."

"He *always* exaggerates. It was maybe only half the night, and before that was capturing Lady Hjelzahn, and before that was when I tried to escape on my own and this happened." Lyrrin gestured to her blood-stained dress. "Wow, was that really just last night? Feels like forever ago!"

Eslinde brushed a hand through her hair. "Which is why you really need to get some rest."

"I'm not tired!" Lyrrin snapped, instantly teary.

Eslinde shot a worried look at Riony.

Riony returned a wry smile. *Welcome to caring for an overtired child.*

There was a knock at the door, which Riony had left open as an invitation for the other reunion Riony longed for. She spun around, eager to see Kess there.

Zeina stood tall within the doorframe. "Can I talk to you for a moment? Sorry to interrupt."

"That's okay." Riony gave Lyrrin a smile, and then checked with Eslinde. "Do you think you can manage this?"

Eslinde gave Riony a fearful look.

Grinning toothily, Riony backed away. "I won't be gone long. There are some clean clothes in that room and there's food through there, in the cold chest."

"*We have a cold chest?*" Lyrrin's eyes bugged wide, and she bolted, Eslinde chasing after.

Riony met the Rebel Rider at the door, and they stepped outside together.

The well-lit hallway was short, off the main looped path of Delver's Circuit. There was only one other round doorway down that hall, directly across from them, that led to the Hjelzahn's chambers.

I hope they're doing okay.

Zeina folded bare, muscled arms across her chest and smiled in a way that would have left Riony in a puddle on the floor not long ago. "Your friends really did it. Rescued the girl right from under the Dragon King's nose. I'm impressed."

"Yeah, me too."

Riony had spent every day since the others had left on the mission with a deep, nagging icy feeling in her gut. A sickening worry that none of them would make it home again. That she'd lose Aishena, Benjin, Dashiel ... that she'd lose Kess, when Kess had come to mean so much to her.

That feeling hadn't left yet. Not entirely. It seemed to pull at her insides, desperate to see Kess again, to prove that she was really there, prove it with her eyes and with her hands, as though physical touch was the only thing that could relieve her worry that none of this was real.

Zeina raised dark eyebrows at Riony's heating cheeks. "And the siege is over?"

Riony cleared her throat. "Word travels quickly."

"Niskina gave me the rundown already, about your deal with the riders." Zeina leaned a hip against the wall. "Which is why I'm here. Gleem is desperate to get out of this cave, and now that we can, I thought I could go and do something useful."

Riony blinked, trying to comprehend through her overstimulated brain.

Zeina continued. "If things are that bad out there, we're going to need more numbers. I know it's not the army we need, but I can go and bring in the other Rebel Riders. There are two other small groups, four in each."

Eight more riders. It wasn't many, in the scheme of things. But Riony's brain had been stewing on something, burbling away between all the other excitement of the day.

She chewed her lip, thinking. "Are their dragons tamed or wild?"

"Wild, all except one which was a rescue."

"Get them to untame it, if they're willing." Riony pulled her vial of silvernix from her pocket and pushed it into Zeina's hand.

"You think it's a good idea? That I should go?" Zeina frowned over her golden eyes.

"It is. And I thought you wanted to?"

"I do …" Zeina wet her lips. "Unless you want me to stay."

Oh … sparks. Riony had so rarely been in the position of needing to let someone down gently. Let alone *a Rebel Rider*. She struggled for words, gaping.

A movement at the end of the hallway where it intersected with the main loop drew Riony's attention away. The shadowed form of Kess stalking past on Griskin.

Heart picking up to a gallop, Riony took one step that way before she'd even noticed her actions. She shook her head, turning back to Zeina.

"Sorry. I … um …"

Zeina followed her line of sight as Kess disappeared around the corner again.

"Don't worry. I get it." She huffed a sigh. "She is impressive, after all. Listen, just promise that if things don't work out with her, you'll consider me again."

Riony offered the stunning woman a brash smile, her feet already leading her away backward. "Are you calling me a quitter?"

Zeina barked a laugh. "You? Never."

Riony turned and sprinted down the hall. There was no sight of Kess from the intersection as the tunnel curved away sharply, and Riony bolted along it, running up behind the wolf and girl around the next corner.

"Kess!"

She swung around, her pale eyes flashing. "What is it? Is everything okay?"

Her hands were already moving to where she kept her knives, as though Lady Hjelzahn were about to emerge from the shadows and slit their necks.

Riony stopped by Griskin's side, in line with where Kess sat in her saddle.

"Everything's fine. I just wanted"—Riony's eyes locked on Kess's lips and she swallowed hard—"to talk to you."

"About?" Kess tucked her flight tangled hair behind one ear, and Riony's gaze traced every touch of the motion.

Sparks. Was she always this beautiful?

Riony replied, "I don't know, maybe about how you almost just died saving my sister for me?"

Kess smiled crookedly. "Is this supposed to be you thanking me?"

"I'm getting to that! Stars ..." Riony took a step closer, her thighs pressing into Griskin's fur as she searched Kess's face, trying to translate every change of expression and what it might mean. "I just wanted to make sure you're okay first. You were hurt. Badly."

"I'm better now, thanks to Dracuni."

"But you *were hurt*. What happened to the silvernix I gave you?"

"I used it on Griskin."

Riony coughed a bewildered laugh. "And you called me a sympathetic fool for saving Dracuni in her egg."

"You wouldn't have done it for Griskin?" Kess tilted her head judgmentally.

"You know I'd do anything for the big pup."

Growing serious, Kess leaned closer, her words a low hush. "And I'd do anything for you."

"Sparks, Kess. I don't want you as a bodyguard. And it's hurting me more seeing you kill yourself trying to be." Riony stepped closer again, one leg on either side of Kess's hanging in her saddle.

She brought a hand up and cupped Kess's spotted cheek. "I just *want you*."

Kess's breath caught audibly. "You want me?"

Breathing labored, Riony leaned in, her nose brushing Kess's. "I need you. I ... *raze it all* ... can I just kiss you now?"

Kess's answer came back on a breath that warmed Riony's face. "Please."

A fraction closer, and their lips brushed each other's.

Then with a desperate grunt, Riony fell upon Kess like a starved animal. Her hands grasped around Kess's waist, fisting into the blood-stained leather and pulling her closer. Kess's own hands reached back, clawing into Riony's back through her shirt. They each kissed the other as though they might die if they stopped.

Griskin rumbled a warning growl.

Riony's lips remained over Kess's. "Go on, bite me. I don't care."

She lifted Kess from her saddle, turning her to face her

fully, then pressed back into the kiss until Kess was caught between her and the wall.

Riony kissed her with every ache of longing she'd endured during their time apart, and Kess returned it with a yearning strength that seemed so much more.

In a gasping gap as they drew breath, Kess whispered, "Is *this* you thanking me?"

"I haven't even started thanking you. This is all for me."

Kess chuckled, a soft, gentle laugh that felt like a rare and precious gem.

Riony lost herself in the hazy pleasure for a long moment, where nothing in the world existed beyond Kess's lips against hers. She placed a flutter of soft kisses over the corners of her mouth, then delved deeper, enjoying Kess's whimper in response.

"Riony?" Eslinde's voice, panicky and high, echoed down the corridor, breaking them apart. "Are you there? Are you coming back?"

Riony groaned, rolling her neck to look toward her chambers. She ran her fingers down Kess's arms, then squeezed her hands.

"I have to go back." She didn't want to let go. "Come with me. Come and stay with me."

"Riony? Where are youuuuuuu?" Lyrrin's voice followed, unnaturally piercing and edged with upset.

Kess, breathless and flushed, shook her head. "Go. You need to be with your family."

Riony turned away and her heart panged deeply, pulling her back to Kess. "You're my family too. I want you with me."

"REEEEE-OH-NEEEEEEEEEE!" The echo of Lyrrin's cry pummeled the tunnel walls.

"Sparks." Riony winced dramatically.

"It's okay. I understand." Kess squeezed Riony's hands with trembling fingers and then let go.

Riony's nose scrunched up with the effort needed to turn away. Every part of her screamed with the need to pull Kess into her arms again.

But she had other responsibilities to put first, always, above what she wanted, or needed. Maybe, one day, things would change. But with all the threats still surrounding her and those she loved she wasn't sure that day would ever come.

EIGHTEEN

Lyrrin had a map of Elundrae laid out on the main table of her chambers, and all the guests she'd invited in sitting around it, and it was getting later and later into the evening and Riony still wasn't back.

The front door held all Lyrrin's attention as she glowered at it, willing it to open.

Food soon? Elumon asked from under her chair.

Soon, Lyrrin thought back, trying to stop her frustration and worry also reaching the hatchling.

Eslinde leaned over and said in a gentle voice, "I'm sure she's fine. The factory raids simply take as long as they take."

Niskina stifled a yawn. "She's been on one every day for weeks now. She's an expert liberator of dragons at this stage."

Beside her, Jaym reclined in his chair. Today's raid was the first he and Niskina hadn't also joined, citing the excuse that they were too sparking exhausted, thanks, and needed a break.

Dracuni, also tired from all of the blood she'd been providing recently, was resting in her own room nearby.

Everyone was working so hard. Since returning, Lyrrin had been with Riony every moment she wasn't out on raids, which wasn't much.

Lyrrin didn't like how hard Riony had been pushing herself, but she understood why. If they had any chance of weakening the shadow dragon's curse, of weakening the revenant army before it reached the capital, they had to untame as many dragons as possible, as quickly as possible.

A couple more seats along the table, Priyune and Yrik whispered together briefly in their own language. Across the other side, Lady Hjelzahn sat with a hunched back, her face bowed and hidden under a now loose tangle of black hair, covering her face like a waterfall. Aishena and Benjin sat stiffly on either side of her like wardens beside a prisoner more than children beside their mother.

The room fell silent again as an awkward tension built.

"Maybe I could serve some food while we wait," Eslinde offered.

Food? Elumon's head popped up near Lyrrin's lap.

With a soft, grinding noise, the circular doorway rolled open.

Lyrrin shot up to her feet. "Finally!"

Riony froze in the doorway, her face smudged in soot and blood. "What's going on? Were you having a party while I wasn't home? Because first of all, rude, and secondly, you need more friends your own age."

"We're having a meeting, remember? I told you this morning. About my plan."

Nodding once in a wobbly, exaggerated motion, Riony said, "Right. Yes. Your plan. Sorry we're late."

Sighing, she stepped inside, with Kess following in on Griskin close to her shoulder, looking equally haggard and battle worn. There was a seat left for each of them across the ornate, carved crystal table from each other. Riony leaned her sword beside her chair and winced as she sat down. Kess slid from Griskin's back into her chair without her usual elegance, landing with a thump.

Riony eyes were glued to Kess's ever motion. "You probably don't need to be here for this. You should go and rest. You need it."

"Like you can talk," Kess's gaze also remained on Riony. "I'll sleep when you sleep."

Riony's nostrils flared and her eyes sparkled with an intensity Lyrrin couldn't quite read.

"You know, I will go and get some food. I'm sure these two are hungry after their mission." Eslinde rose and fluttered to the kitchen.

"Bring a knife to cut this tension with too," Niskina

whispered not so quietly to Jaym.

"All went well, then?" Aishena asked. Although she'd only been on a few raids, she sounded as tired as the rest of them.

Without looking away from Kess, Riony replied, "Aside from one dragon who decided to take its years of captivity out on us, just perfect."

Benjin shot his sister a look. "We should be helping more."

Aishena's gaze flickered between him and their mother. "We have other things to look after right now."

"It's okay, we've got it covered." Riony did part her eyes briefly from Kess, frowning at Lyrrin. "I'm surprised you haven't been asking to come along."

"I would, if you'd like me to." Lyrrin straightened up in her chair, a flush of pride over her cheeks that Riony was now considering her someone who could be invited on missions.

I hope that means she agrees to my plan.

"But I'm plenty busy here too." She grasped her crystal-studded staff, once Benjin's, and showed off three new runed stones embedded into it. "Yrik and Priyune have been teaching me so much! I learned five new runes this week. Five!"

Eslinde returned with a platter piled with cold rope-worm slices, golden goat cheese, and root flour flatbread.

"Right here, thank you very much," Riony patted the

table in front of her.

Elumon skittered under the table to assault Riony with pleading hatchling eyes. Eslinde handed the platter over, then returned to her seat.

She smiled sadly at the staff in Lyrrin's hand. "I do love seeing what you create with the crystals. The way you carve runes reminds me of your father's handwriting. He used to write poetry for me in Alderkin."

Lyrrin pouted back. She had seen one rune carved by her father, and the curves of his lines had the familiar shape of her own. "I wish I could have met him."

Eslinde smiled more, scrunching up her eyes as they glimmered wetly. "Me too. Now, let's get to your plan."

With one hand, Riony piled food indiscriminately onto a large piece of bread, then pushed the remaining platter across the table to Kess. Before taking her first bite, Riony also flicked a slice of rope worm under the table, and happy emotions zinged from Elumon to Lyrrin.

As the two of them ate, the rest of the group looked to Lyrrin. Her worry had shifted to nervousness, now faced with all these people waiting to hear her plan. She wrung her hands in front of her.

"Go on," Eslinde whispered.

"I was thinking ... I had the idea ..." Lyrrin cleared her dry throat. "When we were talking about removing the Dragon King, one of the reasons it would be better if he was gone was because he's the only person who knows where his main supply of silvernix is kept. But what if he wasn't?"

Faces all around watched her silently, the only sound Riony's chewing.

Lyrrin continued. "If we could find his stash and take it from him, we would take almost all of his power. And also, we'd be able to use that silvernix for untaming all the factory dragons, and more, instead of relying on Dracuni all the time."

Eslinde's smile faltered. "That would be amazing ... but the location the king keeps his silvernix has been sought by many for decades, with no luck."

Jaym reached for the platter, poked at it with a frown, then pushed it away again. "We gave it a good crack a couple of times, for the same strategic reasons. But alas, no secret hoard of silvernix was found."

Turning from the Rebel Rider to the heir-killing grayglim, then the Alderkin and the King's own daughter, Lyrrin said, "But we know more now. Between what all of us here know about him and Elundrae, we've got the best chance ever."

"Where would we even start?" Niskina asked.

Lyrrin stood up so that she could reach over the large map in front of her, pointing out locations.

"When I was at the palace, the king said he needed to get more silvernix than they had on hand, and that night I saw him flying his dragon to the northeast, which would take him to his private palace."

Jaym folded his arms and shook his head sympathetically. "One of the first places we checked. Searched the place top to bottom while he wasn't there."

Priyune straightened in her chair, eyebrows raised. "All the way to the bottom? Are you sure? There is a deemfret under where the unicorn slayer built his detestable structure."

That perked Benjin up. "A deemfret? Do you mean an Alderkin depths, like this one?"

"Not quite the same," Yrik said. "It's far smaller. A solely sacred space rather than one built for community. A place of crystal as dark as the night sky, unlike anywhere else in these lands."

Jaym sucked air through his teeth. "*That* we did not find."

Eslinde had paled, and her hands tightened on the arms of her chair. "Alleem never mentioned it. I've been there plenty of times too and never saw any sign of it."

Lyrrin stabbed the location on the map with her finger. "And if you didn't find it, who's to say the silvernix isn't there? The king could be keeping the silvernix underground in the deemfret."

Priyune let out a weak wail, as though even the concept of the unicorn blood being stored in their holy space stung her. She leaned into Yrik, both whispering in distraught tones to each other.

Everyone else held expressions that had changed from

skeptical to warily enthusiastic.

Except for Riony, who was chewing her lip and still staring at Kess. One of her legs bounced, fidgeting rampantly.

"Riony? What do you think?"

"Hmm?" She blinked at Lyrrin. "Yeah, finding the silvernix would be good."

"That's not ..." Lyrrin sighed gruffly, shaking her head at Riony. She had to forgive her sister. She was clearly exhausted to distraction.

Turning instead to the once-murderous grayglim, Lyrrin lowered her voice as though calming an animal. "Lady Hjelzahn?"

The woman flinched slightly. "I no longer deserve that title."

"Kverra," Lyrrin corrected. "Did you see anything? Do you remember anything from your time ... following the king and heirs around? Anything that might help us?"

"My ..." Kverra's voice broke, and she remained hunched over, not looking at any of them. "Aishena has explained to me what is happening in our land, why our king no longer deserves my loyalty. I find it all hard to believe ..."

Her voice dropped, husky and wavering. "But my own actions over the past years defy belief far more. I have spent my days obsessed with killing the king, my king, and all his bloodline, and now I am expected to continue working against him? I don't ... I don't know how to believe what

I feel and see anymore."

"But if you saw anything—"

Lyrrin cut off as Aishena gave a sharp shake of her head. She noticed then how Kverra's shoulders were shaking violently.

"I'm sorry. I think we should go." Aishena pushed to her feet, and Benjin followed, throwing Lyrrin an exaggerated apologetic expression.

The two of them supported their mother from the room.

Lyrrin sighed and dropped back into her chair. "I really thought she might know something that could help."

Eslinde's smile had returned. "You've already done so well. Bringing us all together like this to share information. I think you might really be onto something."

"Well, that brings me to the next point," Lyrrin said, trying to sound older than she was. "I want to lead this mission."

That got Riony's attention, finally.

Eslinde also gasped softly, "Lyrrin ..."

"Before you say anything, remember how many times my plans and my magic saved us. I can do this, really." Lyrrin firmed up her jaw, staring them both down.

"No." Riony shook her head, drowsily awed. "You're right. I'm sure you can. But we can do it together."

Lyrrin winced. "I don't think we can. You can't come on this one."

Riony leaned back in her chair, smirking. "Oh, so *you're* excluding *me* now? Is that how it is?"

"Given your own plan, and your promise to Mestra Lerris, and the need to keep Dracuni safe, you and all our best dragonriders need to stay here. Same with Yrik and Priyune—this deemfret and the people here need them. I'll still take help, of course. Aishena and Benjin, probably; they were amazing when they came to rescue me before."

"And me. I'll go," Eslinde said, reaching for Lyrrin's hand. "I know my father's private palace. I've spent time there."

"You've really thought this all through, haven't you?" Riony pushed her chair back and came to stand beside Lyrrin.

With a firm jaw, Lyrrin rose to face her, prepared to continue defending her plan.

But Riony bent over, bringing Lyrrin into a hug. "I think it's a really solid plan."

"Thank you," Lyrrin said, muffled by Riony's shoulder. "I'm sure it won't be nearly as dangerous as what we've faced before."

"Don't jinx it." Riony backed away, giving Lyrrin's hair a quick ruffle.

"Well, it seems we have a lot of preparations to manage." Eslinde stood as well, watching her daughter a little teary-eyed.

Lyrrin grabbed her sister's hand and swung her arm

back and forth with enthusiasm. "I still have more details I want to go through. Will you help?"

"Of course, little moon."

"We'll be off, then," Niskina said.

"Glad I could help, although I'm not sure I entirely did." Jaym chuckled and offered Lyrrin a small salute. He caught up to Niskina and they exited shoulder to shoulder.

Yrik turned his hand Lyrrin's way, curving it through the air in an elegant gesture. "We'll take our leave too. We have much to do."

He and Priyune followed the others out.

Kess was still in her chair, watching Riony like a child might watch a beloved toy dropped in a stream drifting out of reach.

She whistled softly, bringing Griskin to her side. "I'd better get going too."

Riony returned an equally strange expression to Kess, cheek twitching and chest heaving.

"Actually," Eslinde said brightly, "I was thinking that maybe Lyrrin could have a sleepover with me tonight? If that's okay?"

"A *sleepover*?" Lyrrin wheezed. "Can I?"

Riony's jaw dropped as a breath rushed out of her. She answered with her eyes on Kess, who had frozen in her chair, hands on Griskin's saddle.

"Um. Yeah. Sure. That would be okay with me."

"Wonderful. Come on, let's go now. I want to keep

planning with you, since I'm on your team." Eslinde's eyelashes fluttered at Riony, and she smiled as she put a hand on Lyrrin's back, ushering her out.

"Elumon! Come on. He can come too, right?"

The hatchling loped across the room to follow them.

"Of course."

Lyrrin beamed up at her mother. It was still a concept she was getting used to, having a mother again. Riony's amma, growing up, had been Lyrrin's as well in every way, and Riony had cared for her as much as any mother would since then.

But having Eslinde around was different. Lyrrin was so excited to get to know everything about her, to share all of both their lives they'd missed out on experiencing together.

I hope we stay up all night talking!

She glanced back to wave to Riony as they reached the door, beaming from the successful evening, only to find her sister with an expression that looked desperately distraught. She was stalking toward Kess in a way that looked almost murderous.

"Is she ... okay?" Lyrrin asked, her smile dropping.

Eslinde pressed her hand into the middle of Lyrrin's back, pushing her into the hallway. "She's fine."

"She's not angry at me for wanting to have a sleepover, is she?"

"No, I don't think so." Eslinde chuckled and closed the door behind them.

NINETEEN

Kess woke from sleep like crawling out of a thick, warm syrup that pulled back against her every time she tried to reach consciousness.

She wasn't even sure why she was fighting it.

I want to stay like this forever.

She lay on her side under a cloudy tangle of blankets. Riony's body was curled around her from behind and warm like the touch of summer sun, one heavy arm draped over Kess's middle.

Riony was so rarely stationary. She seemed perpetually in motion, rolling her shoulders or shifting from leg to leg as though her body feared the concept of stillness.

To have her there, so comfortable, so trusting in Kess's company that she was completely at rest, was such a deep, aching honor that it made tears well in Kess's eyes.

The gentle inhale and exhale of Riony's sleeping breaths were sweeter than a love song.

She's really here. Really here, with me.

With the lack of natural light in Riony's bedroom it was almost impossible to tell what time of day it was, but Kess's body clock roused her as equally as the exhaustion of the previous week and late night fought to pull her back to slumber.

Kess's heart had awakened to Riony's touch as well, pattering quickly in a way that would be hard to calm again.

Sleep or not, Kess was content to lie there in that moment for as long as she could. She reached down to shift one of her legs into a more comfortable position, and Riony's arm instantly tensed. Then both arms snaked around Kess and pulled her tight to her chest.

"Don't go," Riony mumbled into Kess's hair.

"I'm not going anywhere." Kess closed her eyes as an electric energy thrummed through her at being in Riony's embrace. "I'm sorry I woke you."

"Am I awake?" Her voice was thick and soft with sleep. "Let me check."

A warm kiss pressed to Kess's bare shoulder where her undershirt had slipped down. Riony sighed heavily around the second kiss before planting the third.

Kess forgot how to breathe. "Yeah. You seem awake to me."

"I don't know. Pretty sure I'm dreaming."

Kess couldn't disagree. Everything felt dreamy and soft-edged and unreal.

Because how could she have this? How could she exist in this moment of raw, peaceful joy? It felt like the moment of calm before the nightmare takes over the knife twists.

She'd never known a time when the knife didn't cut away her happiness. A shiver of dread overtook Kess's body. Already overwrought with emotion at everything about her current situation, she couldn't suppress it.

Riony's drowsy kisses along her back grew more forceful, and she crushed Kess tight to her again.

Then she stopped and ran a hand down Kess's arm. "You're shaking. Are you okay?"

"Yes ..." Kess squeezed her eyes closed. "No."

Riony shuffled behind her, lifting up onto one elbow and leaning over her. "What's wrong?"

There was no judgment in Riony's expression, no annoyance or anything other than concerned care, and it only made Kess shiver harder.

How could I deserve this?

She wanted to make an excuse, to flee, but had no easy way out. Griskin had been closed out the night before. They were alone in what was now Riony's bedroom. Alderkin finery woven like liquid from cave silk in blues and purples was mismatched with an earthy collection of worn and singed blankets.

A well-loved doll with a red ribbon sat on a chair beside the bed, and although there was another bedroom in those chambers for Lyrrin, Kess was sure the young girl slept in this room with Riony most nights, as they must have for years in the smaller apartment they'd had before.

Riony waited patiently, and Kess steeled herself. Even if she didn't deserve this, she owed her courage to Riony. She owed her truth.

Kess worked to find her words. "Doesn't it scare you? *Having* anything. Happiness, friends, family, love. Aren't you terrified it will all be taken away?"

"Only every razing moment."

Kess rolled onto her back, staring up into Riony's multihued, ineffable eyes. Riony, who had grown up with her loving parents and still had her sister and friends who would do anything for her. She had lost so much but still had so much more she could lose.

Kess asked huskily, "How do you handle it?"

"Badly, mostly, and with as much inappropriate and ill-timed humor as possible." Riony smirked, but then her smile softened, and she lowered herself down, propping her head up on a fist. "I wish I could tell you it was easy, but I can tell you it's worth it, to have those things in your life."

Kess rolled over onto her side again, facing Riony. Her fiery-red hair was trimmed short all around one side where it had been burned, but a mop of unruly curls still tumbled over her face.

She had always been the most beautiful thing Kess had ever known, right from the day her parents had cruelly gifted Riony to her as a slave. There was no way to ever leave all of the injustice and trauma of their past behind, but the way Riony watched her now felt new.

It wasn't with the feigned respect of a belligerent slave, or pity, mere tolerance, or outright hostility. Not any of the ways Riony had once looked at her.

Kess's trembling eased, and her breath grew steadier again.

Riony's free hand found Kess's, toying with her fingers. "Is that what's worrying you? Not me? I didn't do anything wrong?"

"Never."

Riony lowered her eyes, her lashes shadowing them. "Really? Because I'll openly admit I am brand new to all of this. Outside of the theatre of my own mind and reading Rebel Riders, I mean."

"You haven't been with anyone else like this before?" Kess shook her head, confused. "*You*?"

"Thank you for the expression of shock. But nope."

"Me either." Heat flushed from Kess's collarbones to her cheekbones. "Was it ... okay for you?"

"Okay? *Okay*?" Riony dropped Kess's hand, her expression aghast as she sat fully upright.

"You made me question if I'd ever understood the word pleasure before. You made sounds come out of me that I

didn't even know were *in* me. You made me feel like I was filled with exploding starlight. Sparks, Kess. The slightest touch from you makes me dizzy with how much I love you."

Kess's thoughts blanked out entirely as though her head just took a great blow. "You ... love ... me?"

Riony lifted one shoulder. "What do you think we're doing here?"

Seeking comfort or relief or simple recreation? Kess had a hundred excuses in her mind for why Riony had turned to Kess the way she had recently. She'd never assumed love. She couldn't ... even if it was the reason she'd said yes in return.

The time they had spent together, the closeness and kisses and bare vulnerability was one thing, but to hear those words, *those words* from Riony ...

Kess's mind flared back to life with a surge of frantic emotion and she sat up to face Riony.

"I love you too. I've loved you for so long, longer than I could ever admit, because I never knew love. I couldn't perceive it, couldn't *accept* it. And when I finally realized ... I've caused you so much suffering. I don't deserve to love you and could never, ever deserve for you to love me in return."

Riony's head tilted as though she were considering this. "But I do."

"But I've hurt you. In so many ways. My selfishness, my family, my mistakes I've made while pursuing my

foolish dreams."

Riony frowned yet smiled at the same time, soft and determined. "But I do."

Kess's voice rose higher. "But I have so much blood on my hands. I'm not a hero like you. I looked after myself and only myself for too long. I would have torn this land and every heart in it apart for what I wanted, and I still would, only I have learned to *want* better. But I've done too much to be loved."

Riony leaned forward into Kess's space. "But. I. Do."

"But I'm ..." Kess's words broke off.

I'm not enough. I couldn't ever be enough.

Riony brushed a hand across Kess's cheek, smearing wetness there. "Do you think you can talk me out of this? Stars, Kess. All the things you're saying are all the reasons I *do* love you."

Kess scoffed in a way that was almost a sob. "Maybe you're the one who doesn't understand love, because they aren't good things."

"That you're a survivor? That you're driven? Forthright and passionate? Sly, confident, and effortlessly capable?" Riony leaned her forehead onto Kess's. "And *especially* how overly dramatic you are."

More tears spilled from Kess's eyes as she laughed. "You're the one who just said *filled with exploding starlight*."

"No drama. Just facts."

Kess leaned away from Riony, chewing her lip and

giving her an assessing look. "Might be something that needs to be tested again, for accuracy."

Riony huffed a breath and lunged onto Kess, knocking her back onto the bed with a giggling yelp.

Their hands were tangled beneath each other's clothing, and their mouths hot and raw from kissing when someone pounded at the door.

"Hey, you two!" Niskina's voice bellowed from outside. "Hate to interrupt whatever's going on in there which isn't obvious at all, but you're going to be late for today's mission."

"Sparks, already?" Riony groaned.

She lifted herself off Kess into a plank above her and yelled over her shoulder, "We're not here."

"Did you really think that was going to work?" Niskina replied, muffled through the stone.

Riony sighed, leaning down again and hiding her face in Kess's neck. "Just one day. I want just one day off before we either save the world or die trying."

"We could barricade the door," Kess offered.

"Give me your cutting athame and I'll make sure it never opens again."

"Sounds good to me. Although, we'll eventually starve."

Riony pressed a long kiss to Kess's neck. "We'll die happy."

Niskina pounded on the stone again. "Also, this wolf

of yours is real upset at being locked out here!"

Riony and Kess sighed as one.

"Fine," Riony yelled. "We're getting up. But we're not happy about it."

There was some incoherent muttering from the other side of the door, drifting off as Niskina left.

The bed was a low platform of stone, softened by a quilted mattress. Kess shuffled to the edge and dropped her legs over, looking around for her clothes, armor, and weapons that were strewn on the floor amongst Riony's.

"Let me fix that up for you." Riony moved behind her, running fingers through her tangled hair. "Considering I'm the one who messed it up."

Riony's nails combing against Kess's scalp and pulling the hair into braids made goosebumps rise over her skin. It had once been one of Riony's duties as Kess's carer, to braid her hair. Her hands still moved surely with the muscle memory, and the feeling of it brought a swell of mixed emotions rushing into Kess.

She murmured, "I can do it. You don't have to."

"Listen. Anything that means I get to keep touching you, I'm all in." Riony continued twining the hair into neat braids. "I can also help you with your leg exercises, if you'd like. I think I remember how."

In an even smaller voice, Kess echoed, "You don't have to."

Riony stopped then. She reached around and cupped

Kess's chin, turning her to look back. Her expression was serious. "You know people who love each other do things for each other. No bargaining or debts. You know that, right?"

"I'm ... still getting used to it."

Riony shook her head, and one hand traced lines over Kess's shoulder where her undershirt had fallen away. "You did this for me. You took these scars for me."

Kess hadn't seen the marks left from her brother's whipping herself but had been told they were there by Dashiel who had checked on her back on that night. Thin, barely there, white lines that the silvernix had closed, but not soon enough to be unmarred.

Kess met Riony's eyes. "That was different."

"How?"

"You already have too many."

Riony didn't say anything but began placing kisses across all the places she'd traced.

"We're never getting out of here if you start that again."

"It's very, very hard to stop."

"I know." Kess turned all the way around, catching Riony's kisses with her mouth.

A deep warmth of unfamiliar emotion consumed Kess. *Happiness.*

Pulling back for a breath, Kess said, "Do you remember when we went to Heithorn estate to rescue Dracuni, and before lifting me onto the dragon you told me you were

going to give me everything I ever wanted?"

Riony's lips quirked under Kess's. "I do say a lot of dumb things, don't I?"

"But you have. You have given me everything I ever wanted. I never thought this sort of happiness could be mine, and it's all because of you."

Riony pulled Kess off the edge of the bed and back onto the covers and into her arms.

Kess laughed. "So we're choosing *die happy*?"

Riony's voice was a lazy growl. "You always used to say to me that you'd watch me die one day."

Kess pulled back, frowning. "I'm sorry I did that. It wasn't what I meant, really. I think, even back then, I just always hoped that we'd be together that long."

Riony pouted. "Aw! But also, you know that's the worst possible way of expressing that sentiment."

Kess ran her nose up Riony's cheek and pressed a kiss to the corner of her lips. She felt Riony shiver under her touch. "I hope I've improved since then at expressing my sentiment."

"You have indeed."

It was at least another hour before they emerged from Riony's bedroom, still groggy and red-cheeked. The happiness that filled Kess felt as though it could burst her rib cage with the sheer immensity of it.

Riony loves me.

But further down, in the pit of her stomach, a chill

grew as they once again picked up their weapons.

Even yesterday's mission had some close calls. How much longer could their luck last? Would it end on today's mission, or tomorrow's? Or the next?

Despite all of Riony's reassurances, Kess still found it hard to believe she deserved any of this, which made her fear even stronger that it was all going to be taken from her soon.

TWENTY

Dragons fought in the distance. Tiny silhouettes swirling around each other, puffing bright flame. Riony kept her eyes on them from the plateau outside of the undercity.

Don't you dare get any closer.

Since the siege broke, a few riders still loyal to the Dragon King had tried to return to their mission of capturing Dracuni. Mestra Lerris and those on her side had so far kept them away.

Eslinde walked up beside Riony, dressed in full blue and gold scale mail, her thin blade at her hip. "I think Lerris got the better numbers and riders when she led her mutiny. It bodes well for the battle to come."

Riony hummed grumpily. "A battle they will have us

to help with too, thanks to their neat bit of extortion."

Eslinde kept her eyes on the distant aerial combat. "Extortion or not, wouldn't we have tried to help anyway? Knowing one of the last and biggest sanctuaries for human life in our land was under threat? We have to take a stand at some point, and if not then, when? When there is nothing left to save?"

"Just because you can make lots of good points doesn't mean I have to be happy about it. I know it's inevitable. I know it's what we have to do if anything in this world is going to change."

Riony looked around the plateau and everyone there, thinking about all they'd given, all they might still give. Waiting just out of sight inside the entrance tunnel with the Alderkin, Dracuni had given the most lately. The number of scars of bloodletting on her were multiplying rapidly.

Viska and Ambri, gold and orange, sat nearby as Lyrrin and her team said their goodbyes. Viska was alert, focused on Vance in silent conversation, and Ambri, still tamed, sat still and unthinking. Nobody knew just how long this mission would take, so supplies and packs were loaded onto the dragons.

They could be gone hours, days, weeks. They could be gone forever.

"But I still hate that other people let it get to this point and that I and those I love have to fight and die for other people's mistakes and wrongs." Riony gestured to where

Lyrrin was saying goodbye to Niskina and Dash. "Where my sister, your daughter, is about to fly into danger even now."

"I'll be with her this time. I'll do everything I can to keep her safe," Eslinde said.

Aishena, Benjin, and their mother were also leaving with them. The hatchling, Elumon, was going too, since Jaym recommended it would be best for his and Lyrrin's bond that they remained together.

It was a strong group, but Riony still worried.

Riony turned to Eslinde and held out a hand. "Look after yourself too. Everyone comes home safe, okay?"

Eslinde brushed the hand aside and stepped in to hold Riony tight. "Same goes for you."

Riony returned the embrace, and when Eslinde pulled back, she smiled and tucked Riony's flop of hair behind one of her ears in a way that was so similar to how her own mother once had that it left a lump in her throat. Oblivious to Riony's swell of emotions, Eslinde turned away to say goodbye to Vance.

Lyrrin ran in toward Riony then, and Riony knelt down to catch her in a hug. "All ready for your big mission?"

"Could you make that sound any more patronizing?" Lyrrin scoffed. "But yes, I think we are."

Riony squeezed her tight. "You're going to do great. I love that you're going to be the one who steals your grandfather's ill-gotten riches from him."

"That might have been part of the reason why I planned all of this." Lyrrin chuckled wickedly.

Letting her go enough that she could look into her bright-blue eyes, Riony swallowed hard. "Before you leave, there's something I wanted to tell you."

Lyrrin assessed Riony's serious expression. "It's not bad news, is it? Why would you save bad news for right now?"

"Not bad news. Good news? I suppose? More like … something I want your approval on." Riony hesitated, then swallowed again. "It's about me and Kess."

Lyrrin stared back. "Are you two fighting again? You looked so angry at her the other night."

Riony flushed red. "No. We're together."

"Together how?" Lyrrin asked.

"As a couple."

"A couple of what?"

Riony huffed. "We're together *romantically.*"

"Oh!" Lyrrin seemed to consider this, then pulled a face. "You and her? Really?"

Riony's heart sank. She wasn't sure what she'd do if Lyrrin didn't approve of the relationship. "You don't like her?"

Lyrrin looked over Riony's shoulder to where Kess waited near the undercity entrance. "No, she's okay, and I love Griskin. I just thought you hated her."

Not long ago that had been true. "Feelings have changed, and it was a surprise to me too how much everything has changed."

"Romantically ... With like, kissing and everything?" Lyrrin's face scrunched up with disgust. "I could see you were looking at her differently, like an intense sort of way, but I didn't know what it meant. All you older lot look at each other like that all the time ..."

Shaking her head, she looked to where Vance and Eslinde were saying a long goodbye, eyes locked longingly on each other despite the tense distance between them.

Lyrrin gasped scandalously. "Them too? It's them too, isn't it?"

Riony had seen it before, the simmering emotions underlying Vance and Eslinde's interactions, but nothing had ever seemed to come of it.

"Maybe they need a sleepover arranged for them too," Riony muttered.

"What?"

"Nothing." Riony poked Lyrrin until she turned back around to face her, then gave her one more hug. "Now, I know you've got everything planned, but be careful, okay? Check in through gateways when you can."

"I don't think we'll be gone that long. I'm sure the silvernix is at the king's private palace, and we have everything we need to get in. This is going to be the quickest mission ever, better than any of yours." Lyrrin squeezed Riony once, then backed away to go and say goodbye to Dracuni and the Alderkin.

"Always has to be a competition with her," Riony murmured as Dashiel and Aishena walked over.

"Are you sure I shouldn't be going with them?" Dashiel looked to Aishena with harrowing puppy dog eyes.

Riony refused to be swayed. "We need all the best riders with us. That means you and your brother."

Kess had offered that morning as well to go with Lyrrin and keep her safe for Riony, and Riony had to point out that she and Lyomir were among their best riders too, which left Kess very thoughtful and red-faced.

"I might argue I'm one of our better riders too," Aishena smirked but was distracted by her mother moving past to load a saddlebag onto Viska, and her expression turned steely again.

The woman had cleaned herself up greatly since the last time Riony had seen her. She wore her full grayglim armor, and her hair was back in its long whiplike braid.

Riony raised her eyebrows. "You're sure taking her is a good idea?"

"She's a grayglim first, regardless of anything else. If put to task, she will perform." Aishena lowered her voice then, fidgeting with the guard armor she wore, stolen during their last mission. "Mostly though ... I don't trust leaving her behind alone. She is ... a threat to herself."

"I'm sorry things haven't worked out better for you and your family." Riony moved in, clasping the stern young woman around the shoulders and pressing her forehead

to Aishena's.

Aishena grasped Riony's arm in return. "She needs time. We all do."

"Then I hope you all get that time."

As Lyrrin, Aishena, Benjin, Eslinde, and Kverra mounted the two dragons, waved one more time, and took flight, Riony continued wishing all of them would have more time.

Niskina patted her on the back. "I'm sure they'll be okay. We've all survived worse. And look on the bright side ... at least you have your bedroom to yourself for a while now."

Smirking, Niskina backed away, returning into the undercity, joined by Vance and Dashiel. They passed Kess along the way, who waited at the entrance for Riony.

A great roaring wave of love filled Riony, as it always did now when she looked at Kess and saw Kess returning that look.

Riony had imagined being in love, had longed for it for most of her life. She'd crushed hard on more beautiful girls than she could count. But something had always gotten in the way of any romance growing, so she had only ever gotten as far as dreaming.

She never thought it would feel like *this*. This insatiable inferno of need and the desire to fulfill her love's needs in return.

She never thought it would be with and for Kessara

Heithorn.

But that fire was quelled by the chill of fear for those who had just left.

Riony sighed. Letting her shoulders roll back with a long exhale, she stared at the retreating dragons in the distance. The soft shifting of dirt underfoot heralded Griskin and Kess appearing beside her.

Kess said nothing, asked for nothing. Only remained waiting beside Riony as they watched until Viska and Ambri vanished from sight.

Riony leaned into Kess then, her head on Kess's shoulder. It still left her dumbfounded how this wild girl who was once her tormentor always seemed to know exactly what Riony needed.

But what Riony needed most was to not lose anyone else she loved, and that was feeling more and more impossible with what was coming.

A pummeling gust of icy wind sent Dracuni barrel-rolling through the air.

"Whoa. Get your wings out. Steady!" Riony clung tight to the tumbling unidragon.

With a crack like wind hitting sails, Dracuni's wings

caught the air again, leveling them out and slowing them down.

Sorry. I didn't expect that.

"Yeah, wind is a thing outside of caves. That's why we're out here, so you can get used to it," Riony replied.

She didn't return into the undercity with the others after Lyrrin left. She needed some space with her feelings, and Dracuni also needed practice flying in the open skies. As the distant dragon battle had ended and all seemed quiet, the two of them took flight over the white-topped mountains.

They remained wary as they skimmed around one tall peak. Snow disturbed in their wake glittered in an icy stream.

I understand the concept of wind. It was just stronger than I expected.

"And you're even stronger. You're doing amazing." Riony patted the opalescent mane down Dracuni's neck.

The unidragon had proven to be fast and agile in their practice, more than anyone had expected after her slow start to flying. But her endurance was still lacking. Whether it was because she had to work harder to fly than other dragons or whether she was already tired from the bloodletting, Riony wasn't sure.

Even now, Dracuni's flanks heaved with strained breaths. The wind picked up, howling and battering against them both.

Riony recognized the landscape beneath them and called out, "Come on. Let's take a break. Land down there."

Is it safe? Dracuni's ever-present, underlying worry laced her thoughts.

"There's no one else around. Except Kess and Lyomir."

The purple dragon and Kess kept their distance, circling high above, keeping watch over them while still giving them space.

Reluctantly, Dracuni landed in the thick snow, and Riony jumped down beside her, boots crunching as she sank down to her calves.

She shivered, rubbing her bare arms. She was dressed for the temperate atmosphere of the undercity, not for being out flying or trudging through the snow, but there was something she wanted to see.

"Come on, this way."

Where are we going? Dracuni gave another nervous glance at the sky.

"I wanted to show you where you came from." Riony followed the slope down, scanning the drifts of sparkling white for the entrance to the ice cave.

Where I was made ...

The sadness in those words landed hard on Riony. "I'm sorry."

You saved my life. You didn't know what that would mean for my future.

It didn't make Riony feel much better.

281

How could Dracuni ever be able to live freely, when her own blood put a target on her?

So much about the upcoming battle relied on Dracuni and would only put her under even greater threat. Even if they saved the capital and ended the curse, Dracuni would continue to be at risk for all her life.

The mouth of the cave appeared, half-buried behind a soft drift of snow. The two of them pushed inside and the howling wind cut off.

Staring around the cave, Dracuni's lilac eyes glistened. *Sometimes I wonder if I should cut my horn and my mane. It would help me stand out less.*

Riony's chest contracted with sadness. That Dracuni would have to change herself to remain safe felt wrong. But maybe it was something Riony should have done far earlier. She'd disguised Lyrrin to keep her safe. But she also knew how hard that had been on her sister.

"The nest was a bit farther in," Riony said, leading the way.

Dracuni took a step, and her leg slipped from under her, wobbling before she steadied again.

"You okay?"

Just tired.

"You've been giving too much blood lately. We should slow down."

We don't even have enough for the plan yet.

Dracuni's steps were timid and shaky, and her chest

heaved, still catching her breath from the flight. Her eyes seemed dimmer than they usually did.

Riony shook her head. "It's too much. If we don't have enough, then we don't have enough. Even if we can't heal all the untamed dragons."

As though you aren't giving everything to the cause? Wouldn't give everything? I'm doing this because I want to. Dracuni snorted. *Because why should it be dragons who are the ones to suffer and die to fix what humans did?*

"They shouldn't. But if it's between you and them—"

Then we choose them. Just because they've been enslaved doesn't make them any less. Without the spike in their brain, they would be as intelligent and feeling as I am. I'm going to do everything I can to help them survive this.

Dracuni locked eyes with Riony. Her pale rainbow-sheened scales seemed to glow in the cool light of the ice cave. Riony leaned in and hugged the unidragon around her snout, patting her on the cheek.

"You're right. I just wish it didn't cost you so much."

Dracuni's thoughts held a hint of smugness. *We all have to decide at some point what is worth destroying ourselves for.*

Riony flinched and backed away. "Were you ... did you hear all of that?"

Dracuni huffed something like a laugh.

283

"You didn't! What else did you hear?" Riony acutely remembered the desperate, awkward, but passionate kiss that had followed that conversation.

Dracuni's eyes narrowed cheekily, and she wandered away, farther into the cave. *You asked for little sister's approval, but not mine?*

"I was getting to it ..." Riony muttered, chastened as she hurried after.

Dracuni glanced at her over her shoulder. *I approve. I haven't really seen you happy much. But this makes you happy. That's good.*

Riony pressed a hand to her chest, wondering just how much of her happiness and love overflowed to Dracuni for her to feel it too.

"I am happy, and I feel so loved. And just imagine what all our lives and this world could have been if we'd all felt happy and loved from the beginning."

Dracuni nudged the tip of her nose to Riony's cheek.

They reached the place the nest had been, but the area was filled with blown-in snow, melted in patches on the outcrop of warm earth that emerged there.

Only a few old shards of broken egg remained. Riony kicked around through the snow and muck for a while, but the tiny vial that had held the silvernix that created Dracuni couldn't be found. She continued searching a bit longer, so there was time for Dracuni to rest more fully before they took to the air again.

The moment they stepped back outside, a red dragon was visible, flying in toward the undercity entrance.

Mestra Lerris.

Riony and Dracuni flew swiftly down to meet with her, and Kess and Lyomir landed close behind them.

The bulky woman didn't bother dismounting from her dragon. Her face was drawn, pulled tight around her mouth and eyes. She called across the plateau to Riony and Kess.

"The revenant army has reached the capital. It's time."

Riony inhaled sharply. "Now?"

"Now. The undead already attempt to breach the walls. They came upon the city faster than expected in the last stretch. The shadow dragon flies with them, driving them to a frenzy."

Riony's heart hammered. Lyrrin and the others had only just left. They weren't ready. Even with Dracuni's insistence to do so, they hadn't yet bottled enough blood for what would be needed in the battle. Riony had wanted a dose of silvernix in the hands of every dragonrider out there, and they weren't even close.

Mestra Lerris turned her dragon sideways, as though already preparing to fly back the way she'd come.

She yelled with a harried urgency, "My riders have all received the crystals you supplied for them. I have a higher confidence that they will be able to stay on their dragons than you seem to have, but we are grateful. But do we also have you? Will you follow through on your promise and join us now?"

"Are the revs burning?" Kess called from her seat on Lyomir.

Lerris's expression stretched tighter. "They aren't yet staying dead."

Stars, no. Something inside Riony seemed to crumple and die.

With everything they'd done, with all the missions, all those factory dragons untamed, and still there was no sign of the shadow dragon's curse ending, or even weakening.

Maybe it can't be. Maybe it can't be reversed at all.

Riony pressed her hands to Dracuni's scales and pulled herself together. "We're with you, either way."

The mestra nodded once and was in the air again a second later.

Riony's heart beat like war drums, signaling the fight about to begin. One they had no hope of winning if the revenants still didn't burn.

There was still the backup plan, the final, apocalyptic gambit only for use if it came down to a situation where survival was already unlikely. Because if that plan worked, it would likely be the last thing any of them ever did.

TWENTY-ONE

Lyomir growled beneath Kess as the battle came within view.

Uncountable corpses in ashy gray and earthen reds formed an ocean, crashing against the walls of Draekhanhelm.

Hundreds of dragons flew above, evading and clashing with flying revenants while also attempting to burn those on the ground. Their flaming breaths were no more than small sparks of light, consumed by the mass of the horde. Sputtering candles in the darkness.

The living corpses of massive carrion birds and bats, down to smaller pocket-hawks and owlettes swarmed the skies. Any revenant whose wings were still intact enough to fly.

Above and below, everything swirled—a living storm cloud of smoke and fire, chaos and corpses. And flying above, casting a dark pall over everything beneath, flew the shadow dragon itself.

"I think the technical term for that," Riony yelled from nearby on Dracuni, "is a shit show."

Kess couldn't disagree.

After receiving Mestra Lerris's news, the undercity team rallied fast. They were armored and armed and in the air with the speed their drills had trained them for.

Niskina and the Alderkin remained behind, preparing for the aftermath of the battle, whatever that might be. Griskin had fretted when Kess took off without him, but considering what they were flying into, she preferred he stayed safe. She wasn't intending on leaving Lyomir's back anyway.

Kess still felt strange wearing delver's armor. She had become so used to her ratty leathers over the years. She'd been offered rider's scale mail from Eslinde's supplies like most of the others wore, but she preferred the flexibility of the delver armor and the anchor points on the harness for tying herself to the saddle.

It also felt strange to have a large, flat slab of runed crystal strapped to her back, the way everyone in their group except for Riony had.

In the front of their team, Jaym flew on Hux, and Vance rode Kife's left behind snowflame. It could no longer

breathe its liquid fire without risking its life, but it could still fly well, and Vance preferred Viska go with Lyrrin and Eslinde to keep them safe.

Dashiel had taken Norallei's white dragon, Iffyr, with Shiff flying beside, still too small to carry a rider, but able to assist. And behind them the thirty-odd newly trained riders followed on treedarts.

Kess frowned at the battle they approached. Their numbers weren't even close to enough to make a difference.

The main mass of the fight filled the fields to the west of the dragonkeep, lit by the orange light of late afternoon, but the revenant army had the walls entirely encircled.

There are so many of them.

Vance signaled from up ahead, and he, Dashiel, and Jaym took the new riders with them directly into the fight. Kess raised a hand to signal back, and she and Riony split off, avoiding the aerial warfare and heading over the city.

Spotting a flat-topped building that looked clear, Kess caught Riony's attention and pointed to it.

Riony frowned back. "I should stay with you and the others."

"You know that you shouldn't. That's not the plan. You and Dracuni need to stay safe for later," Kess yelled over the gusting wind.

Jaw set tight, Riony adjusted her flight goggles, then turned away. Myrwa's shawl was tucked around her neck, one end fluttering behind her, the dull red looking like

blood in the afternoon light. She and Dracuni glided down and landed on the crenelated tower top.

Kess circled twice, watching the skies around them for threats, then she and Lyomir flew to join the fight.

"Are you ready?" Kess spoke the words aloud and pushed them through her mind connection to her dragon as well.

Brave little one, don't question me. Lyomir growled and picked up speed.

Coming back over the city walls, Lyomir swooped low, sending a roiling fireball at the revenants climbing the steel and stone. The flame exploded as it hit, sending a handful of undead creatures toppling down into the masses below.

Kess stared, aghast, as the hole Lyomir had burned in the revenants' ranks closed over instantly. Even if the revs that were hit died, it made less impact than plucking a hair from a giant's head or a single star from the sky.

A mourning hopelessness filled her. She wasn't sure how much was from the immensity of the task before them or the effect of the shadow dragon itself, circling above.

Still, she didn't slow, didn't turn around. They were there to make a difference. She wasn't giving up.

Kess braced as Lyomir flew them into the thick of battle. A burst of orange flame came from the left and Lyomir swerved away from it, then under the lunging claws of a haggard plains eagle.

For each dragonrider in the sky there seemed to be a

dozen or more undead creatures assaulting them. Kess couldn't spot Dashiel, Vance, or Jaym among the mess. She could barely see what was right in front of her.

The nearest rider had a massive carrion bird locked in chase with them, and Kess turned Lyomir to assist. The rider wore the king's colors, but that didn't matter anymore. The only fight now was between life and death.

Kess leaned close over Lyomir's purple scales as he shot in fast. With a thunder-crack crunch, he caught the undead bird in his jaws.

Mangy feathers burst from the creature, gusting in the wind over Kess. With a wide swing of his head, Lyomir threw the crushed body of the creature away, into the path of a smaller swarm of flying creatures, scattering them.

Even with its bones shattered and feathers torn, the carrion bird rev continued flapping and squalling hideously as it fell to the ground.

Kess and Lyomir passed ahead of the rider they'd cleared the tail of, and the woman signaled her gratitude.

A swell of pride filled Kess, and something that tasted almost like hope.

Grinning fiercely, Kess opened herself to Lyomir's thoughts and feelings and shared all of hers in return. They wove through the battle as one.

To the left, Kess would think, and Lyomir would act almost faster than thought. The thrill of their connection, the speed of their flight, each life they saved by snatching

away the hunting revenants, filled Kess with a deep satisfaction.

This was it. This was what she'd always dreamed of, to be a dragonrider, fighting the undead scourge with her peers. It was bittersweet, to have this moment, when the chances of surviving beyond it felt so low.

But now she had this, she had Lyomir, and Riony, and she was doing what she had always known deep in her bones that she was made for. She wasn't giving it up. She would do everything she could to survive and to keep everything that had been so hard won.

Below her, two riders in Skaella's red and blue were caught in a midair wrestle with something huge, bigger than the treedart-sized carrion birds.

Blessed sun ... it's a dragon. A revenant dragon!

Kess had never seen one before, in all her years aboveground. Whether it was because dragons themselves often burned up when they were downed or some other reason, the shadow dragon hadn't seemed to raise them before.

Another sign the curse has only worsened? Kess shuddered.

The dragon had dark, rotten flesh with scales still holding on only in patches. Tears in its wings fluttered in the wind, but otherwise it was whole, and massive.

Lyomir snarled. ***Abomination. We will destroy it.***

They dove, spear like through the sky. Afternoon sun glinted on Lyomir's purple scales, and Kess's braids

whipped behind her. Lyomir landed on the back of the death-blackened dragon rev and sank his claws in. Then he barrel-rolled.

Kess held tight, prepared for it, but the speed still stretched and strained the leather strap buckling her to her saddle. The undead dragon below roared, torn away from the others it was attacking. In the outer arc of his spiral, Lyomir released the creature, sending it flying.

Steadying out again, Kess came up between the two riders in red and blue. Their faces registered shock as they took her in, looking over her to Lyomir and his lack of taming spike, and Kess was shocked in return to see she recognized them.

The two riders who had been partying with Kife the night she found him to ask for help to hunt Dracuni. Kess couldn't remember their names. But it was clear they recognized her too.

The woman offered her a nod and a salute. Kess lifted her arm to return the gesture, when a burning eagle crashed down over the rider, sending her tumbling to the earth in a spray of ashes and sparks.

Kife's other friend went after her on his dragon.

Kess had to duck under the cloud of scorched feathers, and as she came clear on the other side, the revenant dragon was there again, coming back toward her.

Kess felt Lyomir's urge to dive under the revenant, and she pushed back hard.

Over, over! Panic filled her, remembering Norallei's fate.

At the last second, Lyomir twisted upward, cutting in between the deathly dragon's wings. It turned, unnaturally fast, and was right on their tail, bearing down fast.

Dive now, away from the army. We need to get somewhere clear if we want any chance of outrunning this thing.

Lyomir dropped suddenly, sending Kess lifting in her saddle. She held tight, teeth gritted as the army of land-bound revs came up toward them. Flying away from the city, Lyomir veered north to where the air and ground were clearer. The undead dragon screeched a rattly roar as it snapped at his tail.

It was easily as fast as Lyomir and it would never tire, never slow down.

We need to get behind it. We've got to ground it.

I will tear the thing to pieces.

Lyomir lifted, bringing his body up vertically with wings out wide to break the wind. The undead dragon shot beneath him, then he and Kess lunged downward, onto the undead dragon's back.

Lyomir got all four claws clutched around the ragged corpse, and the rev twisted and whipped its head back, trying to bite him in return. Its wings beat awkwardly without their full range of movement.

Lyomir snapped his teeth around one and bit clear through the bony structure. With a squeeze of his claws, he ripped the other wing free from the shoulder. He roared

with triumph, and then in pain, as the rev landed its own bite into one of his front legs.

The weight of both dragons had them plummeting, and the ground flew toward them. Kess could feel Lyomir cursing through their thoughts as he tried to pull free from the revenant's teeth.

Crush it! "Crush it!" Kess screamed, inside and out, as hitting the ground became imminent.

Lyomir stretched all four legs out in front of him with the revenant within them and used his wings to slow their descent as much as possible.

They still hit hard, skidding across charred plains with the revenant beneath them. Ash and dirt plowed up around them, choking Kess. She jolted roughly in the saddle, and there was a snap as the leather strap buckling her in snapped. She clung tight to Lyomir's neck.

Somewhere in the landing, Lyomir and the dragon were freed from each other's hold, and he pumped his wings once, twice, bringing them out of the dust cloud.

Are you okay? Kess's heart pounded in her throat.

Lyomir growled, and Kess could feel his pain. **Merely a scratch.**

Kess leaned out over his side to look down. The undead dragon lay in a twisted mess, black scales and limbs scattered in the long trail their landing had left.

And yet it still moved.

What will it take to stop these things?

Lyomir brought them higher again, with great effort. They'd been in the fight mere moments and he was already injured and exhausted.

Kess shook her head as she looked down over the ocean of undead before them. It washed up like a tide against the walls of the capital, surging higher and higher. Soon, they would spill into the city itself.

And the shadow dragon circled lazily overhead.

A chill of mourning filled Kess as she watched the battle they moved to rejoin. The riders were all working so hard, but the revs still weren't dying by fire, didn't seem to be able to be put down at all. They weren't making any impact on the army.

Raze it all. This is an awful stalemate at best, and a slow death at worst.

Kess knew what had to be done. There was no choice left.

Call to Hux and Shiff. Tell them to retreat, bring Vance too if they can find him. We'll meet at Riony's location.

I can keep fighting.

I'm sure you can. But it doesn't matter if that fight gets us nowhere.

Grumbling, Lyomir took them through the thinner edges of the battle, skirting around and back over the city. As they came in toward the tower, Dashiel arrived from the other side on Iffyr, Shiff leading them in, and Vance trailing as well on his dragon. Jaym and Hux were farther

back, the red dragon burning their way clear of a flock of undead birds.

Riony paced like a stalking wildcat on the flat tower top, glowing sword in hand and Dracuni at her back, sitting patiently. When she saw them incoming, she moved back to give them room.

Lyomir landed in the center of the roof beside Riony, and Iffyr and Shif landed perched on the crenelated edge.

Kess took a moment to catch her breath and brush ash off her armor, and Riony ran to her.

"Are you hurt? What's happening?" She looked up from the ground, so much smaller for once from Kess's high vantage point.

"Nothing's happening, which is the problem. Nothing is dying, nothing undead, anyway." Kess wanted to climb down to her, to hold her, but there was no time. She couldn't even reach her hand from her saddle.

Vance arrived then, taking up a perch on the other side of the tower, the stone cracking under the snowflame's claws. There was no space left for Hux to land. He circled above.

I will let them know our plans, Lyomir thought to Kess.

Vance adjusted his position on the saddle, shaking out one of his arms. "Why did you call us back in?"

"Were you managing to make any difference out there?" Kess asked in return.

He shook his head roughly. "Saved a few of our greener riders' lives, but if you mean in number of revs we actually stopped, I don't think we were doing a damned thing."

Kess took a deep breath and turned back to Riony. "It's time we use the summoning rune."

"Already? Are you sure?" Dashiel blanched, making a smudge of blood over their cheek stand out starkly.

Riony looked equally uncertain. "If this works the way we hope it will, we could lose every tamed dragon out there. Which, in case you forgot, is *every dragon,* except ours here."

Kess looked over the battle again, at all the riders who had abandoned their loyalty to the king in order to do the right thing, at all the riders who had remained loyal, but were out there fighting for their lives and others now anyway, at all the new and not nearly experienced enough riders they had brought from the undercity.

They could all die. Their dragons could all die.

They had prepared their own undercity riders as well as they could for this outcome. Kess had been amazed at how much Dracuni had given, how much the Alderkin had given, to make sure everyone had a chance to survive, but still, it was only a chance. And all the riders who weren't on their side that morning didn't even have that.

Kess sighed. "We can't stop the revenants as is, and this is our last chance. We have to weaken the shadow dragon if we want any hope to stop this army before it adds everybody

in the capital below to its numbers. Whether this works or not, there's nothing else we can do."

Riony's head swayed almost drunkenly. The self-doubt in her eyes hurt Kess physically, and she had to clutch her saddle with white knuckles to stop from throwing herself down to hold her.

Riony's voice wavered as she asked, "And if it doesn't work? If the curse can't be reversed at all?"

Vance growled. "Then we are condemning every single rider and dragon here."

"They're already dead if we don't." Kess's eyes stayed pinned on Riony. "This is our only hope. This is what you've worked so hard for, to make this happen. Because you do believe it has a chance. Keep believing."

Riony's nostrils flared and her eyes glimmered wetly, but she reached to her belt pouch and drew out the summoning stone. Not the one they had taken to the undercity, altered to make tamed dragons unresponsive.

A new one, freshly carved by the Alderkin with the original summoning rune.

"Big dreams, bold deeds." After a long, steadying breath, Riony traced the rune, and the stone lit up in a rich green, like an unburned forest. She held it aloft over her head.

Beneath Kess, Lyomir stiffened and growled, head swinging sharply toward the crystal. Shiff and Dracuni followed, each of the wild dragons mesmerized by it, eyes

locked and chests heaving and claws digging into the rooftop's stone as the magic drew their focus. Hux flew down from above, clinging to the side of the tower to get closer.

Lyomir? Kess called to him through their connection.

There was no reply, only a sense of urgency, need, command.

Dashiel looked from Shiff to the skies over the city. "How long is this going to take?"

Kess was about to reply when she followed Dashiel's gaze. From the direction of the palace, a small group of dragons flew their way. Three of normal size in red and white, led by one immense silver and gold beast.

The Dragon King.

Riony gave a forced laugh. "You don't think they're coming to help with the battle, do you?"

"Nope," Kess whispered, because nobody needed to hear it.

The king and his team's trajectory was clear. They were flying straight toward the tower. Straight for Dracuni, who remained stunned senseless by the summoning rune's power.

TWENTY-TWO

"The revs are scaling the walls." Lyrrin lowered her seeing stone. She didn't want to watch anymore.

Nasty creatures, Elumon thought. He had flown on his own for a while but was currently resting on Viska's back.

Lyrrin sat in her own saddle behind Eslinde, with Viska flying them carefully northeast toward the king's private palace, which took them within view of the capital and the army of revenants that marched upon it. The living corpses had moved so fast, like an avalanche of undead pouring across the ground.

When they first saw how close the army was to Draekhanhelm, Eslinde had even suggested they turn back, to warn the others, to help them as they would surely be entering that battle soon. But the rest of them agreed it was more important they continue on their mission.

And more important than ever that they find the king's silvernix, and fast.

Aishena, Benjin, and their mother flew on Ambri, just behind Viska.

Thin wisps of white hair, pulled free from a tight bun by the wind, whipped around Eslinde's flight goggles. "Are your sister and the others there yet?"

"I can't tell; we're too far away now. But there are a lot of dragons in the sky."

Elumon pressed his snout under Lyrrin's arm from behind, then snaked his neck around to look up at her.

Big dragon friends are coming. I hear them.

Lyrrin closed her eyes for a moment and the visions of the massive undead army, of all the human and animal revenants roaring for human blood, remained burned in her mind.

You worry?

Yes. I worry. We have to get the silvernix. They're going to need it.

"This is good, in a way." Eslinde turned around in her saddle to face Lyrrin. "All defenses will be sent to the capital. The private palace should be less guarded than usual."

Lyrrin chewed her lip. "Do you think the king will leave it completely unguarded, though, if the silvernix is

there? Even if nobody else knows where it is, the king must keep some guards around."

Or maybe he just relied on it being secret. Everything the Rebel Riders could tell her about their time searching the place suggested minimal staff and security even in normal times.

Lyrrin's stomach churned. Something didn't feel right.

"We're going to be fine. We've got your magic and what almost amounts to three grayglims with us." Eslinde measured up Benjin with her eyes. "Maybe two and a half."

Lyrrin tried to smile in return but her lips twitched crookedly. Something nagged at the back of her thoughts.

Don't worry. I help too.

Elumon tucked himself in at her side and put his head on her lap. His emotions felt just as worried and fearful as her own.

Lyrrin patted him distractedly.

Eslinde's brow furrowed, and she tilted her head. "How do you feel about having Lady Hjelzahn with us, after what she did to you?"

"What, stabbing me?" Lyrrin dismissed it with a wave of her ungloved hand. "She was possessed then. I don't think she's going to do it again. I'm more worried about her for Benjin and Aish."

"Do you think she's a threat to them?"

"No, I just don't think they quite got their mother back the way they wanted."

Despite having their mother with them and no longer trying to kill anyone of Draekhan bloodline, they'd all been sadder since.

Eslinde remained quiet for a long moment, looking over her shoulder at the Hjelzahn family on the dragon behind them. "I had a talk with Kverra ..."

Lyrrin waited, and Eslinde paused for another long few seconds before continuing.

"She told me she doesn't know how to be a mother again, after everything she's done. She is mourning her husband, a son, and a daughter as though their deaths were fresh, deaths that were by her hand, even if not by her heart."

Lyrrin couldn't imagine how that must feel, to know you'd done something terrible, but against your own will. Nobody blamed Kverra herself, not really, but all of the hurt still remained.

Eslinde's voice grew softer, barely carrying over the wind. "She also told me she wasn't sure she ever knew how to be a mother. When her husband told her he wanted Aishena trained to be a grayglim too, Kverra had to stop being her mother entirely and become her mestra instead. She doesn't know how to be what her children need right now."

Lyrrin shrugged. "But it's easy. They just need her. I know she's sad right now and maybe that's making them all sad, but they just need her to be there."

Eslinde's face scrunched up as though in pain, and smoothed again.

Lyrrin glanced back at the Hjelzahns. Aishena rode up front, controlling the tamed dragon, with her mother behind and Benjin at the back. It seemed they rode in silence, but every few seconds, Aishena would turn back to check on her family.

Lyrrin said, "When I first met Lady Hjelzahn, in the depths, I could see how much Aishena wanted to trust her, how much she wanted her mother to be there for her."

Eslinde turned away to face their heading. She adjusted her flight goggles, wiping beneath them. "I feel as though it's rare for mothers to be everything they wish to be for their children. And even when so much is out of our control, it's too easy to feel as though we can never be forgiven for that."

Lyrrin's own eyes flushed wet as she watched the tense angles of her mother's thin frame. She leaned forward in her saddle and hugged around her waist from behind, pressing her cheek to Eslinde's back.

"I forgive you, for not being there when I was growing up. If you need that. But I was never angry at you. It was never your fault, and you came and found me as soon as you could. You left your kingdom behind for me!"

A restrained sob shook through Eslinde, and she half turned again, holding Lyrrin in return. "And I would do it again. You are *everything* to me. You have all your father's

magic and wisdom, all of Riony's fire and temerity, all of the kindness and joy of the parents who raised you."

"And all of *your* courage and cleverness," Lyrrin squeezed her amma tight.

Eslinde laughed brightly. "Do you think so?"

"Of course!"

Eslinde kissed the top of her head. "Then we have everything we need to succeed."

Lyrrin smiled, but the worry nagging at her returned. The winter air was cool, and even a blazing afternoon sun didn't take the chill off as they flew, and it seemed to sink deep into Lyrrin's bones. In the distance, a high single spire emerged from the smoky haze. The Dragon King's private palace, Draekhan's Rest.

We're almost there. This has to work.

Elumon, put out at having had to move when Lyrrin hugged Eslinde, had curled up behind her again.

He lifted his head suddenly. ***Something ... calls ...***

Beneath the saddles, Viska shivered strangely, then growled, long and low. Without warning, she turned sharply, back the way they'd come.

"Viska? Viska!" Eslinde yelled, but the golden dragon made no response.

"They've activated the summoning stone ... already?" Lyrrin gasped.

Elumon stretched out his neck, holding his horned head high.

Lyrrin prepared to throw herself bodily on the hatchling if he looked like he was going to take flight.

Are you okay? You aren't tempted to go?

It calls, but not for me.

Lyrrin sighed. Yrik had assured her that the summoning stone only summoned fully grown wild dragons. At no point in the past was it ever useful to them to summon hatchlings, and they would have considered it cruel to do so.

But they were still on Viska, being drawn in by the magic.

Aishena brought Ambri, tamed and unaffected by the call, around beside them. She yelled over the wind, "We need to get you off Viska, or you're going to end up back at the battle!"

Eslinde looked between the two dragons, then at the ground far below. "Oh, blessed sun."

Aishena called out, "I'm bringing Ambri in as close as I can."

"Maybe we should have made float runes for all of us too," Lyrrin mumbled through her fear.

With slow and careful movements, Aishena brough Ambri in from behind and above, laying the orange dragon's head and neck along one side of Viska's back, between her wings and close to Lyrrin's saddle.

Benjin and Kverra lashed cave silk ropes around them, then climbed down onto Viska's lower back, just at the start of her tail.

"Come down to us, Highnesses. We will help you up," Kverra called, clutching tight to her rope and swaying between the spines of the dragon's back.

"I'm right behind you," Eslinde said to Lyrrin with an encouraging nod.

Lyrrin brought her legs in beneath her and shifted around in her saddle. She didn't mind so much being up high on a dragon when she was seated comfortably and strapped in, but undoing the rope that secured her left her hands trembling.

Elumon stood beside her. *I can fly, but I'll walk with you.*

Thank you. Lyrrin placed an arm around his neck and rose up to stand.

The dragon's spine ramped down like a path between a twin row of spikes, but fear trapped Lyrrin's feet.

Come on. It's only a few steps away.

She lifted one foot and stumbled awkwardly forward, clutching Elumon for stability. Gusts of air rocked the dragons like rowboats in a storm, threatening to tip Lyrrin over the edge.

Eslinde caught her by the back of her coat when she staggered too far to the left and brought her back to the middle again. Viska's golden scales shone like a second sun in the afternoon light, and Lyrrin felt dizzy as she slipped down the last couple of steps and into Kverra's waiting arms.

"Easy now. I'll boost you up. Ready?" Lady Hjelzahn's

voice was commanding and even, but without the unearthly cold it had once held.

Lyrrin nodded once, then was lifted beneath her armpits up onto Kverra's shoulders. From there, Aishena reached down and pulled her the rest of the way up onto Ambri.

Heart pounding, Lyrrin dropped into one of the saddles and clutched it with rattling fingers. A moment later, Elumon flew behind her.

That was fun!

"Sure. Fun for those who have wings."

A scream pierced the air from below, making Lyrrin jolt upright. Viska was diving. With no warning, the golden dragon dropped out from beneath Ambri and the people standing on her back. The saddles all tugged to the side with the twang of rope.

"Amma!" Lyrrin leaned out from her saddle, and Aishena caught her, holding her from going too far.

She could see hands, clasped not far below, holding on to the dragon's side. A dark-skinned head with shorn white hair. Benjin.

"Where are the others?" Aishena bellowed as she reached down to haul him up.

Lyrrin's eyes followed the second rope, pulled taut, down, down …

Kverra Hjelzahn swung at the end of it, with Eslinde caught around the waist.

Lyrrin gasped. "We have to pull them up!"

Benjin had reached the saddles, and once he secured himself, both he and Aishena grasped the remaining rope and pulled. But the angle lay wrong, making the spinning weight of the two women below hard to drag up.

Lyrrin tore open the pouch at her belt, dragging out two of the largest crystals she'd brought with her. Unmarked ones, ready for any contingency. She scratched out the symbols in a hurry—a float rune on each—and activated them.

She held them out to Elumon. "Can you take these down to them? One to Eslinde first, then to Kverra."

The hatchling cowered. *Me?*

Lyrrin could feel his fear woven between her own so the two were hard to distinguish. *Please, you're the only one who can.*

Elumon gave a solemn nod and grasped a purple glowing crystal in each of his front claws, then swooped down off Ambri's back. ***What if I can't? What if I can't?***

Lyrrin wasn't sure those thoughts were meant to reach her, but the hatchling's worried repetition came through clearly.

Eslinde and Kverra were spinning wildly at the end of the rope, and Kverra was using both hands and all her strength to keep a hold of Eslinde.

It took a few tries before Elumon could get close enough for Eslinde to reach. He would fly forward, then back out fearfully again as a leg almost smacked across his face. And it took longer again before Eslinde snatched the float crystal from him.

Benjin let out a whoop of celebration, but Lyrrin still held her breath.

The crystals were small. Only enough to reduce their body weight a little. But as Eslinde held her crystal, Kverra was able to readjust her hold on her, freeing up one of her arms. She caught the second crystal Elumon brought in to them.

"Pull!" Aishena ordered as soon as both women had a crystal in hand.

She and Benjin tried again, and the rope slid upward, reeling Eslinde and Kverra in. Elumon remained flying beside them, nudging them with his nose to keep them stable.

It felt like two long lifetimes before Eslinde and Kverra were on top of Ambri, panting as though they'd been drowning.

Eslinde crawled into the saddle beside Lyrrin and the two of them held each other fiercely.

Elumon landed behind them, shaking all over.

Lyrrin gave the hatchling a warm smile. *You saved them. Thank you!*

I saved them? His thoughts were still clouded with worry, but a tinge of pride broke through.

From over Eslinde's shoulder, Lyrrin thought she saw

Benjin and Aishena move to embrace their mother as well. But then Aishena reached past her mother and brought Benjin up into the front saddle with her.

When Kverra sat in the middle saddle, Eslinde slapped a weary hand on to her shoulder.

"I am in your debt," she said.

Kverra shook her head, braided hair swinging. "Your highness, it is my duty."

"Duty or otherwise, I'm glad to have you here with us. I think we all are."

Aishena brought Ambri circling around in a slow glide back toward the private palace again.

She cast a quick glance over her shoulder. "We will be glad if we all stay alive for the rest of our mission."

"I am sure that will be the most excitement we'll see." Eslinde handed the float crystal back to Lyrrin, but Lyrrin refused it.

"Hold on to it, just in case."

Eslinde huffed a small laugh. "Well, the private palace isn't far ahead. We'll be back on the ground soon."

The nagging worry awakened in Lyrrin again. "Did you ever look for the silvernix there?"

"Not myself. I was never interested to find it. Some of the other heirs did, though. Ylva had a few times and never found anything. But they didn't know what we know."

"Kverra? Did you ever spend time there? See anything?" Lyrrin asked warily from how her questioning had gone last time.

Lady Hjelzahn remained stoic, with only her voice betraying her with a crack of emotion. "I did stalk the king there, a number of times, in my ... attempts to kill him."

A muscle in her jaw jumped. "But he was never alone, thank the sun's blessing. He would oversee mining that was being done there, but never alone. He didn't even fly his dragon there alone. He always brought grayglims with him."

Lyrrin's mind raced. It didn't make sense. If the Dragon King was the only person who knew where the silvernix was, then he'd have to be alone when he went there.

"Was there *anywhere* you ever saw him alone?"

"If there was, he wouldn't still be alive," Kverra said flatly. "There was only one place he ever went into entirely alone, and it was always too heavily guarded from the outside."

Lyrrin's eyes popped wide. There was only one place. A place she had seen him remain alone in.

She called out over the gusting wind in a rush, "We're going the wrong way!"

TWENTY-THREE

Riony scanned the horizon all around, seeking any sign that the summoning stone had worked. Apart from keeping Dracuni, Lyomir, Shiff, and Hux lured in by its compulsion, there weren't yet any signs of other wild dragons approaching.

What if they've already moved too far away and aren't coming?

Only the Dragon King on his massive dragon, followed by three more, were flying toward them fast.

"We have to get Dracuni out of here." Riony still clutched the summoning stone in one hand and hauled herself hastily onto the unidragon's back.

But Dracuni didn't respond to her urgency to leave.

Kess leaned over Lyomir's neck, looking equally

worried. "I don't think any of our dragons are moving while the summoning stone is activated. They can't think about anything else."

"Then deactivate it!" Jaym yelled from the side of the tower where Hux clung, hanging vertically.

His pocket-hawk flittered around the red dragon, making Riony flinch away. She was glad she hadn't been asked to go out into the aerial battle with the revs before. *So many birds. Ew.*

Dashiel brought the tamed shimmerdart they rode in close and extended an arm out to Riony. "If we deactivate it too soon, the wild dragons won't come all the way into the battle. But we can still keep away from the king. Throw me the crystal."

Riony did without hesitation. "What are you going to do?"

Catching the glowing green stone, Dashiel shrugged and half smiled. "The dragons will follow it, right? So let them follow it."

The white dragon's wings thrust down powerfully, sending it and Dashiel shooting into the sky. A second later, Dracuni jolted forward, launching off the tower as well and into pursuit.

Riony shot a glance over her shoulder. Kess and Lyomir, Jaym and Hux, and Shiff on her own were all flying after the summoning stone as well. Vance, on Kife's old snowflame, went the other way toward where the Dragon King and his riders weren't far behind.

He must be trying to buy us some time. It was foolish, though. The snowflame couldn't breathe fire anymore. Kife had burned it out with misuse.

Vance and the white dragon rushed headlong at the pursuers, weaving like an eel through water as the first gust of fire from the king's massive silver and gold etherflame burst around them. One of the three riders with the king broke off, chasing Vance, but the rest remained on target.

There wasn't much Riony could do other than hold on tight. Dracuni and the other mesmerized dragons chased after Dashiel and the crystal as though their lives depended on it. And maybe they did.

And all their lives were in Dashiel's hands.

Come on, keep us away from the king, just a little longer.

Dashiel led them on a winding chase through the city, skirting between towers fluidly, bringing the trail of wild dragons behind them. The king's huge beast barreled after them, less agile but unstoppable. It hit a spire, sending shattered stone crashing down onto the streets below, and it didn't even slow down.

They were away from the larger battle with the revenants, but some of the flying undead had crossed the walls and circled around, flying down to pick off any human foolish enough to still be outside.

Dashiel kept them moving at a dizzying pace, and the Dragon King remained close behind, his dragon's wings beating like rhythmic thunder. *Fwoomp, fwoomp, fwoomp.*

Dashiel must have decided to change tact, lose the larger mass of the king's dragon with an uphill climb as they all shot higher at a steep angle toward the ashy clouds above.

A swarm of undead bugs hit Riony and she swatted them away as they picked at the skin of her face and tried to dig through her armor. Clearing the air again, she squinted out to the horizon. More flying revs? Or …

A dark shape flew straight at her, dropping in from above. The living corpse of a carrion bird, as big as a Dracuni, claws outstretched as it aimed for Riony.

Terror zinged through her limbs and her face twisted in disgust. She dropped sideways in her saddle, hanging out to the side by her fingernails, to avoid the collision. The flash of sharp beak and rotten feathers as it shot past left Riony shuddering.

Gross, gross, gross!

Then a short, sharp yelp came from below her, followed by a longer scream in an all too familiar voice.

"Kess!"

Riony whipped around in time to see the carrion bird rip Kess from her saddle. Lyomir didn't even blink, continuing after the summoning stone.

The revenant flapped hard as it angled its head around, trying to peck at the prey it had captured. Its beak clacked against the float rune on Kess's back, then ripped it free. The unactivated stone hurtled sickeningly down.

Kess cried out again, dangling and twisting in the revolting creature's grasp, so high above the city below.

A hum of fury and fear roared through Riony.

She gritted her teeth, gave Dracuni one final concerned look, then she jumped.

Riony plunged toward Kess, dodging Lyomir as he flew up past her, making the air swirl and buffet against her. Through her flight goggles, Riony could see Kess swing her glowing yellow cutting athame. But even if she could strike a blow that would kill the awful thing, it would only leave Kess falling faster.

In a burst of ashy feathers, Riony hit the revenant. The impact sent all three of them spinning through the air.

The rev's wings whipped hard, now with twice the burden, trying to keep them all airborne but caring more about tearing its prey apart than falling.

Heart pounding and hating every second, Riony grasped at the horrible creature's body, climbing around it until she could reach Kess in its claws beneath.

"Riony?" Kess gasped.

"Fancy ... meeting you ... here," Riony ground out between panting breaths and gritted teeth.

She wrapped one arm around Kess, and with the other, she wrestled against the scaly gray legs that were dug into Kess's delver armor.

Riony pulled one claw free, which then lashed out and scratched her across the face. Pain lanced over Riony's

forehead, and her flight googles were pulled free, falling out of reach.

The cutting athame flashed, parting the bird from its other foot, and then Riony and Kess fell again.

"Riony!"

Kess's hair whipped in Riony's face as she kept her clutched tight against her chest.

"Activate my sword! Can you reach it?" Riony screamed over the rushing air and lifted Kess higher over her shoulder.

The rooftops of the city below raced toward them. Riony's hands shook as she held Kess, terrified more of losing her grip than what awaited them on the ground below if Kess couldn't reach the rune.

"Got it!" Kess yelled, and a purple glow illuminated around them. Their descent slowed, but not by enough. With the weight of both of them and the speed they were already moving, Riony guessed they'd just downgraded from imminent death to immense pain.

A dark, red-tiled roof came up beneath them. Riony angled her legs toward it and held Kess cradled in both arms.

Tiles cracked as they hit, and a horrific crunch came from Riony's first leg to land. It buckled beneath her and the second leg twisted awkwardly and she did everything she could not to crush Kess as they went rolling over each other across the roof.

The pain hit before they came to a stop in a clatter of ceramic shards. Redness blurred Riony's vision from the blood in her eyes.

Hissing air through her teeth instead of screaming, Riony lay on her back, her crystal sword still glowing and uncomfortable beneath her.

She reached an arm out for where Kess had come to a stop beside her. "Kess? Kessara!"

Hands found hers. "Stay still!"

She's okay. She made it. The words pounded in time to her heartbeat.

"Are you hurt?" she asked through a whimper.

Broken roof tiles clinked and clattered away as Kess shifted closer. "Am *I* hurt. Am *I* hurt? You absolute maniac. You didn't even ... and it was a *bird* ... and ... I would slap you for doing something so foolish if your pain wasn't the sole cause of my own."

"I wasn't losing you. No matter what." Riony grinned weakly. "Of course I'd fall for a girl like you."

Kess's hands moved around Riony, brushing rubble off, and at least once, pulling a piece out from where it was jammed into her armor. "Stop using all your energy on being so razing charming, or I may still slap you."

"Weird way to propose. But yes."

"I'd say you were delirious, but you're just being you." Kess tsked and brushed a finger through Riony's hair before her hands moved away again.

Riony rolled off her sword and onto her side. Pressing up onto one elbow with a groaning wince, she worked to

wipe the blood from her eyes. Across the other side of the city, the smudgy shapes of dragons continued their chase.

Kess leaned over her, pushing her back onto the roof with a hand on her sternum. "I said, stay still."

"I need to get back to Dracuni."

"I know. But you're not going anywhere like this. Your legs are bending in unnatural ways."

"Are you flirting ... with me ...?" A wave of pain engulfed Riony and her words petered out.

A soft kiss brushed over one of Riony's cheeks, and a hand cupped the other. In a gentle voice, Kess whispered, "Stay. Still."

And then the familiar coolness of silvernix dropped onto Riony's forehead.

As the magic kicked in, Riony bucked upward as far as the sword strapped beneath her allowed. She cried out and Kess caught her, holding her through the pain. Light exploded around them, shimmering from Riony's skin as Dracuni's bottled blood wrought her whole again with a violence equal to the fall that had broken her apart.

Riony pressed her face to Kess's, foreheads and noses squashed together as though they could merge into one and then lips followed, kissing over a closed mouth scream drenched in starlight.

Because the pain was nothing, nothing at all, if it meant Kess was still there with her.

As the glow faded, the two of them remained panting,

mouth to mouth.

"You need to get back to Dracuni," Kess whispered.

"Yeah." Riony stretched her legs out, testing them and glad to find them both still whole.

She rolled sideways to unpin her sword from beneath her, then rose to her knees.

Scrubbing her eyes clear, she gave Kess a long look, making sure she wasn't secretly injured as well. Some of the leather of her delver armor had been torn, but there was no sign of blood pooling. Kess's flight goggles lay on the roof beside her, along with the dismembered bird claw. *Yuck.*

In Kess's hand was her spent vial of silvernix.

Riony moved to pick Kess up, but Kess shook her head.

"I'll only slow you down. I'll be fine here, and once the summoning stone is done with, Lyomir will come for me. But you need to go and help Dracuni, now!"

Riony grunted, turning between Kess and the distant dragon chase. The king was right on top of Dracuni and the others. Dashiel was doing their best to keep away, but that was all they could do. They had no other defenses, and Vance hadn't returned to help either.

Riony drew her sword into one hand and gave Kess a pained look.

"Go," Kess urged.

Riony threw herself back toward Kess, catching her in a long, bruising kiss, forcing into that moment every hope and wish and dream that the two of them would somehow make it out of this, that this wouldn't be the last time they touched, the message that Riony loved her with a depth greater than the darkest caves and higher than any dragon flew.

Each of them had only been rationed a single dose of silvernix each. Riony slipped hers into her hand, then pressed it into Kess's. "Stay alive for me. I'm not losing you. Not today, not ever."

Then they broke apart, and Riony ran.

She skidded down the slope of the broken tiled roof and launched off the edge, flying high over the rooftops below with the power of her sword's float rune and her own strength.

The shapes and layout of the city below were so unfamiliar, but years of navigating the undercity roofscape had made that method of travel second nature. She bolted across flat ridges and kicked off tower walls, keeping her footing as she spotted the next safe landing and leaped forward again.

The float rune kept her moving fast, gliding over the ghost-town streets of the capital, where only the occasional flicker of movement passed beneath. Humans still seeking shelter and the flying revenants who had moved in to hunt.

Even those revs are ripping through everything they can find. If the rest of them get in ...

Riony searched the skies again as the battle around the walls raged.

Dashiel was bringing Iffyr and the following dragons swooping down again. They weren't far ahead, and Riony tensed, sprinting faster. One of the smaller dragons along with the king was shooting down like an arrow at Dracuni.

Catapulting herself off a rooftop, Riony arched through the air and intercepted the rider with a knee to the face.

The man swung in his saddle from the blow. He wore grayglim armor, and a sharp curse word betrayed his surprise, but that didn't stop him from getting a dagger into his hand and bringing it up to where Riony clung on to him.

She fell backward onto the dragon's neck to dodge the strike, and the tamed dragon jolted, confused by the apparent jumble of orders. The grayglim readjusted, bringing the dragon from its dive into a flat glide, then he drew a second, longer blade.

From on her back, Riony kicked out both feet into the man's chest before he could swing his sword her way. He lifted from his seat, knocked into an uncontrollable somersault down the length of the dragon and off the end of its tail.

Riony scrambled upright again and into the saddle. She sheathed her still glowing sword onto her back and pivoted around to gauge the current situation.

The tamed dragon beneath her was continuing on with its last command, taking her away from the chase with Dracuni and the king and out into the larger battle again. Riony poked at the creature's neck the way she'd been taught, but the red and white dragon didn't respond.

"Sparks, turn around!" Riony yelled.

Had it been trained differently somehow? The dragon wasn't responding to anything Riony had been instructed on in the event she found herself alone on a tamed dragon again. But Dashiel had said not all dragons were taught to respond to the same orders. Different trainers had different methods.

She was only getting farther and farther away from Dracuni, who still had the king and one other rider chasing her.

I could go back over the rooftops again ... Riony looked down, her eye caught by movement. A flood of revenants spilled over the keep's walls and through the streets below. Panic filled Riony as she got her bearings.

Where was Kess? Where did she leave Kess? She spotted the rooftop. It wasn't far from there, and a horde of revenants plowed that way. And Kess didn't have Lyomir, she didn't have Griskin. She was trapped.

Riony roared, trying to physically turn the dragon's neck to change its direction.

A shadow darkened Riony, and she braced for the attack of another flying revenant.

The blow didn't come. The attacker instead smashed down onto the tamed dragon's head, a writhing bundle of green scales and leathery wings, screeching in wild fury.

TWENTY-FOUR

The first few wild dragons were visible on the horizon as Aishena flew Ambri toward the capital. By the time Lyrrin could hear the battle raging around the keep, the sky was filled with scores of untamed dragons brought in by the summoning crystal.

The calling has stopped now, Elumon informed Lyrrin.

She nodded, a little dazed. The summoning stone had done its job. The others must have deactivated it once all those wild dragons were close enough.

Lyrrin was awed at the sheer number of them. *Riony did so much over the last few weeks, untamed so many dragons in factories around the capital!*

This was good and bad.

It was good because the plan was working exactly the way they had hoped it would. All the recently untamed dragons were drawn in, and they were behaving the same way Lyomir had when presented with tamed dragons. They were attacking and trying to pull the taming stakes from their kin.

It was also bad, because the plan was working exactly the way they had hoped.

And because Ambri was still tamed.

There were easily as many newly wild and wrathful dragons as there were tamed ones with riders, and they were throwing themselves into a wrestling, midair battle with each one they could catch. Piercing shrieks cut through the sounds of beating wings and screaming riders.

Flying revenants tangled within the chaos as colorful dragons swirled and chased each other, and the shadow dragon loomed far overhead, circling like the promise of death to all below.

In the middle saddle, Kverra Hjelzahn stared up at the creature, her expression blank, dark eyes edged red with emotion.

Lyrrin pulled her own gaze away from the mourning spirit and back to the battle ahead. She watched, her jaw dropping, as they flew closer.

"Riony will be fine. She's on Dracuni; the untamed dragons shouldn't go after her." Eslinde, still in the saddle with Lyrrin, gave her a squeeze around the shoulder. But a deep frown cut a line between her eyebrows.

Vance was on a tamed dragon, and so was Dashiel. Lyrrin didn't need Eslinde to say it to know that's what she was thinking. Or about their own risk on Ambri.

"I'm going to have to take us through that if we want to reach the palace," Aishena yelled over her shoulder.

"Do you think you can?" Eslinde held Lyrrin a little tighter.

"Do you want to turn around?" Aishena shot back.

"No, we need to do this," Lyrrin replied.

"Then we're going to find out." Aishena's angular shoulders lifted up around her silver hair as she leaned closer to Ambri and brought them into the battle.

So many creatures. Elumon tucked in close behind Lyrrin, shivering.

Lyrrin braced as Ambri suddenly flung left, almost tossing her from her saddle. Snapping dragon teeth filled her vision, then were gone just as fast, replaced with the flutter of fetid feathers. A flock of undead birds trailed across their path, and Benjin sliced three of the smaller ones from the sky with his twin blades to clear them away from Aishena.

Lyrrin knocked a final one away from her and Eslinde with her crystal staff.

It didn't fall, just swirled around in the air behind them, then sought a new target.

There are still so many revs. Aren't they burning yet? Lyrrin turned her face upward to the shadow dragon. Thin streams of inky darkness swirled down from the entity like reversed smoke, seeking dragons whose spikes had been torn free.

One etherflame, head bloodied and body limp, fell from the sky directly in front of them, and Aishena swerved Ambri steeply to avoid hitting it.

Across to the right, another dragon lit up brightly as their rider used their provided dose of silvernix on it, preventing it from dying midair from the open wound in its brain. A second, smaller glow of purple lit up as that rider then bailed with their float stone from the dragon's back as it roared furiously.

But only the riders who had come with them from the undercity had silvernix and knew what to do with it. None of the other riders were prepared for this assault. Lerris's team had been given float runes, but didn't know why, didn't know what was coming.

They had argued for days about whether or not they could trust them with the plan and the silvernix needed to save their dragons, but it hadn't mattered anyway. There wasn't enough time to provide Dracuni's blood to them all.

That's why we have to find the king's supply. Now.

The palace came within sight, the half-circle structure of it looking like a broken jaw lying in the middle of the keep. Aishena brought them lower, cutting through the streets and around towers to lose a massive dark-red flamesong on their tail.

The ground below churned, streets filled with revenants of all shapes and sizes, charging and tumbling over each other as they encroached into every part of the keep, seeking human blood. They skittered over rooftops and piled against doorways and gates until the sheer mass of them crashed through.

Screams echoed up from within buildings.

Eslinde watched in horror and turned Lyrrin's face away from it when she saw that she was watching as well.

"Flight deck is up ahead," Aishena barked. "Hold tight, we're coming in fast!"

Another dragon emerged from the cavernous entrance, blue and white, rushing toward them, spear like. Aishena turned Ambri, but the other dragon also turned away, fleeing past them.

The blue and white dragon angled out toward the harbor. The flamesong that had been tailing Ambri turned on it and snatched it from the air within its claws. It brought the blue and white dragon, and its riders, crashing down beneath its weight onto a rooftop below.

Eslinde swiveled around to watch with a gasp. "That was Prysha's dragon ... my sister ..."

"Nothing we can do. Hold on!" Aishena ordered again, and the orange ash-tinted sunlight vanished as they went into the flight deck.

The vast polished stone floor screeched beneath Ambri's claws as they skidded down the length of the space. Lyrrin thrust forward, bumping into Kverra's back, and Elumon tumbled against Lyrrin's as Eslinde tried to hold them all steady.

They all lurched forward again as Ambri came to a complete stop.

"You did it! We made it!" Lyrrin cheered, pulling off her flight goggles.

"I won't ever question your flying again," Eslinde sighed the words out.

"Or anything else, I should hope," Aishena muttered as she slipped from her saddle and leaped gracefully to the ground.

Kverra remained silent as she followed, but a small half smile appeared on her lips, vanishing as fast as smoke dispersed in the wind.

Eslinde brushed Lyrrin's darkened hair back from where it had stuck to her temples around the goggles.

They had no more time to recover from the flight or landing as their presence raised a rally of cries in the flight deck.

Ambri had stopped a fair distance into the space, not far from where a mid-sized silver and red dragon was being loaded up with luggage.

A half dozen grayglims stood guard around a dark-haired woman in their midst. The queen.

Her utterly repulsed expression as she stared back showed she had identified those on the orange dragon in return. "What are *you* doing here?"

Eslinde helped Lyrrin down from the dragon, then stared back at her mother, hard-eyed. "We're not packing up and running, which it seems is what you're doing."

Hissing her disgust, the queen waved both arms as though shooing animals.

Addressing her grayglims, she snapped, "Go on, get them! Clear these intruders out of our way!"

The six grayglims broke into motion, rushing their way.

"You know the drill," Lyrrin called out, lobbing a crystal toward the gray-armored guards in an underarm throw.

Eslinde, Aishena, Benjin, and Kverra closed their eyes, and Elumon covered his face with a wing as the flash stone burst with bright light in front of the charging grayglims. Lyrrin's vision glowed red through her eyelids, and she waited for it to fade before looking again.

Queen Vellira cried out, covering her streaming eyes with both hands, and the guards slowed their approach, faces grim as their gazes searched blindly for their opponents.

Elumon crouched into a pouncing pose but shuffled backward behind Lyrrin rather than forward. *I fight?*

The little hatchling's inner voice was tinged with fear.

No, leave it to the others.

Aishena, Benjin, and Kverra danced in between the grayglims with deadly silence. The hilts of swords and unlit athames cracked into vital places—knees, sternums, the backs of heads—and grayglims fell in a tumble.

Five were down, when the sixth, panicked at the sound of falling bodies, lashed out with a wild thrust of his sword. It was luck alone that meant Aishena had her back in line with the attack.

"Watch out!" Benjin yelled.

Aishena spun toward the threat, then a body collided with her side, pushing her away from the thrusting blade. The length of the sword instead clinked against scale mail and sank into Kverra's stomach.

"Mami!" Aishena gasped the word and downed the final guard with a cracking blow to his jaw.

Lyrrin ran to join Benjin and Aishena as they dropped beside their fallen mother.

"What's happening?" Vellira cried, turning around blindly. "Do you have them?"

"No. We have you." Eslinde stepped in front of the queen, tapping the point of her thin epee against her chest until she stilled.

Kverra had both hands clutched over her stomach. As Aishena pried them away, Lyrrin expected to find the wound clean and dry, the way Kverra's body had been while she was possessed, only half alive and unbleeding.

But as fingers were drawn back, a spill of red oozed

from the deep wound.

Aishena hissed. "I was going to parry that blow. *You* should have been able to parry that blow. What were you thinking?"

Kverra turned her face to the side, jaw tensed.

Aishena grasped her mother's chin, turning her back, not gently.

Her voice trembled as it rose, loud enough to echo within the flight deck. "Did you think you could go out in some heroic moment and be absolved of all your guilt? All you would have done was take yet another member of our family from us!"

Kverra's dark eyes flashed, and her head shook with small motions of denial.

Aishena's expression grew cold and still again. "We all have silvernix with us. You're not dying today, as much as you may have wanted to."

Benjin was already rummaging through his belt pouch.

"Don't use your own. Save it. We have some more available right here," Eslinde called over.

She stepped closer to the queen and brought a hand to the golden necklace hanging over her collarbones. With a quick tug, she tore it free and tossed it over to Aishena.

Kverra coughed, and a small splatter of blood sprayed. She choked on her words. "I'm ... sorry."

Aishena examined the necklace, then pulled free a small vial from within the gem-encrusted pendant.

"Don't be sorry. Just *be here*. For us."

Benjin put his arm around Aishena as she applied the silvernix to their mother, and the woman's dark skin shimmered with light.

Vellira inhaled in outraged. "That was mine!"

Lyrrin remained kneeling beside the healing woman and yelled back at the queen, "You shouldn't be using it anyway if you're pregnant."

Vellira's eyes narrowed and her back went ramrod straight. "You think I am?"

"Surely, you wouldn't be, given there were meant to be no more first heirs, even before me." Eslinde circled the woman who barely seemed older than her, trailing the point of her blade after her. "Or did you and Fadda decide it was time to start out fresh?"

"My husband makes his own decisions. If he or others think I am pregnant, all the better for me to be included in his decisions." Vellira shrugged carelessly as she eyed Eslinde's sword. "Your king, our Dragon King, will be back soon, and you will suffer for mistreating me when he returns."

Eslinde stilled then and shared a worried look with Lyrrin. "Where is he now?"

"He has taken his dragon to help with the battle."

Lyrrin scoffed. There was only one thing out there the king cared about.

Dracuni.

Please don't let him catch her.

Vellira continued, haughtily. "But he will be coming back for me soon, so he can protect me when we leave, together."

The glow of the silvernix healing Kverra faded, and Aishena and Benjin helped their mother back to her feet.

"Leave to where?" Kverra straightened but didn't push out of her children's hold. She locked eyes with the queen. "All the years I gave to being a grayglim warden, to protecting the Draekhan line, only to see now this is all you are ... Cowards who would flee their people when things are most dire."

"We are not cowards! We are only doing what is sensible."

Lyrrin imagined her grandfather, out within that mess of revenants and wild dragons and other riders, and Riony and Dracuni, and all the damage he had done or could yet do to the world and those Lyrrin loved.

All he had ever shown any care for was finding his new source of silvernix, of maintaining his health, youth, power. But also that of his wife. The only other thing Lyrrin had seen him care for.

Standing up, Lyrrin called Elumon to her side and nodded to Eslinde. "We have to keep moving. Bring her with us. She could be useful if the king does return."

Eslinde quirked an eyebrow, but acquiesced, giving her mother a small shove on the shoulder to get her moving.

She led the way at a swift march into the corridors of the palace.

The queen huffed petulantly. "Where are you taking me? What are you even doing here?"

"We've come to take all of my grandfather's silvernix," Lyrrin declared.

Vellira loosed a cackling chuckle. "And you think it's here? Don't be ridiculous. He doesn't keep more than a small supply in the palace at any time."

"You're right," Lyrrin agreed. "He doesn't keep it all here. But we are in the right place."

Lyrrin had explained her thoughts on where to go to Eslinde and the others on the flight, and Eslinde had agreed it was promising. The only place the Dragon King was ever alone. A room well-guarded and barred, where only a few select people had ever stepped within.

A room which held broken remnants of Alderkin magic that may not have been as broken as first appearances suggested.

They hurried for the silvernix chamber, Eslinde leading them confidently through the long glossy corridors of dark stone.

The palace was empty of the usual bustle of guards and nobles, and as Lyrrin became familiar with where they were, she took the lead.

They rounded the next corner, and in the eerie cold light of the dragon-powered lamps, a mixture of strangely shaped figures shambled at the other end of the hall.

Low growls filled the air, and clacking, skeletal heads swiveled their way.

The revenants had reached the palace.

TWENTY-FIVE

Riony clung to the saddle of the red and white dragon she'd commandeered as it pinwheeled out of control. The tamed dragon wasn't responding to any of her commands. Even if she could work out how to ride the thing, her efforts were entirely hampered by the wild dragon wrapping itself around her dragon's head.

The gold-green treedart was one Riony remembered from one of her factory missions. Most of the dragons they'd untamed were etherflames, etherdarts, and flamesongs— good firebreathers used for smelting.

But one glass factory had a whole team of treedarts that were being used to haul sand from an adjoining quarry.

It had infuriated Riony, seeing the powerful creatures being used that way.

Tamed and enslaved, just to be beasts of burden.

The treedart didn't appear to recognize her or care one bit that there was a human clinging to the red and white dragon it attacked.

It only seemed to care about ridding that tamed dragon of the spike that kept it enslaved.

Which is great. Just great. Exactly what we were hoping for. Except I wasn't meant to be on a tamed dragon when it was happening.

She didn't even have a dose of silvernix anymore to heal the poor red and white dragon with once the treedart got its stake out, and she wasn't looking forward to falling down into the revenant army below along with it.

Dizziness swirled through Riony as they continued circling in a horizontal corkscrew and it was all she could do to hold on. Her flight goggles had been lost earlier, and the bitter, cold wind left her eyes watering. She wiped them clear.

All around, more dragons arrived. Dozens and dozens. Riony had counted their efforts with the factory dragons at around one hundred freed, and it seemed as though almost that many had responded to the summoning stone.

Dashiel must have deactivated it when they saw it had worked, because the wild dragons weren't all flying the same way toward it. They were careening throughout the battle in every direction, seeking their targets.

Riony stared, aghast.

Whose tamebrain idea was it to bring one hundred wild and angry dragons bent on ripping the taming stakes from their kin into the most tame-dragon dense area in the land?

Oh right, it was mine.

It had seemed like a good idea, at first. What better way to quickly untame dragons en masse than recruiting dragons to do it for them?

But the reality of it was a bloodbath.

Spatters of dragon blood rained over Riony as the green treedart shrieked. The red and white dragon finally stabilized. Riony sighed with relief, then ducked as a ball of fire shot over her head.

She shook off the dizziness and tried to get her bearings. If the summoning stone was no longer activated ...

Dracuni? Riony cried loud in her mind.

Where are you, big sister?

Green wings flapped, clipping Riony's shoulder as the treedart flew away, and Riony realized why her dragon had stopped spinning. A deep hole showed in the middle of its forehead, and it hung limply in the sky for another moment before its wings crumpled in and they plummeted together.

I'm on a red and white dragon, near the walls, going down fast!

Riony clung to her glowing sword, looking for a place to jump to safety, but the sky was a riot of tangled dragons and revenants.

I see you!

Dodging beside a whopping flamesong, Dracuni burst into view, racing after the falling dragon and Riony. With three long steps across the red and white scales, Riony leaped high into the air.

Dracuni ducked beneath her, and Riony caught her saddle as she came over the top.

Getting herself properly seated, Riony patted Dracuni's neck. "Nice catch."

Sorry I didn't come sooner. One of the king's riders was still chasing me.

Riony checked behind them. "Nobody there at the moment. I think you lost them. But we should deal with that dragon ahead of us. I couldn't heal it. I don't have my silvernix anymore."

Why? What did you do to yourself this time?

"Nothing. I gave it to Kess." Riony shied away from the details.

With a surge of determination, Dracuni dove fast toward the red and white dragon. As she came up behind it, the unidragon huffed a short burst of silvery fire, lighting the injured beast up just as it crashed down into the revenants below.

Hopefully they soften its landing. Revenants rarely went after dragons and animals. Only humans. With the hole in its head healed, the red and white would have a good chance of surviving.

"Where's Lyomir?" Riony yelled over the rush of

flying, worried to her core about someone else's chances of surviving.

Flew away fast when the summoning stopped calling us.

Did he get to Kess? Has he got her?

I can't hear him now. Too many voices.

"Sparks," Riony grunted.

They were out within the main battle now, far from the rooftops of the keep where Riony had left Kess. *I should have brought her with me. I never should have let her go.*

Riony wanted to ask Dracuni to take her there, to go back and make sure that the revs crawling through the city hadn't found Kess, but she couldn't. She knew their place was right there, within the heart of the chaos.

It was the only reason Dracuni had been brought into the battle at all.

To save as many dragon lives as they could.

Gritting her teeth, Riony pulled her focus away from the deep ache in her heart toward the work before them. She scanned the messy skies.

"That way, the yellow etherflame!"

Dracuni shot toward the falling dragon, catching it in a short puff flame.

It revived quickly, wings swishing wildly as it got the air back under it again. Another two dragons followed in quick succession as Dracuni pitched up and down through the air between them.

A familiar purple and icy-blue treedart came in beside them, followed by a white shimmerdart.

Dashiel waved, beaming from its back. "You're okay!"

Riony gave a casual salute in return. "Thank you for keeping Dracuni okay, too."

"And Kess?"

Swallowing hard, Riony kept her eyes away from the keep and the revenants crawling all over it. "Survived the fall. Fine the last I saw her. Where are the others?"

"Vance and I have mostly been playing keep-away with the wild dragons. Luckily, the Dragon King also backed off when the wild dragons came in. A heap of them went straight after his dragon." Dashiel pointed out over the harbor where the silver and gold monstrosity circled.

A couple of smaller dragons still harried it, like owlettes trying to bring down a bovin. The tamed dragon moved almost with the speed and precision of those who could control their own actions. Riony figured that synergy between beast and rider must have come with eighty odd years of the king flying it.

Its head swiveled fast, snapping efficiently at its attackers, catching them in its teeth.

"Haven't seen Jaym since the summoning rune stopped. I was over the city a moment ago. The revs have reached the palace. The whole city is filled with them. If they don't start burning soon ..."

"Then we're all totally boned." Riony didn't bother

yelling that loud enough for Dashiel to hear.

She still held on to the tiny scrap of hope that this madness was going to work. That all the dragons around them being forcibly untamed would be enough. Enough to finally weaken the shadow dragon's curse.

All throughout the sky, dragons were lighting up with the healing power of silvernix. That alone filled Riony with pride and awe that those from the undercity who had been entrusted with Dracuni's blood for that very purpose actually followed through.

Everyone there knew exactly how high the stakes were.

And with each healed dragon, another curling shadow was threaded free from the shadow dragon above.

Riony could still feel the heavy weight of the entity's mourning, trying to infect her.

The glow of float runes from riders having to bail from newly wild dragons also peppered the battle.

They had provided those crystals to every rider they could, undercity and Mestra Lerris's riders alike. They would be saved from falls, but that didn't help them a whole lot when they were falling into an army of revenants below.

A purple glow of a falling rider passed in front of them.

Dashiel signaled their goodbye. "I'll catch that one. Good luck!"

"Stay safe!" Riony and Dracuni turned the other way, racing toward another wounded dragon.

A giant bat revenant screeched, coming for Riony as

Dracuni puffed her healing breath again. Lighting up her sword with the burn rune, Riony swatted the horrible creature away. Its dry, leathery wings caught alight, and it fell away in a trail of smoke.

Riony watched as carefully as she could through stinging eyes, trying to tell whether the revenant was falling because it had expired from the burning or whether it just didn't have enough wing left unburned to remain airborne.

As Dracuni healed another dragon and another, Riony's chest tightened over her thumping heart. There were so many to heal. All of Mestra Lerris's team and all the dragons from riders still loyal to the king didn't have silvernix or any idea what was happening and why.

They were the ones who most needed Dracuni's help, but it also meant with every breath of healing flame, Dracuni was exposing herself and what she could do to everyone who could see.

There was no coming back from this.

The next dragon Dracuni healed was a familiar snowflame.

"Vance?" Riony yelled.

She could see no sign of him falling alongside the snowflame. Riony craned around, checking all the nearby dragons and revenants Dracuni dodged through. A flash of gold streaked by.

Viska's back. Dracuni's thoughts were edged with exhaustion.

Lyrrin and Eslinde aren't with her? Riony panicked, worried they'd activated the stone too soon and brought the others back along with the golden dragon.

No. Just Viska. She has Vance.

Dracuni was breathing hard, her wingbeats arrhythmic and weak.

Riony ran a hand down her neck, finding it feverish. "We can stop whenever you need to. You've already saved so many."

Dracuni snorted. **What would you say if I said that to you?**

Riony scrunched her nose and then steeled herself. "That there are still so many more to save. Just ... small puffs, okay? Conserve your strength."

Dracuni raced on to heal her next target. Riony caught glimpses of Hux and Jaym a couple of times, catching falling riders. She still had yet to see Kess and Lyomir.

Riony lost count of how many more dragons Dracuni revived. The unidragon moved sluggishly, her eyelids drooping over lilac eyes. Riony clenched her teeth over her words of worry, wishing she could infuse the unidragon with her own energy, her own life, the way Dracuni had so often done for her.

Riony felt Dracuni's guilt and pain as she didn't reach a sunflower yellow dragon she was heading for in time and it crashed hard to the ground below.

There were too many obstacles in the air, and the more

tired Dracuni got, the harder it was to navigate.

A flock of smaller revenants blocked their way ahead. Dracuni tried to swerve but her wings faltered, struggling to hold a glide let alone the push needed to switch directions at speed. Riony brought her sword up, ready, when a swirling vortex of air cleared their path.

"Hey! You miss me?" Zeina swept in across their path on her shining aqua seasong.

Riony grinned from ear to ear. "Took your razing time!"

Zeina waved behind her, where more Rebel Riders swooped along on a colorful mix of dragons. "And it looks like we got here just in time. This is a shit show."

"Right?" Riony laughed, but it came out more like a sob.

"What do you need?" Zeina asked.

Riony needed Dracuni to be at full health, full energy again, to not have expended so much of herself. But she couldn't do anything about that. Zeina had left before they'd distributed silvernix, so she wouldn't have any.

"The riders on tamed dragons need help, and we need these skies to be clear of revs."

"We'll see what we can do." Zeina lifted one arm into the air, swirling it, then pointing in a gesture to the other Rebel Riders.

Each rode a wild, untamed dragon, unbothered by the factory dragons as they formed a V-shaped wedge in

front of Dracuni, with Zeina at the lead. Gleem released her gusting breath again, knocking both revenants and dragons clear.

Then the formation split up, fanning out from Dracuni, plucking flying revenants and falling riders from the smoky air.

Tamed and untamed dragons still tussled fiercely all around them, but the battle cleared enough for Riony to identify where the dragons who most desperately needed healing were.

"You ready to go again?" Riony lay a hand on Dracuni's opalescent scales.

Only a faint sensation of affirmation returned as Dracuni followed Riony's direction to the next target.

She managed to heal almost a dozen more, then her wings started to slip in the air like fingers grasping a soapy ledge, lacking the strength to hold air beneath them.

"It's okay, it's okay." Riony's voice lifted in panic.

She deactivated the flame on her sword, leaving only the float rune active. But if Dracuni fell, that magic would offer little help.

Dracuni's thoughts came to Riony only in drifts of blurred exhaustion, a sensation of fading away.

As she cast around for a friendly face to call in assistance from, she caught a glimpse of red and white behind them. "Sparks, really?"

The king's rider chased toward them. Riony cursed

at the loyalty of the rider to persist in their mission, even given the utter chaos around them.

"We've got a tail again. We need to move!"

Dracuni shuddered, letting out a whimper that solidified into a roar, and she stretched her wings with painful effort. But they didn't hold.

"Sparks," Riony hissed.

The king's rider was still a way off but had clearly spotted them and was coming in as directly as they could through the battle.

Riony leaned over Dracuni, pressing her forehead to the back of Dracuni's neck. *I know you can do this. Come on. Just a little bit more, then you can rest.*

The unidragon stretched her wings again, and they held, just enough to glide. Riony used her own body weight, leaning out from the saddle to help turn them, aiming back into the thick of the battle, hoping to find one of their companions for help within.

But the king's rider gained.

A bristle of emotion shivered down the unidragon's neck and into Riony.

Dracuni lifted her head, seeking.

"What is it?"

Familiar ... voice ...?

Blinking her watering eyes clear, Riony squinted at a large shape coming in beside them, her heart rampaging with the hope of seeing Gleem, Hux, Viska, or any friendly

dragon at their side.

Instead, it was one of the larger wild dragons. It flew calmly and apparently wasn't driven to maim the tamed dragons like the others were. It hovered curiously at Dracuni's side.

Riony thought it was a flamesong at first, based on the size.

But as she took in its colors and patterns, she realized it wasn't one of the dragons she'd untamed at all. It was a seasong, silver, with a few flecks of black.

"It's your amma ..." Riony exhaled the words huskily.

A deep pang of emotion rang back from Dracuni.

A long, low growl rumbled from the seasong in return. Riony kept her sword clutched tight in one hand warily. The last time she'd seen the mother dragon, it had tried to kill both her and Dracuni. And she was no longer emaciated and weak as she had been then.

Dracuni's wings fluttered, and she and Riony dropped suddenly, sending Riony's stomach up into her throat before they stabilized again. The seasong rumbled a growl, head flicking their way, sniffing at the air with flared nostrils.

Dracuni thrummed, then opened her mouth to release a stuttering, whimpering song.

Tears filled Riony's eyes. *You can sing?*

The mother dragon growled and then returned the sound, just two humming notes of the haunting melody.

And then the snap of dragon teeth behind them broke off the sound.

The king's rider had reached them.

"Come on, we need to get out of here!" Riony yelled over the wind, but she could feel within her own bones how drained Dracuni was. It was a miracle they hadn't already fallen from the sky.

The silver and black seasong swung her head around to the pursuers, eyes narrowed. Then she roared so loudly it should have blasted the clouds from the sky.

In a fluid motion like twirled ribbon, she curved up and over Dracuni, then set upon the king's rider and his tamed beast. The smaller etherdart's wings crumpled within her claws.

Riony watched in awe for a moment, then Dracuni dropped again, farther this time, before her wings caught the air with a wet-fabric clap.

I'm ... sorry. Dracuni's thoughts seemed hollow, echoing into Riony like a sound from the distance depths of a cave.

Riony's hair whipped into her eyes, and she clung to Dracuni. "It's okay. It's going to be okay."

The unidragon's wings gave again. They were so close above the revenant army now that Riony could hear the clack of their bones as hundreds of claws and teeth reached up toward them.

A dark shadow dropped down in front of them, faster

than Dracuni's faltering fall. The shadow dragon. Riony clenched her teeth against the anguished cry its presence made her want to loose.

The cursed mass of dragon souls bellowed a thunderous roar, and Riony held her breath as she watched and waited, hoping ...

Please don't work. Please be weakened.

The ground beneath churned.

The first new revenant to rise was the red and yellow dragon Dracuni hadn't reached in time. Purple lights spotted through the masses as downed riders revived as murderous undead. Flickering orange trails of smoke rose from revenants who had been burned and continued to march on.

Riony's heart dropped into an icy well.

And Dracuni dropped again. Riony clung to her, patting her neck through tears.

It's okay. You did so well. So well. You saved so many lives.

There was no response from the unidragon as they crashed down into the sea of monstrous undead.

TWENTY-SIX

Skeletal claws and ragged, rotten flesh skidded on the polished floor of the palace corridor as the revenants charged toward Lyrrin and her team. The human and animal corpses formed a thick wall, like a flood of gray water rolling their way, glinting with sharp teeth and pale, dead eyes.

Elumon's fear spiked though Lyrrin so strongly she had to clutch the nearby wall to stop from falling over.

Queen Vellira stood frozen in the revenant's path. "They've made it to the palace? How? It's impossible."

"If you had any idea what was going on out there, you wouldn't be so surprised." Eslinde grabbed her by the elbow and tugged her onto the nearby stairs. "Move! Everyone! We need to get to the silvernix chamber."

Lyrrin's attention snapped away from the raging creatures' approach. The silvernix chamber was just down the stairs. She hopped down the first few, only to find Elumon didn't follow. His moonlight wings fluttered as he trembled.

Come on, we'll be safe down there. We can lock them out.

With a small yelp, he bolted down the stairs, almost bowling her over on the way.

The little hatchling had never seen revenant up close before. Lyrrin wanted to reassure him that they probably wouldn't hurt him, but she didn't know for sure and didn't want to test it. Either way, the creatures were terrifying.

Aishena, Benjin, and Kverra brought up the rear as they all galloped down the wide flight of stairs, coming up to the barred gateway below.

Lyrrin had been faint with pain and blood loss the last time she'd been there. She remembered there'd been guards waiting within to open this gate, then the more solid door beyond it. But no guards remained on duty now, whether they'd been called to some other tasks or simply fled.

Eslinde reached the gate first and grasped on to the bars, giving it a hard shove. It rattled, remaining closed.

"It's locked!"

Elumon circled around Lyrrin's feet, panting. **We're trapped. We're trapped!**

"I might be able to pick it, but it takes time," Kverra said.

"We don't have time." Aishena pulled an athame in each hand, pointing to the top of the stairs, where the first, fastest revs had reached.

She lit up the yellow blade and slashed down through the lock, cutting the latch.

With a kick to the gate, it swung open.

"Go, go!" Eslinde herded everyone through.

They crowded into the small space between the gate and the solid vault-like doorway, designed just for a couple of guards at a time. Aishena and Kverra slammed the gate closed as the revenants tumbled down the stairs toward them.

"We can't lock this again!" Kverra said.

Aishena leaned her shoulder to the bars, pulled a coil of cave silk rope from her belt and began lashing the gate closed. A canine-shaped revenant bounded down the last few stairs, smashing against the metal. It snapped yellowed teeth at Aishena's arm as she reached through the bars to loop the rope again.

Aishena screamed as its jaw locked around her wrist. Kverra barged in beside her, thrusting both arms through the bars. She grunted with effort as she wrestled the revenant's mouth open.

The quilted guard armor Aishena wore tore through as she wrenched her hand away. Blood dripped around her fingers.

Kverra finished lashing the rope and backed away from

the bars as the rest of the revenants crashed against them. Spindly arms of sinew and bone clawed through, trying to reach them.

"That's not going to hold for long," Aishena said.

"Are you okay? Do you need silvernix for that?" Benjin hovered around his sister.

Aishena cradled her bleeding wrist. "It's not going to matter either way unless we get through to the next room soon."

Eslinde stood near one of the two keyholes on either side of the door, running her fingers over it with a distraught look. "It requires two keys, turned together, of which we have neither."

"I could cut through again," Aishena offered.

Eslinde shook her head and knocked on the solid metal. "Try, but the latch mechanism is deep within the door."

"Move aside," Lyrrin ordered, then put a hand out for Aishena's cutting athame. "Can I have that for a moment?"

Aishena handed the blood-smudged crystal over. The bars behind them shuddered and rattled as the revenants scrambled to reach them.

Lyrrin activated the cutting athame and plunged it straight into the middle of the metal door, creating a thin, deep hole. She then pulled a long, finger-sized crystal from her belt, activated it, and jammed it in.

Eslinde leaned in to see what she was doing, and Lyrrin pushed her back away. A popping explosion made the metal door clang and groan, and dark energy consumed all the internal cogs and mechanics within the lock into a swirling void. Air howled and sucked in, ruffling Lyrrin's hair, and then the small crystal ran out of charge and the magic cleared.

Eslinde gaped. "That ... The Alderkin taught you *that*?"

"I wanna know how to do that," Benjin grumbled.

Lyrrin pushed the door, and it swung freely, the entire locking innards obliterated. "A pretty powerful combination, isn't it!"

Eslinde helped open the heavy door wider and hurried through. "I'd say. I'm happy they've been teaching you, although I have to admit I'm a little concerned they taught a child how to do *that*."

"I'll only use it for good." Lyrrin smiled with narrowed eyes. "And maybe the occasional prank."

The bars behind them rattled again, weld points groaning and snapping. The whole thing was going to come off the walls before the rope tying the gate snapped.

"Quickly," Eslinde called from inside the silvernix chamber.

Lyrrin urged Elumon to go in, then followed. He seemed equally terrified of the creepy ossuary ahead as he was the revenants and kept so close to her that he risked tripping her. Aishena, Benjin, and Kverra followed in, pushing the heavy door closed behind them.

The structure of the metal had remained solid after

Lyrrin's magic, only a bit bent in places, but there would be no way to lock it again.

"Get whatever you can to barricade it." Kverra pointed to the stone pillars holding skulls and the heavy stone shelving in the center of the space.

"Not the shelves," Lyrrin said. "Don't touch them."

A great smash and clatter came from the other side of the door, ringing like broken bells, and revenants roared. They were through the gate. The force of their bodies struck the inner door, rattling it. Aishena and Kverra put their shoulders into holding it as Benjin wedged bones and unicorn horns beneath it to jam it closed.

"Float rune," Benjin yelled from beside one of the low display pillars.

Kverra tossed him the crystal Lyrrin had carved for her earlier, and he activated it. Holding it and the heavy stone together, he lifted the plinth enough to drag it over to the door, propping it against the metal.

Eslinde did the same with another block of stone. "That might hold them for a little while, but it sounds like they are tearing right through the metal on the other side. I hope you're right about there being a way out of here."

Want out too. Don't like it here. Elumon tucked his head under a wing.

Lyrrin bit her lip. She hoped she was right too.

The round room otherwise had no visible doors or windows, only walls covered with intricately arranged bones and unicorn skulls.

Lyrrin moved into the center of the domed chamber where the two narrow shelves stood, arched over the top with the broken remains of a gateway geode.

She'd been too unwell to really consider the doorway-like structure the last time she'd been in there, to really look at it. The geode oval was broken in half, but the shelves it sat on were made of a dark, glossy stone, struck through with lightning streaks of pale crystal.

Could they work the same way as other crystals?

Lyrrin had seen the stones the Alderkin had created the new shrine with in the undercity. They weren't pure crystal either, but rather limestone with crystal veins.

Stepping between the shelves, carvings along the inner sides became clear. Delicate swirls that felt familiar to Lyrrin, almost like looking at her own handwriting, lined up both edges of the twin shelves and along the floor between them.

"Look! There are runes," Lyrrin cried.

She kneeled down, running her fingers over a larger one on the floor where a gateway's main activation rune usually sat.

Eslinde rushed to her side. She gasped when she saw it. "I never ... I never came in here. I hate this room so much. If I'd seen this ..."

"The king probably counted on nobody who knew what runes looked like coming in here." Lyrrin frowned

as she looked over the carvings. "I don't know what this bit is, though. It's not normal magical runes."

Eslinde's face scrunched with emotion. Her voice came out small, almost lost under the clamor of revenants trying to beat their way inside. "It's Alderkin language."

"Can you read it?"

Eslinde shook her head, but it didn't seem like a denial. "Not all Alderkin writing. But I can read this. It's something Alleem used to write for me, on every message we shared."

Lyrrin's breath caught. "What does it say?"

Eslinde brushed her fingers over the words as though caressing a lover's cheek. "Love beyond barriers. Although, that is a poor translation of the true meaning. In Alderkin, this word's meaning encompasses not just physical boundaries, but time, emotions ... life and death."

A tear splashed down from the tip of Eslinde's nose onto the glossy stone.

Lyrrin's eyes stung with the threat of her own tears. She already knew that the carvings there must have been done by her father. She'd heard how the Dragon King had taken him away, forced him to work and share his magic, tried to get him to share gateway magic.

His last words were that he'd never shared it. That he found another way.

Lyrrin swallowed the emotions away. She had work to do.

She examined the carvings of the main rune.

The Alderkin had assumed the king wanted gateway magic in order to use it to move around the kingdom, to rule it even more fully, to have that power for himself along with all his others.

Then Lyrrin started thinking maybe he wanted the gateway magic for something else. A way for him, and only him, to reach his main supply of silvernix.

And he set it up in a place where he always kept just enough silvernix stocked on the shelves to keep the magic charged. I should have known earlier!

"It's close to the usual gateway rune, but a bit different here," Lyrrin pointed to where the strokes were changed.

"Can you activate it?" Eslinde asked as she wiped her cheeks.

Benjin rushed over from where his sister and mother guarded the entrance. "You'd better! That door is coming off its hinges. Hurry!"

With a nod, Lyrrin ran her fingers over the lines cut into the stone. The song was muffled, dull compared to runes carved on pure crystal. But it was there.

She tried the normal sequence, running her long-nailed fingers up around the main lines, down through the central V line, then up and around, but nothing happened. She tried a variation. Nothing. The thundering crashes at the metal door and roaring from beyond overwhelmed the song from the stone, and she wasn't sure where she went wrong.

"Cover my ears for me?"

Eslinde's eyebrows wrinkled in confusion, but she placed a palm over each of Lyrrin's ears.

Taking a deep breath, Lyrrin tried again.

This has to work. Riony, Dracuni, and the others need us. They need us to get the silvernix for them. Pabba, let me hear the song you created.

Lyrrin moved her fingers slowly, letting the sounds of the stone hum through her, listening deep within. She trailed her fingertip over the final line, and magic lit up in front of her.

Benjin let out a whoop, and Eslinde gasped.

Lyrrin looked up, seeking any symbols they could select for their destination. But there were none. The gateway had opened already, only a single location available.

A gloomy chamber was half-visible through the wavering magic.

The metal of the door wailed like a vengeful spirit, buckling in on one side, and grasping claws thrust through.

Aishena and Kverra backed away to join the others at the magical portal.

A human revenant pushed its head through the broken door, teeth gnashing.

Eslinde turned Lyrrin's shoulders, pushing her toward the gateway. "Wherever this leads has to be better than here. Go!"

Elumon? Come on. Lyrrin waited as the hatchling came quivering to her side again, and they stepped through

together. All the others rushed after, as the metal door crashed down behind them, revenants tumbling into the silvernix chamber. They were on their feet in seconds, racing for the humans.

Lyrrin held her breath as she traced the rune on the other side, and the gateway closed, cutting them off.

Darkness surrounded her. She scrambled for the light stone on her belt and activated it within its netted bag. Cyan light spilled out, revealing the familiar layout of an Alderkin shrine. But not any of the ones Lyrrin had visited in her travels so far.

The gateway in front of her had been changed. The usual rune was carved out, replaced with the altered one that only paired it with the shelf structure in the palace. Her father never revealed the magic of gateways to the king, only this one, different way.

There were gasps and mutterings behind her, and as Lyrrin turned to see the rest of the space, her own jaw dropped.

The stone walls of the shrine building had been hollowed with long niches—shelves filled with hundreds of bottles of silvernix, maybe thousands.

Elumon sniffed hesitantly at the shimmering glass.

"I never thought he'd still have so much," Eslinde exhaled the words in a rush.

"Blessed sun. We really found it. I can't believe it." Kverra shook her head.

"*Lyrrin* really found it," Benjin said.

"I couldn't have without everyone's help, without what everyone knew." Lyrrin blinked a few times, making sure she was really seeing what she was seeing. There'd be enough silvernix there for every injured dragon and rider. If they could get back to them in time.

"Gather up the silvernix quickly." Aishena shook out empty cloth bags and handed them around.

Kverra and Eslinde began plucking the vials and carefully filling the bags.

Aishena grabbed a nearby bottle, and a moment later her dark skin glowed. She groaned and shook out her injured hand.

Benjin had circled the space, then went to look out the doorway. He came back in notably paler. "We still have a problem."

The silvernix collection paused as they all went to see outside. Everything was shadowed, even outside the building, as though night had fallen early. As Lyrrin squinted out beyond the ring of standing stones, the reason for the thick darkness became clear.

The shrine was entirely encompassed with a writhing mass of inky black magic and revenants.

"The first taming ..." Lyrrin whispered. "We're at the shrine where the first taming happened."

They'd seen it once from a distance. A beshadowed, cursed place. The revenants gurgled and growled all around, not just encircling the ground where the standing stones created a protective barrier, but also climbing above them, as though over a glass dome. Only the odd patch of sky showed between them.

Benjin offered a wry half smile. "At least the revs can't get in."

The sheer mass of bottled silvernix stored there no doubt had something to do with that. Keeping the shrine and its protective barrier active.

Lyrrin's own lips puckered. "Yeah, but we can't get out, either."

"How are we going to get the silvernix back to the others?" Eslinde's shoulders slumped. "We can't go back to the palace. And if this is the site of the first taming, we're almost on the other side of Elundrae ..."

"Lyrrin could adjust the gateway!" Benjin said, bouncing with enthusiasm at his idea. "Make it go to one of the other ones, somewhere safe."

Aishena shook her head. "Safe for us, but there aren't any close enough to the capital, and we'd be on foot. We wouldn't be able to get all of this where it needs to be in time."

Benjin wasn't deterred. "Then we send Elumon. He could fly from somewhere closer, carry at least some silvernix with him?"

Elumon whimpered and ducked behind Lyrrin. *Not on my own!*

"It would still be a really long way." Lyrrin turned away from the cursed shadows surround them, stepping back into the shrine.

Cyan light twinkled off the carefully stored bottles of precious fluid. They had more silvernix than anyone could ever need, enough to save everyone, but no way to get it to them that was safe.

Lyrrin ran her hands over the geode crystal, thinking about the shelves of stone that formed the doorway on the other side, the room now flooded with undead. An idea started to form. Utterly reckless. Unlikely survivable.

Riony would approve ... if it were anyone but Lyrrin doing it.

"Maybe it's time we stop trying to be safe ..." she whispered, mostly to herself.

Louder, she said, "Keep loading up all the silvernix, and fill one bag for Elumon to carry. I'm going to open the portal back to the palace, and he's going to carry the silvernix to the others from there."

Eslinde shook her head, pale eyebrows drawn tight together. "That room is filled with revs. They'll set upon us the moment the gateway opens!"

Lyrrin was already picturing what would happen when the magic connected them to that room again. Would they even have a chance to push Elumon through before the revs flooded them? Would they have a chance to fight back? Would they be able to close the gateway again?

Lyrrin pushed away her fear. "It's our best chance of getting silvernix to the others. They used the summoning stone. You know what that means. There are going to be a lot of people and dragons out there who need this. Dracuni included."

The five of them stood in silence for a long moment.

"You're right," Eslinde said finally. "It's what we should do."

Elumon stared up wide-eyed, inhaling sharply through his nose. **No. No, I don't want to go alone.**

His fear stabbed through Lyrrin's mind like a cutting athame. She knelt down beside him, cupping his snout in her hands and locking eyes with him.

I know it's scary. I'm scared too.

Elumon's nostrils flared, and he whimpered.

I'll do everything I can to make sure you'll be safe. And that we will too. And what we're doing here ... it could save so many others too. It could save Dracuni, big sister, all our friends.

You're always brave. Always easy for you. I'm always scared.

Lyrrin half smiled. *You know that's not true. You can feel how I feel. I'm always scared too. I just have to act brave so Riony and Eslinde let me do things.*

Elumon snorted, and his eyelids snapped closed and open again.

"Will he do it?" Eslinde asked gently.

Lyrrin brushed her thumbs over the hatchling's cheeks. Her own little dragon, bonded to her. She wished she could take away all his fear, but she knew he had to learn how to manage it himself. So she just waited for his response.

With a big inhale of breath that puffed out his chest, Elumon nodded once.

Smiling beneath wet eyes, Lyrrin brought him in for a hug. "Aishena, Benjin, Kverra, they'll all keep the revenants off you and me while you get away."

Lyrrin looked to the others for confirmation, and they all nodded.

"I can't say how long we'll keep that many revs at bay, especially if they aren't burning. But we'll do what we can," Aishena said.

Getting back to her feet, Lyrrin stared at the gateway, imagining the room beyond. "I have an idea that might help. But we have to open the gateway again. We have to try this. We need to get the silvernix to the others ... no matter what."

TWENTY-SEVEN

Dracuni came to a plowing stop amid the revenant army.

The crackle and crunch of bony bodies beneath her was louder than a roaring waterfall. Splinters of osseous matter hailed everywhere. Dirt stained black from decades of dragonfire stirred up all around, choking and blinding Riony as she clung to the unidragon's neck.

Not even the pain of the landing channeled through from Dracuni to Riony. She had become so used to sharing her mind with the unidragon's emotions that now without them she felt empty inside.

Opalescent scales slipped under Riony's sweaty hands as she felt for life.

"Come on, you're going to be okay."

You have to be.

A faint thud of a heartbeat still tapped under the scales, but there was no other response.

A growl rumbled from Riony's side. The revenants were undeterred by the dragon crash-landing in their midst. She barely had time to lift her sword, angling the flat edge like a shield as the first of them hit.

Decayed, yellowed claws lashed through the settling dust as undead clambered carelessly over Dracuni to reach their human prey.

"Get off her!" Riony roared.

Wiping grit from her eyes, she swung the thick crystal blade in a wide arc. Glowing purple light trailed after it and one human revenant's head was separated from its neck with a satisfying crack.

Looking around from her perch atop Dracuni, Riony was struck with a gut-clenching terror. An endless mass of undead swarmed her way.

They wouldn't hurt Dracuni themselves. Revenants only went after humans. But that didn't mean many other terrible things couldn't happen to Dracuni if Riony left her there and tried to escape.

As though Dracuni had sent that thought through, urging her to flee, Riony snapped back, "I'm not leaving you!"

Dracuni's head lay on its side in the dirt, eyes closed. Her chest lifted in weak, fluttering breaths.

A horrifically small human revenant scrambled up Dracuni's back, and Riony balked, skidding down the unidragon's neck to the ground away from it. She smashed her sword ahead of her like a battering ram, clearing a path to beside Dracuni's head.

If all the revenants were coming after her, she couldn't let them climb all over Dracuni to get to her. She positioned herself with Dracuni's head to her back and prepared for the next surge of ravenous undead.

Just hold them off until someone comes to help.

Riony batted a scaly white-eyed dreer away, then pivoted to block the grasping claws of more human revenants, both skeletal and far, far too fresh.

A charging bovin revenant crashed into all of them from the side. Its thick-boned skull hammered Riony's shoulder and cheek before she could roll away from it. She came back up onto one knee.

Her heart pumped at a raging pace. She spat dirt and blood. Her face and arm heated from the blow, and she was rolling her shoulder socket to confirm she hadn't lost any motion when a weasel revenant skittered up her back and sank sharp teeth into her neck.

She snatched it in one hand, throwing it off her.

Revenants tumbled in from every direction and crushed over her, burying her in gnashing teeth and scratching claws that poked through her armor and ripped at her face. Riony swung her sword in wild, cutting arcs, cracking through

bodies indiscriminately and desperately.

The area cleared for just long enough for Riony to draw a breath that ached all the way down. She managed to get back up to her feet, and then the undead hit her again. A revenant latched on to one of her arms and she wrenched it free. She just had to keep fighting, just had to keep swinging, keep the revenants off her and Dracuni, just a little longer.

Someone had to have seen her and Dracuni go down. Someone had to come for them. Zeina, Vance, Dashiel, Jaym ...

Kess. Where are you?

Daring a look back at the sky, there was still no sign of the purple dragon and his rider.

Riony's chest squeezed around her panting breaths, caught in the fear that when she'd left Kess on that rooftop, it was the last time they'd ever see each other.

Something sharp stabbed into Riony's back, piercing the armor. Searing pain and the trickle of warm blood followed. She spun blindly and smashed her sword down like a hammer on an anvil over the tusked revenant before it struck again.

The wound was just over her left hip, and her leg wobbled beneath her. She grunted, steeling herself and standing strong as every part of her body screamed.

Then the beat of wings above made the breath in her throat catch.

A white dragon. Iffyr! With Dashiel still riding.

"We're here! Here!" Riony's voice cracked around the words, lost in the roaring battle.

But still the shimmerdart swooped their way and Riony laughed with relief.

The undead assault on her didn't slow, and she backed up closer to Dracuni, waiting and hoping for the shimmerdart to come in and rescue them. If Dashiel was still on the tamed dragon, then they still had their silvernix with them, unspent.

Would it be enough to revive Dracuni? Get them airborne and out of this cesspit of frenzied bone and rotten flesh?

Riony chose to believe it would. Her arms felt heavy and solid as stalagmites as she swung her sword again and again.

Then the shrieks of fighting dragons came from above, and her heart frosted over. A wild flamesong had Iffyr in its claws, wrapping the smaller shimmerdart entirely and wrenching at its taming spike.

Dashiel dangled from the tip of one wing, being flung side to side in the midair wrestling match.

Shiff flew close, darting back and forth, but unable to get through the whirlwind of tails and wings to reach Dashiel. The three dragons and Dashiel went over the capital's high walls, crashing downward into the city on the other side.

"Sparks, no!" Riony wailed.

The stickiness of blood spread across her lower back and every swing of her blade tugged on throbbing wounds all across her body. Blood trickled down one side of her face and the muscles in her arms stung so fiercely she wasn't sure how much longer she could keep fighting.

Above, the battle still raged between tamed dragons, wild dragons, and flying revenants. But the sky seemed clearer now. Whether that was due to newly untamed dragons leaving the area entirely or dying, Riony wasn't sure. A wishful part of her hoped it was because there were fewer undead in the skies.

Then at least her friends still up there on their dragons had a chance.

If they were still up there.

Dragonfire, in shooting darts, fireballs, and streams of flame, made the world glow orange and red. There was more than before ... what were they doing?

Like a meteor crashing to earth, a burning ball of carrion bird hurtled down into the revenants in front of Riony. It smashed apart in a spray of flaming feathers, catching the undead around it on fire as well.

Riony shielded herself as sparks blew across her face. She turned away to keep off the next creature attacking her.

But then she shot a glance back again.

The carrion bird revenant wasn't moving. It wasn't getting up again, feathers or not, to scratch its way across the field to tear into Riony.

It was down. It was dead. It burned and it stayed dead.

Heart pounding, Riony fumbled exhaustion-locked fingers over the burn rune on her sword. It lit up in combination with the float rune, creating flickering hot-pink flames all up the blade.

Muscles screaming from overuse, Riony put her whole body into her next swing, smashing through the wall of undead in front of her. Desiccated flesh and aged bone smoldered and caught alight, and a line of revenants went down with a shrieking roar.

It's working. It's working! The revs are burning again. Do you hear that, Dracuni? We did it. You did it.

Riony sobbed from wonder and relief and the ragged exhaustion of her aching limbs and pain of the jagged scratches in her flesh.

The revs were burning. They were dying by fire and staying dead.

Casting watering eyes upward, Riony sent a thank you to all the factory dragons who had come in and untamed their kin, to all the riders who had risked their lives to heal their untamed dragons, to the stars watching down from above.

They'd done it.

They'd untamed enough dragons to make a difference. Finally.

Even if this was the end for her, for Dracuni, they had

weakened the curse enough that there would be hope for those left behind. Some may survive. That was something. That had to be enough.

Distracted in that moment, Riony missed the next attack. Snapping jaws crushed around Riony's waist, long fangs digging in between the scales of her armor.

She roared with pain, bringing her flaming sword around to knock the revenant off her.

It gurgled a scream as it backed away from the burning sword, angling around to strike again from the other side.

The large, four-legged predatory creature was so mangy Riony couldn't tell what it had once been. It snapped at her again, catching her wrist as Riony tried to dodge a snarling human skeleton.

For every revenant she struck down with fire, a hundred more were there to take its place, and everything hurt. Sweat mixed with blood and ash and ran into Riony's eyes, smearing the world into a gray and red nightmare.

Her heart and lungs were ready to give up and Riony trembled all over from overworked muscles and exhaustion. And the revenants kept coming.

A flapping sound came through the turmoil, small and distant, barely louder than the thudding pulse within her own ears.

Could it be Dashiel? Did Iffyr get free, or maybe Shiff? Riony shot a look over her shoulder, desperate with hope.

"*Elumon?*" Riony gasped.

The small hatchling's wings worked hard to keep it up as it flew unevenly overhead, carrying a loaded sack in his claws.

"How did you ...?" Riony grunted as claws lashed down her cheek, and she turned her focus back to the fight around her, burning the next line of revenants away with a wavering, clumsy swing.

The momentum of the attack sent her broken body tumbling, and she cracked down onto one knee.

Elumon was there, carrying something.

It has to be silvernix. They found it. Lyrrin found it!

Riony didn't know what was going on, why he was alone, how the hatchling had flown all the way there from the private palace so fast.

Had she been fighting for that long? It felt like forever.

"Here! Down here, quick!" she bellowed into the air above, waving her flaming sword in a circle to get his attention.

The hatchling pivoted, changing direction and dropping down their way.

The small pale dragon looked so much like how Dracuni did when she was younger, and a hot sting of tears scrunched Riony's face.

A human revenant grappled her from one side, pinning her sword arm to her body as it tried to chew through the armor at her shoulder, crunching scales and leather in its stinking maw.

On her knees, Riony braced as another skeleton grabbed her from the other side. Her fist cracked against its face, but it was on her again a moment later.

Elumon flew closer. The little thing looked terrified, hovering over Riony.

She wished she could communicate with him, the way she could with Dracuni. But she had to hope he could just hear her anyway and cooperate.

"Dracuni first," Riony gasped out in a scream as the revenant chewing her shoulder moved up to her neck. "DRACUNI FIRST! HEAL HER, NOW!"

There was a startling, tearing sound at her neck and pain exploded through Riony, blurring out everything else.

All she could think was *get to Dracuni. Heal her.*

Dracuni needed to be saved. But it was so long since Riony had been able to spare a glance her way, she didn't even know if the unidragon was still breathing.

Claws dug deep into the back of her scalp and a heavy weight of bodies crushed over her, pushing her down onto her stomach. She tried to fight them off, but every limb was weighed down, heavy with exhaustion and sticky with hot blood.

More and more revenants covered over her, all trying to reach through and dig into her skin and pull her to pieces, creating a thick mass over her, squashing the air from her lungs and blocking out all light above, leaving Riony drowning under the churning wave of undead.

TWENTY-EIGHT

"There's more over there." Kess leaned over Lyomir's neck to the right, leading him toward the huddle of humans in the alleyway below.

They were backed into a dead end, and a horde of revenants stampeded their way, a tornado of snarling jaws and scrambling limbs.

With a gruff snort of air, Lyomir swooped low, catching on to the side of the building with one claw above the screaming people, lowering the other leg over their heads and down between them.

Kess called from her saddle, "Get on!"

The people jumped up onto Lyomir's talons, clutching around his leg in a tangle, all holding on to each other and the dragon as he lifted them into the air again.

With the humans cleared, Lyomir blasted a fireball down into the space. It hit the incoming revenants, the fire rolling along between the stone walls of the narrow street.

Kess watched, grinning viciously as the revenants burned. They crumpled under the scorching heat and didn't move again.

Riony's reckless plan had worked. Finally. *Finally.*

Another burst of screams came from the rescued people below as flames licked around them, but Lyomir flew them clear. He turned sharply, heading toward the high, glossy stone tower in the center of the palace where they'd left all the other survivors they'd plucked from the chaos below.

The sloped roof was perilous but still safer than being on the ground among the revs. Lyomir hovered above it as the newest batch of rescues climbed off, assisted by those below, all clinging to each other to keep anyone from toppling off the steep edge.

The tower was tall enough and smooth-walled enough that it would be safe for a while longer. Depending on when the battle turned. If it ever would.

The revs were burning, but few riders remained in the air who could do that, and there were so, so many revenants.

Kess gave a worried glance over all the people there. Both civilians fished out from within the city and riders with float runes thrown from their newly untamed dragons. They wouldn't fit many more on.

Most of the city was clear of people, and Kess hoped it

was because they were all hiding, like Kess had told them to do. But enough people had either not heard the message, not listened to it, or were caught out to keep Kess busy saving them from the revs.

Kess and Lyomir had been scooping people up nonstop since he'd found her on the rooftop where Riony had left her.

They hadn't even had a chance to get back into the main battle. Kess saw Riony fly by on Dracuni once, but it was a while ago. Her mouth was dry and heart felt raw with worry.

"Up again. Let's see who else we can find."

How many more? Lyomir thought back like a groan.

"All of them."

We can't save them all, little thing.

"But we're going to try. Come on. You're not saying you're tired, are you?"

Lyomir scoffed in a gust of smoky air and took them high above the city.

The sky over the battle surrounding the walls was clearer, and down within the roiling field of undead, something large lit up bright.

Probably another tamed dragon being healed after its stake was removed. But it was already down on the ground, which meant its rider would need help.

Kess tapped Lyomir on the neck to signal their heading, and he shot that way with a gusting beat of his wings.

Kess squinted through her flight goggles as the light below dimmed, and her heart flung itself into her throat, cutting off her breath.

Dracuni.

"Faster! Go faster!" Kess cried.

The unidragon lay within a mass of bodies. Many weren't moving, scattered around the dragon and still smoking. But in front of Dracuni, a pile of revenants squirmed and fought over something like a flock of gulls over a fish out of water.

No, no, no. Riony! It couldn't be anyone else drawing the revs fury. Only Riony would be so razing stupid to have stayed there with Dracuni amid all of that.

Faster. Faster! Kess pleaded. She couldn't see Riony herself within the piling bodies. If she was under there … they weren't going to reach her in time.

Lyomir pushed faster anyway, and as they swooped down, Dracuni stirred. The unidragon lifted up tall, wailing a growling, sorrowful cry, and then she breathed.

Silver flame rushed over the mound of revenants in front of her. Agonized, inhuman cries filled the air and the undead twitched and writhed under the blast of healing magic.

Kess held her breath as Lyomir brought them down, crashing over the revenants on the other side of the reforming mountain of corpses and silver fire.

"Riony? Riony!" Kess yelled. She wished she could

leap down from Lyomir's back and search through the butcher's yard below to find the woman she loved more than anything else. To find her alive.

She's underneath. The little bright one said.

Kess's blood turned cold.

Dracuni's flaming ended, and she heaved deep breaths, legs wobbling beneath her. On her back, Elumon clutched on to her saddle, cowering and wings trembling.

Kess stared wide-eyed and numb at the pile of bodies as tall as Lyomir. "We have to get her out ... She ... she ..."

Kess's worries filled her head with screams.

Would Dracuni's flame have reached Riony under there? Would it even matter if she was crushed again?

Was she even still alive to have been healed?

The army of revs roared all around them and it was nothing compared to the roaring of Kess's own heart.

Lyomir turned on the spot, sending a quick succession of fireballs out into the approaching army around them. It blasted the revenants back, creating a clearing around them ringed in fire.

Kess shifted to the side to climb off Lyomir, and he shrugged a shoulder roughly, pushing her back into the saddle.

Stay. It's dangerous.

With a snap of his jaws, he picked up the top layer of corpses and flung them away. Dracuni worked on the other side, dragging bodies off the pile with her teeth and claws.

Together the dragons dug down through the smoking mound, fast at first, and then more carefully as they got closer to the bottom layers, to the ground and what lay beneath.

Kess flung her flight goggles off so she could wipe her eyes.

As the charcoal-stained dirt below came into view, so did the glint of gold and blue scale mail and a vibrant flop of red hair.

"Riony!" Kess squealed her name and launched herself off Lyomir's back.

He gave a warning growl but didn't stop her that time.

She slipped down his shoulder, landing on soft bodies of healed revenants. Panting hard through clenched teeth, Kess crawled swiftly over to Riony's side.

Dracuni cooed songlike sounds, nudging her nose against Riony's shoulder. The scale mail and padding below had been torn clear away there and across her middle and around her neck. The bare skin beneath was slick and red but whole, no gaping wounds showing.

Still, Riony didn't move.

Kess fell on top of Riony, grasping her face in both hands and pressing a salty kiss over her forehead. The ground all around was muddy with spilled blood.

"Wake up. Come on. You can't leave me now. Not now. We did it. The revs are dying. You broke the curse. You saved us, and you need to be here to see what you've done."

The sounds of more fireballs being shot out to keep the revenants back roared over Kess's shoulder, but she could only look at Riony's closed eyes, her crimson-spattered cheeks, searching for any sign of life.

Kess bared her teeth in an effort to fight off tears. "I love you. Don't leave me."

A soft, low groan parted Riony's lips. Her voice came out rough and scratchy. "Not ... going ... anywhere."

Kess sobbed in relief.

Riony's eyes remained closed. Her shoulder shifted as though trying to lift her arm, and she grunted and lay still again. "Sparks. I feel like I've been entirely pulled apart and put back together again."

Kess peppered her cheek with teary kisses. "I think you were, you razing, tame-brained maniac."

Overhead, Dracuni grumbled and huffed as though in agreement.

Riony smirked. "Glad you're okay too, Dracuni. Also, like you can talk."

Finally, she opened her eyes, lids peeling back slowly, and she grunted as she raised a wobbling hand.

"I was worried about you." Her fingers brushed over Kess's lips. "Is it over? Did we win? Did I kill all the revs? I feel like I killed a lot."

Kess laughed and eyed the smoldering bodies around them and the still flaming sword lying to Riony's side. "You took down a few."

"A few?"

"Don't worry. I'll make sure you get your 'killed the most revs single-handedly' prize later." Kess's eyes were locked with Riony's, her insides roaring with relief that she was still with her. "Just a few hundreds of thousands still to clear up and we're done."

Lyomir sent out another volley of fireballs. All around, the crackle of fire echoed and a gust of smoke made Kess's eyes sting.

"Is that all?" Riony winced as she sat upright. "Back to work, then."

Kess held her shoulders, helping to steady her, and Riony slumped forward, resting her forehead on Kess's shoulder.

"Take a breather. You're exhausted. Lyomir is keeping the revs off us."

Riony's head shook, rolling against Kess. "The battle isn't over until a bard writes an epic ballad about it."

"I'll get Jaym to work on that." Kess wrapped her arms around Riony, feeling her warm and tacky with drying blood.

Riony lifted her head, tilting it toward Dracuni in silent conversation.

What is it? Kess directed to Lyomir.

A tamed dragon with your human friends is coming in. Little bright one hears his bonded child. Lyomir flicked his snout skyward.

Kess followed the direction, seeing an orange dragon coming their way.

Kess hadn't thought much of Elumon's presence there a moment ago. The hatchling was the least of her concerns while Riony was buried under bodies. But she turned her eyes to him again where he sat atop Dracuni.

His wings fluttered with excitement as Ambri got closer and he had a cloth sack beneath his claws, filled with clinking glass.

A bag full of silvernix? They'd found it. Lyrrin and the others must have found the king's supply.

"How did they ...?"

Riony squinted. "Not sure. Dracuni is trying to pass on what Elumon is saying, but the kid is way too overexcited to be making much sense. But he's guiding Lyrrin here."

The orange dragon glided in, circling once before coming to land in the cleared area around Dracuni. Aishena rode up front with Benjin, Eslinde, and Lyrrin at the back, and Kverra Hjelzahn was in the middle, holding a sixth passenger beside her.

Her dark hair was coiffed in intricate braids to highlight the white streaks in the front, her fine gown wrinkled, and she glared petulantly.

"You stole yourself a queen?" Kess raised her eyebrows.

Eslinde climbed down the dragon's side. She held up a bag, heavy with vials. "Her and more."

Kverra Hjelzahn pushed the queen down next, and

Eslinde clamped a hand on her mother's shoulder.

Riony said, "Lyrrin's grandmother? Can't say it's a pleasure."

The queen snarled and looked away, then seemed to take in the horde of revenants around them and her face blanched.

Groaning all the way up, Riony got to her feet, stretched, then loped over to help Lyrrin down from the dragon's back. Benjin jumped down beside them.

Aishena remained in the saddle, directing the tamed dragon around and burning a rush of incoming revs. "There are still tamed dragons in the sky and others downed we might be able to help. Are you okay here?"

Riony nodded once. "Go. Dashiel and Iffyr went down over the wall, that way, not long ago. Do what you can."

Aishena's dark eyes glinted, her chest heaved, and she took Ambri speeding back up into the air, Kverra going with them.

Kess remained on the ground. Her thundering pulse, brought on from the fear Riony had been lost, was only just easing, when the news of Dashiel sent it racing again. She began making her way back to Lyomir, pulling herself up onto his back. Riony had been right before; there was still so much to do.

Riony had Lyrrin scooped in a crushing hug, and when she put the girl down, her blue eyes were wide with disgust as she looked over Riony's shoulder at all the bodies of revenants around them.

"What happened here?"

Riony shrugged. "You know, the usual. What about you? How did you get back so fast from the private palace?"

"We didn't go. I realized the king didn't keep the silvernix there. He kept his access to it here in the capital palace." Lyrrin's voice was high and clipped with excitement.

Kess paused as she reached the saddle, looking back. "The one that was filled with revenants?"

Benjin bounced, making the twin swords at his hips jangle against his armor. "Lyrrin got us out! She worked out how she could use the very stone the palace was made from like crystals."

Lyrrin smiled bashfully. "Well, they already sort of were crystal, partially. The pale streaks in the marble held enough crystal to channel the magic. That was how my father made the gateway for the king, so I didn't really work it out myself. I just did what Alleem had done."

Kess shook her head, not quite following the rambling children.

Benjin crowed, "She made the whole floor one giant magic crystal by carving a rune on it! A burn rune!"

Lyrrin shrugged modestly. "It was lucky we had all the bottled silvernix to charge it up."

"It roasted every rev all the way along! Like PHWOOSH! So much fire! I think I lost my eyebrows!" Benjin lifted his arms in the air, mimicking an explosion.

Eslinde laughed softly. "It was deeply terrifying. But it cleared the way back to Ambri."

The hatchling jumped down from Dracuni's back then, pale wings fluttering, and he ran up to Lyrrin.

She crouched beside him, smiling. "But we sent Elumon ahead, because we weren't sure at first it was going to work."

"I'm glad you did," Riony said. "He arrived just in time."

Kess settled herself in her saddle and wiped the remnants of tears off her face. "We should get moving again. Get all that silvernix where it will do some good and—"

Lyomir tensed beneath her, and a vast shadow flashed over them through the clouds of smoke.

"No!" Riony cried, running toward Dracuni.

A massive silver and gold shape dropped over the unidragon, grasping her in talons like scooping her in a net. Dracuni bleated, squirming in the king's dragon's hold as it lifted skyward again.

"Let her go!" Riony roared.

Yeonard Draekhan, the Dragon King, turned his enormous dragon around to face all those below him, and flame flickered in its mouth.

"We have Vellira! We have your wife!" Eslinde's voice boomed over the scrambling sounds of Riony running for her sword and Lyomir growling beneath Kess.

Eslinde grasped the queen by her shoulder and pushed her in front of them all, beneath the silver and gold dragon's jagged, old teeth.

"Give Dracuni back, and you can have her," Eslinde yelled.

Vellira's expression brightened, and she reached both arms up toward her husband.

The threat of flaming ended, and the dragon's mouth closed. From atop the saddle, the Dragon King peered down at his wife and daughter with a cold, hard expression. Something akin to disappointment.

Then he turned his dragon around and flew away, taking Dracuni with him.

"My king? My king!" Vellira cried out.

"Dracuni!" Riony scooped her sword up, but the long wings of the dragon had already lifted them far out of reach.

"Up here, quick!" Kess called to her, and Riony came running.

Vellira's head was shaking, her face scrunched in denial. "No. No! My king, you're taking me with you. You have to take me with you!"

She shook off Eslinde's hold on her, running after the flying dragon, stumbling over the bodies littering the ground.

Riony jumped, landing heavily onto Lyomir's back behind Kess.

But Kess's eyes were on the queen's mad rush. "Watch out. Catch her!"

The woman was running blindly into the surrounding

mass of revenants.

Eslinde charged a few steps after her mother, but Lyrrin grabbed her hand, pulling her back. A surge of revenants braved the wall of flame around the clearing as the queen drew near, the lure of her human flesh too strong.

They burst through, the first undead creatures burning and collapsing around the screaming woman, but their bodies smothered the flames the fell on, clearing a gap and more poured over them. They dragged the shrieking woman down and her screams cut out.

Eslinde yelped a gasp and pulled Lyrrin in, turning her head away from the sight. Benjin stood in front of them, both swords drawn.

Lyomir snarled, shooting another fireball toward where the revs were breaking through.

Lyrrin turned her head while staying within Eslinde's arms. Her vibrant eyes glimmered with tears but her expression was firm.

She yelled up to Kess and Riony. "Go! Go and get Dracuni!"

"What about you?" Riony yelled back, her eyes locked on the king's escaping dragon.

"Viska's coming in. We'll be okay. Go!" Lyrrin cried with her full chest.

Kess glanced back at Riony for confirmation.

Riony held her flaming sword low in one hand, as though too tired to lift it properly. Her blood-smeared

face was crumpled, and she turned a pained look from her sister to Kess and nodded.

Kess joined her thoughts with her dragon. *Go. Go fast. You can catch up to them, can't you?*

Lyomir growled in reply. He stretched his purple wings wide, breaking into a running start so fast he churned up the dirt and bodies beneath him. They cut into the air at a dizzying speed.

The shape of the king's dragon was already small, far ahead in the dimming sky. Yeonard Draekhan flew out over the water, away from the harbor. Away from the capital. Away from Elundrae itself. Leaving all the devastation behind.

Twenty-Nine

Riony crouched behind Kess as Lyomir sped them across the water after the Dragon King and Dracuni, every muscle in her body strained.

Even with having been healed by Dracuni's flame, Riony's limbs all ached down to the bone from exhaustion and also probably also from being crushed under the hundreds of revs that had died reformed on top of her.

She shook out her arms, stretched her shoulders, and clenched her jaw, trying to will enough energy to return. Lyomir was gaining on the massive silver and gold beast the king rode, and she *would* get Dracuni back. She could feel the unidragon's fear from there, stabbing into her heart.

I'm coming. It's going to be okay.

"What's your plan?" Kess's voice blew to Riony on

the smoky wind.

She pointed with her glowing purple sword. "I'll hack that dragon's legs right off if I have to."

Kess drew the cutting athame Riony had given her from where it was concealed in her armor and handed it back. "You get Dracuni free. Lyomir and I will try to keep the king and dragon busy."

Riony stared at the body-warmed crystal knife in the palm of her hand. The day she'd found it was the same day she first saw Dracuni's egg. She closed her fingers around it so tight the chipped edges dug into her skin, then she tucked it away safely.

Kess pulled her flight goggles off from where they were sitting atop her head. "Have these too. You're going to need them more than me."

Riony took them gratefully since hers were long gone and she was going to have to get over to the king's dragon somehow. She didn't want to be squinting into the wind while she launched herself through the air.

She wiped her eyes as clear as she could from the dust and tears and blood and yanked the goggles on. Holding her breath, she looked over her shoulder to where her sister, Eslinde, and Benjin had been left behind.

A wall of fire surrounded them, offering some protection from the revs, and Vance and Viska had been close, but Riony's heart still rattled with the fear of leaving her loved ones behind in the middle of all those monsters.

Air rushed out of Riony's mouth in relief as she saw the golden dragon on the ground, collecting her family, but that relief faded fast as a red and white dragon and king's rider swooped toward Riony from the side.

"Watch out," she called to Kess and Lyomir.

The purple dragon banked hard as the snowflame sent a jet of liquid fire their way. The two dragons spiraled around each other, and Kess sent a couple of blades flinging toward the rider. They clinked off the grayglim's armor. The snowflame angled over them, forcing Lyomir down and away from the chase toward the king.

Swooping low, Lyomir skimmed the waves of the harbor with one wingtip as he came back around. The king's rider stayed close on his tail, matching every move.

"We're not losing this guy easily." Kess narrowed her eyes as she watched behind them. "And he's slowing us down."

Riony hefted her sword up, glaring at the king and his dragon up ahead. "Just get me close."

Kess nodded, and Lyomir dived toward the white-caped sea. He sped down so fast that Riony had to cling tight to Kess to avoid being left behind, and then the dragon's wings shot out and they catapulted back up high into the air. Leathery wings pumped hard and icy, salt-spray wind whistled around them.

The burst of speed brought them up behind the king's massive dragon. Dracuni hung within its claws, her tail and head and one wing hanging free from the cage of talons. She squirmed and bleated.

Big sister! It's too tight. I can't get out.

I'm coming to get you.

Be careful.

Me? Always.

Dracuni's emotions surged unchecked through Riony. All her desperation and anger and worry for Riony washed through like a burning tide, leaving Riony's exhausted mind dizzy.

As Lyomir came up higher, over the gold and silver tail, Riony put one hand on Kess's shoulder, squeezed, didn't want to let go, then did.

She jumped, careening through the air. Jumping, and falling, had become second nature to her, and she angled her body, bringing her feet around and bending into the landing.

Riony's muscles screamed in protest as she landed hard on the shimmering scales of the king's dragon, and for a moment, her exhaustion, the gusting wind, and the combining emotions of Dracuni's hope and fear all threatened to overwhelm her. She slipped, landing on hands and knees, grasping on to the back of the king's saddle to avoid tumbling off the dragon's back entirely.

Are you okay?

I made it. Just one old man to deal with and I've got you.

Dracuni's emotions surged again, but the bitter edge

of fear had gone. Now there was only the warmth of hope, of love, of trust shared between them.

Riony let that power run through her, warming and revitalizing her body. She shook her head, steeling herself.

The Dragon King turned to her with cold precision, his silver-bright and midnight-dark eyes gleaming unnaturally as they landed on Riony.

His voice boomed. "*Who are you?*"

Riony rose to her feet, holding her sword out like a challenge. "Hi. We've never met. But you've tortured and killed so many of my loved ones that I really feel as though we're close, you know?"

His eyes narrowed, and intricate silver braids whipped in the wind.

Riony lifted her chin at him. "Now let go of my dragon and I might go easy on you."

"You've made a mistake, ridiculous child," he drawled. "I have not ruled this land for eighty years by being weak."

In a languid motion, the king stood up on his saddle, drawing a gleaming steel sword.

Riony scoffed. "Mine's bigger."

The king swung at her, neat and practiced and so fast Riony almost missed it. She deflected the strike with her crystal blade, but the king was already bringing another blow around toward her middle, where her armor had been torn away.

She had to jump backward to avoid being gutted. She

slipped down the dragon's spine and grabbed one of its spikes to steady herself.

Sparks, he's good.

Even with the training Aishena had given her, Riony realized the disadvantage she was at. What was a year of lessons compared to decades and decades of practice?

Riony considered simply running, climbing down the dragon's side and cutting Dracuni free. But while ever this cruel monster of a man before her lived, Dracuni would never be safe. And as the king marched down the dragon's spine toward her, it was clear he didn't intend to let her go either.

"You're the one who created this creature, who has kept it from me." He tilted his head as he looked her up and down, lips curled.

"And I'm the one who's going to beat your ass until you learn you can't just take anything you want."

Riony rushed him, barreling in so recklessly toward the man it caught him off guard. He dodged sideways and Riony pulled her swinging blade after her, connecting a hit. The blow struck his shoulder, sending silver and red scales from his armor clattering away, cutting right through.

The king scowled, glaring at the swell of blood staining his skin. He slapped one hand against the hilt of his sword. The rings he wore clacked against the metal, and he lit up with the glow of silvernix. The wound was sealed before Riony's eyes.

The light hadn't even faded before the tip of the king's blade caught Riony under the chin, leaving her jaw stinging and bloody.

She had no silvernix left to heal every blow. She should have taken some from the stolen supplies, but the urgency to fly after Dracuni was too great. Pain was something Riony was familiar with though. She'd take as many hits as she had to, would keep fighting through all of it, to save her Dracuni.

She raged, throwing everything she had left against the man. Swing after swing she met his sword, but every time she got a blow through, the crack of breaking glass and glow of silvernix followed. Every time the king struck her, she bled more.

He carefully targeted the torn away gaps in her armor, jabbing the point of his sword into her belly, slicing across her shoulder, nicking her neck.

Desperation flared in Riony's chest. Her arms shook, weaker with every swing. Her breath came in ragged gasps. Every muscle in her body burned hotter than dragonflame. She smashed her sword toward the king again, only to have it deflected with an effortless parry.

Back across the water, Lyomir still clashed with the king's grayglim. The rest of the battle was far behind, the city and all the people and revenants warring within just a smoky smudge on the horizon. Nobody else was coming to help.

I can't stop now. I can't give up. I won't.

The king would run out of silvernix eventually. He *had* to.

With a roar, Riony flung herself at him again, blades clashing in a flurry of strikes. The king's movements were smooth and easy, while each of Riony's felt like dragging her limbs through quicksand.

Her body wanted to give out, but she kept pressing, pushing through every ounce of pain and exhaustion.

She landed a hit on his thigh, her sword biting deep. The blow sent the king reeling, and he fell onto his knees, then back. Another crack came from his rings, and he growled as the silvernix took effect.

But Riony wasn't going to wait for him to heal again. She stepped over him, bracing against the howling wind, raising her sword to strike.

"Carve! Ten point, left, upper!" Yeonard Draekhan bellowed, eyes flashing.

Riony hesitated. "What?"

The dragon's shoulders shifted, sending Riony scrambling backward to rebalance. Then its head came whipping around at a terrifying speed, jaws wide.

A sharp snap echoed through the sky as its teeth clamped down, right where Riony had been standing a moment ago.

She would have been swallowed whole if she hadn't fallen back.

But that wasn't much consolation as the dragon still managed to catch on to her leg.

Pain shot through her like wildfire, and she screamed, feeling bone grind beneath the dragon's crushing teeth. Her sword fell from her hand, clattering uselessly against the beast's spine and dropping off into the waves below.

No!

The world spun and darkened at the edges.

A great, wailing scream was torn from Riony's throat as the dragon whipped its head forward again, taking her with it. She hung like a rag doll from its mouth, her left leg from the knee down trapped between immense, crushing teeth.

Dracuni's fear spiked, and the world burned bright.

Riony cried out as the unidragon's flame flickered around her in a puff. The healing magic stung as it closed the multitude of bleeding wounds across Riony. It tried to fix the splintered bones and shredded flesh of her leg, but the limb remained trapped in the dragon's bite, crushing it again as swiftly as it healed, trapping Riony in a repeating loop of agony that shattered her senses.

Roaring through gritted teeth, Riony fought to stay conscious. She couldn't stop. She couldn't give in.

Dangling upside down, Riony was in line with where Dracuni was trapped in the dragon's claws. From somewhere above, the king laughed and called another strange order to his dragon.

Riony braced, reaching wildly for her sword before the creature swallowed her whole.

It's gone. My sword is gone.

The gold and silver scales of the dragon's jaw shimmered in the fading sunset as it opened. And then smashed closed again.

Riony shrieked as pain lanced through her. The dragon's jaw chomped again and again in a mechanical chewing action.

A terrible thought turned Riony's insides cold. *He's toying with me. He's going to let his dragon chew on me as long as he can.*

Dracuni keened a songlike cry. A puff of healing flame gusted around Riony again as she felt herself fading, the magic renewing her just enough to feel every crushing bite acutely again.

And still the dragon chewed, breaking bones as fast as they healed.

Stars swirled across Riony's vision, and sickness swelled through her. She heaved breaths to stay conscious. Blood ran down her leg, her stomach, splattered on her face.

Stop. Dracuni, stop! I have to get free. You're only going to use yourself up otherwise.

But you're hurting, you're hurting! The panic cut deep into her thoughts.

Riony wished she had the wherewithal to keep her emotions and pain in check, to stop sharing them with

Dracuni, but it was all she could do to not simply scream and scream and scream.

I have to get free.

Riony blindly patted around her pockets and withdrew the cutting athame with trembling fingers. Her vision blurred as she traced the rune, fumbled it, then finally got the sequence right.

Roaring with effort, Riony folded at the waist, bringing herself up. She pressed her hands against the scaly lips of the massive creature. Saliva and blood hung in strings all around as she grabbed on to the lower lip with one hand to hold herself up. With the other, she slashed with the cutting athame at the dragon's teeth.

The aged, yellow fangs her mangled leg was pinned between were already jagged and broken from decades of use, but each was as thick as a tree trunk. The glowing athame cut long, crisscrossed gashes through them.

Riony swung from the motion of flight and her vision darkened and she couldn't hit the same place twice to cut deep enough to free herself.

A combined scream and sob of frustration ripped from her.

Let me heal you again. Let me!

No. No! Riony could already feel how weak the use of the flame had made Dracuni. She'd expended so much since using it on the pile of revenants.

Riony clung on to the dragon's lower jaw, panting

through bared teeth, tears filling the tight seal inside her flight goggles. Her head shook as she realized what she had to do.

No. Don't heal me yet, she thought to Dracuni. *Soon. You'll know when.*

Her fingers trembled as she drew a steadying breath. She knew what she had to do. If she didn't act, she wasn't going to last much longer anyway. She had one last chance to get free. And she had to, to save Dracuni, to see all those she loved again. She *had to.*

For Dracuni and the world and what Dracuni meant to the world.

She had to.

Riony looked up to the sky, bruised by dusk and smoke, hoping to see her ancestors, her parents in the stars to give her strength. But the rallying reply to her wishes came from within her.

A warmth, a tugging pull of powerful love.

All the support and strength she needed came from the love she had for those around her, Lyrrin, Aishena, Benjin, Niskina, Eslinde, Dashiel, Vance, Zeina, Jaym, Dracuni, and Kess. And the love they gave her in return. She would do anything for them.

Anything.

Riony brought Myrwa's shawl up from her neck, filling her mouth with the fabric and biting down. Then she swung the cutting athame again.

And plunged it down through the flesh above her knee.

Bile rushed up her throat and searing pain sent her reeling as the crystal sank through like a knife through mist. Skin, bone, skin again. Riony's skin flushed hot and cold all over and her hands shuddered as agony blinded her.

The athame slipped from her grasp. Her leg ... what was left of it, fell from the dragon's mouth.

Her body swung free heavily, jarring her, and she felt her grip on the dragon's jaw slipping as well.

In a roaring cry, Dracuni's flame engulfed her. Riony's fingers slid over wet scales as the magic worked down her leg like molten metal through her veins, knitting torn flesh and regrowing bone. The wound closed, neat and round over a partially reformed knee, and then the pain ended.

Riony's hands scrambled for purchase, clinging to the mouth of the creature as though it were a life raft while it continued to chew on the parts of her that were left behind.

Your leg! What did you do?

What I had to do.

I'm sorry.

It's not your fault.

Even though the pain ended, Riony's head swam with exhaustion. She felt every bit as chewed up and spit out as she was. She had no weapons left. And if she fell ...

We're finishing this. One way or another. I'm not stopping until you're free.

Dracuni trilled sadly, her tufted tail and loose wing

struggling futilely against the giant dragon's talons.

It was a long way up to get on top of the dragon's head again and then a risky path down its neck to reach the king. Maybe she could try to throw herself over to Dracuni instead, but she'd lost the cutting athame.

Turning her face upward, Riony prepared herself to climb.

The dragon continued chewing, and above one of its dull eyes, a polished length of wood jutted out.

The tale of the first taming, the mural in the undercity, flashed through Riony's mind. How Yeonard Draekhan had thrown a spear at the dragon summoned by the Alderkin after he'd murdered a unicorn. The spear covered in silvernix. It was still in there, just like a taming spike.

Riony knew what she had to do. She flung her first arm up, clasping fingers around the ridge over the dragon's upper lip.

Do you have another healing breath in you?

Dracuni's thoughts had grown dim since she healed Riony's amputation. ***I think ... one more?***

That's all we need. Be ready.

Riony groaned as she reached her other arm up beside the first, dragging her body over the dragon's mouth. Her fingers cramped and were slick with sweat and dragon spit.

Stars, I can barely hold on.

She brought one foot up onto the dragon's bottom lip and tried to bring the other up to meet it. She slipped as

her phantom leg, only air, failed to hold her.

"Sparks!" She pressed herself to the dragon's snout to stop from falling.

Dracuni yelped.

I'm okay. This is just going to take some getting used to.

Teeth bared, she climbed again. She clung from her fingertips onto the dragon's nostril ridge, edging her way up. Cringing, she got one foot into the corner of the dragon's eye. It didn't react, didn't even blink as she hoisted herself over its eyelid.

But then it stopped chewing.

"How did you ...?" The king's voice boomed her way, outraged. "Skyward, buck!"

The dragon's head flicked upward. Riony's foot slipped, and her body flung sideways as she clung tight to the creature's eyelid. She grinned viciously as the motion brought her higher. She let go as the dragon nodded its head down again, rising up over its eye ridge and landing beside the spear.

She knelt there, unevenly on mismatched legs, both hands wrapped around the aged, polished wood as the dragon's head flicked up again.

Keeping her fingers wrapped tight, Riony wrenched at the spear. The brittle wood crackled in her grasp, sliding with a slow, painful suction. Riony leaned backward, putting her whole body into the motion as the dragon bucked up and down, trying to throw her off.

"Come on, come on!" Riony screamed over the whipping wind and whomp of massive wings.

And the spear slipped free.

Now! Riony rolled down the dragon's snout, grasping for purchase as her final pull left her unbalanced. The dragon bucked again, and she tumbled into the air over its head, then slammed down onto her back between its eyes.

A gust of silver fire hit the massive dragon from below.

Riony stared up at the sky as the dragon stilled, and a long, winding ribbon of black smoke rushed down toward them. It passed right through her, and then the dragon roared.

The sound rumbled beneath Riony like sky full of thunder.

"No, no!" the king yelled. He slapped his hands over the dragon's back, yelling a stream of commands.

The dragon was no longer listening.

Riony rolled onto hands and knees, staring with a vicious smile down the dragon's neck toward the man.

The dragon's head flung upward sharply again. With the spear dislodged, Riony had nothing to hold on to, and she was sent flying high above.

Riony held her breath, eyes narrowed, fingers still wrapped tight around the spear she'd pulled free. She arched up, body weightless for a moment at the summit. Then she angled around, targeting her landing.

Falling had become so easy for her.

Riony steadied the spear as she plummeted down again. The Dragon King stared back from his saddle, mouth open in horror as his newly wild dragon writhed beneath him, and Riony came crashing down over him.

The tip of the spear hit him in the center of his chest, plunging right through the armor, and out the other side.

The ageless man howled, pressing up to his feet and stumbling backward down the dragon. "You can't … you can't kill me. Nothing can kill me."

Sprawled on the dragon's neck where she landed, Riony smirked up at him. "Anything can seem impossible until it happens. And I've always had big dreams."

Silver light burst from the king's skin again as he used another dose of silvernix. He gurgled as the spear shifted around his healing organs but remained skewered through him. He cracked another ring, pushing against the end of the spear, trying to force it out of him as the light glowed again.

The dragon swerved sharply. The king stumbled, slipped. He rolled, clattering down the length of the dragon's back and off the end of its tail.

Riony clung to his saddle, her breath panting like sobs as the king screamed and cursed as he fell into the air, silvernix making him glow like a falling star.

With that much silvernix, he could survive the spear … Could he survive the fall too? Riony pushed herself upright. She wanted to get to her feet, to dive after the man and make sure he didn't make it, even if she went with him, but her single leg scrambled uselessly beneath her.

The silver and gold dragon roared again. The sound was filled with fury and vengeance, like the wails of newborn life combined with the power of the ocean, so loud Riony's ears ached.

The beast veered suddenly, diving after the king. Riony cried out, wrapping herself around the saddle to hold on. What was the monstrous creature doing?

Whatever it wanted. Riony swallowed hard. She and Dracuni had to get out of there.

Dracuni?

No reply came.

Are you okay? Dracuni?

The silver and gold dragon's massive jaws hinged open as they came up behind the falling king. The teeth slammed closed around the man who had kept it enslaved for eighty years. Bone crunched and blood sprayed up over the dragon's snout.

Riony's eyebrows raised. She was fairly certain there was no surviving that.

She wiped her goggles clean with her palms, casting her gaze around frantically. *Dracuni?*

Off the side of the dragon, back the way they'd come, a pale body tumbled in the air. Dropped. Falling. Unconscious.

"Dracuni!" Riony screamed.

She kicked off the back of the dragon with her one leg, rolling headfirst into the air. Salty wind ripped at her as she sped downward, trying to reach the unidragon in time. She had no float rune, no silvernix. She had nothing left. But she couldn't lose Dracuni too.

THIRTY

The ring of fire surrounding the clearing dimmed, smothered by the undead surging around it. Lyrrin's feet felt stuck to the ground as a rotting bovin and far too fresh human corpses, bloodied and blistered, broke through and raced toward her.

She'd never been as brave as Riony. She'd fight when she had to, but the shivering underlayer of fear never went away.

Now, Elumon's fear added to it as he wove around behind her shins, stepping out boldly, then backing away again in repetition.

You've done so well. You saved Dracuni and Riony! And we're together again now. I'll keep you safe.

Want to keep you safe too.

Lyrrin's heart warmed. She smiled in the face of fear.

Maybe it's time you try out that flame of yours.

Elumon growled softly and emerged again from behind her, raising his head. Lyrrin eyed the approaching revenants and grasped her staff, activating the burn rune on it.

Benjin moved beside her, twin swords raised. "I don't suppose your magic works on metal too? I could really go for some flaming blades right now."

"I don't think we've got time to test that at the moment. But let's try it later."

"Vance!" Eslinde's strained scream came as she drew her thin blade in one hand and used the other to pick up the bag of silvernix beside Elumon.

"We've got you!" Vance's voice yelled from above.

Air gusted around them so furiously it almost blew Lyrrin to the ground. Viska's golden wings arched over their heads, turning the world a warm yellow as the setting sun shone through the thin membrane. Lyrrin coughed as dust and ash and the smell of death swirled all around. A revenant growled close by.

A bright silvery flash shot across Lyrrin's grayed-out vision.

Elumon, did you—?

Then the world was engulfed in sun-bright gold as a jet of fire roared overhead. Viska blasted the approaching revenants with a relentless, charring burn.

"Climb up, quick!" Vance called.

Eslinde grasped Lyrrin's hand and brought her to the dragon's shoulders, giving her a boost.

Lyrrin scrambled the rest of the way. Viska still had multiple saddles from their earlier flight toward the private palace and she climbed in behind Vance, then reached down to help pull Benjin up and into the saddle beside her. Elumon flew up and landed behind them.

"I'm on, go!" Eslinde called from below, still clinging to Viska's scaly arm.

Vance leaned sideways to grab both of her arms as the golden dragon thrust her wings down, taking them off the ground.

The moment they were in the air, Lyrrin turned her eyes the direction the Dragon King had flown, trying to track where he'd taken Dracuni and where her sister and Kess were.

But a darker shape blocked the view.

A heart-wrenching sadness hit Lyrrin as the shadow dragon descended down over them. It came so close a sweep of its umbrous wing passed right over Viska, washing them all in inky shadows and darker grief.

Elumon tucked his head in under her arm, whimpering.

Benjin sobbed beside her, swatting at the tears on his face. Lyrrin let hers flow. She kept her bright eyes on the swirling, living darkness that formed the cursed entity.

All those dragons, all their spirits, separated from their bodies, tangled together and mourning. She reached out a hand, her blue tipped nails brushing the last wisps of black that trailed over them.

"I'm sorry," she whispered, as salty tears dripped into her mouth.

Riony had untamed so many dragons on her missions recently, and so many more had been untamed that day. Lyrrin felt good at how many they had healed, how many dragons could live their life freely again. Whether they'd broken the curse from doing that or not, it was good to have helped them.

But the curse had been weakened. The revs could be stopped with fire again—Lyrrin had worked that out in the palace—and even the size and bulk of the shadow dragon had decreased. She could see the threads of darkness weaving it together now, fraying and bare in sections around a single, larger core.

As the shadow dragon touched the ground, everyone on Viska held their breath. As it lifted its head and roared, Eslinde whispered a prayer to the sun and a repetition of, "Please, please, please ..."

Lyrrin watched the field of corpses in the clearing below, burned by Riony's sword and dragonfire.

The shadow dragon's cries echoed all around, its grieving sound rattling through Lyrrin's bones, calling, calling the dead. Calling for their vengeance. Calling for their aid.

But they didn't rise again.

The roaring continued, growing louder, as the shadow dragon turned on the spot, whiplike tail swishing like a ribbon of smoke behind it.

Again and again it called, and the dead didn't respond.

"It worked ... It worked," Eslinde rasped. She made a sound between a laugh and a sob and leaned into Vance's side. He wrapped an arm around her, pressing a kiss to the top of her head.

With one final sky-rending scream, a large curl of shadow tore from the cursed creature, right from its middle, and flew out toward the harbor where Riony and the Dragon King had flown.

What's happening out there? Lyrrin chased it with her eyes.

Tiny dragon-shaped smudges moved in the distance. Lyrrin turned her staff around, reaching for the seeing stone at the top.

"Look," Benjin said, pointing below with one of his swords.

The shadow dragon had stilled, grown quiet. So much smaller and less substantial than before, it rose back into the air, wafting past Viska and vanishing into the dusky sky above. Not gone, not entirely, not until every last dragon was freed. But it had lost its power.

"Now we just have to clean up the rest of the revs!" Benjin cheered.

"Hmm, easy." Vance leaned over, looking down at

the patchy landscape of undead and fire beneath them. "Where's Dash? I haven't seen them in a while."

Eslinde pointed toward the walls of the capital. "They went down over the city. Aishena and Kverra went after them a while ago."

"On Ambri?" Vance growled, shooting a worried glance that way.

Viska aimed her path at the city.

"No, we have to go after Riony!" Lyrrin traced over the rune on the seeing stone. "We have to help get Dracuni back."

"The king took her. We have to stop him getting away," Eslinde added with a gentle touch to Vance's shoulder.

With teeth bared, he shook his gaze away from the city and nodded.

Lyrrin brought the seeing stone up in front of her eyes.

"What's happening?" Eslinde asked.

Through the magnifying crystal, it took a moment to pinpoint the action in the expanse of sky over the sea.

Lyrrin gasped, as the first thing she saw was Dracuni falling. Her shimmering, moonlight-toned body was limp, lifeless. Lyrrin scanned around, spotting Riony, also falling, just above her. There was no glow of purple magic around her.

Lyrrin tried to explain what she was seeing but only a panicked squeak came out. Then there was a flash of purple through the seeing stone.

Lyomir, with Kess on top, diving toward the falling bodies. She couldn't see the king or his dragon; she could only track as the bodies of Dracuni and Riony and Lyomir went down toward the ocean below.

Viska turned again suddenly, and Lyrrin lost her target. "They ... they're ..." she stammered.

"Look out!" a familiar voice yelled from nearby.

Orange scales streaked past in front of them, forcing Viska to turn again to avoid a collision. Ambri sped by, with Shiff close behind, a trail of a dozen wild dragons chasing after.

The tamed orange dragon had a crowd of people clinging to her back. Lyrrin recognized Aishena, Kverra, and Dashiel, along with Mestra Lerris. The others wore dragonrider armor in a range of colors.

Viska joined the chase, speeding in between the wild dragons at the end. The gold dragon growled and snapped the air toward them in warning, making them back off.

Lyrrin turned, trying to get a clear view of the harbor again. *Riony ... Elumon, can you hear Dracuni? Can you hear Lyomir?*

Elumon remained silent for a long moment.

Only Lyomir. He says they're coming back.

Lyrrin's heart flopped in her chest with a burst of relief. *Are they all okay?*

Elumon looked up from under her arm with large lilac eyes but didn't answer.

Viska wove left, then a sharp right, making Lyrrin focus on the chase in front of them. She cast her gaze over the battle.

The skies were almost clear now. All the flying revs were gone, and the only dragons with riders still on them were wild ones and Ambri. Many newly wild dragons were disappearing over the horizon, but some remained, hovering in a bewildered state or chasing anything that moved with wrathful fury.

The factory dragons that had come in had few targets left. Many of them had also spent their energy and anger, and they rested, perched on the keep walls or were long gone as well.

Those still with vengeance to spare were chasing Ambri, one of the only tamed dragons left in the air.

Viska wove between them, growling fiercely as she checked them with bumps of her neck. The dragons grumbled back, but Viska was larger than most of them. A few smaller treedarts bowed their heads and dipped away from the chase quickly. A flamesong at the head of the chase didn't give up so easily, even as Viska nipped at its tail and wings.

From each side, more dragons approached. Hux, brilliant red, and Gleem, glowing aqua in the dusk. The wild dragons still had their bonded riders, and both had also picked up a few extra passengers along the way.

The three wild dragons pinned the flamesong between

them in the air, muscling into its space. Gleem rumbled a long, warning sound, and the flamesong clicked its teeth at her. When Hux joined in as well, yelping a harsh retort, the flamesong slowed, cowed.

With the last of the pursuers turning away, Viska rose over the top, flying past the flamesong to join Ambri up ahead.

"Viska and the others are explaining things to the wild dragons," Vance said. "Convincing them to stop attacking any remaining tamed dragons."

Lyrrin turned around to watch the flamesong following Hux and Gleem, as a few of the other smaller dragons joined them as well, flying lower over the revs.

Vance pointed. "They've agreed to help burn the revs."

The flamesong swooped, loosing a massive stream of fire across the field below. The fire consumed everything beneath, where revenants swarmed along the base of the keep walls. The metal sheeting over the massive stone walls glowed in startling reds and oranges as plumes of smoke darkened the falling night.

"Thanks for the backup," Aishena called over as they drew near. "I wasn't sure I was going to be able to lose all those dragons."

Dashiel grinned from the saddle behind her. "I didn't doubt you for a moment."

"We wouldn't have ended up with so many after us if Dashiel and Shiff weren't playing hero, gathering up

riders who'd gone down in the streets. Took a while to extract everyone." Aishena pointed to all the other riders clinging to Ambri.

Mestra Lerris shared the back saddle with Kverra, but many other riders hung on between the spikes down the orange dragon's spine.

"Sounds like Dash," Vance grumbled.

Beside Ambri, Dashiel's pale blue and purple dragon did a little loop in the air.

"Are there any more that need help?" Eslinde asked.

"I used my last silvernix on Iffyr," Dashiel called over. "But with what Aishena brought, I think we got the last surviving dragons and riders we could see in that area."

Mestra Lerris shook her head fiercely. "You lot are mad, utterly mad, for what you did! I thought at first the wild dragons were part of the shadow dragon's curse worsening … And then Dashiel explained."

Eslinde said, "I'm sorry we didn't share the plan with you sooner."

The riding master's eyebrows pulled tight over her eyes, darkening her expression. "We lost many today. So many good riders, because they weren't prepared."

Lyrrin cast her eyes down to the ground below, to where Hux, Gleem, and the wild dragons moved over the keep walls and through the city, burning the revenants in the streets. How many had died that day? How many people would be waiting for family that would never come home?

She glanced again toward the harbor, where Lyomir slowly returned, silhouetted by the last rays of sun.

"But many were saved too, by that strange dragon of yours. The one the king wanted all along. And now I can see why." Mestra Lerris shook her head again. "I see why you couldn't trust us with that information earlier. And blessed sun, your plan worked. The revs are burning. The revs aren't rising again. They have been stopped."

But was the cost too high? Lyrrin found tears in her eyes. After so long protecting Dracuni's secret, now every rider in the sky that day saw her magic. A shiver of fear ran through Lyrrin, wondering what that was going to mean.

And there was still so much to do.

Still more dragons to untame. And what would become of Elundrae with so many wild dragons released upon the land?

The curse was broken, and it took so many lives. So many died.

But now, at least, they would stay dead.

Eslinde held Mestra Lerris's gaze across the gap between their dragons, until the muscled rider offered a salute, and she returned it.

"Where are Dracuni and the others?" Aishena asked.

Lyrrin wiped her eyes and pointed out over the harbor. "Elumon said they're coming back but won't say anything else."

Vance frowned. "Viska says the same, that they're on

the way, but won't say any more."

From Ambri, Aishena's eyebrows dropped, and she turned the orange dragon sharply toward the water. Viska followed as they sped toward the harbor.

As they crossed over the city, human figures were emerging, gathered on rooftops to avoid the last of the revenants and the fire. They must have been hiding during the earlier attack, like Kess had told them to do. Her warning had saved a lot of lives.

Lyomir flew toward them, crookedly, one wing ripped.

Something large hunched behind Kess, but it wasn't clear what. It might have been Riony. Lyrrin couldn't see Dracuni. She leaned out to one side, trying to see past those in front of her and around the purple dragon, to see if Riony and Dracuni were flying behind.

The purple etherdart glided down roughly toward the long flat stone of a wharf, and Viska, Shiff, and Ambri mirrored him. They landed on the pier, and no additional dragons appeared behind Lyomir.

"Where's Dracuni?" Lyrrin's voice squeaked out, barely a whisper.

From behind Kess, Riony's head lifted, her red hair bright in the gloom of dusk. Her eyes searched over those in front of her, softening as she saw Lyrrin and Eslinde, and then her expression dropped as she turned to Ambri, seeing Lerris and the other riders there.

She looked exhausted, worn down, and she slouched

down behind Kess again.

"Riony needs help!" Kess yelled from Lyomir's saddle.

"Coming!" Aishena was down from Ambri in a flash, rushing in a sprint to the purple dragon. Lyrrin slid down from Viska as well, running up behind her.

Riony moved, slipping unsteadily down the dragon's side to the ground.

Aishena gasped as she caught her, steadying her by getting under her shoulder.

Lyrrin's run faltered as she approached, stumbling to a stop. Her sister leaned her weight on Aishena, standing on only one leg. Her armor was torn and bloodied all over, and a clean, healed stump hung at the end of one thigh.

"Riony!" Lyrrin burst into movement again, hurrying to her sister.

She clutched for Riony's other side, and her sister swayed her way, wobbling beneath her touch, and then fell forward, despite Lyrrin and Aishena's attempts to catch her.

They all fell, sprawling on the ground beside each other.

"You reckless tamebrain," Aishena whispered, brushing back Riony's hair tenderly as she knelt beside her.

Riony remained face down, on hands and knee. Her whole body shuddered with grief and Lyrrin wrapped her in a speechless embrace.

"What happened?" Eslinde's armor clattered as she joined them.

All the others moved closer, surrounding Aishena and

Lyrrin as they tried to lift Riony again.

Her head shook, and only a rough wail escaped her throat.

Eslinde looked up to Kess for answers. "Did the king get away with Dracuni?"

Kess leaned over from her saddle, shoulders slumped and face grim. "No. Riony untamed his dragon. The king is gone. His dragon is gone. But Dracuni ... she was already so weak, after everything. And we didn't have any silvernix left."

Lyrrin felt hot tears spilling and her head shook, angry at what Kess was saying. "What do you mean? Where is she?"

Riony rose up on one trembling knee and covered Lyrrin in a crushing, sobbing embrace. "She didn't make it. Dracuni's gone."

Thirty-One

Riony still wasn't used to the artificial leg Vance had helped her get. Her thigh ached, and she leaned heavily on the crutches she'd been using while adjusting. The crutches made more people stare at her than if she disguised the loss of her leg entirely.

She didn't care. Let them look. Let them see what she'd lost. She was proud of what she'd done, and she'd do it again in a heartbeat.

But standing for long periods had become painful.

Standing before Dracuni's funeral pyre was even more painful again.

The neatly formed stack of timber had been built on the grand balcony of the palace, overlooking the public square below. Dracuni's body lay on top, scales shimmering so vividly in the afternoon light.

In the few days since the battle, word had spread about how the curse had been broken, how the city had been saved. Soon everyone knew how the strange, magical dragon who had saved them hadn't survived, how her body had been retrieved from the sea.

And now it seemed most of the city crowded into the square below to watch the funeral.

As it should be, Riony thought.

Nerves rattled her as she approached the pyre. Eslinde handed her a flaming torch, and with a deep breath, Riony thrust it into the tinder at the base.

The fire took quickly, flickering around the still body of pale, opalescent scales lying on top. They didn't cover Dracuni's body with a shroud. It was important she was seen.

"In our battle against the curse of death that plagued our land for too long, there were many heroes." Eslinde stood before the fire, her voice strong and resonant as she spoke to those watching below.

Riony stepped back in line with her friends, Lyrrin on one side and Kess, sitting atop Griskin, on the other.

Aishena, Benjin, and their mother were on the other side along with the Zarram siblings. Farther away, a tier down, was Mestra Lerris and all the dragonriders who had survived. Jaym, Zeina, and the Rebel Riders stood with them. The glow of the fire made the scale armor they all wore shine a flickering gold.

Eslinde swept her arm around, gesturing to Riony and all those in line with her. "Heroes who we would not have seen victory without. Many who gave so much to make our victory possible. Many who gave everything."

"Sparks." Riony grunted as a fat tear spilled over one cheek.

Griskin shuffled closer, his fur pressing against her crutch. Kess wrapped her hand around Riony's. Lyrrin, dry-eyed, tsked.

A guard came along the row, handing out lit candles to each of them.

The pyre roared, flames engulfing Dracuni's motionless form in a solid wall.

"We farewell one of our greatest heroes here today. A dragon, born by a unique miracle with the magic needed to break the curse, and the brave and kind heart needed to give herself entirely to that cause."

Riony breathed deep as her tears came fast, dropping one after another down her cheeks and splattering on the dark marble floor.

Eslinde raised her candle. "We send our love with her as she rises to find her way home in the sky, with those who've gone before. Let the lights held by our ancestors, sparkling above, guide her. We send our love to those who hold their own candle in the sky and wait for us, those left behind."

Below in the quiet crowd, flickers of light spread as

candles were lit. A few at first, then more. Sparkles of light filled the square like a sea of stars.

It had been Eslinde's idea to give Dracuni a Rolanian funeral, rather than the Taen one most royalty or riders received. In Rolanian myth, dragons were creatures of tragedy, born from the angry souls of the dead who lost their way on their path to the sky.

To see Dracuni honored as a soul who would sit with her ancestors above, to see the crowd of people below holding light for her, filled Riony's chest to bursting.

Riony sniffled hard, awed by the beauty and sadness of the moment. The tears kept coming, and she leaned into Kess, crying on her shoulder.

She whispered the final words as Eslinde spoke them aloud to the audience. "Keep your candles burning bright. We will be together again."

Soon, Riony thought.

A tickle of worry washed over Riony.

I'm fine.

Are you crying?

Of course I'm crying. It's your funeral. Shush!

Riony turned back to the fire. The flames roared and crackled, heating her face as she stared, no longer able to see Dracuni within.

Eslinde turned and nodded to Riony, signaling her to leave. Swinging her crutches around, Riony limped away from the funeral, her friends falling into single file

behind her as Eslinde remained to present medals to the surviving dragonriders.

Pushing through into the palace, Riony moved faster, dropping the mourning act. Elumon waited just inside, and Lyrrin skipped along with him as they hurried down a flight of stairs and into a private room below.

The Alderkin met them at the door. "How did it look?"

"Perfect." Riony smiled, wiping away the last remnants of tears. "The flames have covered Dracuni now. I think it's safe to end the illusion."

Five thin spears of crystal stood around the edges of the room, where all furniture had been cleared away. Dracuni lay motionless in the middle of the space, in the exact pose the vision of her on the pyre had appeared.

She cracked one eyelid open. *I can move again?*

Yrik and Priyune traced over the symbols on the ring of crystals, and the glow of magic dulled away.

"Now you can," Riony said, stepping in and giving Dracuni a hug as she rose up.

Dracuni fluttered her wings and stretched out a back leg. *I got a cramp.*

Riony chuckled. "It was worth it. I think everyone bought it. The dragon with the silvernix blood and healing breath is gone. Nobody will be hunting you anymore. You're free."

Kess stalked up beside them on Griskin. "She'll be free once the unidragon really is no more. Now that the

illusion is over, we need to get to work, before anyone catches a glimpse of her."

Riony eyed the clippers, cutting athame, and pots filled with dye at the edge of the room.

When Dracuni left this room again, she would no longer look like herself.

"I hate having to change you, just so you can live freely," Riony whispered.

I don't mind. Everybody changes. You changed, so you could live. Dracuni bent down and jabbed Riony's wooden leg with her horn.

Aishena, Benjin, and Kverra Hjelzahn handed out the tools, and Dashiel and Vance came in as well, closing the door after them.

Only the people in that room, plus Eslinde, Jaym, Zeina, and Niskina back in the undercity, would know that Dracuni lived. People Riony trusted. People who would do anything for Dracuni. Family.

Benjin poked at the dark gooey substance in the dye pot he held. "The rumors and stories going through the city after the battle were wild. So many people saw Dracuni's healing flame. Even when we worked on spreading the news Dracuni was gone, there were people saying they were going to steal her bones or her horn."

"That's so mean! And gross!" Lyrrin said.

"If anyone does poke around, they'll find the remains of the other dragon we hid within the pyre," Dashiel said.

"I think we found a really good size match from the bodies after the battle."

"And a horn from the king's skeleton collection," Kess added. "It's a good plan. It's going to work."

Lyrrin picked up a pair of clippers and snipped them menacingly at her sister. "Yeah, only it would have been really nice to have known about your plan earlier! I can't believe you let me think Dracuni was dead!"

Riony held up her hands and backed away. "There wasn't any time to tell you! We only made the plan out on the water, after Kess caught us."

Riony's heart stuttered at the memory. She'd really thought for a while that Dracuni was gone, until Kess healed her with the dose of silvernix Riony had given her. But that was the moment Riony had decided maybe it was better if Dracuni didn't go back with them.

Lyrrin punched her hard in the arm. "You still could have told me sooner!"

"I wanted to, but we had an audience as soon as we got back. We had to sell it."

Lyrrin punched her again.

"Ow! Kess, save me!"

Kess raised an eyebrow. "I'm not getting on her bad side. That kid practically burned half the palace down."

Elumon wriggled in between the sisters, tilting his head at Lyrrin.

His horn had already been trimmed a couple of days

ago, just in case anyone decided he was more like Dracuni than he was.

Lyrrin huffed at the hatchling and put her hands on her hips. "Don't you start. I know you and the other dragons were in on it as well!"

"Speaking of selling it, you sure cried a lot for a funeral you knew wasn't even real," Aishena teased.

Riony pulled a rude face at her. "It might not have been real, but that doesn't mean it wasn't true."

She turned toward Dracuni, cupping her large head on both sides. "Everything Dracuni did for the world, how much of a hero she is, how proud I am of her, and how close she really did come to sacrificing everything ... All of that was true."

Tears brimmed in Riony's eyes again. "With or without her horn, she's magical."

Dracuni sniffled and bumped the tip of her snout against Riony's face. *I learned how to be a hero from the best.*

Aishena really is excellent at everything she does.

I mean you, you big tamebrain.

Smirking, Riony wrapped her arms around the unidragon's head, hugging her tight.

I always wanted to be like you. Strong. Caring. Selfless. Dracuni paused after her last thought, then added bashfully, *Although it was nice to see such a big party being held for me.*

Riony backed up. "Did you peek?"

Just once!

Riony tutted. "Besides, it wasn't a party, it was a funeral. But yes, it was nice to see so many people there for you."

Only having heard part of the conversation, Kess frowned and shrugged. "My father always said more people will go to a funeral than a birthday party because most people would like me better dead than alive."

"Wow," Riony said. "Your parents were the worst."

"No argument there," Kess replied.

Lyrrin, having forgotten her earlier ire, gasped, her eyes wide. "Wait, when is Dracuni's birthday?"

Birthday? Dracuni thought, confused.

Riony's face scrunched up as she tried to work out the dates. "We missed it. Her first birthday would have been back when we were at Eslindekeep."

"Oh no!" Lyrrin looked more devastated than any recent events had caused. "*We missed it*? We need to do something for her!"

"You know what? We should," Riony agreed.

Birthdays were the last thing on Riony's mind during that time. Even now, as the world felt like it had taken a collective sigh of relief after the shadow dragon's curse was weakened, it had been hard for Riony to shake off her anxiety and alertness the trials of the last year and longer had set in her.

It felt as though she'd been running for her entire life. Fighting for her entire life. Trying to keep herself and those she loved alive.

She couldn't believe it had been over a year since she first saw Dracuni's egg, since she first felt Dracuni's thoughts and emotions merging with her own.

She never could have known back then where she'd be now.

Riony smiled as she picked up the cutting athame. "But first, we have a little bit more work to do. It's time for a change."

Dracuni nodded, bowing her head.

A wave of bittersweet emotion filled Riony from inside and out. She wished Dracuni could be free without having to hide herself, just as she wished Lyrrin and the Alderkin could too.

Riony had kept Lyrrin safe most of her life by disguising her, and now she'd do the same for Dracuni.

They all deserved to live in a world where they could be themselves without fear or threat. But the world wasn't quite there.

Not yet.

Riony would keep those she loved safe until it was.

With horn and hair trimmed, and scales dyed to a rich, midnight black, Dracuni flew over the palace. The smoke of the battle still tainted the air, leaving it tangy and thick.

Riony could feel the unidragon's trepidation at being so visible, out in the sky where so many eyes in the city could see her.

But Riony encouraged her out anyway. She wanted Dracuni to experience her freedom, to know she was safe.

They flew together silently for a while over the ruins of the city, where people were working to clean up ashes and rubble. Heads turned upward to watch—there were so few dragons in the skies now.

Hux, Gleem, and the other Rebel Riders with wild dragons kept up patrols, making sure the newly untamed dragons didn't cause trouble, and burning any final revenants that had been missed.

But nobody recognized Dracuni. Nobody tried to chase them or catch her.

And after a while, Dracuni's worry tipped over into joy.

"There they are." Riony pointed to a courtyard in the higher levels of the palace.

They landed in the neatly trimmed, if slightly scorched garden. Lyrrin balanced a big bundle of candles in one arm, salvaged from supplies from the earlier funeral.

She'd been coerced into wearing a dress at the funeral but had since changed into a simple top, pants, and her own hooded coat, hood pulled back.

"We're all ready. You're just in time!" she sang.

Riony hadn't had a chance to change, but as part of her plan to help Dracuni feel confident they were safe, and strip some of her own defenses, she'd taken off her outer layer of armor she'd worn for the funeral. The chilly air left her bare arms prickling, but it felt good.

Aishena, startlingly, had changed into a dress. A very simple gray slip with gold braiding around the neckline that hung expertly over her angular form.

Riony did a double take. "I'm sorry, but who allowed you to look so good in a dress, on top of everything else?"

"Did I ever need anyone's permission?" Aishena asked back, deadpan.

Riony chuckled as she slipped down from Dracuni's back. She landed awkwardly on her artificial leg, stumbling forward.

Kess brought Griskin into her path, catching her. As she helped Riony get her balance again, she sighed. "I had been hoping I'd see you in a dress."

Riony smirked and leaned in closer, muttering into Kess's ear. "I'm just looking forward to when I can get you out of yours."

She ran a finger over the embroidery down the side of Kess's gown. The skirts were hitched up around the saddle, revealing leather pants beneath.

A giddiness had filled Riony, born from joy and relief

that left her feeling lightheaded, and she reveled in it. She ducked in and kissed Kess's neck.

The soft gasp Kess released could have knocked Riony flat on her back if she wasn't being supported in her arms. Kess's embrace tightened and she kissed the cropped hair at Riony's temple.

"Stars, I love you." Riony exhaled roughly and pressed her lips over Kess's.

"Would you two stop already, we're waiting!" Lyrrin yelled.

Riony and Kess broke apart, smiling and flushed.

"Birthday. Right. That's what we were doing." Riony limped over to join the others where Lyrrin had them all sitting on the paving in a semicircle around Dracuni.

Everyone had found neat formal clothing somewhere, leaving Riony feeling shabby in her undershirt and chausses. But as they all smiled and teased as she took a seat on the ground, she knew nobody cared. All that mattered was that they were together.

Dashiel lit Aishena and Benjin's candles for them, and then Aishena turned and lit her mother's from her own.

The Alderkin still wore their long cloaks and hoods, needing them to move about the palace unrecognized, but sat beside the others, chatting amiably.

Eslinde and Vance had trays of food in front of them, covered in metal domes.

Elumon sniffed around them and Eslinde shooed him

away. "Later!"

Dracuni settled down, watching everyone around her, bright-eyed and happy.

"Has everyone got a candle?" Lyrrin asked.

"Except for Dracuni." Riony smiled as her sister organized everything.

They'd only had a couple of birthdays in the undercity after their parents were gone, but Riony always tried to hold them the way her amma and pabba had taught her, and Lyrrin remembered well.

Her little sister moved around Dracuni, flustered for a moment, before placing the candle on the ground in front of her. "That will have to do."

Do I need to do anything? Dracuni sniffed at the small flame.

Riony adjusted her artificial leg into a more comfortable sitting position.

As she looked at the candle in her hands and the people around her, her giddiness changed into something more somber.

Addressing everyone, she said, "In Rolanian tradition, when someone grows a year older, we remember those we've lost. And we ask them to watch over the person whose birthday it is for another year."

Dashiel leaned closer to Vance, bumping shoulders. "Do you remember doing this when we were young? It's been so long since Pabba allowed it."

Vance nodded sadly.

Riony held up her candle. "Dracuni, do you want to go first? Who do you want to remember?"

The unidragon tilted her head, thinking. The dyed black scales made her lilac eyes startlingly bright.

My siblings, lost before they were born. I hope they are watching me.

Riony took a trembling breath and relayed her message to the others.

Aishena bowed her head.

"I remember my parents, Eylin and Farrad. They would have loved you, Dracuni." Riony hugged one arm around herself, wrapping her hand over her tattoo of the rings, swords, and candle.

Kess had climbed down from Griskin and sat beside her. She slid an arm around Riony's waist.

With a heaving breath, Riony continued. "We also remember Myrwa, Kellae and her brother and baby ... all our friends lost that night."

A tremor of sadness from Dracuni joined with her own.

Wiping at her face, Riony indicated for someone else to take a turn.

Eslinde cleared her throat, her silver eyes shining. "We remember the brave riders Thallan, Norallei, and Samor. We remember Shael and her bold kindness."

The Alderkin bowed their heads and together drew a synchronized pattern in the air before them.

Benjin's voice broke as his words jumped out. "Yoskar ... We remember Yoskar. And Fadda and Neif."

Kverra Hjelzahn's face crumpled, and Aishena and Benjin caught her in an embrace.

Over her mother's head, Aishena said solemnly, "Brishan. Jonna. Caed. Daymora. Honorable delvers and friends."

Riony's head hung heavily as each name struck her heart. She let tears fall, for all they'd lost, every one of them. Vance and Dashiel didn't mention their father much, but Riony could see their grief now in how they held each other's hands.

Lyrrin lifted her candle hesitantly, eyes averted and voice low. "I ... I remember Yensen."

"*We* remember Yensen," Riony echoed, nodding to her sister.

Lyrrin smiled tearily back.

A silence fell as they all looked up to the stars and remembered the people they had lost along the way.

Dracuni rose up, dark scales glistening like the night sky, and her chest expanded. Opening her mouth, she sang. A deep, lingering note filled with sadness and longing that reverberated around the candlelit courtyard. Then the tone lifted into a melodious trill.

I feel stronger, Dracuni thought, awed.

Riony smiled at her part seasong, all magical dragon friend. *That's those above we've remembered watching over you. That's the power of their love. And ours.*

Everybody raised their candles one last time, before placing them all in the center of the circle, letting them burn down.

Eslinde opened up the trays of food, sharing around sweet buns and sliced fruit, and a few pieces of meat for Dracuni and Elumon.

"That was beautiful," Kess said, staring at the candles with an intense expression.

"Yeah, it was kind of cool," Benjin agreed. "Taens just give presents."

Riony laughed. "Really?"

Aishena and Eslinde and the Zarrams all nodded.

I could have had presents? Dracuni snorted.

Taking a big bite of cake, Riony spoke with her mouth full. "Maybe we'll do that next year."

They remained in the courtyard together for a while, sharing food and laughing and crying and laughing again. As the night grew darker and air grew colder, people drifted away to their beds.

Soon only Kess and Riony remained, tucked in together against Griskin's fur to keep warm as they stared up at the moon.

"What do you want to do now?" Kess asked.

Riony turned to face her and waggled her eyebrows.

"I mean with your life. With your freedom. With this world that you saved."

"Saving the world really was a group effort. There's no way it would have turned out so well on my own. Much like what I want to do with you."

Kess pursed her lips and gave Riony a hard look. "Would you stop deflecting for once?"

Riony pouted and leaned back against Griskin's side again. Buying time, she reached overhead and scratched his back. The wolf's tail thumped on the ground happily.

"I've kind of been avoiding thinking about it," Riony finally admitted after Kess refused to break.

"Why?" Kess's voice had become small.

"Because I don't know what I want to do. I've spent so much of my life just ... surviving. Doing whatever I had to do to keep myself and those I love alive. I never really thought about the future. Never really thought I'd have one."

A dark emotion flashed over Kess's features, scrunching up her face. "I'm sorry."

Riony shook her head, turning to look at Kess, her shimmering ice-blue eyes and spots like stars over her cheekbone and white-streaked charcoal hair. "I know there's still no guarantee, there's still danger, but these last few days, for the first time in a long time, it feels like I have a life ahead of me."

It felt strange, saying it out loud. Riony swallowed the feeling away, trying to be as forthright and brave with her wants as the woman in front of her. "I have some ideas ...

But I don't want to rush into it. I want to spend some time first just ... breathing."

Kess seemed to echo that with a deep breath of her own, one that released with an expression like heartbreak. "Whatever you want. You deserve any future you want."

Riony reached for one of the salt-and-pepper braids beside Kess's face, wondering how she'd fallen so deeply in love with this wild, passionate woman who had once been so cruel. But as she stared at Kess's beautiful face, knowing all they had been through together, for each other, it didn't seem so strange at all.

"Of every future I could want, of all the futures there could be, I want mine to be with you."

Kess's expressions brightened, her nose still scrunched as though in disbelief. "You do?"

Riony smirked, leaning in to kiss Kess's neck. "You promised you'd watch me die one day. I'm holding you to it. And I'm not planning on dying anytime soon."

THIRTY-TWO

Lyrrin paced up and down the side of the long table she'd arranged to be brought into one of the palace's flight decks. It was laden with trays of flatbreads and dips and jugs of spiced drinks. Eslinde carried in another tray, arranging it between the others.

"Why aren't they here yet?" Lyrrin huffed.

Eslinde surveyed the spread, then took a seat with a tired sigh. "It's still early. Everyone will be here soon."

"Why can't they be here now? It's been weeks since I saw Riony." Lyrrin kicked the leg of the chair next to Eslinde's.

Eslinde tutted softly. "It was only last week. Riony visits as often as she can. And we both agreed it would be good for Riony to have some time for herself."

Lyrrin pouted. She had agreed that it seemed like a

good idea, and it also meant she could spend a lot more time with Eslinde, but she didn't realize she'd miss Riony so much. Even with frequent visits, it wasn't the same as the years they'd spent side by side, inseparable.

She sighed. "I know. But she has to come today, because I did so much to prepare for her birthday!"

"She'll be here," Eslinde said.

Lyrrin paced around the table again to where Elumon was sniffing at the food. He'd grown a lot in the last few months, almost as big as Griskin, but not quite big enough for Lyrrin to fly safely on yet. According to the Zarrams anyway.

But Lyrrin was small too, and she and Elumon had been on a couple of small flights around the palace.

Can you hear Dracuni yet? Are they on the way at least?

Not yet. A sense of longing came with the thought.

Lyrrin knew he missed Dracuni as well. She rubbed a hand over the stub where his horn had been trimmed down. At a casual glance it looked like a scar from a taming spike removal. A lot of dragons had those now.

As he'd gotten bigger, the tufts of hair he'd been born with had been replaced with scales, and apart from his opalescent rainbow tone, he looked just like any other dragon.

The flight deck was otherwise empty of dragons. All tamed dragons in the palace and city had now been freed. Even the dragons that had been powering the palace's strange electric lights were gone. Lamps were now fitted with Alderkin glow stones, giving off their familiar cyan shine.

The polished cavernous room that opened out to the sky at one end echoed with Lyrrin's pacing footsteps. It had been strange at first for Lyrrin, living in the palace where she'd once been held prisoner.

But after the battle, as dragonlords and remaining riders and advisors clamored for leadership within the rubble, it soon became clear that Eslinde was the last remaining first heir still alive. All others had been lost to Lady Hjelzahn, when their keeps fell, or when trying to flee the revenant hordes that day.

Between Eslinde's claim to the throne, her ownership over the king's silvernix supply, and the backup of the few riders still with dragons, all others vying for control soon backed down.

But there had still been *so many meetings* since. Lyrrin was tired of them, and the way her mother looked as she poured herself a drink, she figured Eslinde was as well.

Lyrrin paced back and took a seat beside her, smiling in a way that crinkled her eyes. "This should be fun for everyone."

Eslinde smiled back. "I think so too. It's a lovely idea."

Wingbeats at the end of the flight deck had Lyrrin springing back out of her seat again, hopefully looking for Riony and Dracuni.

A red dragon came in to land, wind rustling the tablecloth.

"Oh, it's just them," she said a little too loud.

"Happy to see you too, little spitfire," Niskina called down the length of the vast room.

She climbed down from Hux and Jaym followed. His pocket-hawk flittered around, then landed amid the red dragon's crown of spikes, preening herself. Hux moved away from the entry to where food and drink had been put out for the incoming dragons.

"Are we the first here?" Jaym asked as he reached the table.

"Yes," Lyrrin muttered.

Eslinde stood and greeted them both with a hug, and Niskina walked past Lyrrin with a wrapped bundle under one arm. She ruffled a hand through Lyrrin's undyed hair.

Both she and Jaym wore rider's armor, dusty and marred from use.

Lyrrin straightened her hair again and patted down the dress Eslinde had encouraged her to wear. Most around the palace and city still wore Taenish grays, but Eslinde had some more colorful dresses made and Lyrrin didn't hate them. She wore a blue one today that matched her eyes.

Niskina hid her parcel under the table and sat down. "Zeina sends her apologies. She's caught up with Gleem and the others trying to manage a group of wild dragons that have been taking their anger out on a town out west."

"You both look like you've been busy too," Eslinde said.

Niskina glanced down at her dirty armor and windswept locks, then over at Eslinde, in a pristine gown with silver hair coifed in an elegant bun. "We didn't have a chance to stop and change. There's a lot to do out there."

Niskina had been on the wing with Jaym and the Rebel Riders since the battle at the capital. As soon as news reached the undercity that the revenant curse was weakened, people began hesitantly moving aboveground again.

With the shrines being recharged by Dracuni, communities were springing up all around Elundrae, living under the sun and sky and stars.

There were still plenty living in the undercity, but Niskina thought she wasn't needed there as much anymore.

She helped herself to some food, swiping flatbread through a plate of dip and oil. "There are a few dragonlord holdouts in the north where the revenant army didn't pass through. We're working through them at the moment, convincing them to hand over their dragons."

Jaym leaned on the table beside her and grinned roguishly. "One way or another."

Niskina gave him a gentle eye roll. "Mostly with diplomacy. Sure, some of them are angry and don't want to give up their wealth and power, but none of them can deny the change in the land since the curse has weakened."

It had only been a few days ago that Eslinde had called

Lyrrin out onto their balcony, staring up at the sky with wide-eyed wonder. Lyrrin hadn't been sure what she was looking at, at first, because the sky was clear.

Then Lyrrin saw it too. *The sky was clear.* No ash fell. No smoke grayed out the sun. The sky was *blue*, a glowing, vibrant azure, with thin streaks of white cloud.

Eslinde gave Jaym a glittering smile. "I've heard your words are doing far more than your aerial battle skills anyway. The new Rebel Riders tales you've been putting out to explain to everyone what happened, and why the dragons were freed, have been doing a good job spreading the word."

Jaym took a seat beside Niskina, draping an arm around her and winking. "What can I say? I've found new inspiration."

Eslinde looked toward the patch of open blue at the end of the flight deck. "I think we all have."

Niskina raised her glass to that, then sighed. "One problem we keep running into is actually *because* of how good things are getting. The last few dragonlords are saying that since things are better, they should be allowed to keep their dragons."

"Of course they can keep dragons," Eslinde said, gesturing to Hux at the other end of the deck. "If those dragons are wild and agree to it."

Niskina nodded. "That's what we told them too. Every last dragon is getting untamed. It's only fair."

Pouring himself a drink, Jaym looked up and down the long, empty table. "This isn't just for us, is it? Who else is coming?"

"The usual," Eslinde replied. "Although Yrik and Priyune are away traveling at the moment and can't make it."

The Alderkin had built a shrine within the palace, as they had at the undercity. Once it was completed, they took their leave, traveling around Elundrae to repair broken shrines and looking for any signs of other Alderkin survivors.

They came back to visit about as often as Riony did, and they sounded quietly hopeful the last time they were there.

It had been good having a gateway in the palace. Lyrrin had gone back to visit the undercity a couple of times. She missed Butterfur, as she'd been unable to lure him through the gateway to the palace with her. He was too busy swimming through the pools of the undercity and raiding bins with his family.

That was where he should be. With family. But she still liked to visit and give him treats sometimes.

Dracuni's coming! Elumon perked up, flushed with excitement. His next message was more of a grumpy afterthought. ***And Lyomir.***

Lyrrin turned to the end of the flight deck to see the two dragons flying in side by side—Dracuni still dyed midnight black, stark beside Lyomir's dusky purple.

They glided down onto the open end of the deck, with nobody on their backs.

"Where's Riony? And Kess?" Lyrrin asked.

Dracuni says they're walking in. They wanted to see some of the city.

"*Walking*?" Lyrrin balked. "They're going to be late!"

Dracuni trotted up the rest of the flight deck, frolicking around Elumon as he reared up to greet her. Lyomir huffed and remained at the end near the entrance.

"Who's going to be late?" Benjin came running in from the palace side entrance. "Are we late?"

Aishena and Dashiel followed him in.

"Riony and Kess are *walking*," Niskina said.

"Of course they are," Aishena replied.

"You're right on time," Eslinde said, standing to greet them all.

Lyrrin joined them as well, giving each a hug.

She backed away from Benjin with a grimace. "Why are you so sweaty?"

He grinned. "Came straight from training so we wouldn't be late."

"I tried to tell him there was time to change. The guest of honor isn't even here yet." Aishena's silvery locks swung loose around her brown face. She and Dashiel both wore neat, casual clothing.

"You could have changed. You should have changed."

Lyrrin wrinkled her nose teasingly.

"Just because you're a princess who can spend her days relaxing doesn't mean we all can." Benjin only grinned more as he wafted his shirt.

"I have been very busy with my rune research and experiments!"

Benjin's silvery hair had been growing out as well and he smoothed it back. "Which is why I need to train hard to be your official grayglim warden. Not that you need a bodyguard. But so I can be around all the time when you're doing more awesome magic! I want my flaming blades!"

Lyrrin offered him a smile of truce and ushered him over to the seat beside hers. She liked the idea that he was going to stay around. Since the battle, it felt like a lot of them had drifted off different ways. But the Hjelzahns all remained at the palace with Eslinde and Lyrrin.

Although Hjelzahn the First had died, Hjelzahnkeep was one of the few not to fall to the revenant horde, but Kverra, Aishena, and Benjin were still many generations and many heirs away from being necessary there.

Lady Hjelzahn had returned to her role of training grayglims, although whether it was on Eslinde's instruction or a change in heart in general, her lessons were far less intense than before, according to Aishena.

When Eslinde asked Aishena to also take a role teaching, it had left her dumbstruck for a while before she agreed.

"I want a new type of grayglim than before. Ones who

can use their wisdom and instinct to make the right choices, beyond their loyalty. I can't think of anyone better suited to bestow that learning than you," Eslinde had said, causing Aishena to blink rapidly, then excuse herself.

The uneven footsteps of an artificial leg swung Lyrrin around again, only to see Vance walking in.

Eslinde popped up out of her seat, thin hands smoothing down her dress. She rushed over to greet Vance, and the two of them hugged awkwardly.

Benjin leaned closer to Lyrrin and whispered, "Are those two still—?"

"Acting clueless about each other's feelings?" Lyrrin whispered back. "Yes. I'm working on it."

Lyrrin knew her mother was still grieving for Alleem, even after all this time, and she didn't really understand the allure of romance that had seemed to spread through their group like a plague. But in the past few months, Lyrrin had seen how happy Riony's relationship with Kess made her.

And she wanted that for her mother as well. There hadn't been a lot of time lately to get Eslinde and Vance alone together since Eslinde spent so much time with Lyrrin. Maybe Lyrrin just needed a night away ...

She gasped, outraged by a realization.

The sleepover!

As Vance reached the table, Viska, Shiff, and Ambri glided in together onto the flight deck. They greeted Dracuni, Hux, Lyomir, and Elumon fondly.

Ambri had been one of the first dragons to be untamed after the battle, once everything had settled down. It was done with both Zarrams and other wild dragons around her, to be there for her as she awoke. As usual, she was angry at first. She left, wanting her freedom, but often returned to spend time with Viska and Shiff.

Vance and Dashiel had been taking care of all the dragons that needed untaming, trying to give them a positive experience as they awoke again, finally freed. They'd taken over the king's dragonhold, working with riders and breeders who were interested in building relationships with untamed dragons, the way the Zarrams had.

"Riony's still not here?" Vance looked at the people already seated.

A grumbling of 'noes' came from around the table.

Lyrrin looked to Elumon for an update, but the dragons were too busy in discussions of their own.

Vance sat down heavily beside Eslinde. "And I thought I was late."

"You are," Eslinde said with a slight smile as she offered him a drink.

"My apologies. I wanted to check on some of the bovin herds we've released onto the plains. It took a bit longer than expected."

"How are they?" Eslinde asked with far greater interest than Lyrrin thought the topic deserved.

"Doing well. Grazing and moving about as though they'd never been penned. Maybe a third are already missing, but that was expected with so many hungry dragons around now. We're working on increasing numbers soon."

Niskina smiled at the news. "We've been seeing some reach the north as well. And more dreer and other animals moving around too. And green ... so much green! Grass and forests are all sprouting again."

Jaym leaned back in his chair and put his feet up on the table. "Been ages since the last time we've seen any revs. People are still hesitant to leave the safety of the shrines for now, though."

Lyrrin straightened in her chair. "Do you think when the revs are all gone, Riony and Dracuni won't need to travel around so much to keep the shrines charged?"

Getting some time for herself wasn't the only reason Riony was regularly away. She and Dracuni made frequent stops at the shrines, ostensibly checking in on the settlements there, but really to keep the shrine's protective barriers active.

"Maybe," Eslinde replied. "Although the shrines are also needed to recharge the Alderkin crystals the communities are using too."

Lyrrin slumped a little. "I suppose."

They had discussed trying to hide small bundles of the king's silvernix supplies at each shrine to keep them activated, but they weren't sure it would be safe.

Niskina shrugged. "Riony said the shrines seem to be lasting longer between visits, with less revenants around to drain them. So I don't know how busy our missing heroes have really been."

"What's this about missing heroes?" Riony stepped in through the nearby entrance, flushed and short of breath. "Do you think they mean us?"

Kess padded in on Griskin beside her. "They might mean you."

Riony grinned. "I think they mean us."

"Finally!" Lyrrin shot from her chair and grabbed her sister's hand, dragging her at a run back to the table.

Riony limped behind her. "Whoa, slow down! Do you know how many stairs I just walked up?"

"Then you should have flown in and not been late!" Lyrrin pushed her down into the seat beside hers.

Riony readjusted her leg, then undid her belt, hanging it and her dragonguard sword on the back of her chair. She wore a loose tunic that left her arms bare, like she always preferred, but the fabric was clean and new, not like the old tatty clothing she'd worn for years.

"Did you enjoy your *walk*?" Niskina asked with a smirk.

Riony wiped a hand over her forehead, brushing back the flop of red hair. It had grown out just long enough to have a tiny braid at the back again.

"Yes, actually. It was nice to spend some time walking

with Kess. I enjoyed seeing more of the city."

Niskina raised her eyebrows.

Riony tsked and shook her head at Kess. "These people, always with their minds in the gutter."

Niskina threw a scrap of flatbread at Riony.

Kess slid into the seat beside Riony, and Griskin bounded away to take a big drink from one of the dragon's troughs. "It was good, though. The city has really rebounded after the battle."

Riony leaned her cheek on one hand, looking at Kess. "Maybe we could stay in one of the buildings by the harbor for a while. It's nice down there."

Jaym scoffed. "Look at these two, on holiday while the rest of us are working so hard."

"Yeah, it's pretty sweet." Riony grinned toothily and reached for some food.

Lyrrin slapped her hand. "Presents first! We've been waiting so loooong."

"Presents?" Riony asked.

Dashiel and Vance shared a sharp look with each other.

Lyrrin sighed. "It's your birthday, remember? And we're doing it Taen style this time! Surprise!"

Lyrrin reached down under the table and dragged out a long heavy parcel wrapped in red cloth.

Riony helped her haul it up the rest of the way, frowning at Kess. "Were you in on this?"

Kess smiled back with narrowed eyes. "Maybe."

"Open it, open it!" Lyrrin squealed.

Riony barely had the first bit of cloth unwound, but Lyrrin couldn't contain her excitement.

"I made it for you myself. I mean, Yrik and Priyune also helped a bit, but it was mostly me, since the glass magic doesn't seem to work for them. But they taught me what I needed to do to harden it all enough to make it work and fuse together the different materials. And there are some new runes on there too!"

Riony's jaw dropped as the final fabric fell away.

She rose from her seat, bringing the hefty sword of glass and dark crystal with her. The high polish and facets gleamed in the cyan light as she turned it side to side in front of her face. Along the shaft of the blade, enclosed droplets of silvernix shimmered. Riony stared, open-mouthed, her head shaking.

As Riony said nothing, Lyrrin grew nervous. "Do you like it? I know how much the one you lost meant to you, and I know I can't really replace it, but I thought you might like this anyway. Do you?"

Riony traced the float rune, and the blade lit up purple. "This is ... this is the second most beautiful thing I've ever seen in my life."

"Second?" Lyrrin pouted.

Kess frowned as well. "It's much nicer than the other sword was."

"Never said it wasn't." Riony put the weapon down

beside her chair and grabbed Lyrrin up in a big hug. "I can't wait for you to show me what the other runes on this do."

"Maybe not at the dinner table," Eslinde said.

She leaned over from the other side and held a scroll of paper out for Riony. "This is from me."

Riony put Lyrrin back down in her seat. She cracked the wax seal and unrolled the parchment, frowning at a wall of tiny handwriting.

"Um ... thanks. What is it?" she said.

"An official declaration. That I, as heir to the Draekhan throne, affirm you as one of my daughters."

Riony continued to hold the parchment, staring at it as her breath came heavy.

Eslinde's pale cheeks flushed pink. "I hope that's not too presumptive of me. But you are already a sister to my daughter. I felt there was nothing more I wanted than for all of us to be family."

Lyrrin held her breath, waiting for Riony's response. Eslinde had run the idea past her a while ago, and Lyrrin loved it. But she also knew how Riony felt about her parents she'd lost before.

Riony's face scrunched up. Her voice came out huskily. "Thank you. I'm ... I'm honored."

Eslinde shook her head. "No. I am."

Benjin huffed. "How are we expected to compete with those presents?"

Aishena rolled her eyes as she pulled a satin bag from

beside her and tossed it over the table. "I'm not calling you princess."

Riony grinned as she caught the lumpy bag. Tugging the drawstring open, she gasped. "No way!"

"What is it?" Lyrrin knelt up on her chair to try to see through the bag's opening.

"No way!" Riony repeated, pulling a couple of shiny red apples from the bag. She grinned and tossed one back to Aishena.

"Thanks, but I had apples just a few weeks ago." Aishena's eyes glittered as she handed the apple to Benjin.

Riony barked a laugh.

"Apples?" Vance asked.

Eslinde shrugged, looking equally bewildered.

Lyrrin laughed too, thrusting her arm into the bag to steal one.

"It's the thought that counts," Aishena said.

Riony gleefully handed apples around to everyone at the table.

Kess held hers in front of her. "I don't get it."

Dracuni wandered over from the end of the flight deck, sniffing at the empty bag and nudging Riony with her snout.

"You remember them too? They were your first meal." Riony and Dracuni spent a moment, locked in private, silent conversation, before Riony turned back to the others, taking a big bite from her apple.

At the other end of the table, Vance and Dashiel wore matching frowns.

Dashiel blurted, "We weren't told we were doing presents. We thought we were doing the candle thing again."

Riony just laughed again. "That's okay. I wasn't expecting anything."

"I'm sure I told you about this," Aishena said.

Dashiel rubbed a hand through their blond curls. "Maybe? I get a bit distracted when you're around."

Aishena smiled wickedly in return.

"Gross," Riony smirked. "You know, even Dracuni got me something."

Dashiel turned a deep red. "I'm so sorry. I'll make it up to you."

Lyrrin looked between Riony and Dracuni. How had a dragon Riony spent most of her time with manage to get a present? "What did she get you?"

"News, from her mother." Riony smiled as she chewed around the core of her apple, right down to the seeds. "She has a new clutch of eggs."

Lyrrin bounced in her chair.

"That is happy news," Aishena said with only sadness in her voice.

Riony nodded to her solemnly.

"More baby dragons?" Lyrrin squealed. "Will they visit?"

"I don't know about that," Riony said. "Maybe."

A short silence fell, as Niskina and Kess held a staring competition across the table. Then Niskina stood up and handed Riony her wrapped gift.

"Ours first. So we can show up whatever she got you." Niskina gave Kess a sly look.

"This isn't a competition." Riony took the parcel.

"We'll see." Kess returned the sly look, relaxing back into her chair.

Lyrrin waited impatiently as Riony undid the ties and pulled back the fabric. She was a little disappointed to see a book inside.

Niskina grinned and sat back in her chair, leaning shoulder to shoulder with Jaym. "It's every chapter of the Rebel Riders in existence, all bound together. Including the most recent stories featuring the popular new redheaded character."

Riony gasped and clutched the book to her chest. "Okay. You two win."

"You haven't even opened mine yet," Kess said.

"Every chapter, Kess. Every. Chapter."

"Fine. As long as I can read them, too." Kess shrugged, pulling a tiny bundle of satin from her pocket, holding it out. "Here."

All around the table, chairs squeaked as everyone leaned in to see what was in the palm-sized pouch as Riony worked it open.

Kess spoke softly. "While we've been traveling, Riony has midwifed at a few births. It's been amazing to see ... her skill, knowledge, gentleness in aiding mothers and newborns through their labor. She's been incredible."

Riony's frantic tugging at the small parcel stilled as it fell open and her eyes glistened with a flood of tears. "Kess ..."

Five silver rings lay on the black satin, sparkling like stars.

Kess bowed her head. "They aren't the same ones handed down through your family. But you still deserve them, to recognize the five generations of women in your line who have brought life into this world. You more than any other."

Riony heaved a deep breath, and her hand closed tight around the rings. She turned to Kess, lunging forward to kiss her deeply.

"I still think our present was the best," Niskina muttered.

"No chance. I got her *a sword*!" Lyrrin yelled back.

Riony and Kess broke apart, laughing, and Riony slipped the five rings onto the fingers of one hand.

Lyrrin grabbed her sister's shoulders, physically turning her back toward her, telling her about all the new magic she'd learned and what the sword could do. They ate together, and Riony wiped a bit of dip off Lyrrin's chin as she talked.

People moved around the table, chatting with each other and sharing food and flicking through the new chapters of the Rebel Riders, arguing and laughing about the details.

Benjin showed Niskina how much taller he'd gotten, and Kess moved a few seats down to chat with Dashiel, both giggling.

Eslinde moved around from the other side of the table to join Lyrrin and Riony. "This has been a lovely night. You did well organizing it."

"She's always been the brains of the group," Riony replied.

They shuffled their seats closer as Lyrrin slumped sleepily in her chair.

Lyrrin hadn't grown much in the last few months. Not shooting up the way Benjin or the dragons were.

She still felt so small compared to everyone else, but as she sat there between Riony and Eslinde, she felt okay with that.

She knew now who and what she was and where she belonged. And she loved that place.

Lyrrin pulled Riony and Eslinde in closer, cuddling up between them, happy she was still small enough to do so.

THIRTY-THREE

Kess waited at the party until almost everyone was gone. Even Riony had left a while earlier, due to her leg being sore from their long walk through the city.

But Kess remained behind, waiting until she was sure she could be alone with Lyrrin.

As Eslinde and Vance cleared the table, Lyrrin sat farther away with Elumon. Kess took Griskin over beside her, lowering the wolf down so she was closer to the girl.

Lyrrin looked up, yawning. "You had such a nice present for Riony."

"You too." Kess swallowed.

She'd always struggled to talk to Lyrrin. She'd started their relationship with so much anger and jealousy that this girl had been loved by Riony when she hadn't been. She wasn't sure why Riony entrusted this task to her.

Clearing her throat, she reached out a closed hand. "Riony and I have a present for you, too."

Lyrrin looked at Kess's clenched fingers. "Really? Is that how Taen birthdays work?"

"No. This is something special, just for you."

Lyrrin reached out her clawed fingers, and Kess placed a tiny empty vial into her palm.

"You found it!" Lyrrin held up the bottle in front of her, staring in awe at the markings in the glass.

Kess nodded, speaking quietly. "When I was scouting during the siege, I took Griskin to look for it. He sniffed it out of the snow pretty quickly."

Kess had almost given the vial to Riony right after finding it. Then she saw how shattered Riony was, having lost Lyrrin. Then Riony had kissed her. Then Kess had left to rescue Lyrrin.

There was always so much to worry about.

"I only told Riony I had it recently, after the battle."

Lyrrin's blue eyes sparkled, enthralled by whatever she was seeing in the minute scratched lines.

Kess half smiled. "Riony asked me to hold on to it since then. But we talked tonight and think you should have it. It makes sense since you created it. Also, I think Riony just doesn't want the responsibility of deciding what to do with it. But she trusts you to decide."

Lyrrin's hand closed around the vial and she nodded.

"I'll keep it safe."

Kess returned a torn expression. It was a big responsibility to be handing to a child. But she'd seen what that child could do and knew she had a heart as big as Riony's.

"Thank you." Kess turned Griskin away.

"Thank you!" Lyrrin called after her. "For making Riony happy. I've liked you being around. Although you could have been nicer sooner."

Kess huffed a laugh. "Rub it in, why don't you?"

Lyrrin stuck her tongue out as Kess waved good night.

At the far end of the flight deck, Lyomir raised his head. *I can eat her for you if you'd like.*

Kess chuckled. She loved her grumpy dragon so much. *Good night, Lyomir.*

Kess stalked on Griskin down the long corridors of the palace. It was late, and only muffled voices sounded here and there through closed doors around her. She balanced Riony's new sword, book, and declaration scroll on her lap. The apples were all gone.

The massive palace was fuller than it had ever been, with Eslinde opening the doors to people who had lost homes during the battle, but Riony and Kess still had a room set aside for them for when they visited.

Just as they had a home in the undercity. And in the new enclaves around the shrines, all over Elundrae. They had a home anywhere they were together.

Griskin brought Kess into the modest living area of their chambers. The doorway to the bedroom beyond was open, and Riony lay on the covers of the bed.

Her artificial leg was off, dropped carelessly on the floor, and she held one hand up in the air over her face, admiring the shine of silver on her fingers.

Riony noticed Kess come in and called out, "Should I get my tattoo redone to add another ring?"

Kess opened the balcony doors, looking up at the risen moon. It was cool and white, a color Kess was still getting used to. It had always been a bloody orange before from the smoky skies.

Then Kess brought Griskin into the bedroom and beside the bed. "I don't know, will it fit in?"

Riony sat up and turned her arm for Kess to appraise the existing tattoo, flexing noticeably.

Kess smiled. "Yeah, it'll fit."

Riony reached out, taking her presents off Kess. "Thanks for bringing these up for me. My leg's giving me trouble again."

"Can't relate." Kess climbed off Griskin onto the bed beside Riony, and the wolf padded away back to the living room to sit in the open air of the balcony.

Riony snorted a laugh. She admired her new sword for a moment, then propped it up against her side of the bed. The declaration from Eslinde was placed reverentially on the nightstand. She kept the book on her lap, flicking through the pages. "Taens might have some okay customs."

Kess just smiled as she moved beside Riony to rub the knotted muscles in her thigh. She'd never received much in the way of gifts from her family. Her birthday was generally forgotten, until it was used as an excuse to banish Kess from her home. With Riony already gone by that point, there'd been nothing at Heithorn estate she missed.

Kess hadn't known until recently why Riony and her family had left, fleeing with Eslinde's newborn, but as much as Kess had felt abandoned at the time, it still made sense. Why wouldn't they want to leave that awful place?

She'd just wished Riony had taken her with them, even though she knew part of what Riony had been fleeing was her. Riony had never been happy in that awful place either. She never could have been.

But now ... Kess was in awe, seeing Riony so joyful, so relaxed. Surrounded by family and love, but no longer crushed under the weight of responsibility to keep them all alive. It was beautiful in a way that ached.

And I get to be part of that.

It still didn't feel real sometimes. Kess had Riony, Griskin, Lyomir, and a home with people who loved and respected her. The world was healing, and she'd played a role in making that happen. She'd been able to be so much more than the dragonrider hero she once dreamed of being.

She had more than she could have ever wanted.

And it was nice to sleep in a soft bed sometimes too.

Although, the way Riony was looking at her, she wasn't sure either of them would be getting much sleep that night.

"Did you see the kids in the city?" Riony leaned back on her elbows.

"Which ones?"

Riony watched her with an intensely soft stare. "The ones riding on other kids' backs as they crawled around, howling like wolves. Because you should have seen their faces when *they* saw *you*."

Kess's hands stilled on Riony's thigh. "I was wondering why they were staring ... I thought ..."

"That they'd all just seen their hero?"

Kess shook her head. Back when she'd imagined herself as a dragonrider, she'd wanted it to prove that she could be as good, or better, than other riders. To win the approval of those who'd always hated her. At some point, that dream no longer seemed important.

Kess was so used to people looking at her with pity, disgust, or as though she were invisible, she hadn't even imagined that the kids playing in the city idolized her.

"Do you really think that was why?"

Riony shrugged one shoulder. "Or, I don't know, maybe they were all stunned by your beauty. I wouldn't be surprised. My new sword came second for a reason."

Kess pictured the scene again in her mind with the new context. The scramble of children playing in the still charred stone streets, acting out a battle as their favorite heroes. Heroes who looked like them.

"I also saw more than a couple of kids with toy peg legs and big stick swords. I thought they were pretending to be pirates."

"*Pirates*?" Riony knuckled Kess in the ribs, making her squeal.

Kess dodged out of the way. "Are you jealous there were more kids pretending to ride wolves than there were pretending to be you?"

Riony pillowed her arms behind her head. "No. Maybe. Wolves are cool, okay? I can't compete with that."

"Lucky for you it's not a competition." Kess leaned back onto the bed beside Riony.

"It was sort of weird to see, though. And there was a market stall selling acorn pendants!" Riony shook her head, laughing. "Maybe we should ask Jaym to stop writing so many details about us."

Kess doubted the children they saw had been reading the Rebel Riders chapters. "I think it's more than that. The story has spread, taking on a life of its own. People know what you did."

"What we did," Riony corrected sternly.

"What me and some pirate did."

Riony gasped in mock outrage and lunged forward, tackling Kess around the waist and pinning her down from above. "Kessara, you always did know how to go right for the heart."

"Yours was the only heart I ever wanted."

They stared at each other for a long moment, breaths coming short, and Riony grew solemn.

"No matter what stories spread about us, we'll always know the truth. What we went through, what we sacrificed, what we lost. What we almost lost." Riony traced a finger around Kess's neck, along the string where the original acorn pendant still hung.

Kess tucked a strand of red hair back behind Riony's ear. "How brave and honorable you remained, every step of the way."

"And hot. Don't forget hot."

"Never."

Riony sat up, flicking through the pages of her bound volumes again. "Jaym hasn't even come close to capturing the true magic and greatness of what we've done."

Kess waited, eyebrows quirked. Riony just stared back sweetly.

"You mean sex, don't you?"

"I mean the sex." Riony nodded.

Kess let out a bright giggle. "And yet you're the one who thought I was being literal when I suggested we *go for a walk* before getting to the party tonight."

She greatly enjoyed the dumbfounded look that hit Riony.

"Wait ... you meant ...?"

Kess just stared back sweetly.

Riony's eyes softened, filled with longing. "I guess we've got to make up for lost time then."

She chucked the Rebel Riders tome behind her onto the side table. It thumped beside the scroll declaring Riony as part of the royal family.

The corner of Kess's mouth lifted. "So, do you want me to call you Princess now? Your Highness? Milady?"

Riony snuggled in beside Kess, wrapping her arms around her. "You can call me whatever you want."

Kess raised her eyebrows questioningly.

Riony nuzzled closer. "Even *that*. It's kind of grown on me, now that things are different. Funny how you can love something you once hated. I wouldn't mind being your Pony again."

Kess shook her head. "I promised you I'd never call you that again."

Riony backed away slightly, frowning. "I don't remember that."

"I might have made the promise to a hallucination … but it still stands. Besides, I don't think I could take all the jokes it would open up."

"Aw, but I have so many. *So many*."

"Never again," Kess teased, and then Riony kissed her on the side of the neck, and all her other thoughts fell away, and all she felt was warm and loved and filled with hope for the future.

Two days ago, while passing by the shrine that had

once been Myrwa's enclave, Riony and Kess had seen the shadow dragon.

It was so much smaller than before, barely as big as a treedart.

They watched it for a while, flying behind it on Dracuni and Lyomir, as its wispy form glided through the clear blue sky. It landed here and there, calling its haunting cry, but nothing crawled out of the ground at its command.

The rush of grief the being's presence caused had also lessened. But Kess still grieved for it anyway. She knew now the creature had never been to blame, that it was only a creation of the greed of humans, taming and enslaving dragon spirits.

It was hard to tell how many tamed dragons there still were in Elundrae, but it wouldn't be much longer before the shadow dragon would be gone for good.

Did the shadow dragon think? Feel? Did it want to end? Did all of the broken pieces that formed it long to be back in the bodies they'd been driven from?

Kess found she held hope for the cursed entity, because of her own experiences. That if a creature so evil, so irredeemable, and so hated could find healing, then surely the shadow dragon could too.

She knew that all those broken pieces could find their place once more and be whole, and happy, and even loved.

THE END

GLOSSARY

Including pronunciation guide

CHARACTERS

Riony Eyfarr (Ree-OH-nee AY-far) – Rolanian, Daughter of Eylin and Farrad, born when servants to the Gyrstein Dragonlords, then sold on as a family to the Heithorn Dragonlords, and since living as fugitive slaves. Trained as a midwife and herbalist. Sword enthusiast.

Lyrrin Eyfarr (Li-rin AY-far) – Daughter of "The Guest", an unknown dragonlord woman, and an unknown father. Taen and Elgarthan? Has some unusual features. Likes animals and magic.

Kessara Heithorn (Kess-AH-ra High-thorn) – From the once wealthy Heithorn dragonlords with strong dragon riding traditions, estranged. Taen. Rides a wolf.

Kife Heithorn (K-eye-f High-thorn) – Elder brother to Kessara, dragonrider. Taen.

Dracuni (Drak-YOU-nee) – Unique hybrid between unicorn and dragon, created from the use of silvernix on a broken dragon egg, and something more?

Griskin (Griss-kin) – Large gray wolf, male, for some reason abides Kess's company.

Aishena Hjelzahn (AYSH-ena Hyel-zarn) – Delver, Middle sibling of three (remaining), fifth generation heir, grayglim in training. Taen.

Benjin Hjelzahn (BEN-jin Hyel-zarn) – Youngest sibling of three (remaining), fifth generation heir. Taen.

Kverra Hjelzahn (Kv-errar Hyel-zarn) – Grayglin warden and wife to Vori Hjelzan, fourth generation heir to the Dragon King. Taen.

Yeonard Draekhan (Yeh-nard DRAKE-arn) – Dragonking, ruler of Elundrae. Taen. First to tame a dragon.

Eslinde Draekhan (Ez-Lind-eh DRAKE-arn) – Last of the dragon-king's first generation heirs.

GENERAL

Alderkin (ALL-der-kin) – a secretive and powerful race of elven humanoids. Masters of rune crystal magic. Extinct.

Alderkin Depths – Massive underground cities once inhabited by the Alderkin. There are five known Alderkin Depths across Elundrae.

Alderkin Runes – Magical symbols carved into crystal items, which, when somehow charged, allow for a range of magical functions. The runes must be traced in the right sequence and direction of strokes in order to be activated and deactivated.

Alderkin War – A twenty-year war between the Alderkin and the Dragon King's forces, ending thirty years prior to the events in these books. Prompted by the human's slaughter of unicorns, and the Alderkin's attempts to protect them.

Athame (Ah-Thahm-Ay) – A dagger of varying size, made from crystal, and powered by various Alderkin runes for utility or combat.

Breachers – Undercity dwellers who brave the aboveground world to scavenge resources, highly dangerous but sometimes required.

Delvers – Undercity dwellers who brave the dangers of the Alderkin depths to salvage useful artifacts to be sold in the undercity. A risky but lucrative profession.

Dragon Glass – Glass manufactured with the use of dragon's fire to melt the base ingredients.

Dragon guards/riders – Those trained to ride dragons, generally for combat purposes. Either born to or hired by Dragonlord families who own the dragons.

Dragonhold – A building with multiple facilities for dragon keeping and raising, including hatchery, stables, and training areas.

Dragonkeeps – Walled in cities protected by dragons. The Dragon King has built and gifted a dragonkeep to each of his first generation heirs.

Dragonlords – Those who have the riches and resources to own their own dragons. Not necessarily royalty.

Elgarthans – A sea-faring race, pale skinned, they will visit and trade with Dragonkeeps for the riches of steel and glass provided through dragon labor, but rarely remain in Elundrae due to the dangers.

Elundrae (Ell-Un-Dray) – The continent in which the story takes place. Nearest neighboring country being Elgartha, across the seas to the East.

Rebel Riders – Title of a popular serial fiction, published and distributed in chapters.

Revenant/Rev/Shadow Revenant – Any undead creature raised by the Shadow Dragon's curse. Generally defeated by fire or dismemberment.

Rolanians – Once ruling large cities throughout Elundrae, most Rolanian settlements were destroyed as the Shadow Dragon curse spread through the land. As very few Rolanians became dragonlords, they had to buy into protection from those who had dragons, often at the cost of their own freedom. Generally presenting with a warm array of darker skin tones, and hair ranging from blonde, through reds and browns.

Shadow Dragon – a cursed and mysterious creature of smoke and sadness that brings the undead blight to the land of Elundrae. Wherever the Shadow Dragon touches ground, the dead rise.

Silvernix – Unicorn blood. Miraculous healing qualities, a single drop can cure a body from near death. Can only be stored in dragon glass, otherwise loses potency within minutes. Opalescent liquid.

Taens – Generally dark-haired and light-to-mid-brown skin-tones, Taens were once a warrior like clan of horse-riders, taking residence through the north-west of Elundrae. When the Dragonking rose to power, Taens became favored and more likely to become dragonlords, and soon became the dominant race across the land.

Taming – The ceremony in which all dragons are subjected to in order to be domesticated, similar to a lobotomy. Performed not long after birth on dragons bred in captivity. Utilizes silvernix in the process.

Undercity – A human settlement, established in the large upper cavern of the Central Alderkin Depths, as a refuge from the dangers of the aboveground world.

Unicorns – Ethereal, horned horse-like creatures. Driven to extinction in the race for the riches of their blood.

Herbs

Carrowmy – culinary.

Corpsefoot – used for contraception, dangerous in high doses.

Genjermint – sleeping tea.

Hennen – for hair dye.

Morass Mercy – powerful sedative with bad side effects.

Plumeberry – tart, seedy berries, poison detox.

Shillgrue – to condition leather.

Tinctoria – for hair dye.

Weftweed – a sticky (both in appearance and sap production) antiseptic.

DRAGONS
Natural subspecies

Etherflame – Plains dragons. Golds and reds, large size. Fire breathing for clearing grasslands/cooking herds, and big wings for hovering. Blood itself is flammable and is aerosolized in breath weapon. Most common dragonrider mount.

Seasong – Sea dragons. Silvers, greens, blacks, largest size, big lungs creates big surge of air/sound to stun schools of fish, and bigger mouth for feeding. There are tales they once sang, but never have in captivity or once tamed. Mostly used for interbreeding and beasts of burden.

Snowshimmer – Mountain dragons. Whites-blues, medium-sized, fast build for snatching up rare prey. Big talons, lightning breath attack, rare and solitary. Used in industry for power and interbreeding.

Treedart – Forest dragons. Yellows, browns, purples, camouflaged scales. Smallest type, with concentrated fire bolts for individual prey. Considered pretty basic by breeders and dragonlords, mostly used for interbreeding. Main/only dragon still in the wild because of size.

Dragons
Interbred selective breeding species

Etherdart – Etherflame/Treedart cross. Medium size, tough but slow, big fireballs. A basic combat dragon.

FlameSongs – Etherflame/Seasong cross. Largest size, high-capacity fire-breathers, used mostly for industrial uses, not used as mounts because they can spontaneously explode.

Seashimmer – Seasong/Snowshimmer cross. Large size, cold, icy breath used in ice making and food storage industry.

Shimmerdart – Snowshimmer/Treedart cross. Small size, with small ball lightning darts, dangerous for single targets but not great against mass undead, bred for speed as scouts/communications/assassinations.

Snowflame – Snowshimmer/Etherflame cross. Medium-large size, white "liquid" fire, fast, considered a great dragonrider mount, but short lifespan as breath weapon deteriorates their health fast.

Treedart/seasong – don't interbreed successfully.

ANIMALS

Bantam Ferrets – Mouse sized ferrets.

Bovin – A large (twice human height) buffalo or yak style creature, docile, used to be in large herds that supported wild dragons. Moved into farming for captive dragons.

Carrion Birds – Massive scavengers with a cry like a wolf's howl.

Cave Otters – A large sized otter with specially adapted claws that allow them to climb sheer walls easily, pale colors to match limestone surroundings.

Cave Spiders – Head-sized spiders, nonvenomous.

Dreer – Deer with Armadillo like scales, that grow as large as giraffes. Also popular prey for wild dragon populations in the past.

Glowflies – firefly-like bugs, finger sized, live in large swarms and light up when disturbed.

Mouse Deer – Cat sized deer with fangs.

Olm – Just like real olm, but larger than human size and carnivorous.

Owlettes – Cave dwelling owls that feed on small rodents and insects within the caves, the size of a small hand.

Rope Worms – Just a worm, but much larger. Delicious when fried.

ALDERKIN RUNES

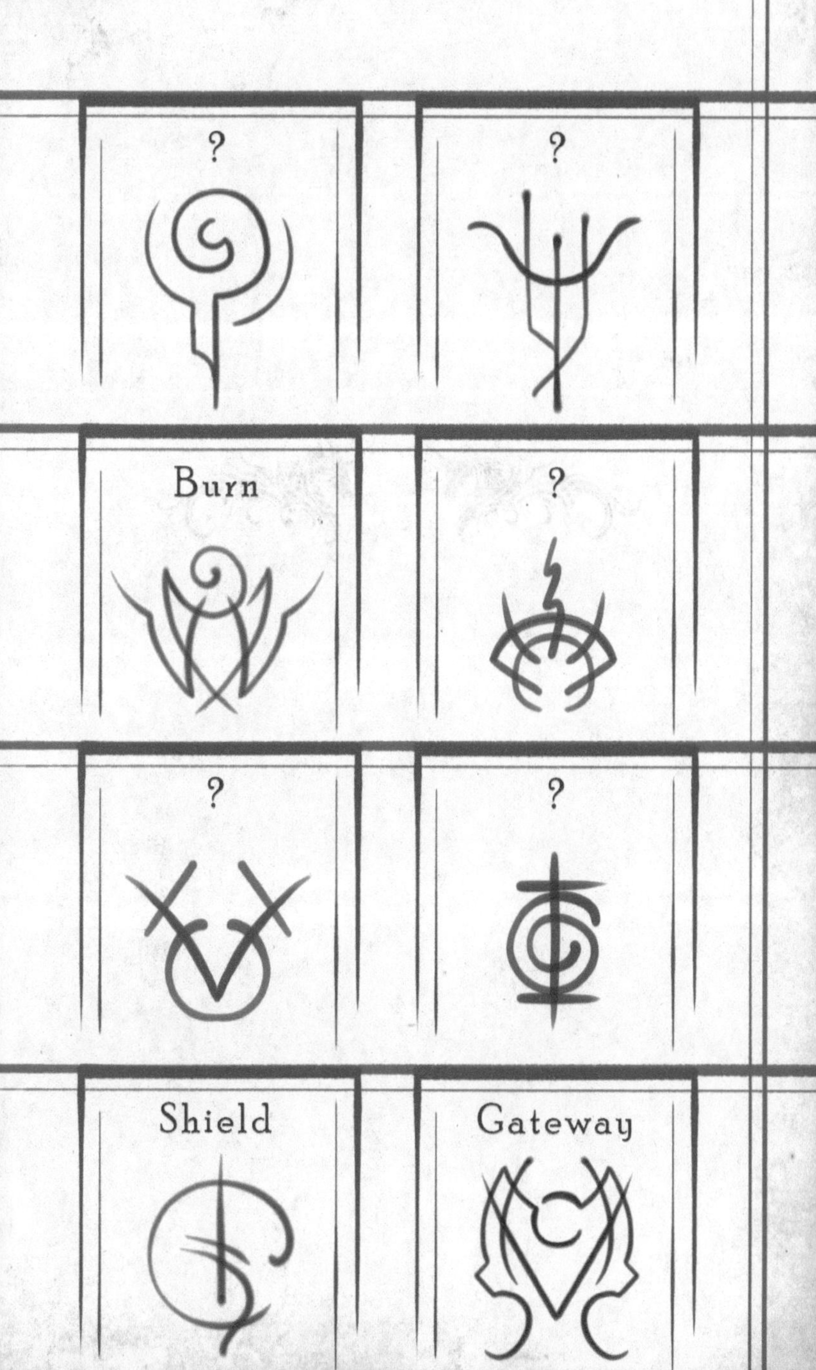

?
?
Burn
?
?
?
Shield
Gateway

About the Author

Professional daydreamer, Selina A. Fenech writes "adorably dark" Epic and Urban Fantasy for teens and adults. Filled with sweet and quirky characters, laugh out loud moments, and perilous adventures, her magical worlds are perfect for readers who love daring twists and happily ever afters.

A cancer survivor determined to live life to the fullest, she is an escape room enthusiast, avid gardener, foodie and self-proclaimed geek, residing in Australia.

In addition to literature, Selina applies her unique take on the dichotomy of light and dark as a professional fantasy artist working under the name Selina Fenech and has published many illustrated books, oracle decks, and colouring books.

Find Out More About Selina

OFFICIAL WEBSITE: www.selinafenech.com

Tree Dart
Sea Song
Snow Shimmer
Ether Flame

Memory's Wake Trilogy

A modern girl lost in and hunted in a fairy tale world.
An illustrated young adult portal fantasy with
Arthurian and Victorian themes.

Empath Chronicles

Teenagers with superpowers fueled by emotions ... what
could go wrong? A young adult superhero romance.

MORE BOOKS BY SELINA A FENECH

Beshadowed

You have been lied to. Werewolves, vampires, ghosts …
they aren't what you think. What is really lurking in the
dark? A spooky urban fantasy.

Fairy Tale Wishes

Enchanting and inclusive standalone fairy tale
retellings.